THE LAMB AMONG ✦ THE STARS SERIES

The Shadow at Evening

BOOK ONE

CHRIS WALLEY

thirsty™

Tyndale House Publishers, Inc.
WHEATON, ILLINOIS

Visit Tyndale's exciting Web site at www.tyndale.com

www.areUthirsty.com

thirsty(?) is a trademark of Tyndale House Publishers, Inc.

Copyright © 2002, 2004 Chris Walley

Cover illustration © 2004 by Mel Grant. All rights reserved.
Title type treatment © 2004 by Nancy Ogami. All rights reserved.

Edited by James Cain and Linda Washington

Designed by Ron Kaufmann

First published as *The Shadow at Evening*, © 2002 by Authentic Publishing, Milton Keynes, England

Scripture quotations are taken from the *Holy Bible*, New International Version®. NIV®. Copyright © 1973, 1978, 1984 by International Bible Society. Used by permission of Zondervan Publishing House. All rights reserved.

Library of Congress Cataloging-in-Publication Data

Walley, Chris.
    The shadow at evening / Chris Walley
        p. cm. — (The lamb among the stars ; bk. 1)
    "Thirsty."
    Summary: In the year 13851, on the planet Farholme, Merral discovers evil beginning to encroach into his beloved countryside, where for centuries it has been absent.
    ISBN 1-4143-0067-0 (sc)
    [1. Christian life—Fiction. 2. Science fiction.]   I. Title
    PZ7.W159315Sh 2004
    [Fic]—dc22   2004010259

Printed in the United States of America

08   07   06   05   04
7   6   5   4   3   2   1

For my parents

• ◆ •

On the basis of ecological or theological ideas that are
not to be lightly dismissed, many people believe that
this present world will end shortly.

But supposing, in this or some other universe, it doesn't?

And I will show you something different from either
Your shadow at morning striding behind you
Or your shadow at evening rising to meet you;
I will show you fear in a handful of dust.

T. S. ELIOT, *THE WASTE LAND*

• ◆ •

ACKNOWLEDGMENTS

The idea for the Lamb and Stars *Sequence originated in Beirut in the early 1980s as I read Iain Murray's fascinating* The Puritan Hope *(Banner of Truth, 1971) during a rather noisy part of the Lebanese Civil War. The encouragement to persist with this project during its inordinately long gestation period came from many sources, most notably my wife, Alison, and in later years, my sons, John and Mark. I would also like to thank my U.S. editors, Linda Washington and James Cain, and all the staff at Tyndale.*

PROLOGUE

Listen!

This is the tale of how, at last, evil returned to the Assembly of Worlds, and how one man, Merral Stefan D'Avanos, became caught up in the fight against it.

But to tell Merral's tale we must begin with the Seeding of the planet of Farholme in the year of our Lord 3140. Eleven hundred years have passed since the long-prophesied incoming of all the children of Abraham and the spiritual renewals of the Great Intervention ended the shadowed ages of the human race. A thousand years have slipped by since the victory at Centauri ended the Rebellion and brought a final peace to the Assembly. Nearly nine hundred years have elapsed since the first of the interstellar seeding expeditions.

The location of the Seeding is approximately three hundred and fifty light-years from humanity's home planet, the blue world that is already becoming known as "Ancient Earth." Here, the long, gray, glinting needle of the Remote Seeder Ship *Leviathan-D* comes to rest around the dazzling whiteness of the cloud-wrapped second world out from the star so far known only as Stellar Object NWQ-15AZ.

Here the vast ship hangs for months, its pitted hull bearing the faded and scarred portrayal of the Lamb Triumphant on the Field of Stars, the emblem of the Assembly of Worlds. The ship spins leisurely on its axis as it watches, analyzes, and calculates every aspect of the sterile and still-nameless world beneath it.

Three times a plate slides open on one of the needle's six sides and ejects a probe. The first swings around the planet in a spiral orbit mapping every boulder on its surface through the billows of gas dust. The next two plunge down into the savage clouds and days later, battered, charred, and corroded, but bearing samples of rock and atmosphere.

There is no haste. After all, on the timescale its makers work on, weeks are nothing. Patiently, the *Leviathan-D* continues to watch, listen, and gather ever more data. It measures the orbital variation of the planet to centimeters. It looks at the local sun in all the ways known to humanity and scrutinizes its output on every wavelength. It stretches out thin, sail-like extrusions to sift the dust in the space around the planet. It maps and forecasts for twenty thousand years ahead the trajectories of the largest million rock fragments within the system's debris belts. And as they hang above the endlessly simmering cloudscape, the ship's computers whisper and sing to each other as they process the data, predicting, discussing, and debating in learned imitation of the flesh and blood that made them.

The results are marginal. Positively, the spectrum, intensity, and variation of the radiation from NWQ-15AZ; the planet's orbital eccentricity; and the value of its gravitational field are within acceptable limits. As these are unalterable, this is good news. Negatively, the meteorite flux is too high, the axis of rotation too tilted, and the speed of rotation too fast. Adaptable as humans are, no civilization has ever thrived on days shorter than twenty hours and here they are only sixteen. However these things, and the sterile nitrogen and carbon dioxide atmosphere, can be altered. After further debate, the circuits reach agreement. If the Everlasting wills it, another home will be made here for humanity.

Now on *Leviathan-D* the quiet hum of long-inactive machinery starts up again. Smoothly, the vast needle breaks into two unequal parts. From the larger segment, a hexagonal disk detaches itself from the end and slides away to one side. The two halves of the needle rejoin to give a ship now a tenth shorter. The segment formed from their splitting begins to expand outward evenly, creating a six-sided aperture at its heart. As an unshielded Below-Space Gate, this hole will be the key to the future of this new world. With it, no subsequent ship will have to make the six-hundred-year-long sublight-speed journey of the

Leviathan-D. If the Seeding goes as predicted, and this savage world is tempered enough for humanity, then long millennia hence, machinery and mechanisms to build a greater Gate with a shielded opening will come through it. Through that, in turn, will come men and women.

Carried on a column of brilliant light, the needle now withdraws from the target planet and releases two small disk-shaped satellites. One descends into a low orbit of extreme precision while the other races outward to take up position six months later underneath the rings of the nearest gas giant. When both discs are in position, the *Leviathan-D* brings into play a Local Gate linkage between the two satellites, and the disk above the planet's surface begins to slowly assume the mass of the planetary giant. The damping and correction of the orbit of the target planet begin immediately.

It is time to begin modifying the atmosphere. Two further Local Gates are released, one landing on the surface of the planet below and the other on one of the ammonia-sheathed moons of the gas giant. The Gate linkage is slowly brought on line, and a hissing and boiling exchange of gases begins.

Computer modeling of the planet for thousands of years ahead suggests that greater climatic stability can be achieved by sculpting the surface to allow linkages between what will become the ocean basins. For weeks, the Mass Blaster of the *Leviathan-D* pounds the planet with repeated energy pulses of overwhelming force, vaporizing millions of tons of rock and hewing and hammering out the channels, straits, and seaways of the future.

As the blast debris settles out of the atmosphere, the computers on the *Leviathan-D* decide it is time for a gentler but no less vital technology. In the sheltered core of the great needle, proteins are assembled and woven into helixes of genetic matter, each strand tuned and programmed to feed and multiply on the scalding gases below. The genes are inserted into biological cells and the cell cultures inserted into five cylindrical polymer cocoons. Then a panel on the side of the ship slides open and the five containers are propelled into space.

There, in the shadow of the great ship, as dwarfed—and yet as consequential—as acorns before an oak tree, they linger, waiting for the word of command to send them to seed the planet.

Then, although there is no one other than God and the angels to hear, the ship speaks. In a dozen frequencies, as programmed by men and women now long dead, the solemn charge rings forth.

> *In the Name of the High King of heaven,*
> *We name this star Alahir*
> *and this world Farholme.*
> *We of the Assembly of Worlds now command you:*
> *Go forth and multiply.*
> *Redeem this waste world.*
> *Bring air and water, land and sea, day and night.*
> *Produce a home for the Lord's people,*
> *to the praise and glory of the Messiah,*
> *the Lamb who was slain.*
> *Amen.*

The response is the faint, silent flickering of lights on the ends of the cylinders as, one by one, they propel themselves away, onward and down into the swirling gases below.

For a final time, a port on the ship opens and a last satellite emerges to take up a high orbit above the newly christened Farholme. This Overseer satellite is to superintend the Seeding and to attend the planet in lonely vigil for the centuries that the work will take.

The needle now begins to move. The decision has been made that what is now known as the Alahir System will be the last target on the mission schedule. The systems scanned ahead by the *Leviathan-D* show little promise. After six centuries between the stars, the survey of fifteen worlds and the seeding of six, it is time for the *Leviathan-D* to return to port. But the homeward journey will be far swifter. Using the trail of Below-Space Gates it has left behind, its journey back will take a millionth of the time and energy of the outward journey.

The ship adjusts itself delicately in space on pulses of light until one end is perfectly aligned above the axis of the Gate. In a movement of slowly gathering swiftness, the needle's tip stabs into the strangely star-free blackness at the Gate's heart. Nothing comes out of the other side. Vanishing from view, the ship slips through the hexagonal aperture with a handbreadth of space to spare on every side. A second after the tail torch nozzle disappears there is the brief, ghostly gleam of a blue aurora around the hexagon and the Gate is empty.

•—◆—•

As the long years roll by, the Overseer satellite high above Farholme watches, without emotion, the spreading smear of green in the cloud systems as the cells begin to absorb and break down the gases. In time new types replace these, each successive generation pushing the atmosphere closer to that in which oxygen-breathing life can live without being choked, boiled, or burned.

And as life grows and increases on the new world of Farholme, the echo of the commissioning charge radiates outward through the Alahir System and beyond into the silent, unvisited spaces between the stars.

. . . To the praise and glory of the Messiah, the Lamb who was slain. Amen.

•—◆—•

And time passes, not just in those petty quantities that we call days, weeks, and years, but in long centuries, and even multiples of centuries. It is now the year of our Lord 13851, and the Seeding of Farholme is ancient history to its thirty million human inhabitants; as primeval and distant to them as the final waning of the ice sheets was for the first space travelers. More precisely, using the language of a long-dead calendar, it is December 22. In short, the Feast of the Nativity is just over two days away, and on over sixteen hundred inhabited planets the nearly one trillion citizens of the Assembly are preparing to celebrate the Incarnation.

The Assembly of Worlds now occupies a zone of space exceeding a hundred million cubic light-years; its farthest inhabited system toward the galactic edge is still Alahir with its single Made World, Farholme. Farholme retains the status that it had at its Seeding of being the farthest world, so that its thirty million inhabitants sometimes refer to their home, with a mixture of affection and gentle pride, as "Worlds' End." With the exception of its extreme position and low population, if there is a typical Made World (and only Ancient Earth is not a Made World), it is Farholme. Here the ancient, crater-pitted landscape vigorously erodes under the new regimes of water and oxygen. On it infant seas gnaw away at old impact scars, lava fields bubble and smoke sulkily as they cool under the novelty of rainstorms, barren dusty plains are slowly buried under the timorous advance of greenery, and rivers and sea and air currents are reluctantly coerced into stable and predictable courses.

But if the landscapes of the Assembly worlds remain restless this eve of the festival, its peoples, with their mutual tongue of Communal and their many dialects and historic languages, know only peace. It is, though, a peace of activity rather than a peace of rest. The Assembly is as vigorous as ever. There are always new worlds to be subdued and older ones to be stewarded. Nevertheless, this day—as every other day in the Lord's Peace that has lasted over eleven thousand years—sees no wars or strife within the Assembly worlds. And as the banners of the Assembly are brought out and checked in readiness for their grateful unfurling on the Day of the Nativity, there seems no reason why the emblem of the Lamb Triumphant on the Field of Stars may not fly at peace over an ever larger Assembly for another eleven—or eleven hundred—millennia.

Hanging high over Farholme this day, as it has for three thousand years, is the gigantic, beacon-framed hexagon of the shielded Below-Space Gate, the only link to the other worlds of the Assembly. Two thousand kilometers away from it, a dozen shuttlecraft drift gently around the Gate Station as their cargo is unloaded from the latest inbound inter-system liner. And far below their activity, night sweeps silently westward across Farholme, and as it does, the lights of a hundred human settlements flicker on.

But ultimately the Assembly is not Gates and worlds, still less banners and emblems. It is people: men and women, flesh and blood, bodies and souls. And as planets swing in their orbits, as the fabric of space is pierced at the Gates, and as atoms are broken in the forges of rocket fires, down on the surface of Farholme, a lone figure rides a horse northward into the gathering twilight of a winter's day.

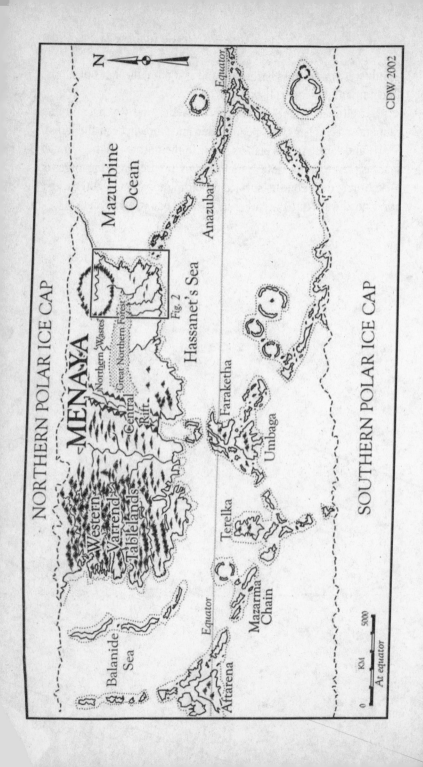

NORTHERN POLAR ICE CAP

SOUTHERN POLAR ICE CAP

Mazurbine Ocean

MENAYA

Northern Wastes

Great Northern Forest

Central Rift

Western Varrend Tablelands

Balanide Sea

Affarena

Equator

Fig. 2

Hassanet's Sea

Anazubar

Faraketha

Terelka

Umbaga

Mazarma Chain

N

Equator

0   KM   5000

At equator

CDW 2002

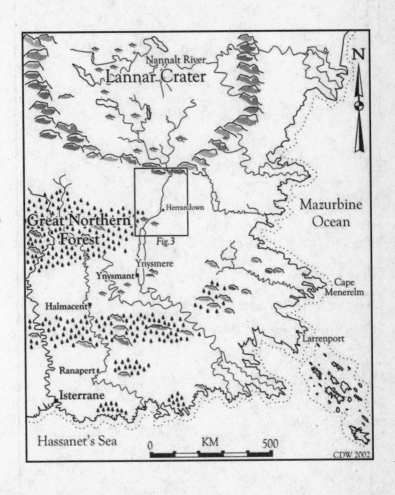

N

Nannalt River

Lannar Crater

Great Northern Forest

Herrandown

Fig.3

Ynysmere

Ynysmant

Halmacent

Mazurbine Ocean

Cape Menerelm

Larrenport

Ranapert

Isterrane

Hassanet's Sea

0   KM   500

CDW 2002

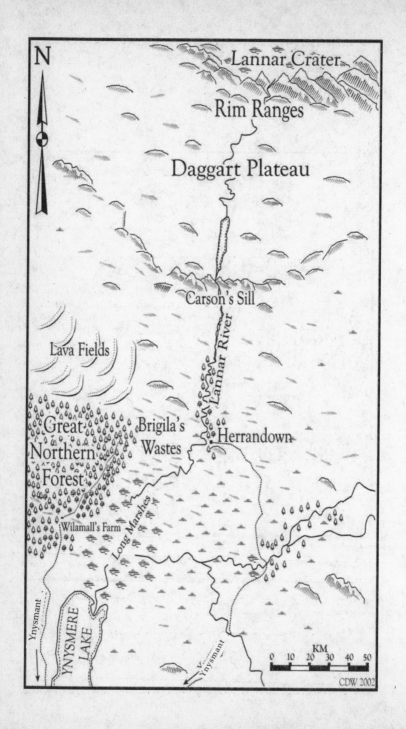

N

Lannar Crater

Rim Ranges

Daggart Plateau

Carson's Sill

Lava Fields

Lannar River

Great
Northern
Forest

Brigila's
Wastes

Herrandown

Wilamall's Farm

Long Marshes

Ynysmant

YNYSMERE
LAKE

Ynysmant

KM
0 10 20 30 40 50

CDW 2002

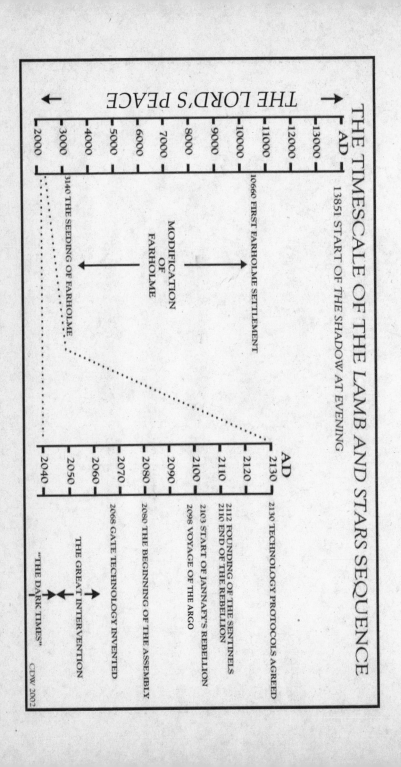

Merral Stefan D'Avanos crested the snow-flecked ridge in the northeastern corner of Menaya, the vast northern continent of Farholme, and reined in his mount. The winter's sun had just set in a great stained sphere of orange gold. He stared at the expanse of gray hills and darker, mist-filled valleys stretching northward to the ice-edged needles of the ramparts of the Lannar Crater.

Above the Rim Ranges, layer upon layer of cloud strands gleamed every shade between yellow and purple in the dying sunlight. Merral tried to absorb all he could of the sights, sounds, and smells of dusk. Down below the ridge, away to his right, crows preparing to roost were wheeling noisily around a pine tree. Far to his left, there was a moving, snuffling grayness under the edges of the birch forests that he knew was a herd of deer. Hanging in the cold fresh air was the smell of winter, new trees, and a new earth.

The beauty of it moved Merral's heart, and he raised his head and cried out with joy, "To the Lord of all worlds be praise and honor and glory and power!"

The words echoed briefly and a gust of wind out of the north dragged them away, down through the trees and bare rocks.

Silent in awed worship, he sat there for long minutes until another chill gust made him shiver, as much in anticipation as in actual cold. He bent down to his horse. "Now, Graceful," he murmured, "good girl, onward."

Obedient as ever, the mare moved forward over the frozen ground.

Merral knew it would not be wise to wait longer. The Antalfers expected him, and the nights of deep winter could be cruel this far north. Besides, as on any young world, there was always the chance of a sudden local weather anomaly. Such an irregularity might be only a few kilometers across—too small to be picked up by a weather satellite—but enough to freeze solid an unprotected man and horse in under an hour.

Merral rode on along a rough snowy trail which wound its way round blocks of lava, toying lightly with the wish that he had been born a poet or painter rather than a forester so that he could better express his love for this place and this life. But it wasn't long before he laughed at the aspiration and pushed it to one side. The Most High had made him what he was, and that was enough.

He peered ahead along the track, straining in the gloom to see the way ahead. The Herrandown Forward Colony was so small—a tree-surrounded hamlet of fifty people in six extended families—that it would be easy to overlook it at night. After some more minutes of cautious riding, he caught a glimpse of a tiny sliver of golden light in the distance. He smiled happily at the thought of his uncle or aunt leaving the shutters open so that the light would guide him in. He patted his mount, seeing her breath in the cold air. "Nearly there, my Graceful, and Aunt Zennia will have something for you."

Five minutes later he emerged abruptly from between the fir trees into the broad clearing that acted as the rotorcraft landing pad and marked the southern margin of the hamlet. As he rode out into the open, the dogs around the farm started to bark, and their dark shapes bounded across the packed snow toward him. Merral reined in as he met the dogs and, reaching down to stroke them, tried to identify as many as he could in the gloom.

"Fastbite, good dog!" he shouted. "Oh, Spotback, it's you! And Quiver, eh? Been having more pups, I hear? Brownlegs? No—it's Stripes. Look, stop licking so much!"

A door slid open smoothly in the ground-hugging building ahead. Light streamed out briefly onto the path before being abruptly blocked by the silhouette of a tall, well-built woman with long hair.

"Merral! Praise be! Children! Barrand! It's Merral! Now, mind the ice over there," she cried, half running to him. "Here, Nephew, give me a kiss!"

For a moment all was chaos as, barely allowing time for him to dismount, his aunt Zennia embraced and kissed him, while the children streamed out to hold and hug him and ask a dozen overlapping questions. And all the while the dogs, barking joyously, bounded in between Graceful's legs.

"Nephew Merral! *Welcome!*" A deep, jovial voice that seemed to echo came out of the door of the house. "Why, it's been months!"

Dogs and children gave way as the large figure of Uncle Barrand, his profile almost bearlike in the gloom, ambled over and hugged Merral to the point of pain as he kissed both cheeks fiercely and repeatedly.

"Excellent! Praise be! Your pack I will take. Thomas? Where is the boy?" His uncle's bulk swiveled around slowly. "Dogs I see, girls I see, but my only son is missing. Ah, there you are, Thomas! Good, you have a coat on. Take your cousin Merral and his horse—Graceful isn't it? Thought so—I'd know her even on another world. Take them to the winter stable. I'd take you, but I'm cooking tonight. Girls! *Wife!* It is cold. Indoors now, and let us finish preparing supper for our guest. He has ridden far. And Thomas . . ."

"What, Father?" piped the small voice from by Merral's side.

"Just take your dog into the stables. Not the whole pack."

Merral just made out a dutiful nod from the figure beside him. "Yes, Father! Here, Stripes! The rest of you dogs! You go off to your kennels! *Shoo!*" With what seemed to be regret, the other dogs drifted off obediently.

Thomas, short but well built for his seven years, took Merral's sleeve and tugged. "Cousin, we have a new stable for winter. An' I helped Daddy build it. We digged . . ." There was a pause. "Dugged? *Dug* it together in summer. Over here."

Merral ruffled the boy's black, wiry hair. "It's good to see you again, Thomas."

"Cousin, the stable is real warm over winter. We got twenty cows, fifteen sheep. When the station says it's gonna be real cold, we even send the dogs in. An' we put all our horses there, of course."

The track they followed went round the side of the low earth banks that gave some protection from the weather to the Antalfers' house and down a ramp into a mound. Merral had seen the plans when he'd come by in midsummer; the bitter cold of the last two winters had made a shelter a necessity. Inside the double sliding doors, the long, narrow structure was warm with the smell of animals. Merral led Graceful into an empty pen, made sure she had clean water and hay, and then spent time checking her over, running his hands over her legs and checking the dura-polymer hoof shields. "Good. She seems fine," he told his cousin. "Always check your animals, Thomas. They are your friends, not your servants."

The child nodded and hugged the dog, which licked his face. "Dad says that. I get a horse of my own in two years. I'm gonna really look after him." Merral nodded and patted the horse's head gently.

"Good girl, Graceful. Well done."

The brown head twisted up from the hay and rubbed itself against his hand as if in mute acknowledgement of the praise.

Merral stretched himself. "Well, I'm hungry, Master Thomas, so let's go."

•◆•

Once outside the doors of the stable, Merral suddenly felt the cold anew. The wind had intensified and was swirling round the building, kicking up little eddies of snow. The last gleam of twilight had gone, leaving the molten fire of the stars and the great belt of the Milky Way splendid in the blackness of the sky above him. Despite the frigid air and his appetite, Merral paused in his stride and looked up in wonder.

"You know your stars, Thomas?"

"'Course! Well, most of 'em. Dad's taught me some. He says we should see twenty with people on 'em."

"Twenty?" Merral thought hard. The naked-eye count for Farholme was supposed to be about fifty occupied systems, but that was from Isterrane; no, the boy was right—this far north you'd see less than half of that.

"On Ancient Earth," he remarked, as much to himself as to Thomas, "they say you can see over two hundred. And almost all the remaining thirteen hundred with a small optical telescope."

"Sol 'n' Terra are over there, just below the Gate." Thomas' voice was quiet.

Merral followed his outstretched hand to the heart of the Milky Way, a few degrees below where six sharp golden points of light marked out a hexagon in the blackness.

"Yes. That's it. Sol and Terra: the Ancient Sun and Earth. Well, time to get in or we'll freeze."

Merral bent down to take the boy's hand, but as he did, his eye caught a movement of the stars. He straightened, watching the approaching speck of light as it grew in size.

"Look, Thomas, a meteor!"

As he spoke, the point of yellow light, expanding a thousandfold, tore northward almost directly overhead. Its brilliance was such that, for a few seconds, the light of all the other stars was lost.

Merral twisted round, seeing the whole snow-clad landscape flashing alight in a brilliant incandescent whiteness. In the brief moments that the light lasted he glimpsed his and Thomas's shadows form and then race away as fading, elongated smears on the snow.

Abruptly the night flooded back.

As Merral blinked, a thunderous, echoing rumble vibrated around them, the sound bouncing off rocks and snow and resounding back round the clearing. The ground seemed to shake gently.

"*Zow!*" yelped Thomas, his fingers flung over his ears. "That was noisy!"

Stripes howled in terror, and from near the house came the barking of the other dogs. The outer door slid open.

"Thomas? Merral? What was that?" Zennia's voice was anxious.

Merral shook himself, the afterimage of the light still haunting his vision. "Just a meteor. I think."

"Come on, Thomas. Suppertime."

•—•—•

They crowded into the hallway, which was bare but beautifully paneled in a light, oil-polished pine, as the double doors whispered shut behind them. Barrand's big red face, framed by his ragged black curly beard, peered out of the kitchen. "A meteor, eh? We felt the house vibrate. 'Ho!' I thought. 'Merral is doing my quarrying for me!'"

"What, Uncle? Cheat you of your pleasure?"

There was the sound of something bubbling. A look of apprehension crossed Barrand's weathered face, and he dashed back into the steam of the kitchen.

Merral took off his jacket and carefully hung it on a rack, relishing the smell of the food and the warmth of the house. He sat on a bench and pulled his boots off, enjoying the feeling of being back in a place that he had always loved. He stroked the wood of the walls gently, feeling its faint grain. Even in a society that prized the right use of wood, Barrand and Zennia's home was special. Since his first visit, Merral had always felt that the house, with its sizeable underground extension, was something that had grown rather than been built. Even if the unruliest of winds struck the exposed part of the building so hard that every timber vibrated, down in the lower parts you could feel as safe and snug as if you were inside the roots of a giant tree.

"But it was a meteor?" His uncle's face had appeared again round the door. Merral sat upright suddenly, his tired back muscles signaling their presence.

"Must have been. But the biggest I've ever seen. It was heading northward. I suppose it probably landed over the Rim Ranges somewhere in the crater."

"Oh, it'll do no harm *there*. End up as a handful of dust."

There was amusement in his gray eyes. "Anyway, you have ten

minutes, assuming this new recipe behaves itself. Your usual room. Just time for a shower."

"A quick shower it is." And with that, Merral picked up his pack and climbed up the stairs to the guest room.

•—◆—•

Some minutes later, Merral was combing his hair and wondering why a shower and clean clothes made so much difference when there was a soft knock on his door.

"Come in!" he called out. In the mirror, he saw a face peer round the door—an oval face with pale blue eyes overhung by an untidy fringe of curly blonde hair. Merral turned round. "Elana! How are you?"

Elana, the oldest and blondest of the three Antalfer girls, was something of a favorite of Merral's. He had a private opinion that she was also the deepest and most thoughtful of them. Although she wasn't fourteen until next month, Merral had felt even on his last visit in high summer that she already had one foot beyond childhood. Now she came into the narrow room and stood under a curving wood beam. She stretched delicately upright on tiptoe and gave him a beaming smile. "I'm fine, Cousin. And you are well?"

Merral looked at her carefully, recognizing in those modifications of her physique the woman so imminent in the girl. "Praise our Lord. I have gained a few more scratches and bruises since I last saw you. And some aches from riding over hard ground. But I am well."

"You rode here just to see us?"

"Sorry! No, I need to talk to your father about his quarry, so my trip here is part of work."

She stared at him, amused puzzlement in her eyes. "I thought you were a forester!"

"I still am. But there's no point in us planting a forest if your dad is going to dig a big hole in it, is there now?"

"No, I suppose not." Elana smiled. "Actually, Merral, I came to say that food is nearly served."

"Lead the way."

He followed Elana to the dining hall, noting a new painting on a wall above a stairway. He reminded himself that he must make time to look at his aunt's latest work. He might ask her to do something for his parents' thirty-fifth wedding anniversary next year. He made a mental note that when it came to planning what to do with his stipend next year, he needed to include the cost of the painting.

The dining hall lay in the deepest part of the house, and although it was the largest room, it seemed already full as he entered. Merral tried to identify everybody. On one side were his aunt, the two younger daughters—Lenia and Debora—and, of course, Thomas. On the other were Barrand's parents, Imanos and Irena, and a young couple from the next house.

Merral made his way to the seat offered to him at one end of the table. As he did, Barrand came in bearing a great pot and the chattering ceased. Quietly, everybody stood up and stepped back behind their chairs. Thomas, too short to see over the solid back of his, peered round instead at Merral.

There was silence. Barrand raised his big, gnarled hands to the heavens. "For your love and presence with us, O Lord, our protector and mighty one, and for your kindness to us, we thank you now. In the name of the Prince, the Messiah, our Savior."

A second's solemn silence was ended abruptly with a chorus of "Amen," and then the scraping and clattering of chairs and talking.

As he sat down, Merral looked around the dining room. The way the side beams sloped inward toward the floor made it easy to imagine that he was deep down in the hull of a boat. It had taken them the ten years they had been in the house to acquire just the right panels, matching in grain and tone, to complete the dining room. Along some of the roof beams, his uncle had started carving animals to what Merral recognized as his aunt's designs.

The meal was like all the many meals Merral had had at Herrandown, with lots of food, endless noisy chatter, and half a dozen conversations bouncing and jumping around and across the table.

Merral was pleased to find that his own substantial appetite by no means outmatched the others at the table. In fact, everyone seemed to be happily hungry. His uncle revealed nothing about the stew other than the fact that the beef-protein had been grown locally and the girls had picked the mushrooms for it in autumn.

Barrand looked up at him. "The family, Merral? You tell us the latest."

"Well, it is five days since I left Ynysmant and I have covered a lot of ground, but when I left all were well, may the Most High be praised, and I have had no news of any change. The only thing is that Great-Aunt Namia down at Larrenport is not well. She is now very frail; she feels she will be going Home to the Lord in the spring. The doctor thinks she is right."

Imanos, a silver-haired man with an air of gentle nobility, spoke. "Namia Mena D'Avanos? The language teacher?"

"That would be her."

"Why, she taught my mother Old-Mandarin; Mama was so proud of mastering it. 'The hardest of all the Historics,' she said." He paused, smiling quietly. "I was very glad to be spared it. But she must be very old now. A hundred and twenty at least?"

"A hundred and twenty-four. But still alert and still praising."

"You'll be seeing her before she goes Home? Please, will you give her our love and blessing." His wife gently nodded agreement, her fine white hair framing a face as peaceful and still as if it had been molded.

Merral bowed his head slightly to acknowledge the taking on of an obligation. "If the opportunity is granted me, I shall indeed visit her before her death and if I do, I will pass on to her your love and blessings."

The elderly couple smiled at each other and then gratefully back at him. A few moments later Barrand, one hand tearing off a piece of bread, caught Merral's eye and gave him a broad wink. His loud voice rang down through the room, cutting across three separate conversations.

"Talking of family matters, youngster. You're twenty-six! What's happening between you and Isabella Hania Danol?"

There was a sudden silence and Merral looked at his glass, conscious that everyone was looking at him.

Zennia laughed and raised her hands in mock horror. "Oh, Barrand! Let him tell us in his own time. He's a shy lad."

"There is really nothing decided." Merral smiled. "Except that my parents and hers are meeting to discuss whether to approve that we proceed to a commitment. That's all I'll say."

"A formality, I'm sure," said Barrand, waving his bit of bread around and smiling at his girls. "We'll all come down for the wedding, won't we, children?"

"Oh yes, please. When? When?" came the chorus from the children.

"This year, next year, sometime, never," interjected Zennia. "Everything is still at the first stage. It's commitment, engagement, and *then* marriage. Now, Barrand, leave the lad alone and tell him about the cows."

"Oh, not half as much fun. But you are right. Now, what with the heat, our cows had a bad summer. . . ."

And so the meal progressed in its animated and somewhat chaotic way, with discussion of the families, farms, animals, life in Herrandown generally, Merral's travels, Barrand's musical projects, and the children's activities.

Eventually even Merral's hunger was assuaged, and slowly, and somewhat heavily, everyone (except the oldest) rose from the table and went to the kitchen to help in the clearing up. Then they went into the family room and heard the children practice their Nativity songs. As tradition demanded, two were in Communal, the universal language of the Assembly; one was in the Farholmen dialect; and one in the historic language assigned to Herrandown. Merral, whose only Historics were French and English, found the Alt-Deutsch quite incomprehensible. Then the neighbors departed, and with kisses all round the children left for bed. Eventually the "senior generation" pleaded age and departed to their own small suite of rooms.

Now the three remaining adults reclined in padded chairs in the small room above the hall and let the conversation drift. Barrand toyed gently with a dark wooden flute of his own carving, occasionally blowing a quiet note and listening carefully to it with a look of suspicion. It was interesting, Merral observed, how the contrasts met in his uncle. To look at him in his work you would think that all he could do was blast quarries and hew out tons of stone. Yet in his wood carving and his music he showed sensitivity and a delicacy of touch. But there were not two separate Barrands, but one: quarrymaster, wood-carver, and musician.

As if conscious of Merral's thoughts, Barrand looked up. "Ah, I'd ask your advice, Merral, but you singers don't understood wood instruments. I'm just not satisfied with this." He tapped the flute. "But it's a delicate business, adjusting. Easy to mar, hard to mend."

Zennia stroked Barrand's wrist, her finger delicate and thin against the muscular bulk of his arm. "All the better then, my dear, to leave it to tomorrow."

"Quite so. Although tomorrow is official work with my nephew the forester. But I will find time. My wife, as usual, is right." He carefully put the flute down. "Nephew, your glass is nearly empty. More to drink?"

"Not for me."

Then they let the conversation drift into a slower, more reflective tempo. In time, they got talking about the arts, and Barrand began to talk with his usual enthusiasm about choral music.

"Oh, Merral, I have had a struggle about what to do for Nativity. Very hard. I've always liked to do something special. It's difficult when there are so few of us, but I don't mind using re-created voices."

Merral remembered that in these small communities, the use of the preserved voices of singers in the past was not luxury in music-making, but necessity.

"As we did Bach at Easter, I thought we'd do something more recent. So it's Rechereg's *Choral Variations on an Old Carol*. You know the piece?"

"Heard of it. It's difficult, isn't it?"

Barrand nodded to his wife. "Our nephew is too busy. Not enough time to listen."

Zennia patted her husband's arm and smiled back at Merral. "Perhaps, dear, in Ynysmant they are too busy making music to listen to it. Remember our blessing of being so remote."

"Wives are always right, eh, Merral? But of course you wouldn't know. . . ." His uncle smiled, showing his powerful, white teeth. "Ho. Where was I? Ah yes, let me see. The Rechereg is very demanding. I will need three re-created voices to handle it. The great tenor Fasmiron—the voice is from 8542 when he was at his peak—and Genya Manners, one of the Lannian sopranos during the great years of their academy. She sounds more like a bird than a woman. But I'm having problems with the female alto. It's a very high part."

He looked into the distance, tapping his fingers on the wood of his chair.

"Who are you using?" Merral asked.

"For the alto?" Barrand stroked his beard. "Hmm, Miranda Cline perhaps. But does she have the range? Just ten years of singing. It was so fortunate that she agreed to let her voice be copied so she could become a re-created when she did. She came and went like a meteor. . . ."

He stared at the wall-hanging opposite. Abruptly, he looked at Merral. "Nephew! A change of subject entirely. Your meteor. Have you considered why the Guardian satellites didn't pick it up and destroy it?"

Merral thought for a moment. "It crossed my mind briefly. It seemed large enough to have done damage if it had hit anything. So the 180 East or the Polar Guardian should have intercepted it, you think?"

His uncle ran his hand through his beard again. "Me? Oh, I don't know. I've never given the Guardian satellites a thought. I know there are four, that they're as old as the present Gate, and that they destroy any meteor or comet coming in on a threatening trajectory. And that is it. They work. So we forget them. . . ." He fell silent, his fingers maintaining a gentle beat on the arm of his chair. "But, Nephew, what I was just wondering was this: Now suppose one or more of the Guardian satellites did see it, but they just plotted the trajectory and then said 'Oh, the Lannar Crater. Uninhabited waste,' and let it pass. What do you think?"

"I think I see where your logic takes you." Merral sipped the last of his drink. "With Herrandown being the farthest settlement north, that's fine, but inside a decade or two we might have a Forward Colony up to the margins of the southern Rim Ranges—at least if the winters don't get any worse."

His uncle nodded, his heavy brow furrowing. "Hmm. Exactly. I just hope someone tells the Guardians. But Nephew, surely the Guardians aren't smart enough to determine an impact trajectory to such precision that they can let it go over our heads like that?"

Suddenly tired, Merral found himself stifling a yawn. "Oh, sorry, Uncle. Yes, you may have a point but my brain is too fatigued. It would be an interesting thing to know. I'll talk to someone when I get back."

"It's not just you who is tired. Zennia looks asleep."

At her name, his wife started, opened her eyes, and shook her head so that her brown and silver hair flew around. "I'm—Oh, what an insult! I am sorry. I really ought to go to bed. If you gentlemen will excuse me."

Merral got to his feet. "I think, Uncle, if you will excuse me, I'll go too."

Barrand waved a hand dismissively. "Of course. Zennia, I'll be up in a moment. But I've just had an idea about that alto."

• ◆ •

In the small guest chamber with its single skylight, Merral undressed. Fighting off sleep he sat on the bed, pulled the small, gray curved slab of his diary off his belt, and noting the illuminated message logo, thumbed it on, switching to speech mode.

"Nine-fifteen P.M. Eastern Menaya Time today. One message:

13

Nonurgent. Voice from Lena Miria D'Avanos." The words were flat and metallic.

Pulling out his night-suit, Merral spoke to the diary. "Play, please. Let's hear my mother."

"Message begins. . . ." The coldly sterile tones of the machine were thrown into abrupt contrast by the soprano of his mother's voice, with her haphazard stresses.

"Merral dear. This is not at all urgent. Not at all! But do thank Barrand and Zennia so much for their good wishes for the Nativity. Zennia's card was lovely. Merral, I am so blessed to have such an artistic sister. Lovely. I shall be writing, of course, but do please invite them down again. Those dark winter nights up north! Of course, I'll do it myself, but the personal touch is the thing! Oh, and Merral, I saw Isabella today. She asked after you. 'When is Merral coming back?' she said. Father and sisters send their love too. Love from your mother."

The metallic voice returned: "Message ends. No further messages."

"Okay. Go to today's notes."

"Ready."

"Add 'Final Observations' as follows. . . . "

For the next five minutes, Merral listed what he had seen on the last part of his journey north. He would tidy up the report when he got home. Then he briefly outlined what he hoped to achieve with his uncle tomorrow before he rode south again. Finally, he switched to screen mode and continued his current evening reading of the Word before bringing his praises and concerns before the Most High.

Then Merral slid in between the sheets and lay there listening to the silence of the house and the soft creaking of the wooden frame as the night winds swirled around it. There was, he felt, something extraordinarily satisfying about being tired: the draining of energy from limbs, the leisurely and ordered shutdown of body systems.

On the verge of sleep, he realized that he had not recorded in his diary anything about the meteor. He would, he told himself, do it tomorrow. Toying with the image in the last moments of wakefulness, he played back through his mind the brief glimpse he had caught of it—the ball of light, like some great firework, racing overhead.

As he did so, it struck him that something about it was odd. But what? He ran over the vision again and again, now faster, now slower.

His last thought as he plunged finally into sleep was that, for a meteor, it had been moving too slowly.

Far too slowly.

That night Merral dreamed in a way he had never thought possible. Normally, if he did dream, all he would remember of it on waking was a short-lived, gentle, and vague memory. But that night his dream was of an extraordinary intensity and unpleasantness.

He was standing alone on a dark, endless sandy beach at the edge of a sullen, night-colored sea, whose slow, heavy waves never broke, but seemed to just crawl up the shore and die before sliding back with a quiet, drawn-out whisper. Somehow, there was something swollen and infected about the sea. The cloudy, sunless sky above was lit with an overcast, tepid yellow light that seemed sickly. In the far distance some dark-winged objects, which he knew were not birds, wheeled and dived ominously.

It seemed to Merral that he stood there for an age, a lone figure looking at a sick sea and a dead sky, watching the oily ebb and flow of the waters. There was an atmosphere of expectancy, a feeling that something was on its way, something impending. It was as though the waves in their slow, lapping decay were saying in words just beyond hearing, "*Wait. . . . Wait. . . . Wait. . . .*" He knew, with a strange certainty, that there was something out there in the waters. Something that was waiting out its time before emerging.

Then, in a fearful moment, he saw the faintest of movements begin far out on the water. An unhurried train of circular ripples began to spread out slowly, and the waters seemed to bulge.

As this happened, Merral felt a strange compulsion. He wanted to run away. Indeed he knew that he had to, but somehow he couldn't. Instead, half of him seemed to want to stay and to watch what was going to come out of the water. There seemed to be an invitation, a beckoning, even a command for him to stay, to watch, to somehow be present at—

At *what?* Merral didn't know. He felt trapped in lonely terror and expectation, bound against his will to watch and await whatever it was that was emerging from the growing ripples.

Suddenly Merral felt he was no longer alone. Someone else seemed to have joined him, some invisible person who tugged at him so that he was forced to turn away from the mesmerizing sea. As he turned away, he felt suddenly released from his bonds. Driven by an overpowering sense of peril, Merral began to run over the loose sand away from the rippling waters. And in his fleeing, he woke up with a start of terror.

Merral lay still for some minutes, wet with perspiration and aware of a thudding pulse in his head. It took him some time to come to terms with what he had experienced. It had clearly been a nightmare, a thing not entirely unknown in the worlds, but almost always in rare psychological ailments or in various poisoning accidents. He switched the light on and went over to the hand basin where he washed his face and checked himself over. To his surprise, he found no evidence of illness. He had no swollen glands, no spots, no pustules, and no distended stomach. Recovering something approaching calm, he went back to bed, switched off his light, and lay down, conscious of a racing pulse. He was vaguely aware of the wind gusting strongly against the walls and heavy footsteps from his uncle and aunt's room next door. Then he committed himself again into the hands of the eternal Father, the great King, the maker of the heavenly glory, and fell asleep.

This time he slept in peace.

◆-◆-◆

Over breakfast, Merral's dream nagged at the corners of his mind. He had been talking over with Barrand some of Thomas's stories from school when Zennia, robed in a warm blue gown, came in and reminded the children that it was time to leave for school. As they left in turbulent good cheer, Merral's aunt sat at the table and turned to him.

She stared at him, her eyes showing concern. "Did you sleep properly, Nephew? You still look tired."

Merral put down his cup slowly, perplexed at realizing that he wanted to avoid her question. "Er, no, Aunt. No, not really. The bed was fine, but I just had . . . well, a dream."

Merral was aware out of the corner of his eye of Barrand, standing against the kitchen shelves, and as he said the word *dream*, he had the strongest feeling that a look of surprise or dismay crossed his uncle's face. But when he turned to Barrand, all he could see was a mild expression of quizzical sympathy.

"No! I *am* sorry," his aunt replied, her voice full of consideration. "You mean a nasty dream? About what?"

Merral found himself embarrassed. "Well, nothing much really. It was an oddly sort of static dream. Almost . . . well . . . a *nightmare*. I just . . ." He hesitated. "No Aunt, it's too silly, really, to talk about. Perhaps it was something I ate." Then he realized what he had said. "I'm sorry, I didn't mean to suggest that your food was—"

"No, I know what you mean," she answered, giving him a caring look.

Barrand turned to Merral. "Perhaps . . . perhaps it was the mushrooms." His normally smooth deep voice was now ragged.

Then, as Merral watched, his uncle swung away toward the wall and began to move a plate along a shelf.

"*I've* never known them to have that effect," Zennia commented, sounding slightly puzzled. "We all had them, didn't we? Husband, you slept all right, didn't you? I do remember you getting up."

For a moment, Barrand, apparently engrossed in finding dust on the plate, didn't look up. "Oh, me?" he said eventually, in a level, flat tone. "Oh, *I* slept fine. No, nothing like that."

"Bizarre," replied Zennia. "Have you ever dreamed like this before, Merral?"

"Never, thankfully."

Barrand turned toward them, his face expressionless. "Now, don't rule out mushrooms. Fungal biochemistry is very complex. And they evolve in such a bizarre way; you get new strains all the time. There was a case some fifteen years ago: A whole community of sixty perished out in one of the Lenedian planets. Do you remember it?"

"Vaguely," Zennia slowly replied, looking at her husband as if there was something she did not recognize about him.

Barrand, who had now swung away again and appeared to be examining the kitchen shelves, nodded to himself. "Yes, well, that was put down to a rogue gene in a fungus. But anyway, no harm done here."

Merral, unsure of what to say, tried to soothe the situation. "Well, that's true. No harm done. Whatever it was, I'm fine now."

Barrand put down the plate he was still holding onto the shelf so awkwardly that it rattled alarmingly. Then without looking back at either Zennia or Merral, he said, "Excellent! Well, dreams or no dreams, we ought to get down to business, young Merral. My office in ten minutes?" But before any answer could be made, he had left the room.

Zennia stared after the departing shape of her husband with an air of puzzled unhappiness, looked at Merral, and made as if to say something. Then she seemed to change her mind and left abruptly, leaving a perplexed Merral in sole possession of the kitchen.

Eventually Merral gathered up his notes on the quarry and stepped outside. It was a brilliantly clear winter's day, and breathing in the sharp, cold air, he stared at the snow-sprinkled landscape engraved in a crisp winter fragility. As he did, the oddly unpleasant atmosphere of the kitchen seemed to dissolve in the fresh air. Soon, though, Merral felt the cold penetrate his indoor clothes, and he strode quickly down the path to the long shed huddled between earth and basalt block banks.

As he entered, Barrand looked up from where he was sitting behind a desk piled neatly with papers and datapaks.

"Welcome to my palatial office!" he exclaimed jovially, waving his great arms so wide that they nearly touched the opposite sides of the room. Merral felt encouraged that the strange mood seemed to have left his uncle as abruptly as it had come.

"Ho! Stop standing there. Do take a seat. I've lost a cross section."

Merral, however, remained standing and looked around. His previous visits had been social ones and he hadn't been in his uncle's office for years. It was a single long room with one end taken up by a south-facing window and the other walls covered with maps, diagrams, and shelves of rock samples. In one corner hung various bits of quarrying equipment, including a cutter beam and a sample corer. Despite all the objects and his uncle's apparently easygoing nature, he found it a surprisingly tidy room.

Merral's attention was caught by a small painting on one wall, apparently out of place among all the paraphernalia of work. It was a picture of an entwined mother and child peering out of the window of something he took to be an inter-system liner, as beyond them a specklike in-system shuttle was beginning reentry into the atmosphere of the green and blue planet below them. Against the margin of the picture was a Gate, its status lights green. The caption read, "A last view of Hesperian. A. R. Lymatov, A.D. 11975."

"Interesting painting," Merral observed, speaking as much to himself as to Barrand.

His uncle looked up from his papers. "Oh, that. The Lymatov. Yes. My great-grandparents were from Hesperian. But you knew that."

He stared at it as if seeing it for the first time, then wagged a finger solidly in emphasis. "Yes, now, Zennia doesn't like it. She says it's too posed. I disagree. Of course it's posed. It's a *posed* sort of painting. But it is flawed. Technically, it's wrong. They would have been seated and strapped in long before they got that close to the Gate, and the windows are too big for a liner. But I like it. Do you?"

Merral looked carefully again at the painting. He noticed that the child's arm was raised in a farewell wave that was somehow ambiguous and that the mother's posture was rather rigid and her face determined.

"Yes. I do. Like it, I mean. It's a well-established genre; you could fill a hundred galleries with them. But I find it moving. There's no father. Did he die, and are they leaving his remains there? It asks questions. I suppose he might have gone on first, but somehow the figures suggest otherwise."

Barrand gave him a knowing nod. "You always did have an abundance of brains. Yes, there is a story. A family of five was planning to go to Granath Beta. Then the husband and the other two children were killed in a freak storm. She and the remaining child went on alone."

He got up and went over to the painting, speaking quietly and intensely now. "It's always been a challenge to me. It says a lot about faith. About what the Assembly is about. What our calling as a family is. *Resolve. Faith.* You know. All those things.

"It is a well-established genre. But all genres are now." He stared at the painting. "Funny business, the Assembly, when you think about it. All the emphasis on a stable, sustainable society. The caution over innovations."

He nodded toward the horse grazing on some hay just in front of the window. "Take animals now. Like Blackmane there. He's a horse, but his genes are different from the first horse that left Earth. Or even that arrived here. Look at him: rounded extremities, reduced ears, nostril flaps, more recessed eyes, thicker hair, heavier hooves. He has adapted to this world with its cold and heat and dust."

"Of course," Merral said. "You can hardly freeze adaptation. But what's your point?"

His uncle creased his large forehead in puzzlement. "My point? Yes. Oh, I don't know. The paradox that we have frozen our culture, but that we have let life evolve. I know it's not a new thought—what is after so long?—but it has just struck me with some force."

"But, Uncle, the wisdom of the centuries is that the stable culture is best. You can't just let a culture evolve; certain limits must be defined. Long, long ago the Assembly decided the parameters in which human beings flourished and set them down. It was a choice; a fixed, conservative, and stable society over one that was open, fluid, and unpredictable."

There was a deep silence as Barrand, his large frame totally dominating the room, stroked his beard in profound thought. Then he gave a grunt that seemed to indicate mystification.

"Absolutely. What a strange idea for me to have." He shook his head. "Ho, to business! Oh, I don't need that cross section. Come and have a look at these maps and let's switch into official mode, Forester D'Avanos."

For half an hour they looked at the maps and imagery, and Merral listened intently as his uncle explained why he wanted to quarry the ridge outside the settlement rather than wait for a new access road to the already-planned quarry site fifteen kilometers to the north. Only he wasn't his uncle now. He was Barrand Imanos Antalfer, Frontier Quarrymaster, and he was presenting his case to Merral Stefan D'Avanos, Forester and head of the team that decided the citing of things such as quarries and forests. *Funny*, Merral thought, *how we distinguish official and family discussions to the extent that it would now be unthinkable for him to call me Nephew and me to call him Uncle.*

Eventually Barrand wound to a halt. "So you see, Merral, we could start in the spring and save two years. And think of the energy saving in skipping that thirty-K round trip. . . ." He tailed off, looking at Merral.

Merral rose to his feet, walked to the window, and looked out at the bare black ridge they had been talking about.

"Barrand," he said, gesturing at the ridge, "let's go and look at it."

Zennia was free to come, and an hour later the three of them were standing on the rocky summit of the hill recovering their breath after the stiff climb up. Merral stared around. Suspended overhead was a cool, eggshell blue sky painted with the most delicate pearl brush strokes of high cloud. To think that they were just water vapor—had the Most High ever made anything so beautiful from so little? There were one or two of the faint corkscrew twists of cloud that revealed local instability in the upper atmosphere layers, but nothing that portended trouble on his ride tomorrow.

Merral lowered his gaze. The farms, fields, and orchards of Herrandown were almost surrounded by protecting woodlands, beyond which lay rough scrub, grassland, and bare rock. To the west of the settlement the bounding fir and alder woods ran into the tree-lined margins of the Lannar River, whose path he could trace northward toward the ranges. Looking northward, from where a cold wind blew that made the eyes water, the ground became increasingly covered with ice and snow. And there, marching along the farthest skyline, were the jagged teeth of the southern Lannar Rim Ranges, gleaming a dazzling white in the sunlight. The notion struck him that this cluster of houses was a vulnerable community. *What a strange idea,* he thought. *Vulnerable to what?*

As they walked down the hill, Merral pushed those thoughts away. Zennia turned to him with a smile. "Barrand has been telling me of your recommendations. You have a gifting of vision and leadership, Merral. You would prefer to disown it, but I think you will use it in the end. If not on Farholme, then elsewhere."

"Elsewhere? I was born here, as you were and all my grandparents were. No one in our family has been off Farholme since, oh, Great-Uncle Bertran traveled forty years ago."

"Do you want to go elsewhere?"

It is an interesting question, Merral thought, *and one that I have struggled with myself.* "I have little thought of leaving, Aunt. I love this place and being here. Farholme may be Worlds' End, but this is my home." He paused. "I believe that my place is here. For the moment at least."

Zennia carefully negotiated a sheet of glittering ice and then turned again to him.

"And tell me, you are happy with the forester's life?"

Merral measured his words. "I am, Aunt. I am happy. There is the challenge of seeing Menaya change and unfold as we work on her and with her."

She smiled, encouraging him on.

"I love it," he said. "It's the combination of art and science. I look at the ground, the lava ridges, the sand sheets, and say to myself, what can I do with it? What will best bring out the uniqueness of the land? Here a beech wood, there a pine forest."

"I see the attraction; it is like painting."

"Indeed, it is art at the grandest scale." Merral smiled. "One of the great purposes of the Assembly—to take brown-and-gray, dead worlds and turn them into blue-and-green ones alive with life. Thus, we fulfill the mandate to humanity to garden what the Lord has entrusted us with."

Barrand waved an arm in agreement. "Oh, absolutely. But let *me* ask you a question. Have you *really* no ambitions beyond all this?"

A hard question. My ambition is not something I normally think of. "Uncle," he answered after a moment, "I suppose I do have one ambition. More a wish."

"What?"

Merral stopped and looked up. "Well, I would like to see the forests of Ancient Earth. To examine old woods and jungles. Ecosystems that go back, not just for eight thousand years, but millions of years. Unplanned, at least by us. Composed of a hundred thousand species in relative stability, not our five thousand in unsteady, unpredictable, and changing relationships."

Barrand grunted, but it was Zennia who spoke. "Yes, I could see that. All Made Worlds are imitations, as best as we can make, of the one original Earth. But I have heard that many of Ancient Earth's forests were badly affected in the Dark Times; they have been reconstructed."

"True. They are not as they were when our First Father and Mother walked in them. But I would like to see them once."

The house was in sight now and the dogs were coming out. Barrand, his teeth bared in a grin, turned to Merral. "And perhaps, Nephew, one day you will."

"Maybe, Uncle, but it's a long walk from here."

And as the dogs romped around them, they laughed again.

•◆•

That night Merral borrowed an image projector and went up to his room early to work. He wanted to get the ideas for the ridge tidied up before the Nativity holiday and knew that there would be little time on the next day to get anything done. If he got to the Forestry offices at Wilamall's Farm by dusk as he planned, he should be back in Ynysmant by eight on the regular ground transporter. And as that would leave little time to write up anything, it was best to do it now. So he linked his diary to the image projector and used it to draw an elegant, scaled 3-D model of the proposed quarry that appeared hanging over the desk like a gray whale painted with gridlines.

As he adjusted the edges of his model, he paused. Was he really working up here just because he had to get the work done? Or was there more to it than that?

He felt there was something that he didn't understand in the house, something intangible and impalpable that he preferred to avoid; something he wanted to be away from. Somehow, the house of his uncle and aunt had ceased to be as welcoming as it had been. As he sat there in the room, Merral felt drawn to consider again the mysterious problem that had afflicted Barrand that morning. Had it been resolved, or had it simply been pushed to one side? Certainly, during the evening, his uncle had become more withdrawn and terse.

Merral was sitting there, idly rotating the diagram as he considered his uncle, when there was a gentle tap at the door.

It was Zennia, bearing a glass of warm milk for him. She smiled. "I thought you might like this before you went to bed."

"Why, thank you very much, Aunt! I hadn't realized how late it had become."

He took the glass and placed it carefully on the desk. As he began to mention his plans for the morning, he saw a glint of emotion cross her face, a look that came and went so fast that it was hard to recognize. But, fleeting as it had been, Merral felt it to be one of concern, and he knew that it confirmed his own unease. There was indeed something wrong in the house.

Zennia, apparently realizing that she had revealed some secret thing, turned sharply and made to go to the door.

"Aunt, wait a moment," Merral said. "Uncle . . . how is he?"

Zennia stopped, her hand on the door, and looked at him, her eyes showing unhappiness.

"He is tired, Merral. He's gone to bed."

"He's not unwell? Any symptoms?"

"No. Just tired." She paused as if uncertain whether to continue. When she spoke again, it was in puzzled tones.

"It seems . . . it *seems* as if he dreamed as well last night—something strange and not very nice. He won't say what." She moved again as if to go.

In his surprise, Merral said without thinking, "Oh, I'm sorry to hear that, Aunt. But I thought he said he hadn't dreamed."

Zennia, looking away from him, remained still, her only movement the agitated twisting of her fingers on the door frame. When she spoke it was in awkward, hacked phrases. "Well . . . I really can't—I'm not sure . . . exactly what he said."

There was a clumsy pause in which both were silent. Then she turned, gave him a cool formal smile, and left, calling gently over her shoulder as she pulled the door behind her closed, "Good night and blessings, Merral."

The door was closed by the time he had begun to return her benediction.

• ◆ •

With his mind in total confusion, Merral clicked the diary off, and the image looming over his desk instantly vanished. He sat back in the chair, arms behind his head, trying to unravel his perplexed thoughts. So, Barrand had had a foul dream too. That was curious. One bad dream in a house was odd, but for two people to have one on the same night was very mysterious. Yet the dream was not what worried him or, he suspected, Zennia. No, what was making his mind reel was that this morning Barrand had definitely said that he had slept well and

CHRIS WALLEY

had had no dreams. He had said it plainly. And Zennia's unhappiness when he had pressed her had confirmed it. She avoided answering his inquiry because she couldn't face the fact that her husband had lied earlier in the day. And with that answer came a terrible awareness: Could it really be that his uncle had lied?

Under the thrust of the word *lied* Merral got up and paced the small room in agitation. The very word *lie* was unfamiliar. To deceive, to willfully alter truth; he knew theoretically—as everyone did—what it meant. But understood it was never practiced. You might sometimes mislead people in sport, like in Team-Ball games, where you made them think you were going right not left, but that, of course, was not lying. Nor was it lying to pull a verbal surprise, as in a joke or a riddle. And even when asked a question where the answer would be hurtful to the hearer, it was easy enough, at least in Communal—the historic languages were harder—to give an answer that allowed it to be understood that, for whatever reason, you preferred not to commit yourself. True, the idea of lying came to you on occasions, particularly when you had made a mistake. But you just pushed the idea aside. Since the time of the Great Intervention, the temptation to willfully deceive someone had had little real force. Jannafy's rebellion in the first days of the Assembly had probably been the last instance of large-scale deception.

No, Merral concluded, the idea of lying was hateful. The entire edifice of the civilization of the Assembly of Worlds was built on truth and on its counterpart, trust. The lie was the enemy to all that. As he lay down on the bed, he reflected that it was an axiom of the whole era of the Lord's Peace from the Intervention till now that no one lied. Truth had been sacred since the Dark Times, over eleven thousand years ago.

And yet, the thought nagged at Merral until sleep finally fell on him; the conclusion seemed inescapable.

His uncle had lied.

CHAPTER 3

Merral was up early the next morning, and after donning his jacket, slipped outside to look at the weather. Although the sun should have been rising there was only a dull glow in the east, and in the gloom he could faintly make out that during the night the wind had changed and was now coming out of the barren wastelands of the west. At least, he comforted himself, from that direction neither rain nor snow would come.

When Merral entered the kitchen he found Barrand sitting at the table. There was an unhappy look on his face, and after the briefest of greetings he blurted out, "Merral, I'm so sorry about yesterday! The whole thing was ridiculous! Zennia said you were worried because I seemed to have well—*contradicted*—myself. It could, I suppose, seem like that. The fact is that . . . well . . . I did dream, it's true. But I had—I suppose—pushed it out of my mind. When you spoke about having a dream, I began to remember it, but I was unsure about it." Here he paused, as if uncertain what to say next. "I mean I was unsure about whether I had had a dream. If you follow my meaning."

Uncertain how to respond, Merral just nodded, and his uncle went on in an unsteady fashion. "So, anyway it was just later on in the day that it all came flooding back. And when I said in the morning that I hadn't dreamed, it was, well . . . true then. But I mean, it wasn't a major dream anyway. So the whole thing is nothing serious. I wouldn't want you to get it all out of proportion."

I need to think about this, Merral thought, recognizing that his uncle seemed to be in serious difficulties.

"I think I understand, Uncle. But actually, if you'll excuse me, I'd better have breakfast and be off—if that's all right with you. Graceful and I have a long way to go today."

A look of relief seemed to cross the gray-blue eyes. "Yes, yes. Now tell me your plans while I get some food out for you."

· ◆ ·

Fifteen minutes later as he came down the stairs with his pack, ready to leave, Zennia was waiting at the outer door. She smiled rather distantly at him. "Your uncle has explained everything, has he? A sort of delay in recognizing that he had had a dream. It all makes sense now. Something about nothing."

Merral hesitated. "Yes, I hope so. I'm glad you've got it all sorted out." He kissed her on the cheek. "I must be away, Aunt. Give my love to the children. I'll be back this way soon."

There was the clatter of feet on the stairs and a slender figure in a fluffy pink robe with a straw-colored mop of hair bounced lightly down the stairs, ran over, and clutched his hand.

"Bye, Cousin Merral. Don't get talking to the trees now."

Merral gave Elana a hug, noticing as he did that she was already nearly up to his shoulder. "Bye, Elana."

There was a heavy thudding on the stairs and Thomas leapt down, slid across the wood floor like a skater, and wrapped his arms around Merral.

"Cousin! You nearly left without saying good-bye."

Laughing, Merral disentangled himself from Thomas's clutches and lifted the boy high so that his head nearly touched the roof. "Owf! You are getting too heavy to do this."

"Have a safe trip, Cousin Merral. Look after Graceful." Thomas giggled as, with a playful tickle, Merral put him down.

"I will. And you look after the dogs!"

Merral turned to his aunt. "I'd best be off before the rest of the family comes down."

He raised his hand. "A blessing on this house." Then he pressed the door switch and, as it slid open, stepped out into the raw grayness of the dawn.

It was still little more than half-light when, ten minutes later, Merral rode Graceful southwest from the hamlet. The route he had planned was a long one. He intended to travel first west over Brigila's Wastes, keeping south of the still-barren lava seas, then south along the Long Marshes before swinging back through the eastern tip of the Great Northern Forest. From there, a track should allow him to make Wilamall's Farm, the most northerly forestry base, by midafternoon at the latest. There he would leave Graceful in the stables while he took the daily overland transporter down to Ynysmant. There were more rapid routes home from Herrandown, but Merral wanted to see as much as he could. Sampling and observer machines made regular survey trips across these lands, and drones flew overhead to monitor for changes, but he knew that there was no substitute for walking or riding the ground.

Fifteen minutes later, having carefully crossed the solid ice of the Lannar River on foot and ridden up the sparsely wooded western bank, Merral squinted across at the wastes before him and wondered why he had been so zealous.

Ahead was a desolate and empty landscape across which a cutting wind whistled hungrily around him. Facing into it, he found that there was little escape even with the glare goggles on and the face baffle of his jacket up round his nose. As he rode on, with Graceful picking her way across the frozen tussocks, he decided that there was little to choose between the west and the north wind. While lacking the polar chill of the wind from the north, the west wind had its own cruel character. Here every turbulent gust that struck carried a reminder that it was drawn across five thousand kilometers of treeless waste, much of it a dry, salty, and sandy desert. At least, he reminded himself, in winter there was still enough moisture to remove the dust. In summer, the dry and baking west wind was filled with dust, silt, and static, and became the scourge of machinery and men's lungs.

Merral, trying to keep his face averted from the wind as much as he could, found little compensation in his route. Here only the thinnest skins of frozen soil and turf covered hard black volcanic rock. There were patches of powdery snow and, every so often, dangerous stretches of colorless ice over which dismounting was necessary. The only vegetation was clumps of rough tussocky grass with occasional straggly bushes of hazel and willow. Given the scarcity of the vegetation and the harsh weather, Merral found no surprise in the fact that he saw little life in the wastes. Every so often he put to flight a party of migrating tundra hares, pale in their winter coats, and once he came across a herd of grazing reindeer, which stared at him stupidly before turning away and shuffling off to resume their foraging. Once a pair of great Gyrfalcons circled above him, ghostly below the clouds, then drifted away southward. But that was all he saw.

Soon he found that he was in a featureless landscape where the gray of the ground faded into the softer grayness of the sky to give an elusive and unchanging horizon. Merral decided that here he could not afford to be lost and set his diary to check the route: a thing he rarely did. So his progress was marked by periodic noises from the diary, a deep long beep for a deviation to the left, a short high one for one to the right, and a bell-like chime for a correct course. Like all Forestry horses Graceful understood the signals enough to steer herself. So together, horse and man progressed slowly over Brigila's Wastes, the silence broken only by the whistles of the wind, the clip-clop of Graceful's hooves, and the occasional interruption from the diary.

For the first half hour or so Merral was preoccupied by what had happened at Herrandown. He was unsatisfied by what both his uncle and aunt had said this morning. Something odd, alarming, and even wrong had happened yesterday. But what? No hypothesis he could invent would make any sense. In the end, Merral reluctantly decided that Zennia and Barrand must be right: It was some sort of psychological oddity that they had mishandled between them so that it had become completely distorted. After all, human beings were complex. On that basis, Merral pushed the affair out of his mind.

Yet as he rode on, he felt a strange feeling of disquiet that seemed to have nothing to do with the weather. More than once, he found himself looking around or even over his shoulder, as if some invisible shadow had fallen upon him. But, other than the gently undulating bleak surface under him and the gray billowy sky above, there was nothing to see.

Eventually, Merral forced himself to concentrate on studying the ground and trying to get a feel for these barren lands. He found himself pondering over the wastes, aware of how widespread this sort of landscape was in Menaya. *Here, I can believe this is a half-finished world, with this ripped veneer of soil and scrub over lava and rock outwash supporting, at best, a handful of species.* But that thought came to him as more of a challenge than a criticism. God willing, within a few years there would be trees over much of this area, and with them, a much greater diversity of plants and animals. The issue was how to do it.

As the brown reeds of the marsh's edge came into sight, Merral checked his location from the diary and ordered the active navigation off. He would swing southward down the flanks of the marshes up to the edge of the Great Northern Forest. Not only was there no danger of losing his way here, but the presence of patches of marsh and swamp made such an automated navigation worse than useless.

Merral picked his way along the slope just above where the reed beds started, watching carefully for patches of thin ice. As he rode down along the marsh's edge his journey became easier. The wind blew now at his side rather than into his face, and the sky lightened overhead so that there was enough sunlight to cast a faint shadow. Here there was life: birdsong from within the reed beds, the whistling of the dwarf swans on the lake, and the piercing cries of the gulls. A reed heron scuttled away in front of him. In the distance he saw a herd of gray deer, a pair of otters slithered away into an ice-free patch of water at the sound of Graceful's hooves, and a Raymont's musk ox lurched across his path.

As he drew near the edge of the forest he crossed the distinctive tracks of a half-ton hexapod surveyor. They were fresh and going south with a purpose rare in surveying machines, and Merral wondered if it had been programmed to return to base before Nativity so that the samples could be unloaded before the break. Wilamall's Farm would probably be busy today.

An hour or so later Merral stopped and took another bearing. He wanted to be certain of striking the forest edge south of the limits of the rough lava flows. At the ragged edge of the forest, he reined Graceful in and took a last look over the Long Marshes, a great sea of tan reeds swaying gently in the wind as far as the eye could see, broken only by snaking waterways clogged with brittle ice. He would, he decided, come by again in summer and camp and linger.

Today, though, there was something about the wastes that he found peculiarly unwelcoming, and as he entered under the shadows of the trees, Merral found himself rejoicing even more than usual. He had always loved woods, even in winter when the rowans and gray alders were bare and only the pines were green, and even these impoverished and marginal forests with their gale-tumbled trunks. So he didn't mind that, with the branches low to the ground and the land rough, his journey was a slow one. It took well over an hour's skillful riding to reach the support road, as he skirted around areas of impenetrable scrub and avoided the deeper streams while trying not to depart from his compass bearing. Even so, he was wondering about taking a location check when suddenly he was out of the trees, and the track—a rift of dead, yellow bleached grass between the high trees—lay before him. The road had been made two centuries or so earlier to ease the passage of the ground transporters bringing in the first trees for this part of the forest. Since then, it had been cleared periodically to maintain a line of access into the forest.

Merral dismounted, letting Graceful graze on the remains of the grass. Then, listening to the wind whistling through the treetops, he looked at the track for signs of recent passage of men or machines but found nothing. Any woodland sampling and observer machines were too delicate on their feet to leave traces on hard ground, and if any humans had come through here lately, they had used some zero-impact machine such as a gravity-modifying sled, a hoverer, or, like him, a horse. He was not surprised; he was too far away from any homes for stray visitors and he knew that the current schedule of the Forestry Development Team did not include any visits in this area. No, today the woods were his and he was glad of it. He loved the solitude and was always glad of the opportunity to sing his heart out to heaven's King.

He remounted and set off southward, starting to sing as he went. Today, though, for some strange reason, he found a lack of spontaneity in his singing, and it was only by dint of discipline and effort that he kept himself going. But for the next three hours, as he rode slowly along the old track as it wound its way down and round a succession of valley flanks and ridges, Merral sang, working his way twice through the entire Nativity section of the Assembly song book. It was not, he knew, the greatest singing, and there was little in it of the quality that Barrand's re-created voices would have, but it was genuine and, with a deep gratitude, he offered it up to the One who was the Light above lights.

But even in the singing Merral was keeping a careful eye on the forest. In general he was pleased with what he saw, finding almost all the trees, apart from those felled or beheaded by ice storms or wind gusts, in a satisfactory state. No, he concluded, after its two centuries of history this wood would pass—at least at first glance—the highest test of a Made World woodland and be taken as an original forest of Ancient Earth, albeit one with some unfamiliar species. A closer inspection would, of course, show a much more limited diversity of plants and animals, and some oddities as species adapted rapidly into the new and unoccupied environmental niches. Everything took time, and you couldn't just throw a world together and hope it would work. Everything had to be checked, its every possible interaction with everything else modeled and predicted. And even then things went wrong; like the fungal species that digested dead wood on one hundred and sixty worlds but which, on the hundred and sixty-first, suddenly became one that digested living pine trees. But as they said, "every world sown was new lessons reaped." What had taken a thousand years on the first Made Worlds now took under half that. But there was always room for improvement and no world was ever truly Earth.

As he rode south, Merral noticed, with faint surprise, that his spirits seemed to lift. He put it down to the gentle lifting of the temperature and to getting away from the bleak emptiness of Brigila's Wastes. Yet it was funny, he reflected, that he had never felt such a change in mood before. But he soon shrugged off his puzzlement; introspection was not something that he, or any of his world, ever indulged in for long. He stopped once for food in a clearing overlooking a stream, setting Graceful free to find what she could to eat among the blanched and withered grasses. Then, mindful of the short winter days, he set off again. Yet as he did so, a strange, fleeting thought came to him that he had an anxiousness to be home he had never had before. It was still another oddity for him to consider.

By four in the afternoon he had approached Wilamall's Farm and other tracks joined his. At one junction, Merral waited while a woodland surveyor, six smaller undergrowth analyzers docked onto its back, ambled past on its eight long, metallic legs. As it passed him the machine stopped and turned its slender head toward him. The two large glassy eyes looked at him without expression. Merral raised his right hand vertically to reassure the surveyor that he needed no assistance. The machine raised a front paw in dumb mechanical acknowledgement and continued on its way south.

The sun was hanging low on the western hills as Merral came out of the forest and saw below him the fences, roofs, and domes of Wilamall's Farm. Down by the labs a line of gray samplers full of plant fragments for testing waited with perfect patience to be unloaded, and over by the transport offices, other machines were being garaged. As he watched, a pale long-winged survey drone descended gently through the air overhead, extruded legs, and with a smooth glide, came to rest on the small landing strip.

Merral was met at the gate by Teracy, the assistant manager, who, after warmest greetings and high praise for a recent project he'd undertaken, told Merral that he had a place booked on a freighter going south in half an hour. Wasting no time, Merral took Graceful over to the stables.

A large, stooped figure in a dark gray jacket walked over awkwardly from the small office by the stables. His left foot dragged behind him.

"If you please, Mister Merral!" the man sang out loudly in a voice as rough as broken wood.

"*Jorgio!*" Merral replied, delighted at seeing the broad, tanned, and twisted face of his old friend, who served as gardener and stable hand at Wilamall's Farm. "Greetings! It's good to see you."

"Greetings indeed." Then, careful to avoid crushing a bloodred cyclamen sticking out of his breast pocket, he squeezed Merral in a forceful embrace. Returning the embrace, Merral caught the faint odor of animals, stable, and gardens, and suddenly his earliest memories of meeting Jorgio came back to him. He had been five or six, and he had been taken one cold spring day to see the new lambs near the edge of the cottages where Jorgio lived. At first, he had found the man's large and deformed figure intimidating. Yet, within minutes, Jorgio had put him at ease and they had been friends ever since. Merral had no idea exactly how old Jorgio was; he assumed he was in his sixties but found it hard to tell.

They released each other, and Jorgio, his amber-brown eyes gleaming softly, gave Merral a thick-lipped and skewed grin and then turned his large, bald head toward Graceful. He whistled to her in a strangely out-of-tune way. As she trotted over to Jorgio, it came to Merral again that everything about Jorgio, from his legs to his misshapen shoulders, was asymmetrical. Occasionally he felt his logic was unusual as well; Jorgio seemed to have an odd perspective, almost as if the childhood accident that had damaged his body had also curved his way of thinking.

"Graceful, let's have a look at you," Jorgio said with a surprising softness of tone. "There's long miles you have covered."

He bent down and ran his rough, veined hands over the mare's flanks. Watching him as he made soft whispering noises, Merral knew that it was not just affection that he had for this man; it was also respect. He had long felt that, as if in some form of compensation for his distorted body, the Most High had given Jorgio special gifts. He was an excellent gardener, capable of making things flower in the poorest of soils, and had a deep affinity with animals. His curved logic wasn't wrong; it was just different.

"It's a real blessing to see you, Mister Merral," Jorgio said, glancing up at him. "It really is."

"And for me to see you."

It is interesting, Merral thought, as Jorgio looked over the mare, *how we deal with people like Jorgio, these accidents of life. We always seem to find them something in which they can fulfill themselves, whether it is tending gardens, painting our houses, or minding our horses. He and I do a job, get the same food and housing, have the same stipend to give away or use, and only the Judge of all the Worlds knows which—if either—of us is the more valuable.* Jorgio looked up, his mouth skewed open in a smile. "It is north you've been, eh?"

"Indeed so. As far as there are farms, Jorgio."

"Thought so."

In an uneven singsong Jorgio whispered words to the horse. Then he gave Merral a clumsy wink. "Let me stable Graceful here and you and I'll take some tea together."

"Ah, I'm sorry, old friend. I'm afraid I shall have to skip the tea. I've been put on the next freighter out. Twenty minutes. But I'll help you stable her."

"Tut, tut! No tea with me? If you please, you youngsters are too busy by far. Here, lass, give me a hoof. I'll talk to your horse instead." He stroked a flank. "Good girl, good girl."

Suddenly, as if caught by a thought, Jorgio lifted his face up briefly, his brown eyes showing puzzlement. "Do you know, Mister Merral, as I've been praying for you lately?"

"You have?" Merral replied, struck by the intensity in his friend's face. "Well I value that. I truly do."

Jorgio was now peering at the hoof. "Tut, tut. Ice and sharp rock are nasty things for a hoof. Even with dura-polymer coatings. If they're all like this I'll get new coatings put on 'em. But after Nativity."

He looked up again at Merral, the angle making his face seem even more distorted. "Funny, it was. I haven't been sleeping well lately. Restless. For two weeks now. The other night, last night, I think. Anyway, I'm lying awake in my bed. You've seen my room, haven't you? Nice it is. Cozy; you can see it now. Oh no, you're off away, aren't you? Anyway, middle of the night the King just says to me, 'Jorgio Aneld Serter.' Full name like. So I sits up in bed and says, 'Your Majesty, present and correct!' Well, there's not a lot else to say, is there?"

Sometimes Merral found it hard to know whether Jorgio was trying to make a joke, but this didn't sound like one. "I suppose so," he said, patting his friend on the back. "Not much else indeed. But go on."

Jorgio let the hoof drop to the ground and stood up, screwing his face up as he struggled to remember something.

"So, well, the King, he says, 'That Merral Stefan D'Avanos, he's in a spot of bother right now. I think you ought to pray for him.'

"'Well, right you are, Your Majesty,' I says, and then he's gone. So I starts asking the Most High to look after you. Half an hour I reckoned I prayed. Hard work it was, like wrestling with a bear. Not that I've done that, but you takes my meaning. I was in a regular sweat when I finished. I don't know what the bother was." He scratched a crumpled ear. "Never had that happen. You know what it was about?"

"Last night? I was safely asleep indoors last night at the Antalfers. But *wait*. . . ." Something like ice seemed to run up his spine. "When was this? *Last* night?" Merral stared into Jorgio's eyes.

"Aye, last night. . . ."

"You're sure?"

The old man wrinkled his weathered face and bit his bottom lip in puzzlement. Then he grunted. "Tut. No! I'm sorry. It wasn't. It was the night before."

Merral stepped back, feeling as if a chill hand had touched him. "No, it wasn't a bear," he said, suddenly both chastened and grateful.

"But it was something. I don't know what it was. And I'm very glad you prayed. Very glad."

For a moment, Jorgio stared at him, as if waiting for an explanation. Merral found himself oddly disinclined to say anything about his dream and suggested instead that they stable Graceful.

• ◆ •

Ten minutes later, having said farewell to Jorgio, Merral was still oscillating between puzzlement and thankfulness as he made his way down to the loading bay. There, floodlit beneath the weather shelter, he could see the brick red, faceted bulk of the six-wheeled Light Groundfreighter with the code *F-28* stamped on its side by the Lamb and Stars emblem.

He was striding toward it when his attention was caught by a slender female figure with long black hair tied back walking ahead of him with a strangely familiar pace.

"Ingrida Hallet!" Merral called out.

The woman spun round smoothly and gave a little cry of recognition. "Why! Merral D'Avanos!"

They hugged each other affectionately. Ingrida had been a year above Merral at college, but they had been close friends. Separating himself from her embrace, Merral stepped back and they looked at each other.

"I heard you were here," she said. "I gather you've been riding around up north. Going all right?"

"Fine, but no room to relax. The winters could be warmer, the summers cooler. But what brings *you* here?"

"Ah." She smiled brightly. "You don't know? Of course, you've been out of touch and it's not been posted yet. I've been asked to work here. Forestry Assistant and so on. So I decided to come and look round on my Nativity break."

"Oh, but I thought I'd heard that you were going south. That you'd got the rainforest assignment they have been wanting to fill. I was wrong?"

She shook her head in an amused way and grinned at him mischievously. "Oh, we talked it through. The board thinks this is more suitable. I'm inclined to agree, although this—"she gestured to the farm complex—"will be a bit of a backwater when the enlarged Herrandown village is up and running and the new Northern Forest extension is the front line. No, I think the tropics job requires more than I have got. There's a better candidate."

"I'd be surprised; tropical systems are tough. But I'm sure you'll get on fine here. I like it up north myself."

She gave him the grin again, only this time he felt laughter was just below the surface. "Not too much, I hope."

"Sorry, I don't understand."

"Oh, Merral, you haven't changed. Not a bit! You are the last person to recognize your gifting. *You* are the one they want for the tropical assignment."

In his astonishment, Merral struggled for words, aware that a man in rust-red overalls was waving at him from the side of the freighter.

"Me? This is all news to me. I've always seen it as *your* job."

"No. You are outgrowing here. Ask anybody." She patted him on the shoulder. "Anyway, take it with my blessing, Merral. Do a really great job. Look, that's your driver, you'd better go. Swing by sometime. Love. . . ."

Then Ingrida was gone and the hatch door on the freighter was opening.

•◆•

The six-wheeler took four hours to cover the one hundred and eighty kilometers to Ynysmant, slowed down by patches of ice on some of the ridges, a track washout, and a herd of golden deer that refused to move. Merral spent most of the time in conversation with the driver, Arent, who was an enthusiast for this particular Mark Nine Groundfreighter, which he'd driven for thirty years. Merral liked enthusiasts of any sort, even if wheeled, winged, or finned engines of transport were not a personal interest.

Yet, in a strange way, Merral was glad of being forced to concentrate on Arent's lengthy discourse on the advantages of the Mark Nine over the old Mark Eight. There was too much crowding into his tired brain now and he was glad of a relatively simple distraction. The prospect of the tropical forestry posting was staggering. When, a few months ago, he had originally heard about it, he had expressed regret that it hadn't come up two years later when he felt he might have been ready for it. Tropical forestry was held up as the great challenge in his profession, and only those who had proved themselves in temperate or cold realms were asked to serve in it. The saying was that cold or temperate forest work was like juggling with three balls; but with tropical, it was eight. The many more species gave a multitude of interactions, and everything happened so fast. He wondered whether Ingrida had made a mistake. In the meantime, he forced himself to follow Arent's explanation of why it would take at least another twenty years of careful design before it was worthwhile producing the Mark Ten Light Groundfreighter.

They were winding through the beech woods on what Merral knew was the last ridge before Ynysmere Lake when Arent looked upward through the transparent roof panel. "Tell you what, the cloud's cleared and we are ahead of schedule. Let me put her on nonvisual waveband sensing and slow the speed."

The rapid flickering of the tree trunks in the headlights eased. "Now we cut the lights. We should get a great view of the stars and the town."

Merral had seen it done before, but found it as impressive as ever. For a moment everything outside was total darkness and then gradually his adapting eyes made out the stars, high, sharp, and diamond brilliant above the rushing black smear of branches, and ahead over the ridge, the golden beacons of the Gate and the sharp, clear pinpoint that was the gas giant planet Fenniran clearly visible.

Arent looked upward and spoke in hushed, reverent tones. "Nativity's Eve, Merral. I always feel somehow that high heaven is that bit nearer tonight. But I suppose that'd be the sort of thing you learned folk would smile at?"

"Oh, 'learned folk' indeed, Arent!" Merral laughed. "This night of all reminds us of the folly of that idea. I recollect that it was to shepherds in the fields the angels appeared, not to the wise in Jerusalem. Anyway, I'm not as learned as you are on your F-28."

"True enough."

"And you may well be right, I suppose, Arent. High heaven may be nearer to us tonight—but we have no instruments to measure its proximity." Then, without thinking, he added, "Or that of hell either."

He sensed Arent's face, looking curiously at him in the darkness. "Sorry, Merral. Did you say something?"

"Sort of. . . ." He paused, puzzled at where the words had come from. "But I didn't mean to."

There was a long silence as the road flattened, and then they crested the hill. Ahead and below them in a sea of blackness appeared a cone of tiny twinkling points of silver light, as if some sort of faint human echo of the glory above.

And as he looked carefully at the town of Ynysmant perched on its steep island in the lake, Merral could see how the reflection of the lights shimmered as the lake's dark waters stirred in the wind.

Home, he thought, and the word had a peculiar taste of welcome to it that he felt it had never had before.

Merral left the freighter at the island end of the causeway, thanked Arent, and half walked and half ran up the winding steps into the town. With it being Nativity's Eve there were many groups on their way to parties and concerts, and Merral picked up a sense of excitement in the air.

The lights were on at his house, a narrow three-story unit in the middle of a sinuous terrace with overhanging eaves. Merral pushed open the door, vaguely surprised to find the hall and kitchen empty. There was ample evidence of recent cooking with a tray of small jam cakes on the side table, and the smell made him realize suddenly how hungry he was. Putting his bag down, he took off his jacket and slung it on a chair. He was suddenly aware of feeling tired and sweaty. It had, he decided, been a long day. Eventually the smell of the cakes was too much for him and he helped himself to one, putting it whole in his mouth and finding it as delicious as he had expected. As he stood there, he heard talking in the general room beyond and, swallowing the last cake fragments, pushed the door open.

His mother, dressed in a skirt and blouse patterned with flowers, rose from her chair suddenly at his entry. She gave a little cry of "Merral," came over, and kissed him warmly. As they broke free from each other, he saw behind her a thinly built, dark-skinned man of medium height wearing a neat blue formal suit rising from a chair.

His mother took his arm and stretched it out.

"I'm so *glad* you're back. Merral, let me introduce you to—I think I have the name right—Mr. Verofaza Laertes Enand."

The young man smiled gravely and gave a slight bow. "Indeed," he said. "Verofaza Laertes Enand, *sentinel*. A pleasure."

Merral stared at him, hurriedly trying to wipe crumbs off his lips with his left hand. The name made no sense. There was only one sentinel on Farholme, an old man, and this was not him. Besides which the man's accent was out of the ordinary, but somehow familiar. Merral felt he had always known it.

"Merral Stefan D'Avanos," he said, awkwardly swallowing the last fragments of cake as he shook hands. Then he looked at the guest. "*Sentinel?* Here?" he asked. "But have you replaced old Brenito? He's not . . . ?"

The man stood back, his smile slightly awkward, even shy. *He's young,* Merral thought, *probably my age—midtwenties.*

"No, he is alive and well. I have traveled farther than your capital."

Merral realized that he had answered in Communal, not the Farholmen dialect. He was suddenly aware of his mother tugging his arm and speaking to him in a quiet intensity of excitement. But even as she spoke he knew what she was going to say, for he had understood why the accent was familiar and why he had known it since childhood.

"Merral," she said in an awed voice, "he's come from Ancient Earth."

CHAPTER 4

M erral stared at the stranger. At college, he had once been in a meeting that had been addressed by someone from Ancient Earth, and he had met pilots and others who had trained there. But he personally had never as much as shaken hands with anybody from there. Indeed now, as he scrutinized the visitor, he felt there was something unusual about him. The suit had a strangely severe line, the black curly hair was cut in a peculiar way, and the rich dark brown skin was darker than any he had seen on Farholme. On their own, these things were merely oddities; taken together they said that the visitor was not from his world.

Merral realized that he was staring too much. "I'm sorry, Verofaza. You have taken me by surprise. . . ."

The other man smiled wryly. "It's Vero. Everyone calls me that. I gather you've been traveling all day. That makes us both travelers."

A kind comment, and one that makes me feel more at ease. He found himself warming to the stranger. "I find it generous that you can put my miserable two hundred or so kilometers in the same category as your three hundred and fifty-odd light-years."

"Nearly four hundred in total. I kept careful count." He gave a little shudder. "The only place they could find was on a long route combination."

"It is a mere twenty million million times my journey."

Vero grimaced vividly. Merral decided he had a very mobile face and that he could make a great clown or mime actor.

"I try not to think of the distances like that, Merral. A light-year is somehow manageable; ten trillion kilometers isn't. Please, why don't we sit down?"

"I'm sorry," Merral said. "I should have asked you."

"It's not a difficulty. And you don't mind me using Communal? I seem to understand your dialect easily enough, but I wouldn't dare try and speak it."

Merral felt that the visitor's warm, deep brown eyes were watching him keenly. "There is no problem. Yes, Farholmen dialect has not yet seriously diverged from Communal. Although there are trends. As a sentinel, I expected you to wear your badge."

"The Tower against the Sky?" He smiled. "Oh, I should do, but I find it a bit of a nuisance. Everybody points you out: 'Look, Mum, there's a sentinel.' It's a tradition—not a rule—to wear it. And I choose not to. But I will wear it tomorrow."

Merral turned to his mother, who was still standing nearby. "Mother, will you not sit with us?"

She shook her head, letting her braided silver-flecked brown hair bob on her shoulders. "No, no thank you, Merral. I'd *love* to really. Your father has been delayed at the depot and I really *must* get the rooms ready. And *really,* I have to finish off some things for supper and the meal tomorrow. And would you like something to drink? Perhaps another cake?" She gave him a knowing nod.

Merral, suddenly feeling rather sheepish, wiped his mouth again. "Er, yes. Both please, Mother. I've been traveling since dawn."

She turned to their guest. "Perhaps Vero, a drink of something for you?"

He nodded formally. "Thank you. Just a glass of your excellent water please, Lena."

She bowed slightly, patted Merral on the shoulder tenderly, and left the room.

"Are you fasting?" Merral asked.

The stranger's face acquired a slightly pained look. "Not really. Over the past two weeks I have been through five Gates. And I have found out that I do not like them. I think that my stomach is still several light-years behind in Below-Space and trying to catch up. In fact, I wonder if I will ever be reunited with it."

"You found it unpleasant? People vary, I gather."

"Yes. Very disorienting. Have you ever been though a Gate?"

"I've never even been in Farholme orbit."

"Lucky you." Vero stretched himself back in his chair and flexed his long, smooth brown fingers against each other as if concerned that they were all present and working. "Five Gates in thirteen days, Merral. There was a lot of turbulence between the Nelat Four Gate and Rustiran. You could feel the whole Normal-Space tunnel being buffeted. A weird feeling. And weightlessness wasn't much better. Or takeoffs." He wriggled his face in an almost child-like look of disgust.

Merral found himself enjoying his visitor. "I have lots of questions, you know," he said.

Vero closed his eyes and shook his head slowly, as if trying to fight off a headache. "Ah, that I can imagine. But I'm here—well, in Ynysmant—for three days, and I promise I'll try and answer some at least. In time. Actually, I'm here to ask questions myself."

"You are?"

"Yes."

Merral waited in vain for any further clarification then asked, "What sort?"

Vero flexed his fingers again, stared at them, and then smiled with wide eyes at Merral. "Ah, that is the problem. But my first question is, what sort of journey did you have?"

Merral was just on the point of answering when his mother came back bearing a small wooden tray with two glasses of water and a plate of small cakes. She put them on the low table between the chairs and gave a glass to Vero, who bowed his head in acknowledgement.

"Thank you indeed." Then he took the glass carefully, held it up toward her as if making a toast, and sipped it delicately.

Merral's mother smiled at him. "And it's our *honor* to have you. But, not wishing to interrupt your conversation, I'd better remind you, Vero, that it's not long before you're expected at the house of Former Warden Prendal. There is a party, with a meal and dancing."

"You are right, Lena." Vero glanced at his watch. "And the evening is going. I'd better get ready. Is it far?"

Merral put down his glass. "Ten minutes' walk, a bit more. I'll take you. In say, fifteen minutes?"

"Done."

Somehow, Merral made time in those few minutes for a shower and a change of clothes. He also managed to wonder why there was a sentinel visiting Farholme, why he had arrived here in Ynysmant, and what exactly sentinels did. Then he grabbed his winter jacket and met up with Vero, who was standing self-consciously by the door in a long, thick brown coat that went down to his ankles. Vero caught Merral's glance.

"Ah yes. The coat. Well, I was near the Congo Position when the Sentinel Council suddenly asked me to go. It was all a last minute rush. So I was actually on the way to the launch site when I realized I'd be arriving here in winter. The only winter coat I could get was one from a very tall Nord-European. It is far too long, isn't it?" He glanced down at it again in an embarrassed way and then looked up at Merral. Suddenly, they both found themselves laughing.

Merral shook his head in mirth. "What a mess, eh, Vero? They send you four hundred light-years to the end of the Assembly through Below-Space five times and with expenditure of enormous amounts of energy, and all with the wrong-sized coat! Oh, I love it!" he chortled.

Vero shook with laughter. "Do you suppose . . . ?" he spluttered, pausing for breath between stifled snorts of laughter. "Do you suppose . . . ? No. . . . It's too funny." Here he suddenly seemed to control himself. He turned to Merral with a perfectly solemn face and, in an intensely serious voice said, "My friend, do you think that perhaps I ought to go back and get one that fits?"

Then the facade of seriousness cracked and he broke out with a croaking laugh. Merral, unable to control himself, burst out into renewed peals of laughter. Eventually he clapped Vero on the back and ushered him out the door. Guffawing with mirth together, they set off up the hill.

By the end of the street they had quieted down enough for Vero to begin asking Merral various questions about Ynysmant, such as how big it was and how long he had lived in it. Apparently satisfied, he then said with a quiet intensity, "Now tell me, Merral, are people happy here?"

At first, Merral wondered whether he had heard the question correctly, then he considered whether it was a joke, and then finally he asked for clarification. "Is that an Ancient Earth question? I mean— excuse me for saying it—it barely makes sense."

Vero stopped in his tracks, obviously thinking hard. "Yes, I know what you mean. But look, are they contented? Do they long for, well . . . what they cannot have?"

Merral heard himself laughing again. "Want what they cannot have? Vero, this may be Worlds' End, but we aren't stupid. I mean, what would a man or woman want with something that was not theirs to have? You'd drive yourself crazy. It'd be like . . . well . . . I don't know—a lake wishing to be a mountain or a bird wanting to be a fish."

For long moments the only sound was their feet on the cobbles and muffled singing from an adjacent house. Then Vero spoke, but this time it was in a puzzled, reflective tone. "See, I don't even know enough to know where to begin. This whole thing is . . ." He sighed. "Very difficult."

They walked on without speaking between the high painted walls of the houses and in and out of pools of light and shadow. Barely audible celebratory music and laughter seemed to seep through windows and doors.

"Vero, why did you come here, to this town, to us?"

"Because it seemed right. My task was to visit here and to write a report. It's my first task as an accredited sentinel."

A cold gust of wind whistled down an alleyway, and Merral was aware of his friend shivering.

"What sort of report?"

There was the faintest of pauses. "On how Farholme is doing. There are specific questions but . . . well, it's very open. Anyway, after I disembarked at Isterrane two days ago, I visited Brenito, who had made the request for a visit. And he said I ought to start looking around 'from the outside in.'"

"And we are one of the farthest towns out. So you came here?"

A shaft of light caught the dark, lean face, seemingly huddled down in the shelter of the coat's high collar.

"Here. And of the thousand doors it seemed right to knock on that of your house."

"Well, Vero, I hope it was."

"I feel it was. I feel that we are to be friends."

"Yes, I think it will prove to be so."

He led Vero up a narrow brick path that wound round onto a footbridge that brought them high along the side of the hill so that they looked down over the spired and steepled houses. The only illumination now lay in the directed-downward light of the active yellow strips that switched themselves on as they approached and off as they walked away. Above them they could see the stars flung out across the night sky. At the very top of the bridge, Vero put out a hand in front of Merral.

"May we stop a moment please? I would like to see where Earth is."

Merral pointed out where in the Milky Way, if they had had a telescope, they would have been able to see Sol. Vero was silent for some moments, then he leaned back against the brick parapet of the bridge and stared at Merral.

"So much of your world I find familiar. Which is as it should be— the Made Worlds are made to be as much like Earth as they can be. Then suddenly I catch a glimpse of something that reminds me where I am." He shook his head. "And the stars do that all the time. It is almost overwhelming. I can't recognize a constellation. And no moon. Ever."

"Sorry, no visible moon. Just a small invisible Local Gate with enough mass to give the tides to stir our oceans. That's all."

"No, it's not the same. Our moon is something really special, Merral." He sighed. "Yes, I can believe those three-hundred-odd light-years now."

He seemed to shudder. "And tomorrow is Nativity. Strange to think, Merral, this will be the first one I have had away from my family. And on this side of Ancient Earth I could not have gone much farther away. Actually, it's the cold that I find odd. Nativity at home in Africa is always hot."

For a moment Merral said nothing, trying to put himself in the other's shoes, imagining himself transported somewhere with a warm Nativity, strange languages, and alien stars. He could sympathize, and he reached out and put an arm around the stranger.

"I understand." He paused, trying to think of the words. "And yet, friend Vero, if God is infinite what does three-hundred-odd light-years compare to the infinity that is his? And doesn't Nativity itself promise that we will have the Most High with us?"

Vero clasped his arm tightly in return. "You are right, Merral. I'm sorry for expressing myself that way. It was a mastery of my mind by my heart. Perhaps I should explain—it's no excuse—that we sentinels are supposed to be different. In our training we are encouraged to be sensitive, to be intuitive, to be able to listen to what others cannot hear, to see what others cannot see. And it takes its toll. Particularly after five Gates."

Yes, Merral thought, *I can see that it could. And yet, are you so different from me? Perhaps with your training I would be as you. Maybe the way of upbringing I have had has suppressed such feelings, or rather channeled them elsewhere. But deep down I have them, and if I too were all the worlds away from home tonight, then I might well feel as you feel.*

"No, I understand. I really do. But why are you trained that way? Sentinels are not exactly an important thing here. We know you watch and guard, but for what?"

Vero answered thoughtfully. "Your question is delicately ambiguous. 'For what' indeed? For what do we search or for what purpose? Ah. . . ." Here he sighed gently. "Both are valid questions that even we inside the sentinels ask. Or at least I ask. And neither has a simple answer."

Merral felt there was a curious hint of uncertainty or even doubt in his voice.

"Well, tell me as we walk on."

Vero began to speak using a tone of voice that indicated that what he said had been long thought over. "The sentinels were founded in 2112 by Moshe Adlen, just after the end of Jannafy's rebellion. Moshe Adlen was from one of those Jewish families whose conversion to the Messiah marked the very start of the Great Intervention. Incidentally, you do call it the Great Intervention here?"

"Of course. . . . I mean, why not?"

Vero shrugged. "Every so often someone reminds us that what we call the Great Intervention is really a misnomer and wants to change it. The real Great Intervention in human history, they say, occurred when the Most High took on flesh, died, was raised from death, and returned to heaven. You've heard the view?"

"Oh yes. But then you can argue that the events of revival, repentance, and conversion that we term the Great Intervention were, in a way, merely the outworking of that earlier event."

"Exactly; the two-thousand-year-long infancy of the Church finally ended." Vero nodded. "Here too, Farholme seems orthodox. But back to Moshe Adlen—he was a teacher of theology in a university when the Rebellion broke out, and he joined up. He fought against the rebels and was at the final battle at Centauri, and saw what had happened to the colony. He believed that the Rebellion could have been foreseen. He went to Jerusalem and stood before the three symbols the Assembly created to await the Great King: the empty throne, the unworn crown, and the unwielded scepter. And there he took a solemn oath to the Most High that, in as much as it was humanly possible, he would see to it that no such thing should happen again. So he founded an organization, first to help him, and eventually to perpetuate his work."

As the visitor paused, Merral spoke. "Some of this I knew or had been told and had half forgotten. But surely, Vero, we are nearly twelve thousand years on. Do you still hold to the same vision?"

They were now winding round the sides of the gardens of the elevated levels of the town. The light from the houses was splintered through the bare branches of the trees.

Vero answered slowly, the words coming out as if he was thinking afresh about the issue. "A sharp question. There has been a modification in some ways. We hold the standard view that, since the Great Intervention, the founding of the Assembly that followed, and the ending of the Rebellion that marred its infancy, we are in the era of the Lord's Peace as predicted by the prophets of the Old Covenant. The glories of the Most High King are proclaimed already on nigh-on sixteen hundred worlds and a dozen Cities-in-Space. Evil is constrained to a shadow of what it was before the blessed Intervention. We get ill, we suffer loss, we die, but these things do not preoccupy us and mar our existence as they did our distant forefathers. And we believe that this pattern will persist until the end, when the King will return and evil will not simply be bound but will be destroyed and the fabric of the universe will be transformed. But into what, we—as ever—only foresee faintly."

He paused. "That much you on Farholme believe too?"

"Yes. Of course."

"Quite. If anything else were the view here, then Brenito or the Custodians of the Faith, who monitor what we believe, would have warned us of it long ago. Now when the King's Son will return and all things will be renewed is, as it has ever been since the days of the apostles, a mystery. There are two main views. Some say that it may not be long delayed, and there are others that think that the King's Peace may yet continue for many more thousands of years. Some among the sentinels even speculate that the Assembly of the Firstborn may itself not be complete until the whole galaxy is under his name. After all, did not our Lord plainly say that, at the end, the elect would be gathered 'from the ends of the heavens'? Indeed, it may be that in the history of the Assembly, all that we have seen so far may simply be the first chapter."

"Whether we are at the dawn or evening of the Assembly is

sometimes discussed on Farholme," Merral replied softly, "but we are mostly too busy about the present to be concerned about a distant future. Such questions are not a specialization here. I personally hold no opinion on the timing of the Messiah's Return other than to await it with certainty and hope."

Vero paused in his stride and gestured up with his arms. "Good. And I hold no fixed opinion. Indeed, there is no contradiction. We plan for a much greater Assembly but we are prepared that the Return and the Remaking may take place before tomorrow dawns. But, on either view, most people consider that rampant evil is a thing of the past."

He turned, and Merral could see his eyes shining in the faint light. "Now here, the sentinels interject a note of caution. You see, we believe that the devil—the enemy—is not dead, just cast down; he is not destroyed, but merely bound. We find no guarantee that, even under these conditions, evil cannot return. We insist that the Assembly must watch, listen, and pray. That is the only task of the sentinels: to watch out for a new rise of evil." He paused. "Well, that's the theory."

"I see," answered Merral, struggling with the concepts. "We are nearly there—it's just up these stairs. I suppose I understand that. But what exactly are you looking for? Do you know, when I first heard about sentinels as a child, I thought you watched out for aliens."

"Aliens?" Vero laughed gently. "No, they have never figured in sentinel thought. Even in Moshe Adlen's day humanity had realized they were alone. The probability of intelligent life elsewhere had become vanishingly small. Bacteria, yes, but nothing else. And everything since has confirmed that view."

"Oh, it was a childish fantasy of mine. But what are you looking for?"

Vero's answer was slow in coming and strangely hesitant when it came, "We do not know. Anomalies, oddities, changes."

"Sounds like everything and anything."

There was a long—and to Merral, very significant—silence before Vero spoke again. "Ah . . . that is the problem."

How interesting. He seems to have his reservations. But Merral felt it would have been ungenerous to pursue the matter and gestured Vero onward.

Soon they turned down a small, narrow street with a single line of trees down the middle and flanked on each side by winding terraces of four-story houses. He began checking the names at the doors, but in the end the sound of the dance music gave away the location.

"Interesting, Vero, but I'm still only a little wiser. Anyway, here we are."

"Hello! Guests!" he called in as he opened the door. Vandra, the former warden's wife, squeezed past a crowd of relatives and neighbors and came down the hall to greet them. In the next few minutes, Merral found himself immersed in a sea of introductions and repeated requests to stay for food and for the dances. The hosts had opened the doors between three adjacent houses to make a single, long, extended room, but even so, it was still full and barely large enough for the dancing. As Vero was introduced, Merral gradually slipped back so that he stood against the wall. There he stood watching as the next dance started. When the dance—a very formal West Menayan one involving two lines of partners and some complex foot movements—had finished, Merral made arrangements for someone to bring Vero back. Then, pleading tiredness, he offered his apologies and left.

Winding his way back home, Merral considered what Vero had told him about the sentinels, noting that even after his answers he actually knew only a little more about why Vero personally was here. From that he moved on to think how strange it must be to spend your life doing something so vague and ill defined. It all seemed so very different from his own work with its all-too-tangible trees, rocks, and lakes, and only slightly less solid plans and schedules. But it was strange how talking to Vero had made him vaguely desirous of seeing beyond his own world's horizons. Perhaps one day he would have an excuse to go through the Gate. But in the meantime . . .

Here he began to think about the news of the tropics post that Ingrida had told him was to be his, and he was still working out the implications of this when he entered his house.

•◆•

His father was taking his outdoor shoes off in the hallway. Seeing Merral, he stopped what he was doing and, one shoe on and the other off, hopped over and kissed him. Merral felt his father's beard tickle him, caught the distinctive workshop scent of oil, and rejoiced in the happy memories it brought back.

"Son! My, but it's good to see you! It's been a week."

Merral stood back and they examined each other. *My father looks tired. But then if he's only just finished work, he has a right to.*

His father, as if conscious that his appearance was under review, swept his thin, untidy, and graying hair back and stroked his silver-tinted beard. "Sorry I'm late, but it's been one of those days. Things break down without regard to it being Nativity's Eve."

"Everything all right?" Merral asked, hanging his jacket up.

"Oh, eventually. We had fun repairing a leaking hydrogen tank on an old lifter. A Series Two had a lot of hard use on the delta, so you can imagine the mud. Took off the tank, flushed it, washed it, dried it, tested it, found the hole, fixed it, tested it with nitrogen—fine. So we tested it with hydrogen—fine. Flushed it again, put it back on. Tested it finally with hydrogen again, and what do you know? Well, it leaks! So, we repeated the entire procedure all over again. But anyway, we fixed it by seven o'clock."

My father's tendency for using many words has not deserted him, but I love him for it. "You must be tired," he said.

"A bit. But you've had a long trip yourself. It went well, I take it? How are Zennia and Barrand?"

In a flash, Merral decided that he would not say anything about the difficulties there. Indeed as he thought about them, he now seemed to have trouble discerning what those difficulties were exactly. From here it all seemed such a vague matter. "Oh, everything seems all right with the colony—more or less. It's been a hard winter. They send their love."

"Good, good. Well, you've met our guest. Quite a surprise, eh?"

As he spoke the door opened and Merral's mother came into the hallway.

"I thought I heard both of you. Stefan *dear,* I do hope you aren't too weary?"

They kissed affectionately and he put his arm around her shoulder, a gesture that always struck Merral as awkward, given his father's shorter height.

"Fine, my dear. And your day went well?"

"*Excellent.* Somehow there were no last-minute crises in Housing Allocation this year; no one's long-lost relatives with six children suddenly deciding to spend Nativity in Ynysmant. Mind you, I always think it so seasonal to have housing crises at this time of the year. There's such a precedent. And I miss the satisfaction of sorting them out. But one can quite live without them. . . . Supper is ready."

As they ate, Merral listened to the news of the town and of his three sisters, all of whom were now married and lived away with growing families. Feeling tired, he was content to listen to the conversation rather than to lead it. Whether it was because of his tiredness or for some other reason, it seemed to him that he had never seen his father and mother with such clarity. It was almost, he fancied, as though they had portrait frames around them. His mother, apron now off and hair flying loose around her face, was apparently all brightness and glitter to the extent that you might have thought she was shallow minded. Then abruptly, as when a crack in a brightly painted surface reveals pure metal underneath, she would make some comment that revealed a hard, acute mind. Merral thought it strange that she and the much less impulsive Zennia were sisters.

Merral turned his attention to his father. This evening he was, as ever, a source of verbose—if amiable—stories and anecdotes, large portions of which seemed irrelevant and some of which were so diffuse that he lost his way. But here beneath the dryness, grace and good sense gleamed at depth. And Merral saw that while each partner saw the weaknesses of the other—and, he presumed, themself—they were accepted in a spirit of amused love. Merral was also conscious, but less clearly so, that the same benevolent acceptance was turned toward him.

Over dessert they discussed the guest. His father was enthusiastic. "Well, Merral, I must say, I think it's great. With the girls away we easily have a spare place for tomorrow."

His mother leaned over. "Stefan *dear*. Of course we have a place for Vero. We could take half a dozen guests. And there's *plenty* of food. I've made sure. *Especially* for Vero. No one is going to come all that distance and go back hungry."

Merral, trying not to laugh with happiness, was moved to suggest that it was probable that Vero wouldn't be going back immediately after the meal and that he was unlikely to be short of food after Nativity lunch. "Indeed, it's problems of overeating that are more likely."

As if prompted, his father started wiping his dish with a fragment of bread, only to catch a look of disapproval—tempered by merriment and fondness—from his wife. He put the bread down, winked at her, and turned to Merral. "I hope you get on with our Vero. He's a long way from home and they all say that the Made Worlds are strange for those born and bred on Ancient Earth. 'Disturbingly like but unlike,' someone has said. All that distance must take a toll too, and I can give that floating from Gate to Gate business a miss. If you do have to do it, say to move somewhere else—like a new world—that's all right, but it's a dreadful way of transport. I prefer my feet on the ground, or at least on wheels. But, charity apart, he must know a lot. There may be some question over how valuable sentinels are, but there's no doubt that they train their people well."

"But Father," Merral asked, "why is he here?"

His father stabbed at a stray bit of cheese with his knife. "The problem, my son, with foresters as a profession is that they don't deal nearly enough with machines. With machines you have to be precise, verbally logical. 'Why is he here?' is inadequately structured. In a word—it is ambivalent. Do you mean, *on* Farholme, *in* Ynysmant, or *at* our house?"

"All of them, my good and respected father. I believe in economy of words."

"I can't think where you got that from!" interjected his mother with a chortle.

His father smiled with good humor. "Thank you, my dear. Vero's bright, highly thought of, and just finished well above average in his tests. Incidentally, Merral, I have been hearing excellent things about your plans for the northeastern forest advance. Oh yes—economy of words—so I won't tell what I heard. Anyway, as I understood it, old Brenito said that there was something that needed looking at in Farholme—or words to that effect—and so out he comes and here he is."

"Well, I wonder what needs looking at?"

His father shrugged his shoulders. "On that I have no idea."

"Still," Merral said, "I suppose that answers a little bit more of my questions."

"The rest you will have to ask him. And if he is so minded he may give you an answer. Now let me make some coffee."

They had coffee sitting round the table and, after a brief and unsuccessful attempt by his father to try to interest them in the detailed scope of the planned new workshops, his mother spoke. "Merral, your father and I had a *lovely* meal with George and Hania Danol. . . ."

Ah, I wondered when that was going to come up.

"I used to know George years ago," his father said. "Funnily enough, he was an engineer on the first of the workshops. I suppose we shall soon have to call them the *old* workshops. . . . Sorry, my dear, I digress."

She patted his hand, cleared her throat, and started again. "And, *of course*, the conversation soon turned to you and Isabella. Did we approve? Did we consider that your relationship should be approved, so that you could proceed to making a commitment to each other? Well, it was a *very long* series of conversations."

His father coughed slightly. "There was a lot of appreciation of your talents. . . ."

"In fact, Merral, *that* was the only problem." His mother paused. "Oh dear, really, I'm not doing this well. *Problem* isn't the word. You see, at the end of it all, both we and George and Hania felt . . . well . . . undecided. Isabella is a super girl and very solid and stable. She has such a gift with children, and it's no wonder Education rates her highly. If your life were to lie here in Ynysmant or even just in eastern Menaya alone then she would be just the person. And yet we all felt that your path may run, as it were, higher and steeper. To Isterrane. Or beyond."

Or to the south, Merral thought, trying to take in what his mother was saying. "Well I suppose that's true," he answered. "I am happy enough here, but I do not know what is in store for me."

"Quite so," answered his father, sipping his coffee and staring at his son.

"So," his mother said slowly, "there was much to discuss. For ourselves, we would love nothing more than to have you and Isabella commit to each other and to have you married and living near us, especially with the girls so far away. But we are *very* concerned that the path that is yours to tread may be too much for Isabella to bear. Perhaps in a year the way will be clearer; after all, she is only twenty-three. And she is changing." She sighed and looked at his father.

His father nodded. "So, Merral, to come to the point. Rather unusually, not one of the four of us felt it right to take any steps in that direction. At least, not at the moment. We decided to review things again next summer. I hope that isn't too disappointing."

Merral felt shaken by a confusion of emotions. *So, they are not going to approve that Isabella and I make a commitment to each other. We stay as close friends but not—at least not yet—exclusively committed to each other. How strange. I had somehow assumed that they would approve.*

I see the reasoning, and I suppose, reluctantly, I approve it. Com-

mitments and engagements are always with parental approval; that is how things always have been.

His father was talking again, thoughtfully and with a soft intensity. "You see, Merral—and it's a funny thing to say about Ynysmant—we have become here a place on the edge of maturity, perhaps, you might even say, of stability. The weather's not as predictable as it could be, and there's always the odd earthquake and ice storm, but it's as safe and cozy a place as anywhere in the Made Worlds now. Why, I was hearing only today that the engineers say the Gulder Swamps are now stable enough that they can begin the new monorail route to Halmacent City next year. No more twenty-hour bus trips on bad roads. Anyway. . . . Oh yes, *this*," he waved his arms around, "is Isabella's world. But we are not convinced it is yours. You see—oh, how can I express it?"

He put his cup down, got to his feet in agitation, and paced over to the end of the room. There he swung round to face them and leaned stiffly back against the wall, his face a picture of concentration. Merral saw his mother's eyes following him with understanding.

"I've never said this to you before, Merral, for fear I was misreading the signs. Son, you're a rare breed. At times I wonder if you really are my offspring. Of course you are, and if I search hard within me I can see bits of you in me. Or the other way about. Something like that. But in you everything has come right. You have the vision, the energy, the drive. You can lead men and women too. The youngest forestry team leader ever in Menaya, I gather. I have no idea where you will end up. But I doubt, very much, you will stay a forester here for long."

There was an expectant silence. Merral bowed his head to signify acceptance. *I am surprised and yet unsurprised.*

"Father and Mother," he replied, choosing his words carefully, "I thank you for the care and consideration that has gone into your decision. I am both honored and humbled by the confidence you have in my abilities. I trust that I will not disappoint you. With regard to Isabella, while a part of me might wish otherwise, I appreciate both your judgment and your motives."

His mother grasped his hand with great warmth. That gesture seemed to close the matter, and after some minutes of general conversation, Merral, feeling suddenly tired, decided to go to bed. After kissing his father and mother good night, he went upstairs to his bedroom.

His head was reeling with a hundred thoughts, most of them contradictory, centering on Isabella and on his future. But he felt that, in some strange way, things had worked out. The message from Ingrida about his pending appointment had prepared his mind for his father's views on his career. Equally, being with Vero had aroused within him a renewed desire to see beyond the horizons of this one infant world. No, he could indeed see the wisdom in what they had said. He would have to talk more with Isabella; there was time, and you didn't rush into any of the stages that lead to marriage. From those thoughts he drifted into thinking about what it would be like to work in the tropical ecosystems and whether they were as hot as everyone said.

However, as he was undressing for bed, a strange, unsettling notion came to him about something else. It was so unnerving that he stopped still, his shirt half on and half off, trying to deal with it. Two things had come together. First, Vero had said that the only task of the sentinels was to search for a return of evil and had implied that he had been hastily summoned. Second, according to his father, Brenito had called for someone, saying there was something that needed looking at on Farholme. Now, if you put the two ideas together you got—the fear that evil was breaking out on Farholme.

His mind rebelled at the thought. It was too staggering for words. After eleven thousand years the sentinels were still looking for evil. And surely now and here wasn't likely to be the time or place. No, the obvious answer was simple but sad. Brenito was old and failing in his wisdom, and Vero had been brought here on a wasted journey. After all, if it had been seriously thought on Ancient Earth that evil was breaking out in Farholme, then they wouldn't have sent out someone so young and inexperienced.

Would they?

CHAPTER 5

Next morning Merral awoke to the clamor of trumpets and drums. He lay in bed for some moments listening to the fanfares rolling down from Congregation Hall and echoing over the rooftops, streets, and courtyards of Ynysmant. Then, as every year, there came the answering trumpet blasts and drumrolls from the Gate House and the flag stand on the promontory.

"Nativity Morn," he whispered to himself, quietly rejoicing in both the meaning and the familiarity of the day.

As the fanfares echoed and counter-echoed across the town, Merral rose, drew aside the thick insulating curtain, and opened the window. He shivered briefly in the fresh air and then leaned his head out. The winter's sun was shining obliquely out of a clear sky over the orange-and-brown-tiled roofs, turrets, and copper green spires, leaving the narrow, winding streets below in shadow. From the highest towers and spires, flags—mostly of scarlet and gold—fluttered gently in the breeze and, as he watched, others were raised to join them. Down beyond the roofs, Merral could see the wave-rippled dull gray waters of Ynysmere Lake, with white gulls wheeling over it and catching the sun. Far beyond, still hazy in the weak morning light, lay the grays and greens of the rolling hills that stretched northward.

Merral stared into the distance, hearing the fanfares and drum rolls rise to passionate ringing climax and then die away. After a few moments' silence, from down by the promontory the tolling of bells great and small began, sending pigeons flying skyward. As the sound swept through the town, other bells of different pitches and timbres joined in, until Ynysmant seemed awash with their joyful pealing.

Slowly, one by one, the trumpets and percussion sounded, adding new levels and colors of sound. Intoxicated by the music, Merral just stood and immersed himself in the surging and swelling of the melody until, slowly and irresistibly, the music built itself through a series of crescendos up to a final culmination of exultant blasts of trumpets over a thunderous echoing roar of drums and tolling bells. Slowly, the music died away in ebbing ripples of sound until finally the silence was broken only by the gentle flapping of the flags in the breeze.

Merral stood savoring the dying echoes of music and the cries of the gulls as they swung over the rooftops until he was suddenly aware that, even in his night-suit, he was cold. He closed the window and returned to his bed. There he knelt and spent time in praise for all that the festival meant. The tradition of missing breakfast on Nativity Morn to spend time in private worship meant that he was in no need of haste.

Indeed it was more than half an hour later that, dressed in his best brown jacket and red trousers, Merral went downstairs. He took the stairs so silently that none of the three people in the general room heard him, and he paused on the landing to look at them. His father, looking splendid in the primrose-and-silver tunic of the neighborhood band, was polishing his trombone. His mother, dressed in an ample dress of a rich purple fabric, was pacing the room, staring at a vocal score she held and silently mouthing words. Vero, dressed in a rather drab gray suit in which he seemed ill at ease, was seated at the table running a finger under some words in the old family Bible.

As he came down, they shared Nativity greetings among each other, and his mother put her score down on a table and came over and kissed him. His father, for once with immaculately groomed hair and tidy beard, beamed affectionately. "Very nice, Merral. Very nice, you look. Are you singing this morning?"

"Not in the choir. Being up north meant that I had to miss the rehearsals; next year maybe."

"A pity, but anyway, we need someone to accompany Vero up to the hall."

Vero glanced at Merral with an apologetic grin. "The kind people of Ynysmant have asked me to do one of the readings. I've pleaded shyness and an uncouth accent. But it's no good."

Merral caught sight of the badge on the suit: a gold circle around a stone tower rising up against a blue sky.

Merral's mother caught his eye. "He's doing the Luke 2. It's very appropriate, son. About the shepherds watching their flocks. Just like sentinels."

Vero wagged a finger theatrically. "Ah, but I trust you note, Lena Miria, that what the shepherds were watching for, was not what actually happened." He paused thoughtfully. "In other words, they were watching for the wrong thing. It is indeed appropriate, for it is a humbling passage for sentinels."

Merral's father spoke quietly, his words slow. "Well, I must say, things do have a way of catching us all out. Talking of which, Merral, your mother and I must be down at the Lower Square in ten minutes. So you two follow on down. I've made sure that they are reserving a place for both of you up near the front of the hall. It's easier for Vero to get up and read."

When his parents had gone, Merral sat down facing his guest.

Vero grinned happily at him and stretched out his legs in a gesture of relaxation. "Your parents have made me very welcome."

"Of course. Now tell me, did you have a pleasant time last night?"

"Ah yes. Everyone was so busy wanting to talk to me that I didn't have to eat anything. I had no idea that merely being from Ancient Earth was enough to make me a celebrity."

"Well, we are a long way out."

"Yes, so I realize. The end of the line. I feel there should be a big sign out there in space. 'You are now leaving the Assembly. May the angels go with you!'" He smiled. "So, my stomach and I have been finally reunited. What about you? Did you get a good night's sleep?"

"Good, although I had an interesting discussion with my parents that I'm thinking through."

Vero leaned back in his chair, his face attentive. "Really? May I ask what about?"

"By all means. I was expecting them to approve that my friend-ship with a girl named Isabella Hania Danol go to commitment. But rather to my surprise, they feel that—at the moment—they cannot make any such decision. So, it's all up in the air for six months."

"Oh?" There was a look of sharp inquiry. "Have they changed their mind about the girl?"

"No. It's that . . . well, it's odd. . . . They think that I may be moving on from here and that she may not be so well suited to such a move. They see me as a frontiersman or something."

"I like that!" Vero smiled. "I think of everyone here as a frontier person. But are you?"

"A frontiersman? Well, I'm happy in my job. I could want nothing more. But we shall see. I am open to the will of the Most High."

Vero nodded. "Well said. Incidentally, everyone speaks highly of you. Or they did last night."

My reputation again. How can I escape it? Or should I even try?

"Anyway," Vero continued, "there's no approval about you and this young lady. Not unheard of. But how do you feel about it?"

"Well, odd, Vero. You see, it raises all sorts of issues. But I sup-pose they have a point. I am fond of Isabella; we have a close friend-ship, and I would have liked it to have gone deeper. But I accept their views."

"Of course. Is she in Forestry or Forward Planning?"

"Isabella? No, she's an educational advisor. She monitors the progress of twelve- to fourteen-year-olds against Assembly standards. You know the sort of thing?"

"Indeed. I find it a very interesting subject."

"Well, I'm not sure I do. But it hardly has anything to do with being a sentinel, does it?"

Vero gave a brief smile and uttered the faintest of sighs. "Moshe Adlen said that sentinels were never to overlook anything. Which is fine in principle, but tough in practice. But one model for how we think is this: Imagine the Assembly as being a complex but beautifully balanced mechanical machine going at a vast speed. Like, say, a hydrogen turbine. Now if, within that machine, one part was to suddenly grow even slightly larger, what would happen?"

Merral threw his hands apart. "Explosive disintegration."

"Exactly. So it is with the Assembly: Stability and balance is vital. And the Assembly has within it a number of mechanisms for ensuring that no part gets larger than it should. One of those mechanisms is education. Through it the Assembly tries to make sure that no world gets unbalanced, perhaps by becoming all artistic or all scientific. It's hard, but things like this are partly our concern too. On one model, as the Assembly grows, the more probability there is that a minor imbalance could become catastrophic. Hence a sentinel's interest in all stabilizing mechanisms."

"I see. Well, you may have a chance to meet Isabella."

"I hope so. But take heart. I'm sure it will all work out." He smiled sympathetically. "Of course, I can say this because we sentinels normally never marry before our early thirties. So, I have all this ahead of me." He furrowed his forehead. "Although that too is something that I have asked questions about."

"Do you like being a sentinel?"

There was a pause. "My likes are immaterial. I was born to the job, as was my father and so on before him."

"Do you question it?"

Merral caught a sharp, thoughtful glance from his companion. "Yes, I do sometimes." He paused. "Not seriously, of course. That would be akin to the sin of grumbling and worthy of investigation itself. But I do ask questions. One of my lecturers said to me: 'Verofaza, as someone committed to preventing rebellion, you do a very good job of imitating a rebel.' I have a reputation. If it was not a disrespectful thought, I would say they had sent me to tame me. You can imagine it, can't you? 'What shall we do with Verofaza Enand?' 'Oh, I know—let's ship him off to Worlds' End.'"

Merral laughed. "But what do you question?"

There was a delicate, almost embarrassed, laugh. "I thought it was me who was supposed to ask the searching questions! But . . . "

Vero seemed to choose his words carefully. "You see, in all our time, now nearly four hundred generations of sentinels, we have sat and watched and listened and—"

"Found nothing?"

Vero's head seemed to nod almost imperceptibly in agreement. "More or less. Some argue that evil was trying to break through in the trouble on The Vellant in 12985. It was certainly a very odd malaise, a whole community seized by paranoia and delusions. But we alerted the Council of High Stewards in time."

"What happened there? I've not heard of it in the history files."

"It never made it there. They rotated the population out, checked the air and water, and reviewed the diets. Then things settled down."

Merral felt that there was a rough and uncomfortable edge to Vero's answer. "So, were the sentinels right?"

There was a long pause, as if Vero was making a painful choice. "The currently prevailing view, which is—I think—the correct interpretation, is that the problem was primarily biological. And not spiritual." He gave a quiet little awkward chuckle. "You are thinking it is not much to show for a hundred and seventeen centuries of labor, is it?"

"Well, I suppose I was."

"I would—I think—find it hard to disagree. And I refuse to talk about some of the other cases we have gotten involved in." He shook his head firmly. "The toad plague on Saganat. The library anomalies on Tegranatar. The so-called psychic triplets of Limaned. Best forgotten. Please!"

"I see. But, Vero, surely you shouldn't question what you do? If you are called to do something, then you do it. Whatever happens— results or not. Here on the Made Worlds we build and plan and sow, but we do not know whether or not we will be successful."

"Ah, well said." Vero smiled ruefully. "Oh, I suppose the last two weeks of travel have made me question my vocation a little more."

"Who knows—perhaps your vigilance has been a factor in the preservation of the Lord's Peace."

"A useful rebuke. *Perhaps* indeed. We do not know."

Merral heard, far away, echoing up through the streets, the renewed sounds of percussion and brass. "Time to go. You'd better get your coat. The weather looks nice and the forecast is good, but you never know."

"It is proverbial. 'Beware the weather in the Made Worlds.'"

Outside the house the street had become crowded with people dressed in their colorful best and with an air of exuberant noisiness. All the neighbors wanted to make Vero's acquaintance, and many people on the other side of the street pointed him out to their children. Gradually the sound of the procession became louder and the talking in the crowd died away to be replaced by an eager silence. All eyes turned expectantly to the end of the street. Suddenly, amid raucous laughter, two dogs raced around the corner, wheeled briefly around to look at what was following them, and hurtled up the street, egged on by the cheers and whoops of the crowd. After them, but in a far more dignified manner, came the procession. Three flag bearers led the way, the first held aloft the great Lamb and Stars banner of the Assembly; the next the gleaming blue sphere on a black field for Farholme; and the third Ynysmant's flag, the stylized cone of buildings above a blue lake. After them came the first of the uniformed musical groups, supplied this year by the music college, and following them, the first singers. Three green gravity-modifying sleds borrowed from Agriculture followed, bearing those who by reason of age, pregnancy, or injury could not walk with the procession. After them came his father's band, and Merral and Vero were rewarded by a wink over the trombone. Walking behind them were the first long lines of townsfolk, more flags and banners, and then his mother's choir. Eventually it was time for their street to join the procession. Merral and Vero fell in with the other families.

Half an hour later, they were filing into the vast space of Congregation Hall on the top of the ridge. Merral found the seats allocated to them, scanning the crowd as he did for Isabella. There was no sign of her, but as the hall was such a tumult of people he felt it was not surprising. As he settled into his seat he noticed that Vero was looking around at the roof and walls with an expression of unease. Their eyes met.

"Those are high-load beams. And the doors are airtight and sealable." His voice was low and curious. "A refuge?"

"Of course it is," Merral replied in surprise, but it was only as he answered that the significance of the question registered. "Oh, sorry, Vero. I forgot you're from the only planet that doesn't need them. Welcome, inhabitant of Ancient Earth, to one of the Made Worlds. Yes, it's a refuge, with two months' food, air, and water for the whole town underneath us and a landing zone on the roof."

"I see," Vero said, his voice somber. He looked around pensively.

It's strange to think that it's new to him, Merral reflected, *when it's one of the first things we learn in the Made Worlds. That it may all go wrong and we may find ourselves huddled in here for weeks, breathing, eating, and drinking our recycled wastes while they get the rescue shuttles in through the Gate. And we always know that sometimes even refuges may not be enough.*

"Do you know much about Yenerag, Vero?"

"You read my mind. Standing in a refuge cannot fail to remind me of Yenerag. A thousand years after the planet's core failure, and the volcano eruptions that buried sixteen cities in ash—*sixteen*—in three days. Fifty thousand people remain entombed in Yenerag's refuges until our King of kings returns."

Merral shifted in his seat, feeling in some way that such thoughts were unworthy of Nativity Day.

"It could all go wrong, couldn't it?" Vero said suddenly.

"Yes, we live with that reality." Then a thought came to Merral. "But Nativity helps."

"How so?"

"The universe is so vast and unforgiving that the only way this whole venture of ours—spreading ourselves over thousands of light-years—makes sense is if God is indeed with us."

"A fair point."

Suddenly, with an increasing rapidity, silence descended on the hall. From the floor three people took the stage and stood still, every eye on them. Merral prepared his heart for worship. Then, away behind them at the door of the hall, the trumpets sounded four loud, open chords and, with the echoes dying away, the congregation stood for the invocation.

•—•—•

Almost two hours later the benediction ended the service. Slowly people got to their feet and began to talk and embrace one another.

Merral turned to Vero. "I hope that wasn't too strange for you?"

Vero shook his head gently and returned a warm smile. "No, that was fine. It seems to me that there's nothing wrong with your services."

Merral wondered whether there was supposed to be and was trying to phrase a question on those lines, when someone came to Vero and introduced himself, and then a moment later Merral's attention was occupied by an old school friend. He had just finished his conversation a few minutes later, when he felt a hand gently grasp his elbow.

"Happy Nativity, Merral D'Avanos!"

Merral turned to see Isabella at his side. How typical of her to slip up to him so unnoticed. They looked at each other, and he noticed how her long gray-blue jacket seemed to offset her dark, almost black, eyes.

"And to you, Isabella Danol. I was looking for you earlier."

"I was at the back." Isabella brushed a strand of her long, straight black hair away from her face. "The Earther who read—the one who is staying with you, I missed his name—Vera something, wasn't it?"

"Vero. It's short for Verofaza. I hadn't realized till I met him that on Ancient Earth men's names can end in A. 'Verofaza Laertes Enand, sentinel' is how he introduces himself. Yes, he was one of a number of surprises yesterday."

"I can guess one of the others," she answered, a hint of regret darkening her soft voice.

"Yes, Isabella. My parents told me when I got back. I'm still thinking that one over, but what with Vero and the service today, I'm afraid I haven't really digested it. Six months' wait before approval."

Merral looked at her, realizing that she was revealing no emotion in her expression. *She wouldn't here, and not so soon.* It would take something like an hour's walk in the park to find out what she really thought.

Then she spoke again, her voice businesslike. "If then. But I understand. Do you have any first reactions?"

"Well . . . actually, thinking about yesterday, Vero was the second of three surprises. We were third. The first was fairly reliable news that I am going to be given a tropics posting." He watched her face as he said it, but other than the faintest lifting of a fine dark eyebrow, she kept any feelings hidden.

"You'd like that, wouldn't you?"

She knows me so well. "It's a challenge. Very demanding and horribly hot, especially if it's Umbaga or Faraketha. Oh, I haven't really thought about that news either. But it does seem that my path may be away from Ynysmant before long."

Isabella said nothing immediately but nodded gently. When she did speak it was in a voice that he could barely hear over the chatter in the hall. "Our parents seem to have assumed that this sort of thing might happen." Isabella joined her delicate fingers together in front of her mouth. She might have nodded, but if so it was so faintly that Merral couldn't be sure whether she had.

"We will talk more of it another time," he added, thinking, *Isabella, it's so hard to read your emotions even though I know you very well. It's as if I have to tune my senses to maximum to pick up the signals you give out.*

She smiled delicately. "Yes, I'm sure we will. And I'd like to met Vero if I can."

"Of course. He wants to meet you. But any particular reason why?"

There was a moment's hesitation. "I have a certain professional curiosity, Merral. There is a school of thought that says that Ancient

Earthers and Made Worlders have differing psychologies. Actually everyone agrees on that—it's just how far the differences go. Made Worlders are more assertive and outgoing but at the same time less secure. Partly that is society, partly it is environment."

"I've heard that, but you aren't going to profile him here?"

"No! Of course not!" She laughed. "But it would be nice to talk to him."

"Well, come on, I'll introduce you."

They walked to where Vero was talking with a young man. At a suitable point Merral made the introductions, to which Vero responded with the utmost formality and a slight bow. Isabella smiled at him. "I hadn't realized Ancient Earth had so much civility."

Vero smiled shyly at her. "It hasn't really, but training instilled in us the idea that in a strange culture it is better to be overformal than the opposite."

"And we are a strange culture?"

Vero gave an oblique grin to Merral. "No, madam, not entirely."

They all laughed, and Isabella turned to Vero. "Have you found Nativity here as you expected it to be?"

Vero paused, thinking through the answer. "I can answer both yes and no. I had assumed it would be like home and in some ways it is like that. But there are differences. For example, with us there is silence on Nativity Morn until we are assembled. And there are other things."

As he went on and listed differences, Merral found himself standing back and treating the conversation as if he were a spectator. *It is interesting how Isabella is able to draw out of Vero what she wants.* He watched how she kept her intent, almond-shaped eyes on him and how she encouraged him with the slightest movements of her head.

Merral's thoughts were interrupted by a member of the Team-Ball squad he played for who wanted to pass on news of a match that he had missed. When they parted after ten minutes or so, Merral realized that the hall was now nearly empty. He walked over to where Isabella and Vero were still deep in conversation.

"Sorry to interrupt, but, Vero, we must go."

"You are quite right." He gave a little bow. "Isabella, I hope we meet again."

"And I too. Merral, you will be in touch soon?"

"Of course."

As Merral and Vero walked down from the hall in silence, Merral felt that his new friend seemed deep in thought.

"You had a good discussion with Isabella?" he asked.

"Yes. I think, though, she found out more about me than I did about her."

"Well observed. She is both an acute observer of others and a private person herself."

"I can believe that. A striking face—but you know that. Her family isn't recently from Earth? I mean in the last five generations?"

"No, Farholme for four generations on both sides. Antakaly before that on her father's side, I think; Marant on her mother's. Why do you ask?"

"Because out on the worlds most racial genes have been fairly well diluted and yet, at a glance, she appears to have fairly pure Chinese features. It's more typical of Earth. Did you know that?"

"That on Ancient Earth there had been much less intermarriage across the races? Yes, I'd heard that. I mean, you are much darker than anyone I know on Farholme."

Vero raised an eyebrow in amused acknowledgement. "It has been pointed out. Well, it removes the temptation to go disguised among you. Anyway, Isabella asked some penetrating questions."

"She would do that. And what was the hardest she gave you?"

Vero shook his head gently. "Ah, you have something in common. She asked whether I had found what I came for."

Merral looked sideways at his companion. "To which you said . . . ?"

"To which I said . . . 'No, and I'm no longer sure what I'm looking for.'"

"That sounds bad."

"Perhaps. But then if it isn't here, then not to find it is surely no bad thing."

"I suppose not."

"I am on the point of coming to a decision. But I need to think more about it. I will talk more about this to you later."

They strode on and Merral caught his companion glancing up at the sun.

"You look puzzled, Vero," he said.

"Disoriented. It's just slightly wrong; it's too red."

"Yes, our sun is slightly cooler than Sol. You'll adjust."

"Maybe. Do you ever call it 'Alahir'?"

"As in 'I see Alahir is setting'?" Merral laughed. "Hardly. In formal astronomy, maybe, but to us it's just the sun. Makes sense to me."

Vero shrugged. "Yes, it makes sense. We never call our sun 'Sol,' except under the same circumstances. But I find it hard. I suppose it is as if you were a child and your mother died and your father married again. You might have a hesitation about calling the new woman 'Mother.'"

Merral felt that the observation revealed how deeply Vero felt that he was away from home.

They walked down the west steps and Merral asked his guest whether he had appreciated the service.

Vero paused. "Yes, it was very good."

"I vaguely noted that you were paying careful attention to what was going on."

"Yes. Well, I suppose I had thought that if there was anything untoward, it would show itself here."

"And it didn't?"

Vero seemed to bite his lip. "I saw, heard, and felt nothing to raise an alarm. It was reverent, orthodox, and all the rest. As you would expect."

"You seem almost disappointed."

He shook his head. "No, on the contrary, I suppose I am relieved. But I am puzzled. Anyway, I'll discuss that later." He paused. "Incidentally, the choir was very good. I'm gifted—if that is the word—

with perfect pitch, and a failure to hit the right note hurts. But it was painless on that account. A credit to Farholme."

"I'll pass it on. Now we'd better hurry or we will be late for the meal."

Much of the rest of the day was spent in festivities and eating. There was an apparently endless round of visits of friends, relatives, and innumerable children, and numerous rounds of food and drink. Then there was the time of giving presents. Merral gave his father a new map and his mother a brooch and received sweets and a scarf in return. There were any number of family stories, and presumably because of Vero, almost any incident even vaguely concerned with Ancient Earth that had happened in the last five generations was brought up. Surprisingly, the one everyone found funniest was that of his father's Great-Aunt Margarita, much given to precise and painstaking management of every detail of her affairs, who at a very advanced age had finally managed to travel to see her family on one of the worlds on the other side of the Assembly. On the way back she had found the strain too much and had gone Home to the Lord without warning. But as she had been such a quiet passenger and much given to sleeping, it was many hours before anybody noticed she had stopped breathing, with the result that the death certificate had written on it under "Location" the words, *Not known within fifty light-years.*

Then there were games, including a long and noisy one called Cross the Assembly. Vero revealed, with a certain awkwardness, that when he played it on Earth, everybody hated getting the Farholme card because you could never get to anywhere from it and it was so far from a decent Gate node. The news that, even in games, Farholme had a reputation as Worlds' End was greeted with a great deal of amusement.

Sometime about nine Merral found himself yawning. He felt he had not fully recovered from his long and tiring northern trip and, making apologies, he went upstairs to his room. As he began to undress he put his diary on the table and noted that a nonurgent text message had been transmitted an hour ago. He flicked it on and read the message as it slid across the screen.

Merral,

The Rechereg choral went fine. I hope you enjoy the attached performance. I did use Miranda Cline after all.

Give my love to your family,

Happy Nativity,

Barrand Antalfer

There was a sound file attached, and switching it through the room speakers, Merral began to play it as he rinsed his face in the basin and put on his night-suit. He was about to switch it off when there was a tap at the door.

It was Vero. "Not asleep then? Good. Look, sorry to interrupt, but I was going to tell you that I have decided to leave tomorrow." He paused. "Wait—I know this music." He started waving his fingers slowly in time to it, his face a study in concentration. Suddenly his face acquired a look of recognition. "Of course! Rechereg's *Choral Variations on an Old Carol*. The old carol being the truly ancient 'Child of Mary, Newly Born.' Very fine. Where did you get the recording?"

Merral, his tiredness gone, sat on his bed and gestured to the chair opposite. "Please. My uncle up at the Forward Colony at Herrandown sent it to me today. He did it himself."

Vero nodded appreciatively. "A good job. Re-createds?"

"'Fraid so. They can barely make a string quartet up there. Some good names. Shall I play it back from the beginning?"

"No, tempting though it is. But I wouldn't mind a copy."

"No problem. There are all the details on the file."

Merral switched the music off and ordered the file to be copied.

"Thanks," said Vero. He looked around the room and gestured to a small glass egg perched on a stand on the table. "A personal creation of yours?"

"Yes," Merral said. "It's a tree."

Vero stared at him. "I've known aquaria, fantasy cities, snow-scapes, but a single tree?"

Merral gestured at it. "It's unique. I call it a castle tree. There's a spare pair of glasses there. Put them on and let me show you."

Merral found his imaging glasses on the shelf above his bed and put them on. "Log on to castle tree; real time," he ordered, and in sec-onds the darkness of the lenses cleared, and Merral saw himself near the top of a low hill. The sky above was a brilliant pale blue, and all around, stretching as far as he could see, lay long, dry, brown grass buffeted under the force of a wind he could neither feel nor hear. At his feet was a bare stone surface etched with the words *Castle Tree; Merral Stefan D'Avanos; Farholme. Simulation 4.2b. Elapsed Real Time: 26401.3 hours. Elapsed Simulated Time: 52021.2 years.*

A soft, glistening light at his left showed him that Vero had joined him.

"I see no tree." Merral found the room acoustic of Vero's voice strangely inappropriate with the open scene around him.

"Lock your position with me."

Merral touched the glasses frame and accelerated forward, flying over the blur of the grass toward the crest of the hill. He stopped dead at the summit and heard a gasp from beside him.

Perhaps a kilometer away from him a mass, like some vast broad tower, rose up into the sky. It was pale gray and speckled with green and the summit was strangely serrated as if made up of a thousand spires.

"What is it?" Vero said, his voice ringing with incredulity. "A building? It's enormous."

"It's a tree. But I felt it looked like a castle; hence the name. Do you think it looks like a castle?"

"I have seen the ruins of castles, but they were never this size. Yes, the shape is right. But a tree?"

Merral touched the frame of the glasses again and he and Vero flew onward over the featureless grass. As they did, the awesome size of the tree became more apparent. He could soon begin to make out the great spreading branches of greenery extending from the uneven wall of silvery bark.

Finally, Merral came to rest at the base of the tree beneath a great bent branch and amid great snakelike roots that burrowed deep into the ground. Dead leaves blew around them and strange insects with long silver wings flickered silently past.

"It's more than enormous!" he heard Vero say, in awed tones. "It's bigger than any building. It must be the size of a town."

"Look up," Merral said and swung his gaze upward. Through the gigantic spreading branches that lay overhead, the great tree trunk towered as if it were an overhanging cliff. At the very top, the trunk and branches passed into wreaths of mist.

He heard Vero gasp. "How high is it?"

"About three hundred meters. Three, four times higher than any living tree. But the volume is something else. Let me show you an aerial view."

Merral touched the glasses again and heard a sharp intake of breath from Vero as they raced upward, passing soundlessly through smears of green and brown branches and foliage, up through the mist patches, until finally, they were high above the highest branches.

Merral looked down. Through the wreaths of low cloud and mist, the vast, hollow inner heart of the tree was clearly visible, and below the outstretched inner branches he could make out the gray waters of a lake.

"The tree is a tube?"

"No, a spiral." Merral began a slow swoop down over the foliage. "I designed this tree. It's like nothing in nature. The size is really incidental; I wanted something that would grow in places where there are high winds and frequent dry periods."

"The Made Worlds."

"Exactly. So it starts low and grows sideways as well as upward. But in growing sideways it makes a spiral like snails do. The result is an enormously strong structure—more like a hill than a tree."

Merral tilted his head and dived under some of the topmost fronds.

"Yow!" Vero exclaimed. "Gentle with the maneuvers, my friend. I know it's not real, but no one has told my stomach. The water in the middle? How does that get there?"

"Sorry." Merral slowed his motion. "It's a design feature. The core of the spiral slowly rots, so you get an inner water body. The branches drain down into it. It acts as a reservoir. And do you see how the inner branches are so much bigger and more delicate? They are protected from the winds."

"Elegant."

"Thank you. Seen enough?"

"I'd like another browse sometime. At my own pace. But it's wonderful."

The image went dark and Merral took off the glasses.

Vero was staring at him, blinking. "So, that is what you do in your spare time?"

"Yes. It's my relaxation. I spend my spare stipend in setting it up and renting computer time. That sort of personal creation system is pretty heavy in processing time."

"I can imagine."

Vero put the glasses carefully down on the table. "How long has it taken you to create that?"

"Five years. The early attempts were disasters. Finding a way for a tree to pump water that high is hard work"

"Could we make it for real?"

"It works, if that's what you mean. The world in this creation is accurate. But it is beyond our skill and—as you know—well beyond the gene-engineering limits we impose. Bacteria, fungi, some crops, yes. But to create totally new trees? Hardly."

Vero nodded agreement and Merral continued. "Actually, the real problem is that it takes time. A castle tree would take three thousand years to get to that sort of size. It's hardly suitable for a Made World."

Vero closed his eyes. "A pity. But a wonderful vision, my friend. The city-sized tree. I shall treasure that image: the D'Avanos castle tree."

There was a moment's silence between them before Merral said, "And what do you do with your stipend, Vero? Give it all away?"

Vero smiled. "Ah, there has been much discussion about that. We Sentinels have toyed, as other organizations have, with having no money, but we think Assembly policy is right. Free food, lodging, clothing, and welfare, and a standard stipend for all on top to spend or give away. Totally money-free societies are dull; how can you give a present when it cost you nothing?"

"I'm sorry I didn't have time to get you anything today."

"Send me some castle tree images; they will do."

After a moment's silence Merral spoke. "So, you are off tomorrow? That's sooner than you had expected."

Vero flexed his legs and seemed to look at his shoes carefully. He spoke slowly. "Yes. Sooner."

Merral said nothing, and eventually Vero leaned forward on the chair, his hands clasped together, and looked up.

"What I'm about to say is really for sentinels. But that's advice, not rules. Do you know why I am here?"

"Not really; I have ideas."

"Well, two weeks ago, Brenito—who is very respected by the way—made an urgent call to Earth with a warning. We only have that happen every century or so. He simply said that he had had a vision that Farholme was under threat."

"But what sort—?"

Vero raised a hand and gave a mock grimace. "Exactly our problem. I don't want to go into the details. But he couldn't clarify the danger. 'Under threat,' that was all. Physical, spiritual, mental? He had no idea. So they weighed it all up and, bearing in mind that he is a hundred and five, they decided to send me. Well, everybody else was busy or had commitments."

"You drew the Farholme card?"

Vero smiled slightly. "I suppose so."

"What other options did they have?"

"A full threat evaluation team. So I'm here to try and find what the threat is and whether there is anything really wrong." Vero looked at his feet again.

"And?"

He looked up. "Well, I have to say it's a tough assignment. You see, everything is strange here. The sun, the clouds, the buildings, are all peculiar. I can barely understand the dialect, and some aspects of your society are totally alien to me."

"Really? Such as?"

"Don't sound so surprised. Many things that you take for granted. Like that thing you are wearing now."

"My night-suit? What's wrong with that?" Merral looked down at his one-piece winter suit, trying to find anything odd about it.

Vero grinned and shook his head as if in despair. "See? You don't even realize it! That orange thing is an active thermal suit designed to protect you if you are forced to evacuate your building overnight or it collapses on you. It is visible on almost every waveband from ultraviolet to infrared and has a passive signal emitter so they can find your body under ten meters of titanium or magnesium-cored concrete debris. And it has your name and career and specialization encoded on it should they need to decide whether you are a priority to resuscitate when they find you. *That's* what's wrong with it."

Merral found himself looking at his night-suit in a new way. "Oh," he said.

"On Ancient Earth, Merral," Vero continued, "we sleep in whatever we want. Some of us choose hopelessly impractical soft, fluffy things in pastel colors called pajamas or nightshirts. And we can choose and go to bed with a reasonable confidence that there will still be an atmosphere we can breathe in the morning."

"I see. I suppose that could make a difference. . . ."

"A *difference*?" Vero laughed. "Oh, it does. Believe me. But you see that's what I mean. How can I find out what is wrong here when even your night clothes are odd!"

Merral raised a hand. "Sorry! But you Ancient Earthers are the odd ones out numerically!"

They laughed together until Merral managed to ask whether Vero had found anything.

Suddenly becoming quiet, the sentinel shook his head. "Nothing. Nothing to alarm me, nothing to persuade me that there is something wrong. But then I don't know what I am looking for. No one does. So I have decided to go tomorrow to Isterrane, and there in your capital I will try to see what ideas Brenito has. I may come back here, or I may travel around. But I do need to talk to Brenito."

"I see. Do you think he has made a mistake?"

There was a thoughtful pause. "You are nearly as bad as Isabella with your questions. Yes, I am beginning to think it possible that the good Brenito may have overreacted. I have so far found nothing remotely odd or peculiar. Nothing at all. I'm glad of the chance of seeing Farholme. But I see, I feel, nothing."

"If he has, what will you do?"

"Stay around for a bit, just in case. It was a long journey out, and without an emergency, it will be hard booking a passage on the route back in hurry. I need to write a report, anyway. I will be suggesting better ways of handling this sort of thing. Asking some hard questions."

"Sounds radical."

"*Radical?* That is a familiar word to me. 'Where, Verofaza, is the boundary between being radical and being rebellious?' That was the dean of political history. Anyway, I shall find somewhere that reminds me of Earth and sit down and write a long review."

He stood up. "I'd better leave you. I hope to be off on the early flight, so I'd better be in bed soon too. I'll be in touch."

As Vero stood by the door, Merral went over and shook his hand. "Vero, I'm afraid I wish your mission total failure. But when Brenito confesses to having let his fruit juice ferment, come back and see what we are doing here. And I'll take you out of the town into the country. That's what you should see."

Vero grinned and shook his hand firmly. "Let's indeed hope we can do that."

Then with a quiet "Blessings," he left the room.

After Vero had gone, Merral switched the light off, prayed, and then lay down and closed his eyes. But Vero's conversation had disturbed him and would not leave his mind. He wondered about the odd things that had happened at Herrandown. *Perhaps I should have discussed them with Vero.* However, as he considered them, it all seemed too unlikely to be of interest. The entire case hung on Barrand's words and now he was pushed to remember exactly what it was that he had said. No, there must just have been some misunderstanding there. One or both of them had overreacted, and Vero's arrival at the same time was just a coincidence.

Then he thought about the eleven thousand years of peace that the Assembly had had and that put his mind at rest. After all, one of the many lessons taught by that awesome span of history was that almost all potential crises had ended up being very much less than that.

Quite plainly, there was nothing to worry about.

CHAPTER 6

One morning some three months later, Merral looked up from his work on the map of the proposed northern extension of the Great Northern Forest and gazed out of his office window. The view looked eastward over the waters of Ynysmere Lake, and Merral had positioned his desk so that whenever he glanced up he saw the water and the rolling hills beyond. In winter, it encouraged him to come in early and catch the sunrise. But today the only view he had was one of a buffeting dull gray wetness in which it was hard to distinguish between the spray of the breaking waves, the blowing rain, and the cloud above.

Wondering at the weather, Merral shook his head. Winter had dragged on this year, and spring was more a fickle, fleeting guest than a permanent resident. Dry, sunny weather would come, and for a few days spirits would lift, windows would be opened, and jackets left at home. Then abruptly, out of the north would come a bitter whistling wind, or cold, soaking rains would blow in from the ocean far away to the east, and winter would be back. He consoled himself with the certainty that spring and summer would come in the end. Besides, he thought with a certain amusement, if the tropics posting—now almost certain—did come through, then he would doubtless miss the long wet winters of northeastern Menaya.

He bent over the map again, but as he did so, the diary adjunct link on his watch pulsed gently three times. He glanced at his diary lying on the desk and saw that the screen confirmed an urgent and private call. He tabbed an acknowledgement back, and then got up and closed the door, trying to remember when he had last had such a message. He sat down and rotated the diary so its lens could image him and ordered it to open the link.

The image that flashed onto the tiny screen was that of Barrand and Zennia. They were sitting at the desk in his uncle's cluttered narrow office. The moment he saw them, Merral knew something was wrong. Zennia was plainly agitated, her face pale and taut, her eyes constantly flicking toward her husband while she clasped and unclasped her slender hands. Barrand, by contrast, was sitting still, but his hands were tightly folded together and his stern face had a determined look.

"Greetings, Uncle Barrand, Aunt Zennia."

"Greetings to you, Merral. Thank you for your prompt response."

His uncle's voice had a strange formality, and his aunt's smile seemed weak, strained.

"Ah, Merral. Thank you," Barrand continued. "I'll come straight to the point. We have a problem here. It's very odd. We need some advice."

"I'm ready to help all I can. Tell me all about it."

Barrand looked briefly at his wife, as if for encouragement, and then turned back to the screen.

"It's Elana. The day before yesterday, you remember? It was dry. At least with us. The first such day for a week. What a winter, eh? Anyway, she went out into the woods above Herrandown. Just northwest of us. There she says she saw something." He paused, clenching his hands tight and glancing at Zennia. "Now she describes it as like a small man, only brown and shiny like a beetle. It scared her badly—"

"She's still scared," Zennia cut in.

Merral's mouth dropped open, and he snapped it shut. "Sorry, Uncle. Try it again. She saw what?"

"Something like a small man, only brown and shiny like a beetle." Zennia nodded.

Merral tried to visualize what she had described but failed. "I mean—an obvious point—this isn't some sort of . . . well . . . story?"

Barrand shrugged, but Zennia shook her head strongly and

turned to the screen. "Merral, I *know* my daughter. And if she did make up a story, she scared herself silly doing it. And us. She came running in, screaming. She won't go outside alone and is sleeping next to our room."

They looked at each other. *I have,* Merral realized, *a potentially serious problem up in Herrandown.* Maybe it was already past the potential stage. Usually able to say something in any situation, Merral suddenly found himself floundering. "Look . . . ," he said, "how big did she say this creature was?"

Zennia spoke. "She said it was about her height."

Merral became aware that he was staring blankly at the screen. "Baffling, quite baffling," he responded and realized it sounded banal; but what else could he say?

He paused for a moment. "Well, you both know the problem, I'm sure. We have an inventory of every species on the planet; we may not know numbers exactly but we know what we have. And all the brown, shiny, beetle-like things we have are small enough that you can hold them in your hand. In fact, anywhere in the Assembly to our knowledge. At least to mine."

Barrand shrugged and threw his arms up in bemusement. "Merral, I know. But she's convinced she saw something."

Zennia nodded. "And I think she did."

"Aunt, how is Elana otherwise?"

"Physically fine. The nurse can find nothing wrong. There's no evidence of hallucinatory activity; it's not associated with a fever. Blood tests, neural activity all read normal."

Merral found himself admitting defeat. "Uncle, Aunt, I have to say I'm baffled. Absolutely. She just saw it and ran away?"

Barrand gestured to his wife to speak.

"No; it was staring at her from behind a bush, she says. It realized it had been observed and ran away."

Merral was silent. He threw up a quick request to heaven for wisdom and tried to run through the various options. He had to have more time.

"And what do you two think?"

Barrand shifted on his seat. "I don't know. . . . I suppose it must be nonsense—a dream or something. . . . I went to have a look, but I could see no sign of it. I haven't searched the area thoroughly. But—"

Zennia nudged him into silence and she spoke. "Elana saw something, Merral. And we think there's more to it than that."

Technically, Merral told himself, the guidelines were such that in the rare event of a psychological problem with a colony, a forester would call in specialist help. In his case, Ghina Macreedy. Of course, if it was something in his forests that had caused it then that was a different matter. But this was a curious affair and they were family. Perhaps, too, if it could be dealt with quickly, then a deeper crisis could be avoided.

Barrand was stroking his beard restlessly. "Yes, I'm afraid, Merral, there is something odd here. Or there may be. . . . The animals are agitated, especially the dogs. Particularly since we lost Spotback."

"Spotback! I never knew you'd lost him. He was a good dog. How did that happen?"

"A good question. We saw him one morning about five days ago heading northward from the farm. Then he just vanished."

Suddenly, Merral knew that at least his aunt and possibly his uncle had worked themselves into a highly concerned state. And recognizing that, Merral knew what he had to do.

"The other families?"

His aunt shook her head. "Elana is the only one that's seen it. The others feel the same as we do. You can call them."

"Perhaps. I'll see."

There was one last question he wanted to ask. "What does Thomas think?"

Barrand's face looked pained. "Our son Thomas is, I'm sorry to say, acting scared. He will only play outside the front of the house. And he comes inside well before dusk."

So he's affected as well. That settled it.

"Look, I think I'm going to come up and see you. I'll see if I can't get one of our fast Recon vehicles and be with you tomorrow. Just for a day. Talk to Elana; take a look around."

Zennia's hazel eyes showed gratitude. "Oh, thank you, Merral! We'd feel better for that. See if you can make sense of it. You think it's a good idea, Barrand?"

There was a pause "Ho! Why not? Better our Merral than a host of people we don't know. We might be able to solve it. Yes, come up. As soon as possible."

Then, with abbreviated family news, they closed the conversation.

After the call Merral did nothing immediately but sit staring at the rain and waves and thinking through what he had heard. It was troubling. Forward Colony families were always selected for their ability to handle remote small communities and few facilities. For them to be so uneasy was extremely odd. The whole thing defied analysis. Merral decided that the most likely cause was that Elana, perhaps helped by her active imagination, had had some sort of waking dream or hallucination.

But, whatever its cause, the event had generated some sort of real collective anxiety. And that needed a rapid resolution. Not only were the Antalfers his family, they were also a good team with a lot of experience. If they had to be rotated out, they would be hard to replace.

After ten minutes, Merral got up and walked down the corridor to where his director was working and put his head around the door. Henri was in his thinking pose. He was reclining in his chair, with his lean arms behind his head and his feet up on the desk, staring at the giant map of northeastern Menaya that occupied most of the opposite wall. At the sight of Merral he swung his legs down and gestured him in with a wave of an arm and a genial smile. "Merral! Come in, man. Take a seat." Ten years in Ynysmant hadn't blunted Henri's distinctive Tablelands intonation.

Closing the door behind him, Merral took the proffered seat. "I hope I'm not disturbing any deep thoughts?"

Henri stroked his carefully trimmed brown beard and stared at him with his closely spaced deep-set dark eyes. "Thoughts? Yes, I'll say so. We have just lost a hexapod; got washed away at the Grandell Cleft. It's how to recover what's left of it. And the weather this winter. . . . Ach!" He frowned. "When I started here, they were worried about polar ice sheets shrinking; now they are expanding too fast. This planet is like an unbroken horse; it runs this way today and tomorrow that. But this winter—it's been so long—means there is the danger of us all being way behind schedule. Summers are short enough in our northernmost zones. I'm thinking of ways of saving time when the weather does improve. My other issue is how to replace you, assuming you go. You'll be missed, man. Really missed."

"Sorry. I'll miss being here."

"Ach." He smiled. "Not with this weather. . . . Anyway, what can I do for you?"

"We have a problem at Herrandown." Merral paused, trying to work out how to tell the story.

Henri clucked sympathetically. "Man, that's bad news. I've got your quarry team ready to go to the ridge. But tell me about it."

Very carefully, Merral explained the substance of his call that morning while Henri listened attentively and without comment. "So you see, Henri," Merral ended, "I'd like to go up and check it out personally. I think that way we can best reduce the strain on the family."

Henri nodded. "I can see that. If you can fix it." He stared a moment at the wall-high image of Mount Katafana. "Yes. Ghina is out south; otherwise, I'd suggest you take her. You really ought to go with someone with some psychological background. I mean, that's what you think it is, I take it? Psychology?"

"There doesn't seem much other option, does there?"

His director thought briefly. "No," he asserted, shaking his head. Then Henri looked at the image again and Merral remembered that his boss was planning to climb Mount Katafana this year.

"No, man. I'm at a loss to think of any other explanation." He gave his beard a further stroke and stared at Merral. "You've got much experience in talking to troubled fourteen-year-old girls?"

"Not really. Although I know the girl at the center of the problem." Then an idea struck him "Mind you, I know someone who has experience."

A look of gentle amusement came onto Henri's face. "Ah yes. I should have thought of her. Yes, see if you can get Isabella Danol to go with you. Get a Recon vehicle booked now. Check that they've still got the winter tires. Normally, by now we'd be starting to grapple with dust, not mud. But not this year. Oh no."

"Thanks, Henri. Thanks a great deal."

Merral turned to go. As he did, Henri spoke again in a low voice. "One last thing, man—if it turns out to be serious, then just ask for help. The Antalfers deserve our best efforts."

❖

Back in his office, Merral had an idea. He pulled off his diary and asked it to call "Anya Salema Lewitz, biologist, location unknown." Moments later the response came from the Planetary Ecology Center in Isterrane where a man, who identified himself as Anya's assistant, answered. He apologized and said that she was in a conference, but expressed the confident opinion that she would call him back as soon as she was free.

Merral had better fortune with Isabella, who was in her office. "Isabella, I have had a problem this morning that you may be able to help me with. It's right in your age group. The Antalfers; you remember them?"

She nodded, her thin face thoughtful. "Of course. Barrand and Zennia out at Herrandown. She is your mother's younger sister."

"But very different. My mother wouldn't last a week in Herrandown. Zennia's much more placid. Or she was. Anyway, their oldest girl—Elana—has had a disturbing experience. Two days ago she claims to have seen a creature her size in the wood. It was brown and shiny, hard skinned like an insect."

Isabella said nothing for what seemed a long time. In fact, Merral thought that if it hadn't been for the slight frown on her face he would have assumed that she hadn't heard. When she did speak, it was very softly. "Poor thing. Is she all right?"

That's Isabella: cautious and concerned. Everybody else, me included, leaps in and says the thing can't exist. She thinks of the girl first.

"Apparently, she's pretty unhappy."

"So I should imagine. Hmm. How old is she?"

"Just fourteen. Becoming a young lady."

"I see. And this thing was her size?"

"So she claimed. Of course, as you know, there is nothing like that. What do you think?"

Isabella put her head on one side for a moment and looked back at him for some time before answering. "Sorry, Merral, I can't judge that. It's odd, and there isn't enough data, I'm afraid. I mean, I'd have to be sure that such a thing *was* ruled out. It has to be an illusion? I mean, it's not an escape of something, is it?"

"No. There are no such things in or out of captivity."

She nodded. "Thought so. Well...." She paused, leaning back as if trying to get the best position to think in. "You would have to know her up-to-date psychological profile. And a lot of other things."

"Such as?"

"Physical health, recent diet, allergies, mental state, etc. It's fairly common for temporary and mild psychological perturbations to occur in puberty. But seeing things is a bit odd. I think there would have to be something else. Hmm." She lapsed into silence.

That is what she would say; she wouldn't be so highly rated if she had made an instant diagnosis in a case like this. But then, who could?

"Look, Isabella, I'm going early tomorrow for the day to see them and to try and sort out what's happening. Henri has okayed a fast Recon vehicle. Can you come up with me? We'd be back early evening at the latest."

There was a moment's pause and then the faintest hint of a smile. "Yes, if I work this evening. I'd like that, Merral. It sounds like you might need some help."

"All right. Meet me at the end of your street at half past six tomorrow."

•—•

Anya Lewitz called back just before lunch. She grinned at him from the screen of the diary before he'd even said a word. With her broad, freckled face, sky blue eyes, flaming red hair, and perpetual dynamism, Merral had always thought her pretty in a rather obvious way ever since he met her in college. The image he saw offered nothing to change that view.

"Merral D'Avanos! Where have you been? Still up to your waist in bogs planting trees, eh? Growing roots? It's been so long since we met up. When was it?" The voice was as bright and cheery as ever.

"The last round of planning for Northern Menaya; you were talking about the problems with the introduction of mammals from different Terran continents into a world with a single supercontinent." He remembered that she had had her red hair shorter then.

"Ah yes, the old purity-versus-practicality debate. Do you have either American or Eurasian faunas or do you do what we've done here and just mix them up and see what does best? Yes, I remember it. I'm now on reconstruction work, actually."

"Reconstruction? I sometimes think that I'd like to be involved in that—restoring species and environments that humanity destroyed in the past. That's valuable."

"Oh, nonsense!" She snorted. "So is planting trees, Merral. Bringing back the dodo is neat, but you can't breathe dodos. In fact, I'm told they are rather ugly and stupid."

"True, trees play a pretty important role in the great scheme of things. Anyway, I enjoy my work so I'm thankful."

"That's good."

There was a slight pause.

"Anyway, Anya, the reason I'm calling you is that I have an odd situation." He hesitated again, feeling strangely certain of how his question would be received. "See, I have a girl here on the edge of the

93

Great Northern Forest who claims to have seen something strange. She says she saw a creature like a small man, with a hard, shiny brown skin like a beetle. Is this a case for zoology or psychiatry?"

"The latter, I'm afraid. No question." The response was immediate, and Anya's smile radiated confidence.

"No other possibilities? I mean, Farholme was, of course, dead when it was seeded."

The red hair bobbed as she shook her head emphatically. "The last bacteria here died out a billion years ago; about average for this sort of world. And there is no evidence that anything beyond the usual simple forms developed. And everything was sterile here long before *Leviathan-D* arrived."

"As I thought. And our existing beetles?"

"The biggest beetles on Farholme could fit in the palm of your hand. On the tropical islands." She sighed. "I'm afraid you are talking psychiatrist. Sorry."

"Well, it's what I concluded too. They are my forests. But, as a matter of interest, what would you need to be convinced otherwise?"

She looked surprised. "I'd need a specimen, dead or alive. You've got a full description? skin or cuticle samples? still or video images? even a drawing?"

"Not at the moment. You have all the data I have. I hope to interview her tomorrow. Oh, the thing ran off when she saw it."

The blue eyes flashed with amused exasperation. "Oh, you tree experts! Learn to describe movement! Try to improve on that 'ran off' line. Did it lope, bound, slink, or scuttle? And please—on how many legs? From the description it could be two, four, six, or eight."

"Okay. Thanks for the tip, Anya. I'll remember that. But I suppose it is a hallucination? You've not reconstructed Cretaceous beetles?"

She smiled and tossed her head. "I'm sorry, especially for the girl. No, the Reconstruction Mandate has strict limits. You know them, but I'll remind you. It has to be a species made extinct by man, so we are still arguing over whether or not we reconstruct the mammoth. I'm voting yes, incidentally. But I'm afraid your guess is right. I can state categorically that it was an illusion. For a start, physics gives a finite size to insects because of their breathing mechanism. If you doubled our oxygen levels you might get them a *bit* larger, but a meter-plus high? No hope! And they never look human unless . . ." She moved closer to the screen. "Say, how many legs do *you* have up there in Ynysmant?"

Merral laughed. "You haven't changed, Anya. I have just the usual."

"Sorry, it sounds like a waking nightmare. Talk to the psychology crowd. But if there is any hard data, and I mean *hard*, Tree Man, let me know, and I'll get the lab ready. And I'll lay in a ton of triple-strength cockroach killer. Incidentally, what's this I hear about you and the tropics?"

So it's news in Isterrane too.

"True, Anya. It's being worked on. Almost certainly I'm being posted to Faraketha at the end of summer. Do you know it?"

"Hot, hot, and hot. And that's the cool season; you'll sweat off a few kilos in days. Actually, I've only flown over it. It's very poor quality at the moment, mostly very low diversity jungle. I'm no expert, but I think you ought to use a vortex blaster on it and start over again from scratch."

"I've heard it's an option. But I need to take a look."

"Actually, in fact, I'm going to be working with the Madagascar Project on Terelka. That's only five hundred kilometers south. But milder."

"You are going to be on that? I'm impressed. That's a grand vision."

Anya raised her hands in excitement. "Maybe too big. It's still in the design stage. But here, we think we can risk the ecological purity approach. Specific reconstruction of a whole long-gone subcontinental ecosystem. Lemurs, small mammals, birds, reptiles, vegetation— the lot. It will take a millennium before we know if we have achieved a viable re-creation." She laughed sheepishly. "Sorry, Merral, I get excited."

"That's how it should be! Well, I'd better get on with my work. I'll hope to catch up with you soon, Anya. But thanks for the opinion. It confirms what I think."

"Apologies about that," she said, shrugging. "Giant anthropoid beetles would be interesting, but I think we'd know if they existed. Blessings, Merral."

"Blessings, Anya." The image faded away.

•—◆—•

Merral could only make time for a trip north by working extra hours, so he stayed on at work until early evening. The idea of a community running from shadows dogged his thinking; he felt certain that there was something about the story that was familiar. Just as he was about to leave the deserted building, the answer came to him: Vero. Vero had talked of a sentinel investigation on a world where there had been a problem with a community. It would be useful to see that data. But where had it been?

Through his diary, Merral located Vero. He was on Aftarena Island on the other side of Farholme. With the time difference, he would be asleep for a few hours yet. Merral left a message on Vero's diary, ordered the building lights off, and walked home across the causeway.

•—◆—•

Vero returned the call just as Merral was getting ready for bed. He quickly pulled his night-suit on, sat within view of the diary and switched on the screen. Suddenly the dark, lean face of Vero appeared. He was wearing a lightweight, short-sleeved shirt, and there was bright, low-angle sunlight streaming behind him.

"Merral! It's been quite a few weeks. I'm sorry I haven't called before," he said with an apologetic smile.

"Vero, greetings. No problem. You wouldn't be wearing that shirt in Ynysmant today. Or this week for that matter."

"I've heard your weather's been poor. Aftarena is very nice. I traveled around a lot after I left you, just looking around. And I've ended up here. I like it—it's my sort of climate."

Merral noticed that his Farholmen dialect was now almost perfect.

"I'm glad for you. What we have at the moment would make you miserable. You have to be born here to put up with it. And congratulations on your Farholmen, Vero. It took me a bit to realize that you were speaking it. You sound like a native."

"Not quite."

"It's fine. Anyway, I was calling to ask you about something we talked about. The world where there was the collective disorder and some thought it was evil, but it was just biology after all—where was it?"

Vero twitched his nose and scratched his tightly curled hair. "Ah, that's just an interpretation. Sentinels have debated ever since it happened—which was in 12985, maybe '86. And it was on Vellant. But isn't it rather an unusual topic for a forester?" His face had acquired a look of curiosity.

Merral wondered how much he should tell. "Yes," he replied carefully. "The thing is, I have a Forward Colony where things are getting a bit odd. It could simply be the bad weather. But I thought your case might provide a lead in."

Vero's brown eyes widened and he opened his mouth to speak. Then he shook his head as if trying to dislodge a thought. "Look, I'll send you the best reviews I can find."

"Thanks. Anyway, how is the visit going?"

"Interesting. I'm enjoying it."

"So you haven't found anything anomalous yet."

Vero blinked. "Well . . . just maybe."

"Can you tell me?"

The brown face on the screen stared at him.

"Er, yes. In fact, I was thinking of calling you about it anyway. It's an odd thing. I've been uncertain how to proceed on it. Can I ask you some questions first, questions that may seem irrelevant?"

"Go ahead."

Vero shifted in his chair and then leaned toward the screen. "The Technology Protocols—you would rate them as important?"

A strange question indeed. "More than important—*vital*. The Technology Protocols make us masters of technology rather than the other way about. It is generally believed that the Assembly would have self-destructed without them."

Vero nodded slightly. "Now, can you remember how the Preamble goes?"

"Testing my memory eh? Well, the final A.D. 2130 version has, 'The Assembly of Worlds believes that, in his providence, God has provided technology so that, in some measure, the effects of the Fall may be lessened in this life. However, the Assembly also believes that, precisely because of our fallenness, technology can be abused to the detriment of an individual and his or her God-given personality. The Assembly therefore solemnly covenants that the only technology that will be accepted is that which can be shown will not lead to the loss or damage of individuality or personality.' How was that?"

Vero nodded again. "Flawless. Now, Protocol Six?"

"Six? Oh that one. The shortest. 'The rights of an individual to be protected from direct or indirect technological abuse are not extinguished by death.'"

There was a further nod. "And, Merral, you understand that to mean—what?"

"Well, I have to think back to college. It's mainly that there is to be no rewriting of history. Because it's banned, it's hard to think of an example. Yes, I know, to alter a visual file to make your partner in a Team-Ball game look like a famous player of the past. I must admit I've never understood why it was in the Protocols. It's never seemed a big thing to me."

"You are fortunate. Sentinels have to spend time studying the times before the Great Intervention, and I can tell you there were many serious instances of this problem. But that's the end of my questions."

Vero paused, flexed his long fingers, and sighed quietly. When he spoke it was in a hushed and solemn tone. "I ask you these things, Merral, about Protocol Six, because there is some evidence that it may have been breached."

It took some time for the significance of the last word to sink in. *Does he mean here on Farholme?* "Not here? Surely not? . . . I mean, breach of the Protocols is—" Merral ran out of words as the import of the statement sank in.

Vero leaned back in his chair and Merral was aware of the palm trees behind him. "Was *serious* the word you were looking for?" he suggested quietly.

"I suppose so. I was actually trying to find a more major word."

"You would be right to do so." The face on the other side of the world was grim.

"You'd better tell me about it."

Vero rubbed his flattened nose between his hands and then stared at the screen.

"Sorry, Merral. You won't like this. A voice has told me that there is a problem. Do you know whose?"

Merral, now feeling too perplexed to even try to answer, just shook his head.

"It was the voice of Miranda Cline." Vero paused to let the name sink in and then repeated it, as if listening to it himself. "Miranda Cline. Although dead these three thousand years, she still speaks."

"*The* Miranda Cline? The alto? The one my Uncle Barrand used on his Nativity piece?"

Vero nodded, unhappiness imprinted on his expression. "The same, Merral, the very same. In fact, the problem is precisely the audio file you gave me—the one of Rechereg's *Choral Variations on an Old Carol.* The one with Miranda Cline as alto."

Merral gasped. If it was barely believable that anyone could breach the Protocols, how much more unbelievable was it that such a breach was linked to his uncle? It made no sense at all. But then, nothing at Herrandown did anymore.

Vero was speaking quietly and apologetically, almost as if he was confessing something himself. "See, Merral, I got round to listening to that recording again recently. I liked it, especially Miranda Cline. I'd never heard her sing as well. And one evening here, with nothing much to do, I called up the background to it from the files in the Library and found that there was an interview with Rechereg himself. There he mentioned that the alto part was very hard and very high. And as I heard that, something clicked: something that I should have known. Because I knew about Miranda Cline. While she was unparalleled in the lower and midrange, she kept out of the topmost ranges. She was the classic, low second alto. Yet in the file you gave me she sings right up to top *G* and holds it firmly without breakup for two seconds."

There was silence between them. Outside his room, Merral could hear his father and mother talking softly as they went up to bed. Their world seemed a long way away.

Merral heard himself speaking slowly. "So you are saying that there is no way that her natural voice could have reached that high. But perhaps it was someone else?"

Vero nodded. "Excellent, Merral. That is quite the line I am taking. The file says it is Miranda Cline and it sounds like her. But there could be a mistake. There are a thousand re-created voices."

Merral closed his eyes. "No, he said he was thinking of using her. And when he transmitted it to me the covering note said that he had used Miranda Cline after all." A faint voice seemed to cry out within him that he was condemning his uncle.

Vero stirred. "Well, it could still be a mistake. An error of the machinery. I'm going to have the file checked." He stared at his fingers, as if seeing them for the first time. "I suppose it is just possible that there was some sort of coding error. I'd prefer any alternative to what I'm afraid I think is the case."

"Which is," Merral stated dully, scarcely able to phrase the words, "that Barrand altered her voice in complete defiance of the Sixth Protocol."

Vero looked away, as if unable to face him, but signified his agreement by the tiniest nod of his head. "You see," he said slowly, after a moment, "re-createds are at the limits of what we allow. They willingly give their vocal skills to be copied so that their voices can be reused later. But there is a commitment that we do not abuse that gift. Some re-created voices come with specific restrictions of the donors. Falancia Wollan, for instance, felt that her voice was unsuited to dramatic works like opera. But this is something else." His face became somber.

"Vero, what are you going to do?"

Vero turned slowly back to face the diary. "I shall transmit the file to my office on Ancient Earth. They have the ability there to take the waveforms to pieces. To definitely say whether it was hers and whether or not it was altered. I will do it in the next few days. I needed to talk to you first."

"If it is an alteration?"

Vero shook his head. "Merral, I have no idea. There are no precedents on file. We can hope that it is some sort of psychological problem and treatable." He looked profoundly miserable and after a moment went on slowly. "It all seems so . . . well, disproportionate. A few seconds worth of a single note on a file from a singer who is long dead. I'm sorry, Merral."

As Vero fell silent, Merral felt caught between his own unhappiness and that of his friend. But the issue was plain and he felt it right that he restate it. "It is not a light thing, Vero. And you as a sentinel know it, even if we use re-created voices more here than you do. To be one is an honor, to give your voice for things like the Forward Colonies and the ships. Voices are special. That's why no machine, no diary even, is ever given a human voice, although we could easily do it. The sovereign Lord made Miranda Cline unable to reach those top notes. To have altered her voice so it did—if that's what happened—is a lie, a twisting of truth."

Vero nodded his head gently and seemed to stare for long moments into infinity. "You know, they always say to sentinels at graduation, 'Always pray that you spend your entire life without being needed.' I always thought it funny." Then his focus shifted back to Merral. "But what do you think? Tell me that your uncle's hardware is set wrong, that he's deaf . . . that in the transfer one note got changed by some distortion of the electromagnetic field—*anything*. Tell me, Merral. Tell me!"

"I need to think Vero. Wait a minute. Please."

With his mind reeling, Merral tapped off the video and sound and sat back in his chair. This was too much. He had been worried before Nativity at the possibility that his uncle had lied, he had been made uneasy by this morning's news, and now this. Three things. His options were very limited indeed.

He reached for the diary and the image of Vero in a pale shirt with the brilliant sunlight behind him returned.

"Right. Vero, let me be open with you. I think something is wrong up at Herrandown. I have some other evidence—"

Vero raised a finger. "A question—which you may, of course, refuse to answer. The Forward Colony with the collective instability you mentioned?"

"The same."

Vero shook his head slowly. "Oh dear. Oh dear."

After several moments, Vero spoke again. "On the positive side, Merral, it's fairly isolated. And, at least it's localized. So far. But what to do?"

"Well, I'm going up there tomorrow for the day. I think, though, your fears are probably right. I think it highly probable that he has willfully modified the voice parameters."

Vero rubbed his face. "I do not know what to advise. This is surprising. I assumed that there was nothing here. But now. . . . No, we need more information. I will wait to hear from you before I do anything. Look, Merral, can you meet me in Isterrane two days from now? No, wait—that will be the Lord's Day. The day after, then?"

Merral hesitated, then spoke. "Yes, if you like. If you think that it's that important?"

"My friend, my reading of the data is that we have either a psychological crisis infecting one individual and probably others—which is what I hope it is—or—" He shook his head.

"Or what?"

There was a long silence in which Merral became strangely aware of the perfect stillness in the room, a stillness so deep that he felt he could hear his heart beat.

Vero's voice, when it spoke out of the diary, almost surprised him. "Or, I do not like to say. But I cannot rule out that we are seeing the start of something so significant that . . ." He tailed off and then shook his head. It was only after another long pause that he spoke again. "No, I will not speculate. Keep this to yourself, Merral, for the moment."

"I see. I will abide by that."

"Oh, and be careful when you go to Herrandown. Look out."

"Look out for what?" Merral asked.

"I only wish I knew."

They stared at each other, a tension somehow transmitted around the globe. Finally, Merral forced himself to say the words. "Vero, I need to know. Finish what you said earlier. Or what?"

Finally, as if being dragged out of the depths, the answer came back, syllable by painful syllable.

"Merral, if what I fear is the case, then the rules we have lived by for over eleven thousand years may be on the point of changing."

CHAPTER 7

The weather on the journey north to Herrandown next morning was dull and overcast, although thankfully dry. There was little to see on the road, whose route had, after all, been planned to avoid the more exciting landscapes. Even so, part of the road had been washed away in one place by a rogue stream, and the little Recon vehicle had to make a brief and muddy detour that fortunately added little to the journey time.

As they rolled slowly along a marshy stretch with the pale sunlight trying to penetrate the drifting mists, a particularly protracted silence fell upon them. Merral looked at Isabella, feeling that her slight figure looked incongruous in the large passenger seat of the Recon.

"No regrets about our parents' decision, Isabella?" he asked, catching her eye, wishing to hear her voice as much as to get an answer.

She paused, stretched her legs out and then smiled softly back at him. "No. Not really. Your tropics job is almost definite, and the more I hear of it the more I think I may be best off in Ynysmant. But also, yes. It would have been desirable, in many ways." The smile grew slightly wistful. "Of course, I think that maybe things could still work out between us."

She fell silent again and then she looked back at him. "And you, Forester D'Avanos?"

He thought for a moment. "The same. This is how things are. I could wish otherwise, but what would be the point?"

Ahead of them, a road repair machine sensed their approach,

pivoted its body clear of the road on its four hind legs, and turned its head toward them. Merral raised a hand toward the machine and the silver head nodded slowly in acknowledgement.

"Just so," Isabella said. "What would be the point?"

• ◆ •

Just after ten-thirty the Recon rolled up to the top of a rise on the road and Herrandown came into view. Merral paused the vehicle and switched the power off. He stared down at the sleepy little cluster of houses and fields surrounded by trees in their tentative fresh green foliage. *What do I expect to see? A dark cloud? A visible shadow?* But there was nothing.

He started the power up again and they moved on down quietly to the houses, where he parked near the rotorcraft pad and switched everything off.

The dogs came running out and carefully encircled the machine. *Poor old Spotback. I do wonder what happened to him.* As he opened the hatch and got out on his side, the dogs edged warily nearer, yapping vigorously at him. Merral stopped, struck by their behavior. It was extraordinary how they seemed much more cautious than in the past. *Perhaps, they know better than we do what is going on.*

His thoughts were interrupted as he was suddenly compressed in an embrace by his aunt. "Oh, Merral! Thank you for coming. We are so grateful. . . . We don't know what to think—"

She stiffened suddenly as Isabella appeared round from her side of the machine.

"Aunt," said Merral, sensing the awkwardness, "I brought Isabella. She has more experience with young girls."

A look of incomprehension, or even annoyance, passed over his aunt's face, only to be replaced swiftly by a smile. "Oh. Yes. I see." She grabbed Isabella in a firm and hasty hug.

"And thank you for coming too." Zennia turned to Merral. "Elana is in her room. The other girls and Thomas are at school. Come on in and I'll get you both a drink. Barrand is on his way down from the ridge. He wasn't expecting you so soon. He's making the most of the dry weather."

· ◆ ·

Leaving Isabella to look at some recent paintings, Merral went into the kitchen. "Aunt, I want to apologize. I should have warned you that I was bringing Isabella."

She shook her head. "No, it doesn't matter. It's just that—"

He waited for an answer and reluctantly she continued. "I was hoping, I suppose, that we could keep it within the family. If you know what I mean. Elana's problem. It's . . . well . . . a *sensitive* matter."

"But, Aunt, if she has a problem, then it affects the community. And it may be that the problem isn't with her."

"But it particularly affects us. It will not look good."

Puzzled, Merral replied, "Who cares?"

"*We* do, Merral, I'm afraid."

Oh dear. We never used to worry about what others felt about us. What has happened here?

· ◆ ·

When they had passed on all the news and finished their coffee, Zennia took them up to the room they had moved Elana to. Pleading work, she left them there.

Elana was lying face up on the bed reading a book projected onto the ceiling above her head. She switched it off abruptly after they entered, half got up, and then slumped back onto the bed. Her face was pale.

"Cousin Merral! I heard you might be coming."

He kissed her. "I've brought Isabella to see you. She heard you weren't well."

Elana gave her a mischievous smile. "Some excuse! Hi, Isabella."

After a few minutes of news and pleasantries, Isabella sat by the bed and said in a matter-of-fact voice, "You had a nasty time the other day I gather, Elana."

"Hmm, yes."

"Would you mind—if it doesn't hurt too much—telling me and Merral about it? Slowly. You went for a walk, didn't you?"

Gradually, bit by bit, the story unfolded. Merral, sitting to one side, watched both as they talked and was impressed by Isabella's gentleness and the slow, steady way she worked at the questions. When, as frequently happened, Elana dried up, Isabella would quietly and softly try another angle. The story that emerged, however, was little more than an elaboration of what Merral had already heard. Elana had been on her own, climbing the path to the north-northwest of Herrandown, when she saw the beetle man in the bushes. He made no noise but just stared at her. When she screamed, he vanished.

After praising some paintings on a desk nearby, Isabella managed to get Elana to do a drawing. After some minutes, she had produced a result that, while being crude, was enough to give an impression of what she was trying to describe. The overall picture was of a vaguely manlike figure. It had a narrow face with two eyes and mouth on top of a body with a chest that appeared to be made of plates.

"Like a suit of war armor from the early Dark Times?" Merral asked, but the concept was unknown to her. Further questions revealed a firm and unshakable view that there had only been one pair of hands and legs and that the body casing was brown and shiny, like a beetle's.

"Or like wood?" Merral asked, wondering whether the whole thing was a bizarre illusion based on a fallen log.

"Oh no," she said in firm voice. "Not like wood. Not really. I suppose the surface, the shell, looked like polished wood—dark wood." She gestured to the varnished planks on the wall opposite. "But you see, Merral, the bits moved together, like they do on an insect."

Merral and Isabella shared a bemused glance.

After a few more questions that seemed to elicit nothing new, Elana began to be restless. "Please, Merral, Isabella . . . I'd rather not talk any more. It was horrid!"

Isabella looked at Merral, who reached over and patted Elana gently on her shoulder.

"Thanks, young lady. You'll soon be better. The weather is improving no end. We'll see you before we go." With a few general comments they slipped out, closed the door, and went back downstairs. Halfway down Merral turned to Isabella, expecting her to say something. She merely shook her head.

"Go on," he said.

Isabella shrugged her shoulders. "What do *you* think?"

"Me? I have no idea. If it wasn't impossible, I would believe her. But it's your opinion I value. What do you think?"

"A convincing vision," Isabella remarked gravely. "It's no game or joke. She is certain that what she saw is real."

"Which is different from saying that what she saw was real."

"Quite so. And that is out of my area."

"And into mine. But well done anyway. You did better than I could do."

"Thanks."

• ◆ •

They were talking with Zennia a few minutes later when Barrand came in from outside, his gray overalls heavily stained with reddish brown mud. He greeted them all with smiles. If Isabella's arrival had been news to him, Merral thought that he did not show it.

"Sorry, sorry. Business as usual here. Merral, here, give me a hug. I'm expecting your quarry team any day. Isabella, how lovely to see you. Let's give you a hug too. Excuse the dirt. Thank you both for coming." He sank into a chair heavily and breathed out loudly. "Ohh, I'm getting old. Not enough exercise this winter. How was your journey?"

"All right: a washout at about the thirty-five kilometer post."

"Ah, there. A wild stream again. But a lot of mud?"

"Of course."

There was a long silence that Merral felt obliged to break. "Uncle, we had a long chat with Elana."

There was the faintest hint of a frown on his uncle's face. "Ah yes. So how did you find my eldest daughter?" To Merral his tone sounded strangely lacking in compassion.

Merral looked at Isabella, who hesitated a moment before answering. "Well, Barrand Antalfer, I'm no specialist, but I would think she'll be all right in a few days. She's had a nasty shock."

"I'm glad to hear what you think." Barrand nodded impassively and then looked at Merral. "You are both staying for lunch, I take it?"

There was an awkward pause. Merral looked at Isabella and could see her staring at his uncle as if summoning up courage to say something. Eventually, though, it was Merral who found himself breaking the silence.

"Uncle, Elana said she saw it about this time of day. As the issue of the lighting is critical, can we go and see where it . . . where she had the incident? Could we go and have a look? Now?"

Barrand pursed his heavy lips. "To see the place. Well, yes. I don't see why not." There was a curious hesitation. "Both of you? Anyway, I suppose I'm already in outdoor clothes."

He's either acting or he doesn't care, Merral decided. *And either is bizarre. What is going on here?*

•-•-•

Five minutes later, they were walking up the muddy track to the hill. It was still cold, but the cloud had thinned so that there was enough sunlight to cast faint shadows. Under the trees, however, the shadows remained deep. Some of the spring flowers were out. There was a fine display of little yellow daffodils in places, and along a rockier patch bright pink cyclamens glowed.

Barrand, still apparently cheerful, led the way. "It began to rain shortly afterward. It's been a rotten spring. The worst I can remember. The children have been indoors a lot."

"Elana said it had been one of the first good days." Isabella's voice was unobtrusive.

"Just so. Now, it was up here."

They turned up a slippery path between stringy pines and old, brown, straggling brambles. The way narrowed and they fell into single file.

"Can I go ahead?" Merral asked. "Stop me when we get there."

"Be my guest."

They made poor progress, as every so often Merral would stop to look at the ground. There were few clear impressions. Once he felt he could see a child's footprints, and in another place, boot marks that belonged to Barrand.

They kept on for another hundred meters. Here the trees had grown higher, and behind the shrubs and bushes flanking the path, a heavy darkness lay under the lower branches. Merral stopped, gestured for silence, and strained his ears as he listened. He soon heard the noise of scrabbling as a rabbit fled, far away a distant buzzard mewed, and somewhere nearby there was the faint hum of a power saw at another farm. Carefully, Merral breathed in, but he could only smell the new flowers, the clean aroma of the pines, and the faint odor of the new young garlic.

Nothing he heard or smelled was wrong or unfamiliar. Objectively, there was nothing alarming, nothing untoward. And yet, he had an inescapable feeling that something was not right.

They walked on, gradually climbing up above the hamlet. Despite being chilly, the day seemed oddly oppressive, and Merral felt keenly that he wanted the clouds to open and the sun's rays to break through. He glanced around, noticing Isabella's pinched and strained face, while Barrand bore an expression of unnatural unconcern.

The trees now were hanging over them and Merral looked up at them, feeling disoriented. These woods were somehow unfriendly. The idea puzzled him. It was, he knew, intellectually a nonsense concept. There were no unfriendly woods. They were bright woods and dark, even just possibly gloomy woods, but *unfriendly* was not an appropriate adjective. But yet, today, in defiance of all he knew, he felt that the word seemed appropriate.

Suddenly they turned a bend in the path and there was a gap in the trees to the right with a view overlooking Herrandown with all its patch-work of gray-roofed buildings buried to varying extents in the ground.

"Here,"—Barrand's voice was flat and without emotion—"in those trees. She said she saw it there."

Merral's gaze followed his gesture. The bases of the trees were obscured by brambles, young grass, and some scrubby hawthorn bushes. He went up to the spot and looked carefully, feeling even more out of his depth. He could find nothing unusual. *What am I looking for?* Suddenly the whole expedition seemed stupid. After all, he thought, supposing there was another creature there, what would he say to it? "Oh, hello, do you realize you have frightened a girl?" And what language would he use? Communal, Farholmen, pre-Intervention English or French? He felt vaguely stupid staring at a clump of per-fectly ordinary brambles. *Genus* Rubus, he told himself, as if finding taxonomy a safe retreat from this imponderable puzzle. *And don't ask me the species name; it's probably another new form. We can travel to the stars, but one hundred and twenty centuries after Linnaeus first gave organisms such names, the humble bramble still mocks any attempt at a usable field classification.*

"Well, any ideas?" There seemed a hint of impatience in his uncle's voice.

"None worth stating, Uncle. Let me see if I can get into the woods behind this. You stay here so I know where I am."

Merral walked back into the trees with Isabella following silently behind him. He picked up an old branch and used it to clear a way through the fringing scrubs. Once through the marginal growth, the undergrowth thinned out. Merral paused to let his eyes adjust to the gloom, which was broken locally by patches of brightness where the light entered through the fractured pine cover.

He sensed Isabella come close alongside. He whispered to her, "What do you think? You are very quiet."

"You are asking the wrong person. Woods aren't my thing and I've got plenty to think about." She frowned, her eyes half closed. "But you think there's something wrong, don't you?"

Merral realized that he might have known she would have detected that. "Wrong, yes. But what sort of wrongness and where? I have no hard data. Let's just listen."

So, with pauses to listen, they moved quietly through the trees. Ahead something dark moved among the trees and Merral froze instantly, his hand swinging up to make Isabella pause. A moment later he relaxed and began breathing again as the squirrel saw him and ran up the trunk. Beckoning Isabella on, he made his way slowly round toward the strip of yellow light that marked the boundary of the path. Beyond the trees he could just make out Barrand in his dark gray jacket.

It must have been about here. There was a feeling of anticlimax. There was nothing to see, no sign of a track or trail. He looked around. The view to the path ahead was obstructed by the combination of the low branches and the brambles. She had imagined it all, she must have.

He called out, "So, Uncle, can you see me?"

"Not well. Go further right, though." Merral moved obediently that way but could see nothing.

"About here?"

"Yes, I think so."

For a moment, Merral was nonplussed, finding that here there seemed to be only undisturbed branches. Then he remembered Elana had called what she had seen a "little man." He squatted down.

Suddenly, through a gap in the bushes, he had a clear view of Barrand's ruddy face framed by vegetation.

"How interesting," he muttered, his voice sounding as if it were from a distance. He turned to Isabella. "You have a look."

Merral stood up and stretched his legs, trying to think clearly. He realized now that he had been assuming all along that Elana had imagined the whole thing. But the gap in the branches made that harder to believe.

He heard a sharp intake of breath from Isabella and then her voice, low and intense, drifted back up to him. "Oh. That adds a different dimension. I hadn't realized . . ."

Alerted by her tone, Merral knelt beside the bush again. "What hadn't you realized?"

"That you can see everything."

As she slid out of his way, he looked beyond her. Barrand had walked away, and beyond the path, glinting in the weak sunlight, stretched the buildings of Herrandown. All of them.

He bit his lip. "Oh my. Oh my," he said, almost under his breath.

The implications sank in one after another, like a succession of stones thrown into still, deep waters. There had been something here. Whatever had been here had been intelligent. It had also, it seemed, had a purpose—that of watching the hamlet. He swallowed, his throat somehow dry. An intelligent purposeful watcher: race or kind unknown.

"Isabella, say nothing to Barrand," he hissed, pitching his voice as softly as he could. He didn't want to alarm his uncle and aunt further.

He heard Isabella answer, "I won't," and recognized a quavering note in her voice.

Suddenly a minute color difference just in front of his face caught his eye. He focused on it. It was the yellow cut end of a tiny branch, thinner than a rose stem. But what had it been cut with? Merral looked around on the ground and found what he was searching for. Carefully, he picked up the other part of the thin branch and stepped back.

"What is it?"

"Whatever . . . whoever was here . . . no, that makes no sense." He paused in desperation. "Anyway, there is a branch here which was cut in half. Somehow."

He held the branch end under a shaft of sunlight and looked at it, noticing a strange, sharp, oblique cut. Aware that his hand was shaking, Merral imaged the cut as best he could on his diary.

Isabella watched him in silence. He saw that she had moved to stand with her back against a tree trunk as if it gave her protection.

Merral spoke to her, his voice little more than a whisper. "We'll talk later. I'm confused."

She nodded sharply. "And I . . . I feel strange here."

He forced a smile, trying not to put his unease into words. *I can understand that strangeness; I've been in these woods for years and I have never felt as I do today. I want to get out, and I want to be in the warmth and coziness of urban Ynysmant surrounded by people.* Forcing those thoughts away, he carefully cut off the end few centimeters of the stem with his knife, put it in a sample bag, and sealed it.

If it came here, then there will be a path to and from this place. Having worked with some of the larger mammals like deer, Merral knew a little of tracking. As he looked into the depths of the woods, he felt he could make out a possible trail between bushes running down into a depression.

He called out to Barrand. "Uncle, we are just going for a walk into the woods. Ten minutes?"

The deep voice boomed back. "Yes, yes. If you need to. Fine. I'll wait here."

Slowly, Merral walked back into the woods, looking for any clue as to what had passed this way. Within a few paces he began to have doubts that there was a trail. Surely he was fooling himself into believing that these depressions were footprints? Might it not simply be the trail of a lynx, a fox, or even a deer?

Yet what he felt might be the trail went west in a fairly straight manner and started to drop down toward the Lannar River. A few dozen meters on, just as he was on the point of giving up, the trail suddenly became very obvious. He found crushed grass stalks and what might have been small and rather angular footprints. But of what creature he had not the slightest idea.

"How much farther, Merral?"

He looked at Isabella, aware from her face as well as her tone that she was unhappy.

"Just another minute or two!" he called out and was rewarded by a fixed, determined smile. *She's right though. We should be going back.* Anyway, the going was becoming rougher, as the trail was now leading down into a steep-banked tributary that fed into the main river.

A large fallen larch trunk partly blocked the way and Merral stooped to get under it. The branches had been snapped off in falling so that the underside of the trunk was punctuated by a series of jagged, splintered protrusions.

"Be careful, Isabella, mind your head."

Merral stopped, his attention grabbed by strands of brown hair hanging on a sharp broken branch. He peered at it carefully in the poor light, just able to make out that the fibers were long, coarse, and wiry. Isabella came and peered at it. Merral pushed her hand away as she reached out to touch it.

"No," he told her, "You'll contaminate it. I'll take it for analysis. We'll get the DNA out and it will tell us what we have."

"Of course. Can you do it?"

"Not here, but I'll get the main lab in Isterrane to do it. An old friend of mine, Anya Lewitz, will organize it."

He imaged the hair on the diary, and then carefully wrapped a sample bag around it. As he did he bent over and put his nose to the mouth of the bag. There was a faint, pungent odor, a smell of something unpleasantly rancid, as if food had been left out in warm weather.

Isabella gestured. "Let me. . . ." Her nose wrinkled in disgust. "Ugh! That's horrid! What creature was that from?"

"I really don't know. There's nothing I can think of here that it's from. And look at the height above the ground. Whatever it was is probably as tall as you or me. Taller, if it was stooping."

Isabella shuddered and looked round.

Merral rubbed his face, as if trying to see the situation more clearly. Not only did this fit nothing in his experience or training, it fit nothing that he had ever heard of.

"It makes no sense at all. It wasn't from what Elana saw, but from something else."

Could there be two unexplained creatures? That seemed hard to believe. He wondered whether two impossibilities were more or less probable than just one.

However a more pressing issue was the need to decide what to do next. Merral paused, weighing up all the options. Should he try and pursue the trail? Take a dog or two and follow it? There would be no problem for a dog following a creature with such a smell. But he was not equipped for a trail that could lead to a day's walk or more, and he had to be back home today in order to be in Isterrane the day after tomorrow. Besides, something like that would raise the status of the whole affair and would inevitably make it a major crisis. And, if it was a false alarm, then harm might be done to his uncle's family. He made his decision.

"Isabella, we will go back now. Anyway, we said ten minutes."

"A good idea," she answered, relief in her voice. "What are you going to do?"

"I will take advice in Isterrane. In the meantime, I think we are neutral about what we have seen. The data, after all, needs analysis." Merral began to walk back toward where his uncle was.

"I suppose you are right."

Barrand was sitting on a tree trunk whittling away at a piece of wood with a knife. "Ho! I was wondering where you had both gone to."

"I found something that might have been a track and I picked up some samples for analysis."

Barrand seemed almost uninterested. "Some faunal anomaly, I'll bet. Well, we'd better get back for lunch."

•◆•

Lunch was an oddly subdued affair, especially by comparison with the other meals he'd had at Herrandown. Elana preferred to stay and eat in her bedroom. Barrand and Zennia were pleasant and affable, and the food was good and plentiful, but Merral felt a tension. Every so often Merral noticed glances between his uncle and aunt that hinted that all was not well between them.

After lunch Barrand and Zennia disappeared into the kitchen to make coffee, leaving Merral and Isabella alone in the small family room that he had sat in with his aunt and uncle just before Nativity. That reminded Merral that he really ought to try and raise the issue of the recording. It was not a prospect that appealed, and thinking of the best way to approach it began to occupy his mind. While Isabella sat looking at a portfolio of his aunt's paintings, Merral got up and, trying to clarify his thoughts, opened the window and leaned out, enjoying the fresh spring air.

As he did he realized he could hear what his aunt and uncle were saying. *The kitchen window must be open,* he thought, and the breeze came from that direction. A second or two later he realized that the conversation was also very animated.

His uncle's voice, loud and ill tempered, drifted past. "You shouldn't have got me to bring him in. It's something *we* can handle."

It was such an extraordinary tone that for a moment Merral wondered if it really was his uncle.

Then his aunt replied and, to his distress, her manner was similar. "*We* handle it?" she seemed to snap. "*We* haven't a clue—least of all you. There's something wrong here, Barrand. I keep telling you."

There was a snort, as if an animal were loose. "Don't be a fool, woman. There's nothing wrong here but hysterical women."

"Hysterical? I like that!" His aunt's voice seemed to vibrate with rage. "The real problem is a man—a man who is too proud and too stubborn to admit that there is something badly wrong here!"

Merral, suddenly ashamed both of eavesdropping and of what he was overhearing, abruptly closed the window. He stepped back into the room wondering if his face was burning. He was staggered, even shocked. The words he had heard made sense, but the tone was like nothing he had ever heard before. Things like it were alluded to in the old literature, but for it to happen between a husband and wife? It was hardly credible.

"What's wrong?" Isabella asked.

"I have heard . . ." He paused, finding himself in agonized consternation. "No, I can't say. . . ." He looked at her. "What's wrong here, Isabella? I'm convinced everything is. Badly."

Isabella opened her mouth to speak and closed it abruptly at the sound of approaching footsteps.

•–•–•

The subsequent coffee was a very quiet, even embarrassed affair in which almost nothing was said. After it Merral and Barrand left Zennia and Isabella and went over together to the office.

The big man closed the door, sat down awkwardly at his crowded desk, and stared over his papers at Merral.

"Tell me, Nephew," he asked, "what will your verdict be?" Merral felt that there was a wary, defensive look on his uncle's face.

Merral did not answer immediately, his mind instead running over a range of possible answers. Eventually he spoke. "Uncle, I need to take some advice. I am a forester. I am not convinced that the problem lies in my area. If it does, it goes beyond my knowledge. Frankly, I have no idea what is going on."

Barrand nodded and leaned back in his chair. "So what are you going to do?"

"The day after tomorrow I will go to Isterrane and talk to some people there about your situation."

A clear look of unease crossed his uncle's face. "It's going to go *that* far? I was hoping that it could be sorted out easily. Here. Or at worst, Ynysmant. "

"I had hoped so too, but I think not. I think I need specialist advice. You see, there is always the possibility that the wrong action may make matters worse."

"I suppose so." His uncle shifted his large frame heavily in his chair. "Well, to be honest, Merral, I'm rather regretting my call yesterday. Zennia pushed me into it. Elana had this thing, this vision. By taking it seriously, we have just made matters worse."

"You don't believe her?" Merral asked.

"Believe what?" There was a hard-edged incredulity in his voice. "That she saw a creature that doesn't exist? I wouldn't say it to her face, of course. No, let's just say I'm frankly skeptical—very skeptical. Female hormones, I'd say."

Feeling unsure what to say, Merral said nothing.

"See, Merral," his uncle continued, leaning forward slightly, "I would rather that we kept the whole thing low-key. Not blow it up. This girl of yours, Isabella, now—very nice, don't get me wrong—she may talk and we might have the colony here closed down. And we've worked hard."

He gestured widely with his arms, got up with a lurch of the chair, walked to the window and peered out of it.

"It's not easy here, you know. 'The blessings of isolation,' I think my wife said." He made a strange, almost mocking noise. "Maybe, it has its curses, though. Fifty of us. All together, and such a lousy winter. I wonder if you people in Ynysmant really understand. . . ."

He swung round and shook his large head angrily as if trying to break free of something.

"Strange, Merral. I've never felt this way before. Very strange. Sorry to take it out on you, too. It must be the weather. It's just . . . well . . . in a word, *tough* here."

He paced the floor as if trying to find words to express his feelings. He paused at the Lymatov painting and stared hard at it. "We were talking about this last time, weren't we?"

Merral nodded.

"Well it's saying different things to me now. It asks a question. Is it worth it? Is the whole venture"—he threw his arms wide as if to encompass the colony—"the sacrifices, the blood, the suffering. Is it all worth doing?"

For some time Merral's perplexity was so great he could say nothing. Eventually, feeling compelled to speak, his reply was hesitant.

"I have to say, Uncle, that this question has been debated, well, ever since the Intervention. The verdict has always been that it is. It *is* all worthwhile."

"Well then," his uncle said, in a tone that suggested he was unconvinced, "in the event of the entire Assembly of Worlds versus Barrand Imanos Antalfer I guess I must be wrong." And he sat down so heavily in his chair that it protested. "Sorry," he said, but his tone denied his words.

There was a heavy silence in the room. Merral, wishing he was elsewhere, plucked up his courage. "Uncle, before I go. There is one more thing. I hate to mention it. But I have a question about your concert at Nativity. The one with the Rechereg."

Merral found it impossible to identify the emotion that his uncle's face suddenly acquired.

"Oh yes. *That*. Did you like it?"

"Very much. But Miranda Cline . . . she seems to have sung at a higher pitch than she was able to in life."

Very slowly, almost as if drugged, Barrand nodded his head. "Ah, that. *That*. I'm surprised you noticed." He shrugged.

"My attention was drawn to it. But her range *was* altered?"

His uncle gave a long, low sigh. "In a way, yes. In a way, no. See, she would always have liked to sing higher. I've read her biography. That's the thing. So I was acting—shall we say—in her best interests."

"But we don't know what she actually thought. Or what she thinks now. And the Technology Protocols say that—"

"Oh yes," There was a clear note of irritation here. "Number six, isn't it? But I think she would have agreed."

In the hanging silence that ensued, Merral realized that he was becoming tempted to say that the affair didn't matter. But he knew it *did* matter. He tried to think what to say next but was spared by his uncle. "Look, I was in a hurry and I didn't think it would give offense. But I will destroy the file."

"Probably the best thing." But it was more than a matter of giving offense, Merral knew. It was wrong.

The silence returned, only to be broken again by his uncle's voice, now quiet but vaguely truculent, as if he was trying to reassert himself. "But maybe, Merral, we need to remember something."

"What?"

"That the Technology Protocols were made by men, not God. They're not Scripture."

Merral suddenly realized that they were now in very serious and very deep waters. He knew that he had to get out of the conversation without giving in.

"No, they aren't. True. But they are part of the fabric of the covenant of the Assembly of Worlds, and there has been no serious discussion of the removal of any part of them for over ten thousand years."

Merral decided that he really couldn't get into an argument. He had to talk to Vero about this.

"Anyway, Uncle. I've had a long day. We can discuss it all at some other time."

"Oh, perhaps so. Anyway, you'd best be going."

Barrand got to his feet, his bulk seeming to dominate the office.

"Look, I'm sorry about the business with Miranda Cline. It was stupid. It's just been a long winter." He sighed heavily. "You'd best go. I suspect it will all blow over here. A proper spring is nearly here and summer won't be far away. And I'll feel better when I get the quarry started. But thanks for coming."

Merral chose his words carefully. "Uncle, be assured of this. I support you, and I'm available whenever you need me."

They walked slowly back to the house where they were greeted by Thomas, now released from school, who leapt on Merral with a boundless energy and demanded to clamber over him. Merral put up with it for a few minutes and then deposited the child on the ground. Not only had Thomas become heavy today, his heart was not in it. Instead, he hugged him and let him go. As he looked at him, he realized how much he wanted to have children of his own someday.

"So, Thomas, how are things?"

"Not good, Cousin. Not good at all." He gestured with a stubby and rather dirty hand to the surrounding woods. "There's something bad out there. Real bad. You're gonna fix it, aren't you? You are, for sure. Do you promise?" His round face was troubled.

"Well, Thomas, promises are made to be kept. So it's a serious business to make them. I won't promise to do what I may not be able to. But what I will promise, Thomas, is this. . . ." He paused, thinking of the binding significance of his words. "I am going to do everything to find out what's bad in the forest. I promise."

"Thanks. Thanks. Find out what's in there."

He looked thoughtful for a moment, and then he whispered something to Merral in a voice that was so quiet that no one else heard it.

• ◆ •

And what Thomas said so appalled and disgusted Merral that when he went over everything that he had seen and heard that day, it was Thomas's comment that alarmed him most of all. And when, the day after, he journeyed to Isterrane, it was still a preoccupation.

Again and again, the words that Thomas had whispered to him came back to him. Endlessly, he saw the little lips move and heard the voice whisper to him.

"Find it, Cousin Merral, find it. And when you find it . . . *kill it*."

CHAPTER 8

As the short-haul passenger flier made its unhurried descent through thick but patchy clouds into Isterrane Airport, Merral peered out through the window. As it was fully loaded, the pilot chose not to land vertically, but instead to come in on a gentle curving descent northward over Hassanet's Sea. Although slower, this approach to the landing strip was Merral's favorite as it offered him better views, and today he was not disappointed.

As they dipped below the clouds, his first sight was of the warm blue waters of Isterrane Bay with the high gray cliffs and green woods of the western headland rising beyond. Moments later as they swung round, the sloping red-tiled roofs of Isterrane could be seen, broken up into segments by the green of the fields and parks which ran into the very heart of the city. As the flier came in low and straight for touchdown, the gleaming pale gray wall of the hundred-meter-high anti-tsunami barrier that guarded the seaward margin of Isterrane suddenly seemed to loom up above the town's skyline.

I wonder what Vero makes of that, Merral wondered, remembering the sentinel's unease at Congregation Hall's role as a refuge. *But we must do things like this; on our unstable Made Worlds there is always the risk of some submarine landslide, volcano, or earthquake suddenly displacing a million tons of water landward. And a hundred other perils.* But, as the thought came to him, Merral found his reflection becoming somber as he realized that he had—for all its risks—always found his world vaguely reassuring. True, it had its hazards, but they were all mapped, cataloged, and known. And yet, in the last two days he had come to wonder whether Farholme was such a known world after all.

Could it be possible, he had puzzled, that they might have overlooked something? Might it be that there was something not mentioned in the Catalog of Species loose here? Something so strange that no light could be shed on it by all the millennia of knowledge of the Assembly?

• ◆ •

Both the atmosphere and space segments of Isterrane Airport seemed busy. Away down to the west, on the long rendered-basalt runways of the space strips Merral noted the white squat hulls of three general survey craft and two of the much larger in-system shuttles. Probably as a result, he found there was a lot of land traffic leaving the port, and the allocating computer almost immediately found him a seat in a vehicle going past the Planning Institute complex. So it was barely twenty minutes after landing that Merral was able to let himself into the guest room that had been issued to him. He unpacked his things, briefly admired his view of the Institute's mixed woodlands and the lake with the high white fin of the Planetary Administration Building rising behind it, and then sat down at the table with his diary to try to contact Vero.

The image that he received showed him immediately that his friend was not yet in Isterrane. The picture was shaking. Vero's face was too close to the screen, and behind him were the unmistakable green furnishings of a long-haul flier. Even as Merral extended a greeting, Vero's eyes closed as if in pain, his face bobbed sharply, and there was a thud as the transmitting diary bounced. The brown eyes opened and Vero gave an unnatural smile. "Merral! I am just being reminded of something I once read but had long since forgotten."

"What was that?"

The face jerked again.

"Ah! That atmospheric turbulence on the Made Worlds can be very much worse than that on Earth. And much less predictable. Oh, here we"—the image jarred and the dark skin seemed to acquire a paler tone—"go again. I'll never complain about the Gates again. Never! Look, Merral, I'm six hours away. Where shall I meet you?"

"The Planning Institute. I'll be there all this afternoon."

Vero nodded weakly. "I'll come straight over as soon as I land. *If* I land. . . . Look, I'm going to switch off. On Earth it's very rude to be sick on screen. Oh no!"

The screen went blank. After a few moments of praying for Vero, Merral called Anya Lewitz. She winked at Merral and gave him a broad smile that seemed to split her freckled face. "Tree Man! You made it in from the wilds. Welcome to the big town." There was a boisterousness to her manner that Merral found engaging and heartening.

"Nice to be here and to see you, Anya. I have something for you."

"Great, put it on a lead and walk it over. What does it eat?" Merral's concerns seemed to diminish in the presence of Anya's seemingly boundless good cheer.

"Sorry, it's dead. No, just a couple of samples."

"Shame! You're at the Institute?"

"Yes . . . how did you . . . ?"

"That decor. Terribly dull. No wonder the planet is such a mess; you guys can't even paint your own walls coordinated shades of blue. Look, get on over straight away. We are at the south end of the center. I want to catch up with your news and I've a meeting in a couple of hours."

Using the Institute's transport allocation system, Merral very quickly found himself a lift to the western side of the city, where the various offices, laboratories, and nurseries of the Planetary Ecology Center occupied most of a park the size of Ynysmant town. From the main entrance, he walked along the long, covered path to the Reconstruction Project Station. There, after stopping briefly to marvel at the wall-size holograph system that was today showing *The Blue Whales of Marsa-Mena*, he was directed up to Anya's office.

This turned out to be a charming, extended second-floor room under a high-pitched wooden roof, with wide glass windows and a balcony overlooking the city. For all its size, the room seemed full. The walls were covered with maps and images of animals, the shelving loaded with equipment, datapaks, models, and books, and the spare table and bench space were covered by papers and charts. In one corner of the room a model of a giant sloth, almost Merral's height, stared at him with a haughty air. In the far corner some tree hamsters in a large cage ran up a branch and peered at him with some uncertainty.

Anya gave him a hearty hug and a moist kiss on the cheek. *Very nice,* Merral thought, surprised at the strength of his feelings. She gestured in her lively way to a seat at a low table. They sat down, and she looked at him in the evaluative way old friends do after an absence of years. Merral felt that Anya's notorious playfulness and exuberance had been slightly tempered with growing maturity, but not entirely lost. *No, she has just learned how to tame it.*

Over coffee, they shared news of families, friends, and jobs. Anya's face brightened. "Oh, and while I remember, tonight—come over for a meal. The building over there, Narreza Tower. Fifth—that is, top—floor. It's at my flat; my older sister is in town. You know Perena?"

"Yes, you introduced me at the beach once. The pilot?"

"Ah, a Near-Space Captain now. Anyway, Space Affairs is letting her off for the night, so she's cooking. Theodore will be there too. You've met him?"

"No. I don't think so."

"Tree Man, you've been out in the bush too long. Theodore is a good friend of mine. He's with Maritime Affairs, works on deep-sea currents. Anyway, you'd be more than welcome."

"Thanks. But I've got a guest myself coming in from Aftarena. I'd better look after him. He's truly a long way from home."

"Ancient Earth? Really, oh, you must bring him. Perena would like that. She finished her training there. But who is it?"

"One Verofaza Laertes Enand, sentinel."

Anya wagged her head slowly and seriously as if reading a lot into the answer. "Ah, a sentinel. You are keeping interesting company. I'd heard we had one visiting. Bring him, though. What's he doing?"

A good question, and one that I wonder if Vero can answer.

"Well, he's writing a report. But it's complicated. Ask him yourself, though."

"Oh, I will."

There was a pause and Anya glanced at the clock on the wall. "Time flies, I'm afraid. Now your problem. Tell me about it."

"It may be something or nothing. I'm involved professionally and also because it is family. I have an uncle at Herrandown, a Forward Colony up toward the Lannar Crater. It's his eldest girl who says she saw it . . . this thing."

"Yeah, the more I thought about it the stranger it became. She is sticking to the story, I take it?"

"Oh yes. I'm certain she believes in it. She did a drawing. Look at this." He summoned up a scanned copy on his diary screen and turned it so Anya could see it.

Anya looked at it in silence, her bright blue eyes examining it carefully. Finally, she shook her head. "Like nothing in reality and precious little I've heard of in fiction. I'm no wiser. It's more humanoid than I had thought. But what do *you* think, O great expert of the Great Northern Forest?" Merral noticed a searching look to her face that belied the teasing tone.

"Me? Well to be honest, I'm embarrassed by it. I really don't know. I was set to dismiss it, but then we found that where she said she had seen it there was evidence that something had been there. Watching Herrandown. And it was a good surveillance spot."

Anya looked at him with surprise. "*Watching* Herrandown? How far away?"

"Two kilometers."

She shook a finger at him and grinned. "Oh, Merral, so it's intelligent now. With long-distance vision. Some cockroach! We'd better evacuate the planet quick and blow the Gate behind us. That will give the human race forty years minimum to work on insecticides before it makes the next Assembly world. Assuming it doesn't go faster than light too."

Merral laughed.

Anya shook her head merrily. "Any other data? These samples . . ."

"The branches had been cut to clear the view. I got a sample." He reached into his bag, pulled out the carefully wrapped sample, and handed it over to Anya. "The right angle cut is mine."

She took the clear bag in her hands and held it up to the light. "You've looked at it?"

"Not really. It's not my area. What do you see?"

"Not much. But let me look at it under a lens." She got up and took it over to a desk where a large microscope stood. Merral got up and joined her as the cut piece of wood came into focus on the screen.

Anya peered at it. "Hmm. Need to do comparative studies. But it was a scissors action. From both sides at once; you can see the pressure points on either side. Could be a tool, I suppose. Tiny scoring or scratch marks. See there?" She pointed to part of the image. "Probably two finely serrated scissor blades. But big. That branch is five millimeters thick. Size of my little fingertip."

She paused, puzzlement in her tone. "Let me see the girl's sketch again."

Merral called it up and Anya enlarged the area around the creature's hands. "Odder still." The note of puzzlement was deeper and darker now. "I had assumed that the hands were badly drawn. Let me get a printout."

A few seconds later, they were peering over a sheet of paper.

"Look, Merral."

"So?" he asked, noting that there were fingers sketched on each hand.

"The thumb."

Merral looked again. "Odd," he said. "It's not really there. As a thumb that is. Just another long finger but oddly wider. Is it an accident of drawing?"

"I think not. See how they are symmetrical? Both hands are alike. It suggests a real memory. But interesting . . ."

"How so?"

Anya gave Merral a distant, abstracted smile and held up her right hand with the fingers aligned together. Then she swung her thumb in and out against the fingers in a snipping motion.

"I see," said Merral, in surprise. "You think that . . . ?"

She shook her head so that her fine red hair flicked over her shoulders. "It must be coincidence." She stared out of the window for a moment, then turned back to him. "No. I refuse to fuel silly ideas. I'll get one of our animal people to look at it."

She put it carefully down, but Merral noticed that her thoughtful look had not evaporated.

"What else?"

"Only this," Merral said as he handed over the second specimen.

She looked at him in feigned bemusement. "No, *no*, Tree Man. That's *hair*. Normally only mammals have it."

He smiled. "Oh gosh, Anya, I'd forgotten that. But joking apart, I don't recognize it, and I've seen all our wildlife. That's my job. What's odder still is that it was caught on an overhanging branch above the trail. About a meter seventy-five off the ground, so you can read that as a minimum height. It could have been an even larger creature if it had been stooping."

Anya rubbed her forehead. "So this little anthropoid arthropod suddenly sprouts hair and doubles in size. Oh dear."

Merral shrugged. "Oh, I know."

Anya sucked her lower lip in. "So, we have *two* new beasts. The human cockroach and a big hairy thing."

"That is a conclusion I've tried to avoid drawing."

Anya put the sample down carefully and leaned back in her chair.

"I can see why. Of course, it could be that there was a monkey that sat on the back of the cockroach. There, have you considered that possibility?" She grinned at him.

"No."

"Well, at least we can get the DNA out of this. Assuming it has any. I'll give you the results tomorrow."

She looked at the hair and then back at Merral. "Well, if it's real, then we have a problem, to put it mildly. Everything we do depends on us knowing exactly what fauna we have here. We always worry about new strains, some new mutant mouse with an insatiable appetite perhaps, but a totally new mammal—let alone a physically impossible mega-arthropod—is totally off the scale. And if it's a nightmare or a delusion we need to keep it in check. We don't want people fearing new creatures. You are certain that it isn't a joke or prank?"

Merral ran the question over again in his mind for the thousandth time. "Oh, Anya, I'm totally unsure. The whole thing says that she really saw something. But it just can't be. And yet . . ."

In this room, with Anya's blunt common sense, his fears seemed to almost vanish. Almost, but not quite. He hesitated.

Anya leaned slightly toward him. "There's more than what you've told me, isn't there?"

"Yes, but it's not really biological. More spiritual or psychological. Something's wrong, though."

"So you called in the sentinel?"

"Uh, no. A wrong guess there. He sort of wandered in. A coincidence. In fact, I'm not at all convinced that he can help. Maybe. What do you know of them?"

"Sentinels? A bit. They have contributed to the Reconstruction Debate. Genetic alteration or manipulation has always been an issue with them."

"I hadn't realized that."

"They are concerned about anything that erodes the human."

"Interesting. That fits with what little I know."

"Anyway, bring your friend tonight."

"I will. Just at this moment he may not be feeling like eating much. But by tonight things may be better."

Anya looked at the clock. "Well, my meeting starts soon. I'll drop these into the lab on the way over."

She picked up the specimens and, apparently catching his unspoken question, answered, "Should have the results tomorrow morning. The whole mystery solved. Anyway, see you tonight. Top floor,

Narreza Tower—say, seven-thirty? Cheers, Merral. Great to see you again." She patted his shoulder gently. "It really is."

Suddenly she was gone and Merral was left in the room. Feeling strangely elated, he echoed her statement in his mind with approval.

Yes, Anya, it is great to see you again.

◆

Half an hour later Merral was back at the Planning Institute. There he had a light lunch and met some old colleagues with whom he shared routine news. Finding he still had time to pass before Vero arrived, he sat down in his room, switched his diary through to the wallscreen, and logged in to the Library. The traditional image of the interior of a vast, high-vaulted building with an almost infinite number of shelves appeared on the wall.

What to look up? Merral asked himself. He had so many questions, but where did he start? Psychological disturbances, perhaps? He pushed his finger on the diary as if to walk to the behavioral science section, but as the file-laden aisles with the ghostly figures of the other users sped past him, he began to have second thoughts. There was so much there. Even within the psychology section. Where to begin? He lifted off his finger and found himself halted in front of a bay of a dozen shelves packed with virtual datapaks. The top of the bay was clearly labeled "Assembly Psychology: The Years A.D. 4000–5220: Section 32, The Schools of the Varantid Worlds. Bay 510 out of 870." With the renewed realization of exactly how much data there was available for him, Merral felt suddenly daunted. Access to all of humanity's knowledge didn't seem to help him.

Perhaps, he wondered, he should ask one of the virtual librarians about beetles? or sentinels? or Protocols and their abuses?

I don't know where to begin. He exited the Library and switched off the link. For the next few hours he walked around the extensive grounds of the center, enjoying Isterrane's warmer climate and trying—*and failing*—to put the pieces of the puzzle together.

In midafternoon, alerted by a faint noise high above him, he looked up to see the gull-like long-haul flier come in to land, the wings extending fluidly outward into landing mode as he watched. He paddled over to land, handed back the canoe he'd borrowed, and went back to the center to wait.

Half an hour later Vero arrived. He lowered his heavy bag to the ground and gave Merral a hug. "Good to see you again. And very good to be on solid land," he said with feeling.

"You'll get used to our atmosphere's fluctuations."

Vero shuddered. "Fluctuations! There are gaping holes in your atmosphere. I doubt I'll ever get used to it. Where can we talk?"

"My room?"

"No," Vero said firmly. "I need fresh air. Let's walk around the grounds."

"Fine, leave your bag in the office here. Incidentally, you are invited to a meal tonight. Let me tell you about it. . . ."

•—•—•

Once out under the trees, Vero turned to Merral, his brown eyes wide and solemn. "Look, I'm taking this seriously. I want you to tell me everything that has happened at Herrandown. Everything, every detail. In order. I'll just listen, although I may need to take a record later."

So for the next hour Merral found himself recounting first the request for help from his uncle and aunt, and then the details of his and Isabella's visit to Herrandown. Vero listened and nodded and occasionally asked for a clarification or a repetition. When Merral described the discovery that the site where the creature had been seen overlooked the settlement, Vero looked at him in an agitated way. "You're sure? Overlooking all of them?"

"Of course. It was what made me think there might be something in it."

"Yes. It raises a number of issues. . . ." His face acquired a worried look and for a moment he seemed to be on the point of saying something. "No . . . ," he said, as if addressing himself. "We will discuss that issue later. Continue."

A second point that excited a particular interest was the conversation that Merral had overheard between his uncle and his aunt. It was something that Merral had felt reluctant to mention; in the end he decided that he had to. Besides which, the business had so troubled him that he was glad to share it with someone. Vero frowned darkly when it was described to him and asked for it to be repeated. At the end of the repetition there was a silence in which Vero just shook his head sadly.

Merral broke the silence. "Vero, I almost can't believe I heard it. A noisy, aggressive dispute between husband and wife. Repeating it now, it sounds incredible. Can I be making it up?"

They had stopped walking and Vero rubbed his face wearily with his hand. "You have every right to be disturbed by it, my friend. No, you can't be making it up. For me, it is in its way all too familiar, I'm afraid. As a sentinel we are encouraged, no—required is better—to study personal relationships before the Great Intervention. You, of course, have the Scriptures too, so you know something of this, but we have to look at such things in more . . . depth." He looked embarrassed and after a brief hesitation, went on. "If *depth* is the word. No one now would read or watch such things out of choice but it does—we believe—no real harm under controlled conditions. So what you heard is familiar to me." He rubbed his long fingers through his tight-curled hair. "Familiar, but no less worrying."

Merral then told how his uncle had reacted when confronted with the question of modifying the re-created voices. He and Vero had stopped on a wooden bridge over a stream that fed into the lake and were leaning over it, staring down into the clear water and watching the trout dart about below them.

"So Barrand then replied, 'That we need to remember something. The Technology Protocols were made by men, not God. They're not Scripture.'"

Vero seemed to jolt upright as if an electric current had been applied to him. "He said *what?*"

"That 'the Technology Protocols were made by men not God. They're not Scripture.'"

135

Merral saw that Vero was giving him a look that seemed close to incredulity. There was a long silence and then he spoke very slowly and softly. "*That* was said by another. But a very long time ago...." He shook his head as if stunned. "Extraordinary! Very alarming! But go on."

They set off walking again and eventually, with the account of young Thomas's injunction to kill whatever he found, Merral ended his tale.

"Can you believe it, Vero?"

There was a long sigh from Vero. "Believe it? Yes, I think I can. But I can't explain it." Then he fell silent.

A six-legged transporter robot carrying flasks paused deferentially to let them walk past. "So now tell me, what do you think? And what am I supposed to think?"

Vero stopped and turned to Merral. "As to what you think, you must decide that. For myself, I think many things. Before you told me all this, I was going to say that I was worried that it was serious. And now I know that it is serious. But there are questions."

"Such as?"

"Everything. What's happening? Why? Why there? More importantly, what do I do?"

"Isn't that easy? Don't you just call your people on Ancient Earth?"

"Yes, I have considered that. I am close to doing it." His face radiated unease. "But there are problems. Supposing we have a full-threat evaluation team come in and I am wrong? We will have done damage to your uncle and his family, damage to Herrandown, and damage to the sentinels." He sighed. "The problem on The Vellant that I mentioned did us some harm. And the other cases. There is an old, old story about the boy who cried wolf. You have heard of it."

"Indeed."

They were standing near a fence overlooking the lake. Vero tapped the wood impatiently. "But you see, it's all so different from anything we might have expected."

"Which was?"

"We have been looking for a slow shift in opinions, for subtle changes across a world. So small that only statistics would show. Not for a sudden, isolated event like this. Least of all one with such bizarre manifestations. No, it's too strange. I need more evidence."

He drummed his hands on the fence and stared over the water before looking at Merral with sharp, inquiring eyes.

"When do you get the results back from Anya?"

"Tomorrow morning, she said. Why?"

"What I think is this . . . no, wait. Can you get me a large display of the area? A remote image—decent scale."

Merral gestured to his diary but Vero shook his head. "No, something bigger, projected would do. I need to visualize the area."

"No problem. There's a free office near my room. I can call up the most recent satellite image—that would be last week's—and overlay places on it."

"Good." Vero shivered slightly. "I feel it's getting cool outside here. Let's go inside. I think my blood got used to the tropics."

• ◆ •

Ten minutes later Vero was staring at a projected image that covered most of a wall. It was grainy but clear enough for the individual buildings of Herrandown to be seen. He moved around it, touching parts with a light pointer.

"Your uncle's house is here? Yes. That's the new building for animals in winter. The office. Good. As I'd pictured it." Vero stared at the image and then continued. "And the woods here—this sort of crescent around the side of the hamlet—they run down to the river. The Lannar."

Merral noted that his friend seemed to have rapidly grasped the area's geography.

"Now," Vero said, "show me where the sighting was. And where you found the hair sample."

Merral pointed out the two localities and Vero stared at them.

"There is less woodland up here than I thought," he commented.

"Other than the plantations, it's all confined to the rivers. Where it is quite dense, but otherwise the area is quite bare."

"We are working on it. But in summer it gets very dry with the westerly wind out of the interior. So the best-established woods all follow the rivers."

"Your trail runs north and, if it went along the river, that runs north–south too. And the dog was last seen going north too. North, north, and north."

Vero magnified the image until the woods around Herrandown were a tiny patch of green in a vastness of pale browns and grays, and the sharp arc of the southern mountain ramparts of the Lannar Crater appeared at the top of the image.

Vero turned to Merral. "I mean, do you know what happens in the north?"

"I thought I did. It's a pretty active area. The Lannar Crater averages a rating of eight on the Stellman Scale of geomorphologic activity for Made Worlds. That's out of a high of ten. Isterrane is around two; Herrandown, four something."

"It's unstable?"

"Let's say, stabilizing. The crater is only about a million or so years old. So it was still pretty fresh at the Seeding, with steep walls and a lot of impact fragments around. When the atmosphere switched to being oxygenating and water-rich in the Eighth Millennium there was an enormous lot of weathering and erosion."

"As everywhere on Farholme."

"Yes. But more so here. Pan out to show the whole crater."

Vero nudged the controls so that the entire circle of the Lannar Crater slid into the center and the brown-smudged blue of the sea edged onto the right of the image.

"At first," Merral said, "the crater just filled up with a great pile of debris and became a mass of lakes and swamps but, oh, about two thousand years ago, the crater walls began to be breached by river erosion. The Lannar is the southern system, but you can see the important Nannalt river system going out east into the Mazurbine Ocean."

"The big brown smudge here?" said Vero, gesturing to a protrusion into the sea.

"Yes. The Nannalt Delta. Anyway, so it's still adjusting to massive changes in its drainage. Some of the swamps are drying up; there's a lot of river erosion. I've seen the images, Vero; some areas are almost unrecognizable within a year."

Vero stared at the map again. "That helps me. But it has been visited?"

"Yes. The odd botanical, geologic, and zoological trips. I've flown over. But it's wild country. We tend to leave it alone and let the satellites keep an eye on it for us. There are only thirty million people on Farholme and there's a lot of areas with more promise."

"So, you have no plans for it?"

"No. Not unless winters warm up a lot. Along the higher parts of the Northern Rim glaciers are growing. You can see them on the image. They've done remote seeding of trees and plants, but it's an area we have left to itself, particularly while it settles down."

"So, it isn't visited regularly?"

"No. This isn't like Ancient Earth, Vero. We have no shortage of wildernesses or work elsewhere. There is no archaeology, no undiscovered animals or plants."

Vero gave him an odd smile. "That's what you used to say."

"True. But what are you thinking?"

Vero put the pointer down and began to pace backward and forward. "I am building a delicate chain of logic. Too delicate, but I must go on. Let us suppose that there is something here, something—what shall we say?—exotic. Yes, that's the word. Then it must hide, breed somewhere. The best guess would be to the north. To the south, east, and west are bare open wastes. But the river valley offers cover along its length well into the crater. Do you follow my train of thought?"

"I do not dissent from it. I was thinking vaguely along those lines but was going to wait for Anya's results."

Vero sat down at the table and stared at the image. "Merral, my suggestion is this: Tomorrow, if Anya comes up with anything strange . . . indeed, anything unaccountable at all . . . then the trail you picked up must be pursued immediately."

"It will be cold. Nearly a week old. But I see that you think it can only go one way."

"Correct. Our creature, assuming we have one—or even two—is furtive and loves cover. It has been seen and knows it. I do not think it will venture out into the open. It will have taken the river. It probably came south down it and retreated back up it." He adjusted the image so that it showed the entire length of the river from Herrandown to the Southern Rim Ranges.

"Well, true enough. Brigila's Wastes is no home for such creatures," Merral answered as he tried to assess Vero's line of thinking. For all the unfamiliarity of the concepts, he found it made a sort of sense.

"I think, Vero, that I agree with you. If the results are odd then I will get permission and take off up the river for a few days."

"Can it be done quietly?"

"Yes, I can travel light on foot. If necessary, I can get food dropped to me. I could probably get most of the way up to the Ranges without needing that. But it's rough going, Vero. Remember our landscape is still in an unfinished state."

He gestured to the image, wondering if the yellow and red gashes of landslides and mudflows were as visible to his friend as they were to him.

Suddenly Vero spoke quietly. "And if you do, I will come too."

Merral laughed. "You? Please, Vero. There are no guest rooms there. It's well, tough country. We would be walking, perhaps with a pack animal. You are . . ." He hesitated. "Well, you show no evidence of being able to travel in this country."

Vero stood up. "I may surprise you. I have done my share of walking and camping on Ancient Earth. We have our jungles and mountains too."

On impulse, Merral squeezed Vero's upper arm. To his surprise, he felt muscle.

"Well. . . ." He paused. "I must say, Vero, that company would be acceptable. Strange. . . ."

Vero was looking at him with curiosity. "Why strange?"

"Because I have spent a lot of time in the last five years on my own in woods such as these. I have camped in solitude in all seasons. I have spent as much as a week without talking to a single person. I have never felt the slightest unease or fear. I watch out for bears and I pass by wolf packs. But that is caution, not fear. Yet since Nativity, on the last few trips, I have felt—" Merral hesitated, trying to find the words. "No, I can't describe it, Vero. Only that I have been glad to be back home. Behind walls and doors."

Vero looked at the image again and then turned it off. Then he spoke aloud in a quiet but penetrating voice. "Another tiny thread of evidence. A forester feels uneasy in forests. All tiny threads, but wound together they are forming a solid rope. But attached to what?"

"I have no idea."

"Me neither." Vero handed the diary back to Merral. He rubbed his forehead. "Sorry, I'm tired; it was a twelve-hour flight. I may get some sleep. And definitely a shower before this meal tonight. Brenito will put me up. I'd better be off now."

Merral arranged for a lift for Vero, and then the two of them went to the doorway.

Vero opened the door and then stopped, his long fingers tapping on the glass. "You know . . . ," he said, then paused as if in doubt. "No, I ought to say it. There is one more thing. I am reluctant to mention it, but I am worried about the possibility of danger."

"To who?"

"To your uncle and his family. You see, my dear Forester, you must become a sentinel with me, at least in thought. You and I must ask questions that no one has asked for thousands of years. Try this. What purpose had this creature—assuming there was indeed one— in watching Herrandown?"

Merral felt slightly cold, as if a draught of air had come through the door. "I'm sorry, I hadn't thought that through. I had assumed just curiosity. As when we watch deer or birds. But you mean that it could be with evil intent? with malice?"

The words *evil* and *malice* had a strange, archaic flavor to them, as if they had just been dug up out of the ground.

Vero gave him no answer except a little shrug of his shoulders.

But was it necessarily so, Merral considered, that these terms were fit only for a museum? Maybe the sentinels had a point; perhaps evil was only sleeping. It was not a thought that he cared for. Merral hesitated. "Surely not, Vero? All our history says not. Frontier communities are at peril from floods, bush fires, earthquakes. And such like. But not creatures in bushes. Real or imagined. Over ten thousand years of history and sixteen hundred worlds say the same thing. These things do not happen. That is the rule."

"Is it?" asked Vero softly, with a raised eyebrow.

"Yes. It is statistically improbable that such a rule will come to an end here in Herrandown and in our time. All our history says they are safe."

"I know, Merral, I know. You see, I can use your argument too. There have been—I was working it out last night—nearly three-quarters of a million sentinels since we were founded. All were looking for what I look for. Logic and statistics say to me that I should not be the one to find what they looked for and failed."

Vero paused and turned his brown eyes on Merral. "History does abide by rules, but those rules are set by the Everlasting One. And he can change them if he chooses. And he does not have to alert us first. The revivals of the Great Intervention happened quite unexpectedly, in Earth's darkest hours. The Holy Spirit gave no warning that he was starting a work unparalleled since Pentecost."

"I suppose not. . . ."

"Besides, consider logic itself. If there is a first time for everything, then logically the first time must happen to someone."

"But to my uncle and his family?"

Vero looked at him thoughtfully. "Assuredly to someone's uncle and family."

CHAPTER 9

For many reasons, the meal that evening was an event that firmly embedded itself in Merral's mind. When he remembered it later—as he often did—it always seemed to him that it marked the end of something. When he tried to define exactly what it was that it ended, the answer was always "the Peace."

Anya's flat was small and low roofed, with numerous wall hangings in warm shades of brown and green which made it seem even smaller. Merral felt that the apartment had been hastily tidied and was reminded that Anya had always put neatness well down her list of priorities. Despite the fact that Vero and Merral were, to a greater or lesser extent, strangers who had become last-minute guests, there seemed no sense of awkwardness at their presence. Merral, at least, soon felt at home, and he sensed that Vero had relaxed. Yet somehow, despite being welcomed, Merral found he was more analytical than usual and, at intervals, he caught himself looking round the candlelit circular table at the others and seeing them, as it were, for the first time.

Perena Lewitz sat to Merral's right. Although Merral had met her two years before, he never really got to know her, and he found it fascinating to compare her with her younger sister. In many respects he felt that she was a muted version of Anya. Physically the hair (which, as a concession to work in weightlessness, she wore short) was auburn rather than red, the eyes were a grayer shade of blue, and the face was less freckled and less immediately pretty.

The pattern persisted in the character, in that while Anya was the sort of person everyone noticed immediately, Perena's quieter, more introspective personality meant that it took time for her existence to become apparent. She seemed content to be an observer rather than a participant. It struck Merral as typical that when Perena was quietly persuaded into admitting that she was close to being the Farholme Space Affairs champion in old-time chess, Anya should loudly state that the game bored her to distraction and that anyway, she always lost within minutes. Along with Vero, Perena seemed to be one who was most happy to be dragged along by the flow of the conversation rather than to seek to mold it.

Round to the right of her was Theodore, a big, barrel-chested, and deep-voiced man with short blond hair and a pale moustache. He was plainly in high spirits and was given to frequently nodding his head to signify agreement and shaking it vigorously to denote dissent. On one or two occasions he clapped Vero on the back to make a point, once catching him unawares so that he nearly choked on his drink. He and Anya could easily have dominated the entire conversation, and Merral felt that both of them were deliberately holding back to encourage the others.

Beyond Theodore was Vero. To Merral he seemed very much subdued, and for much of the time he sat slightly back from the table as if physically distancing himself from the conversation. Merral felt that he was finding it hard to resist the temptation to withdraw into himself and slip into the shadows. Whether the cause was tiredness, the effects of his flight, or his worries, Merral could not be sure. But he saw no evidence that Vero was not fully attentive to what was going on. Although his mobile fingers would often reach out and toy gently with some item of cutlery, his deep brown eyes seemed to track the conversation carefully around the table as if he was scared of missing something. *I wonder whether this is his temperament or his sentinel training? And anyway, after so many generations, could the two be distinguished?*

Between Vero and Merral sat Anya, who, despite her sister's role as cook, was very much the hostess. Whenever the conversation flagged, she drove it on with an anecdote, joke, or provocative statement. Every so often she shook her long hair and the highlights in it glinted in the light of the candles. Merral found himself enjoying watching her face for the sheer animation and joy of life in it. Again, he felt that there was something he found very attractive about her. Once, the thought came to him suddenly that, under other circumstances, there might have been the possibility of something developing between them. The idea so disturbed him that he rejected it immediately and found himself in such a momentary state of consternation that he had to ask Theodore to repeat a question.

The fact that three of the five around the table were relatively quiet did not stop the conversation from moving rapidly and freely. There seemed to be no agenda, no concerns, no preoccupations.

Midway through the evening, Merral suddenly found himself thinking about how he appeared. *I have reviewed my friends, but how do they see me? How do I appear to them? Strange,* he decided. *I've never worried about how I seem to others before.* It was almost as though he longed for a mirror in which to see himself. Was he becoming self-conscious? These odd thoughts vaguely troubled him. He felt he was worse than some adolescent. He resolved that when the Herrandown problem was resolved he would take some leave. A week just walking the beaches, cliffs, and woods of Cape Menerelm might help clear out these funny ideas. His reverie was interrupted by Anya asking Vero if he found the food satisfactory.

Vero delicately wiped his mouth before answering and smiled. "The food is excellent, Anya, and a credit to Perena's cooking skills, but I am, I fear, still recovering from having lost and gained several hundred meters of altitude in under a second this morning. Repeatedly."

"All our fault, Vero," rumbled Theodore. "The seas are too shallow. We still can't get the current systems stable. Heat transport is unbalanced. That's what gives you all that turbulence."

Anya winked at Merral. "For the benefit of our new guests, Theodore is the expert on the thermal properties of the deeper sea basins. He wants to use a Mass Blaster to deepen them all another kilometer."

Theodore gave a wide grin. "Only some. It's not really feasible now. But it would have helped when they were knocking Farholme into shape."

Merral nodded. "I've heard that. But it was the early days in making worlds then, Theo. They were still struggling with how to slow rotation speeds so we didn't have to live around a sixteen-hour day. Contouring ocean depths was an imprecise science. We know better now."

Perena looked across at Vero. "Well, I sympathize," she said, her quieter voice somehow cutting across the table in a way that Theo's louder tones did not. "I've seen those equatorial storms bubbling up and I've often given thanks that I'm in vacuum. But space is different. . . ."

She paused, rotating the stem of her glass between her delicate fingers. The company looked at her and she continued, but in a tone of voice that almost sounded as if she was talking to herself. "In fact there are times when you would like some turbulence. It's the sense of void that is striking about space. Of being supported by nothing. Absolutely nothing."

Anya gave her sister a bemused look. "Oh, for a Near-Space Captain you feel a lot. You are too much the poet."

Perena shrugged and smiled as if at a private thought. Then in an even quieter voice she said, "But vacuum kills quicker than either air or water."

There was a brief, stiff silence, and then Anya, in a voice that seemed a fraction too strident, asked, "So Vero, how do you like our world?"

Vero thought for a moment. "For myself, I think I have been surprised how familiar things are. But then, of course, that is the very goal of making worlds. We are—as we have found out—a species that is adapted for one world. To live elsewhere on a lasting basis we must re-create our homeworld as best we can. The standard for every Made World is Ancient Earth. The Assembly has shunned novelty; we cannot take too much strangeness."

"So, what do you miss?" Anya asked.

"I miss the history of Ancient Earth and the richness of its species, but there are many compensations. Above all, I enjoy the freshness, the excitement—the challenge—of Farholme. This is, indeed, a new world."

With nods of agreement the meal continued.

After everybody had finished eating, Perena suggested they all go on the roof. "It is the first clear night we have had for weeks. I need to see the stars."

"You'd think," Anya commented, her blue eyes glinting conspiratorially at Merral, "that she saw enough of them at work."

They clattered up a narrow spiral staircase, lifted a hatch, and clambered onto a flat roof bounded by a metal railing. The sky was clear and the stars shone as brilliant chill points of light. Theodore and Anya walked off together down to the end of the roof and stood looking over the lights of the town.

Perena, looking up, spoke quietly to the slight figure standing beside her. "So, Sentinel Vero, what do you think of our stars?"

"I like them better here than from Aftarena."

"Really? It's not that different in latitude."

"Ah, Perena," he replied, and there was a wistful note in his voice, "from here I can see the Gate."

Merral watched his hand stretch out across the stars and point to the golden hexagon of light high above them.

"Ah yes. I had forgotten that." Perena's voice was sympathetic. "And that means a lot to you?"

"Yes . . . it does mean a lot to me. I have missed it these last three months. Through *there* is home, family, friends. And my father is rather elderly and not in good health."

"I understand. And you would wish to be going through it soon?"

"I suppose so, but duty declares that I should stay here."

"Yes, duty," Perena sighed. "This side of heaven, duty and desire are often in tension. But in my experience they mostly overlap."

"Mostly," he said. "For which we give thanks. It was not always thus."

Merral heard rather than saw Perena reach out and briefly touch Vero's shoulder. He marveled at the paradox of humanity. *We have the* strength to sling ourselves between stars and yet at the same time the weakness that, when we do, we end up lamenting our absent loved ones. And yet it is perhaps appropriate to remember the weakness, he thought, lest we think we are more than we are.

Perena spoke again quietly. "There is a ship coming through the Gate in a few minutes. The inter-system liner *Heinrich Schütz*, inbound from Bannermene with Farholme being—inevitably—the last port of call. Heading back inward in six days' time if I remember rightly."

She walked over to a low cabinet, opened it, brought out a fieldscope, and swung the lenses up to her eyes.

"Yes, the status lights are on the slow red flash."

Merral strained his eyes hard at the six golden lights of the beacon satellites.

A minute passed and they stared at the same spot. Merral remembered his own surprise when he had first visited the other hemisphere of Farholme and found the Gate, with its geostationary orbit forty thousand kilometers over the equator due south of Isterrane, absent. *We grow up with the Gate and its beacons,* he reminded himself. *It is the first thing in the night sky they show us as children. After all, Sol and Terra are not easy to find. "That's the Gate, Son," they say. "Through that your parents, grandparents, or whoever came from other planets and, ultimately, Ancient Earth. Through that, not just people but all our messages go. That's our umbilical cord." And as you grew up you realized just how important the Gates were.*

Merral still remembered the shock of the surprise he had had as a ten-year-old when he had worked out that if, instead of the two-day Gate trip they had taken eighty years earlier, his great-grandparents D'Avanos had set off from Menedon on the fastest ship available, they would still have been en route to Farholme. As someone had said, after the cross—and it was a long way after—the hexagon was the geometric symbol of the Assembly.

Perena's voice broke into his thoughts. "Here we go. Rapid flashing."

He could hear the latent excitement in her low voice. Merral stared up at the hexagon waiting for the flash as the awesome energies involved in taking the shortcut through Below-Space were balanced. As he watched, an abrupt wave of iridescent deep violet blue rippled out from the core of the Gate, briefly masking the fringing beacon lights, and then faded away.

Perena gave a little grunt of pleasure and put the scope down. She turned to Merral, the starlight reflected in her eyes. "Sorry, I get a thrill from that."

"You love space, Perena?" Merral asked.

She sighed happily. "Yes, I do. It's not for what it is itself. Space is nothing, truly nothing. But I see it as the nothing that holds the Assembly together. If that statement means anything." She paused and looked heavenward. "And I love the whole thing, the Assembly, the Gates, the stations, the whole great system of things. Not forgetting, especially, this tiny, insignificant, half-finished little planet. And, most of all the One who made it and sustains it."

Then she turned her face back to Merral and he caught in the half-light an amused grin, almost as if her declaration had embarrassed her.

There was a gentle tap on Merral's arm. He turned to find Vero hugging himself for warmth.

"I'm sorry. I find this a bit cold. I'm going to go down to check the possibility of us getting on the first flight to Ynysmant early tomorrow. Would you be able to do that?"

"Yes, I suppose so. But I thought we wanted to talk to Anya?"

"She can reach us easily enough. There is nothing to detain us here." He dropped his voice. "Sorry, Merral, but I've been thinking over all you said again. I'm becoming frustrated by these fragments of evidence. I think we need to take some action. Everything points to Herrandown and the area to the north of it. My mind is becoming fixed on this Lannar River. Anyway, if we leave it too late the trail could be too cold."

Merral thought quickly. "Yes. I take your point. Let's see if we can do it. You check if there is a flight."

Anya and Theodore seemed also to find it cold and followed Vero down, leaving Perena and Merral alone on the roof. They stood there leaning on the rail for some time, engaged in desultory conversation as Perena pointed out the trail of tiny glinting points that marked the processed cometary ice inbound from Far Station to be stored as fuel for the ships at the Gate and Near Stations.

A faint orange flash at the edge of his vision caught Merral's attention.

"Meteor! Small one to the south. Oh, but it's gone."

"Ah, it burned up before I could see it."

Seeing the meteor jogged Merral's memory. "Perena, three nights before Nativity I was up at Herrandown and there was a very big meteor that came overhead. Going north, with a noise like thunder. Some ground vibration. It was almost as bright as day for a second and it quite shook the ground. Scared the animals."

"That *is* big." She sounded intrigued.

"I was wondering—well, we all were—why the Guardian satellites didn't eliminate it before it came in. They can't have just assumed that the north was uninhabited, can they?"

He saw her shake her head. "No. They deal with such things well beyond Farholme. Typical Assembly policy to play it safe; it allows a second or even third chance to get them. It's spectacular if you are close enough to see it happen. I saw it once. I was near the north polar one. It warned us and we had—oh—fifteen minutes to get clear. There was no real risk. But it was a pretty impressive sight. It instantly vaporized about a cubic kilometer of nickel iron asteroid."

"I don't understand why they didn't get this big one. But then I don't really understand the mechanics of it all."

"Well, they have a hierarchy. Within a hundred thousand kilometers of Farholme they watch everything larger than a small boulder; beyond that they track everything house-sized or larger as far out as Fenniran or as Alahir's corona. Larger blocks are tracked to the system's edge or, if they are comets, well beyond. Anything coming in fast on a Farholme or Farholme Gate impact trajectory they blast. Pulsed protons, UV laser cannon, Mass Blaster. They are actually more worried about the Gate in some ways. With an open Gate you could patch up or evacuate a damaged world. Without a Gate . . . " She shrugged.

"Okay. But—and I've never thought of this before—suppose it's a ship or incoming probe?"

"Oh, these things are smart, Merral," she replied with a broad smile, and for a moment he was reminded of her sister. "They know where every ship of ours is. They need to. In fact for slower ships or static structures, like a Weather Sat, they may protect them if they detect a meteor is inbound. So the only risk is to an unscheduled ship or a probe coming in fast on a particular trajectory. That's unlikely. But if it were to happen the Guardian would always check on the ship identity codes."

"So have you any idea why it let this one through?"

"No. But they always work. There would have been a reason. I've flown the flights that service them. There are endless backup systems. Look, give me the details and I'll run it through the Guardian files and we'll see what happened."

"Twenty-second December, around five-thirty eastern Menaya time. Above Herrandown going north."

Perena noted the details in her diary, and as she put it away, she shivered. "I'm getting cold too. It's all right for you; you work outdoors. Let's go down."

• ◆ •

As they returned to Anya's apartment, Vero broke off a conversation with the others and came over to Merral. "There is a freight flight tomorrow at 6:20 A.M. with space for two. You can manage it?"

"Yes, but there goes my relaxing morning. But certainly. I'll call my parents to make sure that they'll be expecting us tomorrow night."

"Do tell them that it will be for a single night. And give them my love."

The news of their early flight seemed to precipitate the end of the evening. Amid thanks to Perena and Anya, the five split up.

As Merral made to leave, Anya grabbed his hand lightly. "And take care up north. Cockroach men or not, it's tough country. We can't afford to lose you."

He squeezed her hand. "I'll be back. God willing. Whatever's out there."

Then they parted.

On the way back to his room, Merral thought about Anya in a mood that oscillated between pleasure and concerned perplexity. It was one more thing, he said to himself, which had to be sorted out soon.

•—•—•

The flight next morning was uneventful. Mist shrouded much of Isterrane on takeoff and low cloud hid Ynysmant on landing. Merral went with Vero straight to the Planning Institute, and after dropping their bags in his office, they both went over to see Henri, who was engaged in drawing a sequence of graphs on his desk. He turned off the monitor as they came in and gave both of them a warm welcome, his deep-set eyes asking unspoken questions about Vero. After introductions and pleasantries, Merral carefully explained what he wanted.

Henri sat back in his chair and looked from one to the other in a thoughtful manner.

"A week's trip, fine. But a rotorcraft tomorrow? There's not much time to arrange it. . . ." He ran his hands through his thinning hair. "*Ach*, we will have to reschedule other things. But . . . if you really think this is needed?" There was a questioning note in his voice.

"I do." Merral found himself surprised at both the abruptness of his answer and the certainty it carried.

There was silence for a moment and then Henri shrugged and smiled. "Fine, man. I'll arrange it." He stared at a wall map a moment and then looked back at Merral. "In fact, in some ways, I'll be glad of it. The Quarry Logistics Team is up there now and I've already had one comment about Barrand."

A stab of concern pierced Merral. "Is he—are they—all right?"

"Well, yes. But he's put a bolt on the house door."

There was a sharp intake of breath from Vero and Merral turned to him. "A what?"

The dark face was clouded, and Vero spoke in a low, expressionless voice. "A *bolt*. A catch openable from one side only. Like you'd use—I assume you do here—to stop children from getting into machinery. You put it high against a door."

"I see," Merral said, trying to imagine the mental state that would need something like that. He turned back to his director. "You mean, Henri, that he bolts himself—his family—in?"

"At night, I gather. And he walks around with a big stick, too. That's about it."

There was a long silence that eventually Henri broke with hesitant words. "I'm sorry . . . I'm on the point of sending the psychologist up. I was waiting to hear from you. Your uncle is, I suppose, scared." He looked inquiringly at Vero. "Sentinel, do you know why?"

Vero pursed his lips and shook his head slowly. "Everybody thinks I do, but I'm afraid it's not the case. I'm as much in the dark as anybody else. But I *am* determined to find out."

"Good, good." Henri's face expressed a continuing unease. "I don't like it at all. I'll let you get everything ready. Help yourself to gear. I'll arrange the craft for dawn."

◆

After leaving Henri, Vero returned with Merral to his office where they called up maps, photographs, and computer reconstructions of the Lannar River system.

Vero gazed intently at the detailed imagery. "How accurate is this?"

"The resolution is two meters. It's accurate but misleading. I find that it's the fine grain on a landscape that takes time. These images never show things like brambles, thorns, and mud. But you get the overall trends."

"Your surveying and monitoring machines—do they ever get this far north?"

"Infrequently. It's a long way. Sometimes it may get looked at as part of some special project; for instance, we had a region-wide beaver survey last year and the Lannar was covered then. But not much else is done. A drone probably cruises over once a month looking for oddities. As Herrandown develops we will survey it more."

"So, it's little known." Vero looked at the map. "How far would we get in four days?"

"Day one would be around thirty kilometers in the narrow, densely wooded meanders from Herrandown. Day two would be, say, another thirty kilometers in the more open section where the river braids itself. All being well, that would bring you to the foot of Carson's Sill. Now, that bit's tricky."

Vero gestured at the image. "I can see that."

"Yes, that leads up to the Daggart Plateau, which lies in front of the Rim Ranges. That's a climb of at least eight hundred meters— probably nearer a thousand—up and over a lot of steep ledges. Tiring. But then you are on the plateau at the top. With that long lake, the Daggart Lake." He paused. "So that's an easier walk along that. Say we do twenty kilometers that day. Day four, what? Another thirty kilometers along the plateau to the edge of the Lannar Rim Ranges proper. Would I be right in thinking that you would not wish to go farther?"

"Yes," Vero answered as he peered at the image again. "It gets very steep then. Four days will be enough." He flexed his fingers. "Yes, my guess is that we will be ready for pickup by then. One way or another."

They looked at each other. *Funny,* Merral thought, *I can't easily visualize what sort of answer we might find to this set of problems. I wonder whether he can.*

Vero tapped his diary. "I'm puzzled that we've not heard from Anya. It's nearly lunchtime."

"Let me call her."

When she came on screen, Anya looked harassed. "Oh, sorry, you guys. You did well to get out of town and not to wait. The results are a bit of a mess. I can't decide what's going on. I'm going to get a second opinion. And our bug scholar has only just come in out of town."

"Any hints?"

Anya flashed Merral a smile, but he felt it was the forced expression of someone under pressure.

"Insufficient data, Tree Man. I'll call you as soon as I have anything."

◆—◆—◆

Merral and Vero ate lunch outside, sitting under a large apple tree and looking across the lake to where Ynysmant rose up out of the water, its roofs gleaming in the sun. They were both silent, as if the burden of the expedition north had crushed the desire for conversation.

They were crossing back through the compound after lunch when a rough cry rang out. "If you please! Mister Merral."

Merral turned to see a familiar, bent-backed figure lurching across the compound toward him.

"Jorgio!"

Merral hugged him. As he did, he caught again the smell of earth and animal and he felt sorry that, since their last meeting just before Nativity, he had not made the time to go up to Wilamall's Farm. "Let me introduce you," he said. "Jorgio Aneld Serter—gardener, stable hand, and old friend—this is—"

"Verofaza Laertes Enand, sentinel. But—more commonly—Vero. Delighted to meet you."

The two of them shook hands and looked at each other. As they did, Merral saw a strange expression passing across Jorgio's face: a look that was almost one of recognition.

"If you please, Mr. Vero; you are from Ancient Earth?" Jorgio asked.

"News about me must have been spreading," Vero replied with a quiet laugh. "Or is it my accent?"

A smile appeared on the leathery face. "I was told to expect you."

It was Vero's turn to look puzzled now.

Jorgio turned to Merral. "I was looking for you. I have a message for you and Mister Sentinel here. I assume he's come to sort out what's wrong."

Vero looked startled. "Excuse me, Jorgio—before you give us this message—what *is* wrong? I gather the weather hasn't been good."

Jorgio stared at him, his thick lips protruding. "Tut tut! No. Not *just* the weather. Much more than that. There've been all sorts of things wrong. Here and there. As you know."

"*I* do?" Vero stared back at him with an air of intense interest. "Would you like to tell me what you think is wrong? But please, let us sit down."

"What's wrong?" Jorgio said with a pout as they walked over to the seats at the edge of the compound and sat down. "Why, if you please, all manner of things are wrong. Birds, insects, animals. Even the woods are wrong, now. You see, I dream, Mister Vero. I dream in odd ways."

"I see," Vero said gently. "And in your dreams, what do you see?" He leaned forward as if straining to catch every nuance in Jorgio's words.

Jorgio rubbed a hand over his smooth bald head before speaking. "Since Nativity, in my dreams, I have seen shadows under the woods. *Cold* shadows. Things you don't want to see. Eyes, claws, teeth. Things that creep and slide." He seemed to shudder and fell silent.

Vero threw a glance at Merral, and in it Merral recognized a mixture of fascination, fear, and wonder.

"Jorgio, do you know what—*who*—is behind it?" Vero asked delicately.

Jorgio stared ahead. "Evil is back," he said bluntly.

"Can we be sure?" Vero whispered.

But instead of answering, Jorgio turned his head toward Merral. "You know how the Lord speaks to me? Special ways. Mostly, how I can help people. Anyway, last night he came to me as I was sleeping. 'Jorgio Aneld Serter,' he says, 'I want to show you something.'"

Jorgio cleared his throat. "'Amen, Your Majesty,' I says, 'lead on.' Next thing is that I am in this great big room—enormous, it is—with these dark wood walls. And standing on the floor are all these candles. Set on stands. Must have been over a thousand of them and they are all lit."

Jorgio wiped his face with the back of a hand. "Then he says to me, 'Jorgio, whose is the Assembly?'

"'Yours, sir,' I says. 'It is your work.'

"Then he says, 'Do I have a right to test my work?'

"'Of course,' I answers. Because he does—he is the Lord.

"'And test it I will,' is what he says. Then suddenly a door opens and a wind blows and candles start flickering and I think they are going out."

Out of the corner of his eye Merral saw Vero staring with wide eyes at Jorgio. "Extraordinary," he murmured. "Quite extraordinary."

Jorgio spoke again. "Anyway the Lord speaks again. 'Let me tell you what will happen,' he says. Then suddenly, before I could see whether the candles would blow out, the picture changes. And it's as if I am a bird—like one of them gray kites we get round here—flying around and looking down at a farm. It's beautiful. All on its own. Surrounded by trees and fields of wheat and the sun is shining on it. Then I see that there is a storm brewing. Big, thick, black clouds that go up in the sky forever. But it's not a good storm, it's a bad storm; it hates. The wind gets up; the clouds move toward the farm; the sun goes in. The trees start shaking and the rain starts and there's thunder and lightning. And the Lord says to me, 'Will it stand?' And then the clouds sweep across it and I can't see it any more.

"'Your Majesty,' I says, 'who do I tell?'

"'Tell Merral D'Avanos and his friend from Ancient Earth,' he says.

"'What do I tell them?'

"'Tell them what you saw. Tell them to watch, stand firm, and to hope.' And then, suddenly, I'm back in my room."

For a moment there was a still silence. Then Vero shook his head.

"An amazing account. The candles . . . you think they were the Assembly?"

Jorgio stuck out his lip and his brown eyes tightened. "I'd say so."

"And the farm?"

"I reckon it's us. *Farholme*."

"And a storm approaches. Any ideas about that?"

"No."

Vero turned sharply to Merral. "My friend, what do you think?"

"Me?" Merral heard what was almost a note of protest in his voice. "I'm not capable of analyzing this just yet. I need to think."

"The wisest thing. But remarkable. Thank you, Jorgio. I—we—want to think very carefully about what you have said. Merral and I are going north tomorrow. To look for what is the problem. Do you have any advice?"

Jorgio's soft brown eyes looked uneasily at Merral and then turned to Vero. "No. Only that I feel that things have changed round here." Then he looked up at the sun. "I must be on my way. Going back up to the farm now. I will pray for you. But remember that things have changed."

Then he rose to his feet and, with an odd and awkward bow, made his way over toward the vehicle depot. "Extraordinary," Vero said, staring after Jorgio. "Quite extraordinary. Has he done this before?"

"Once . . . last Nativity. He said that I had been at risk up north and that he had prayed for me. I didn't know what to make of it."

Vero stared after the departing Jorgio and shook his head. "A very striking man. How did he get to be like he is?"

"The story I heard is that when he was a child there was some landslide. Must be fifty or sixty years ago now. Down by the coast. His parents were killed; he was badly injured. They did the best for him. But he was always different. He has always been—in his rather different way—a godly man."

Vero nodded agreement. "You know how we sentinels are supposed to be able to sense things? I felt when I faced him that he was a man who knew more than I have ever learned. I had a sense that—

somehow—what sentinel training tries to produce over years is what he already has."

"You think he is naturally gifted with some insight?"

"*Supernaturally* would be better. It is a gift of the Most High. We must reflect on his words as we go north. I do not trust myself to speak of what they may mean. The vision of the candles and the farm is chilling." He paused and then in a half whisper, as if to himself, muttered, "And evil is back." He frowned.

"Vero," Merral asked slowly, "how could evil come back? Would that mean the end?"

Vero looked at him. "Maybe. But maybe not. Jorgio talked of a testing, which is not necessarily the ending. But evil? You are aware that no one, not even the wisest person, knows how evil works. We never have. Not even in the twentieth and early twenty-first centuries when evil was so rampant. We all know that following those events that we abbreviate to the 'Great Intervention' evil became less pressing on us. In a well-worn phrase we 'felt a partial reprieve' from the effects of the Fall."

"But could that be revoked?"

"Merral, it's the Lord's Assembly, not ours. I never heard of any guarantee that this protection from evil was eternal. It has been assumed to be his gift to his people. And, as such, I suppose he has a right to withdraw it."

After a few moments of silence, Merral felt it was time that they returned to their preparations and went over to the stores. A silent Vero, deep in thought, followed him.

Merral already had much of the equipment he needed for himself, but finding suitable boots and a backpack for Vero was less easy. Merral found reassurance in the competent and familiar way in which his friend handled outdoor gear and the sensible suggestions he made about what to take.

Sometimes, however, what he said made Merral think. At one point Vero, his head deep in a supplies cupboard, asked in a low, thoughtful tone, "Merral, if you had to defend yourself from a hostile animal—say a deranged bear—what would you do?"

"It's a rare threat. We coexist pretty well. But sometimes, if you meet one of the big tawny bears and get between them and their cubs, they get ugly and try and take a swipe. And if you have to bring one in for any reason, say for a veterinary or biology study, we use neuro-potent tranquilizer guns. There's one up there."

Vero pulled out the box and read the instructions. Then he looked up at Merral. "I think we should take it and a few cartridges. Put the dosage on maximum."

"Yes . . . I suppose that makes sense."

In another cupboard Vero found a lightweight, twin-eyepiece fieldscope with a variable magnification and low-light capability. "Ah, this looks useful. What do you use it for? Normally."

"Counting deer herds. Wolf packs at night—that sort of thing. It's useful but it weighs half a kilo or so. You seriously want to take it?"

"Yes," Vero answered firmly. "It may help us to keep a distance."

Merral found himself shrugging agreement.

A few minutes later, as Merral was checking a suitable tent, Vero came over to him carrying a short red tube. "I see you have some of these excellent bush knives."

"Careful!" Merral raised a hand in caution. "That blade is sharp. It's molecularly tuned to cut through wood. They are useful for clearing ground."

Vero pointed it away from himself and cautiously slid a catch. Slowly but smoothly, a dull gray blade slid out in three nested segments extending to an arm's length, before it locked open with a soft, precise click.

"I have seen them used in Aftarena. I think we should take two." Vero's tone suggested that it was not a negotiable point.

"Two? There isn't that much bush but, well, you may be right. They weigh little. But be careful in their use. They can take a hand off and without a surgeon nearby—that is likely to be permanent."

Vero slid the catch again and the blade slid softly back into its handle. His brown eyes looked impassively across at Merral. "I know," he said quietly, "but we may need them."

"What for?"

Vero hesitated, seeming to weigh his words before continuing, "Merral, I do not know what we face. I was concerned before today. But after talking with Jorgio I am even more concerned. There is an expression that I am reluctant to use. It has been thankfully obsolete for most of our history. . . ." He stared at the knife for a moment. "But yes, I must—there is no other. Merral, out there, this time, you— we—may be among enemies."

CHAPTER 10

When Merral and Vero had agreed on a pile of equipment and supplies that they felt was the maximum that they could carry over rough terrain for four days, they took the two backpacks down to the rotorcraft hangar and stowed them on board their allocated machine.

Then they went back to Merral's house, which was empty as his parents were still at work. Vero put down his things in the spare room, lay down heavily on the bed, and stared at the ceiling.

"Nice to be back here, if only for a night."

"Better enjoy it. The beds out along the Lannar River won't be as good."

"I can put up with a lot. Sentinel colleges are notoriously Spartan. How is your castle tree by the way? You are still working on it?"

"It's fine; with it running on sped-up time, it's had three winters and summers since you looked at it. Still growing. Mind you, I need now to work out how it reproduces."

"Any ideas?"

"I think it needs to have flowers and insect pollination. That could be fun visually. Imagine the whole outer surface of the tree—tens of kilometers square—all covered with flowers."

"Let me know when you do it. It should be quite a sight."

"I will," Merral said. A moment later he was struck by a thought. "By the way, should we spend any time with the Antalfers? Don't you want to interview my uncle?"

Vero stretched out his arms. "A point I have been thinking about.

Only briefly, if at all. Barrand may simply be a symptom of something. Besides—"

He sat up and gave a deep and impatient sigh. "Besides, Merral, I need *data*. Real data. More than twisted notes on a piece of music. Contact, an image, an *identification*. I do wish Anya could come up with something. Anyway, this evening I'm going to put my notes in order. Before we travel."

Before Merral could comment, the downstairs door was heard opening.

Vero smiled. "Well, it can wait. I think we'd better see your parents. And if I know your mother, I think there will be food."

•◆•

Vero was not disappointed, and after hearty greetings and the sharing of the most pressing news, food was brought out. They had no sooner started to eat than Merral's father, visibly tired from work, came in and joined them. His mother bubbled on about life in Ynysmant, and his father, rambling as ever, talked first about machines and then his Historic, Welsh, and confused everyone in trying to explain the three basic types of the *cynghanedd* form of poetry. As a result there was little space for Merral or Vero to reveal their own concerns.

Halfway through the meal, there was a knock at the door and Isabella came in. She beamed at all and then gave Merral a shy, almost secretive, smile. Merral rose from his seat and kissed her on the cheek.

"I heard you were both in town," she said.

Vero bowed. "Nothing is overlooked in Ynysmant, that is sure."

"I'm afraid," Merral said, "that this is purely an overnight stop, Isabella."

She looked sideways at them. "So you must be going back up to Herrandown. There's nowhere else to go." Merral sensed a vague disappointment.

"Sorry," he replied. "We should be back in a week. Probably very much less."

"I see. . . ." Now the wistful note to her voice was unmistakable.

"Isabella, are you free at all tonight?" Merral asked.

"I have to look after Eliza. That's my youngest sister, Vero; everyone else is out. It's too late to change."

Vero coughed quietly and they looked at him. "Er, Isabella, I was only saying to Merral earlier that I need to work tonight. So, if you and he were to meet, you would not be depriving me. Besides, we *are* going to be seeing quite a lot of each other over the next few days."

Isabella looked from one of them to the other but said nothing.

"In fact, your arrival has rather caught us by surprise too, Merral," said his mother. "I should have said last night when you called but it quite slipped my mind. We are due out this evening, to see the Berens. They are leaving to be with their eldest and his family on the coast. *Permanently.* Tomorrow. It's very sad for us. So we can't really miss it. Can we, Stefan?"

His father shook his head gravely. "No. I mean you can come with us. But Merral, if you want to go with Isabella . . . and I'd understand . . . well, feel free. And if Vero wants to work here, then well, that's fine."

"I see," Merral said, somewhat relieved that he did not have to disappoint Isabella, "the decision seems made. So, Isabella I'll come over for an hour as soon as I can."

• ◆ •

The Danols' house was in a freshly painted narrow four-story terrace high up the eastern end of town. By the time Merral arrived, young Eliza had been put to bed, and Isabella ushered him up to the main family room on the topmost floor with its sparse decor and pale, polished pine floors. As Isabella prepared coffee, Merral went out onto the balcony and looked out at the view over the choppy gray waters of Ynysmere Lake, above which the gulls swooped, their wingtips gleaming red in the rays of a setting sun that seemed to bleed through rips in the clouds.

I feel troubled, Merral acknowledged as he looked out over the warm, glowing tiles and brickwork, the spires, roofs, and deep shadow-filled streets of his town.

He stood there looking at the town he had grown up in. As he did he had a brief and terrible presentiment—too ill defined to be a vision—of everything before him slowly crumbling, as if Ynysmant were sliding brick by brick into the lake. It was almost as though its buildings and houses were just dissolving into rubble, like snow under warm rain. Merral shuddered and clutched the balcony rail. In a flash of cognition, he sensed that his concern was not the loss of his town but of his world.

A gust of wind blew from the north, and he shivered. He went back inside to the Danols' room and sat down on the sofa, trying to soothe his mind by staring around at the abstract paintings and the carefully spaced pottery items on the high glass shelves until Isabella returned.

There, as the last rays of the sun fled the nearby towers and twilight fell, Merral and Isabella sat together on the sofa with their coffee and talked of the news from the town and of the worlds.

Yet as they talked, Merral found that instead of his strange mood being allayed, his unease persisted, but it was now focused in a different area. In particular, he sensed that Isabella was in some extraordinary, fey mood that seemed to defy analysis.

She leaned back into the corner of the sofa and stared at him with her deep dark eyes as if she was watching for something.

"Are you glad to see me?" she asked in her gentle but searching voice.

"Very much so. I would have got in touch with you after supper."

"I know that," she answered, stroking her long, straight black hair.

"I've been pondering our relationship, Merral," she announced a minute later.

"I would have been, Isabella. But I've been busy." Merral slowly put his cup down. "Still, please tell me what you have been thinking."

"Well, it's odd. Hard to put into words. Do you see it going anywhere?"

"Going anywhere? Well it's sort of frozen, isn't it? We can hardly do anything without the approval of our parents."

"No," she replied, but he felt that a strong suggestion of doubt hung over the monosyllable.

"You sound like you don't believe it."

"Hmm." She twisted a lock of her hair. "I'm just exploring things. I mean the whole commitment routine—the traditional formula. Trying them out in my mind. You and I are *special* to each other, aren't we?"

"Special? Yes, we are."

She snuggled next to him, and he was oddly aware of the warmth and softness of her body. "I agree," she said.

There was silence for some time, a silence deeper than conversation. In it, Merral began to think about the relationship between himself and Isabella. Then his mind drifted, drawn away by the thought of the journey he faced tomorrow. *Where will we be in twenty-four hours' time?* A vague feeling of foreboding came into his mind. *What will we be facing? And what did Jorgio's vision mean? Could there really be something in the north? Some sort of wild, malign presence?* Merral wanted to condemn the idea as folly, to throw it out of his mind, but felt he could not. It was strange how the very phrase *the north* was acquiring an edge to it. It was almost as though it conveyed the same sort of chilling force on the mind as the north wind did on the flesh.

He was suddenly aware of Isabella's eyes scrutinizing him. As if sensing that she now had his attention, she spoke in a firm but insistent voice. "The whole thing is ridiculous. We can do nothing."

With an effort, Merral directed his thoughts toward Isabella. "It's the way it is. A parental decision. We wait—what—another three months?"

"And then, will they say yes?"

"Possibly. My parents are very fond of you."

"And mine of you. They would let me go with you as your wife to your jungle project if necessary. Even if we rarely got the chance to come back here."

"I'm sure they would. But that, well, just wasn't the point."

"Yes, but it seems so, well, *sad* that our parents won't approve of us being committed to each other."

"Sad? I suppose it is. I hadn't seen it that way. But I don't see that we can do anything about it. Except wait."

"And hope."

"I suppose so," he answered, wishing that the pending journey wasn't overshadowing all his thinking.

"I was wondering . . . ," Isabella said, a few minutes later.

"About what?"

"About an alternative."

"How do you mean 'an alternative'?"

"Hmm . . . ," she replied, as if having difficulty trying to frame the words. In the silence that followed, she nestled closer to him. Merral found it undeniably pleasant with her soft, slight weight against him. In fact, he decided, pleasant was an understatement. There was an excitement about it, a sense of an anticipatory promise. Suddenly marriage—and all that it brought with it—seemed to be something that wasn't merely attractive to him; it was something so compelling that he felt himself hunger for it.

Isabella reached out, put her soft hand over his, and squeezed gently. "You think it will work out for us?" she inquired in a low, urgent tone.

"I hope so."

"You'd like it to work out?" There was an almost pleading intensity to her voice. He paused, aware that her eyes were wide and soft and tender.

"Yes . . . ," he said. *Funny,* he wondered as the word slipped out, *should I have said that? That yes? I should have qualified it with "if it's right."* But now other thoughts flashed through his mind: *this feels so pleasant, it seems so right, Isabella is my best friend, our parents will surely approve, and our being linked together is inevitable.*

"You see," Isabella said, looking at him, her mouth so red, soft, and close that he could sense her breath. "I was thinking that—on that basis—we could have a private understanding between us."

"'A private understanding between us?'" he echoed, a shadow of disquiet trying to intrude into his mind but making little progress against the whirling torment of emotions.

"Yes. An *understanding*—just between us—that we are, really, sort of committed to each other. Privately. Just waiting for the approval to come."

Part of Merral's mind wanted to tease out further what she meant by an understanding. After all, what was the point of waiting for their parents to make a decision if they were to preempt it? But another part of his mind was preoccupied by the delicious fact that she was very close to him. He could sense her warmth and feel her breathing. She stroked his hand.

"You agree?" she asked, her mouth suddenly welcoming, her white teeth shining in the fading light.

Suddenly it didn't matter; the approval of their parents seemed something he could take for granted.

"Yes," he answered, almost to his own surprise. "I suppose—"

But Isabella had interrupted him by kissing him on the lips. He yielded to her, and the world seemed to explode into something he had never imagined that flooded his brain with sensations for long, immeasurable seconds.

"Oh, Merral," she whispered, her face pressed against his so close that he could hear her breathing and feel her heart beat. "I do love you. *Thank you.*"

Only the committed or the engaged kiss like that, he realized.

Suddenly an urgent note of alarm sounded over the surging flood of excitement and sensation that was flowing through his mind. In a moment's flash of intuition, he realized that he had initiated something—he was now not quite sure what—without the thought and seeking of God's will that was required.

He pulled himself back from her, the urgent words forming in his mind: *Lord, forgive me. Give me wisdom. Protect me, us. From doing anything foolish, anything wrong.*

"Is everything all right, Merral?" she asked sharply, sensing his consternation.

Suddenly there was a triple pulse from the diary adjunct on his watch.

"Sorry, Isabella," he answered, somehow both relieved and frustrated by the interruption. "I'm expecting a message."

He glanced at the screen and saw that the call was from Anya Lewitz. He tabbed an acknowledgement and stood up, shaking himself and brushing his hair smooth with his hand. Then, trying to focus his mind on what Anya might say, he went over to a nearby table, sat down rather unsteadily, and unclipped his diary. He angled his chair so that the background was a blank wall and flicked the screen on.

Anya peered at him over her disorganized desk. She looked weary, and there was little trace of her normal ebullience.

"Hi, Merral. I hope I wasn't disturbing any family reunions."

"No. Not at all," he replied, somehow glad that it was a question he could answer honestly. "No family reunions. But I've been waiting for your results."

"Well, they have come in. At last." She answered slowly. "They are odd. *Very.* I'd like to talk to both you and Vero about them. Is he there? Or shall we get a three-way discussion going?"

Merral paused, suddenly feeling that he needed to be out of this place. He needed time to think about what was happening—what had already happened—between him and Isabella. "Can you hang on twenty minutes or so, Anya? I'm not with Vero. I think we both need to discuss these things."

"Okay, I'm around."

As soon as her image had faded on the screen, Merral called Vero to say that he would be over straightaway. As he clipped the diary back on his belt, he was conscious of Isabella at his side.

"A problem?" she said.

"Sorry, I need to go back down and talk with Vero. We are waiting for some analyses. It may affect our plans for tomorrow."

"I see. I understand." Her voice strongly suggested that while she might understand, she wasn't happy about it.

"Thanks."

"No, thank *you*," she said, and suddenly kissed him softly and fleetingly on the lips.

•◆•

As he walked back down quiet winding streets to his parents' house, Merral struggled to try and impose some order on the turmoil of his feelings. Somehow, inadvertently, without seeking the Father's will, he had made some sort of promise of an understanding of commitment to Isabella. A promise that he was not quite sure he understood the significance of, and one he was not sure that he should have been involved with. But surely it hadn't been a real commitment, had it? He frowned. It was more, he decided, that it had been a sort of commitment to a commitment. He was unhappy with that as a phrase, but it expressed how things were. And put like that it didn't seem quite so dreadful. But he realized that this was another thing that seemed odd. Was all of Farholme now running so oddly?

Back at the house Merral pushed the matter of Isabella out of his mind, telling himself that he needed to concentrate. He joined Vero at the table and called Anya with a diary linked to a wallscreen.

"Okay, you guys," said Anya, rubbing her face in a gesture of tiredness. "It's been a long, long day. Part of the delay has been because I wanted to check the result with Hamich Bantys and he is on the Mazarma Chain and ten hours behind us; I didn't want to wake him." She stared unhappily at the screen. "I take it, Sentinel Vero, this isn't a test to see if we are alert?"

Vero just shook his head.

Anya sighed. "Sorry, just a desperate last resort. Okay, the DNA results are odd. We've checked the machinery and it seems to be running fine, but it doesn't add up. First of all, it is an unknown species; it has never been recorded. We know its high-level taxonomy—I'll come on to that—but it seems to be a novelty. Now, as you know, Merral, the Standard Operating Procedure with a novelty is straightforward."

"Get the Genetic Innovation Team to look at it. We did it with a new thistle last year."

"Exactly. We'd just say that a new species or subspecies has emerged and ask for a GI investigation. Catch the thing—or sample it—and decide whether it is going to be a blessing or a curse." She paused. "But this is quite off the scale. We have the DNA analysis, but on the line where we should have species, subspecies, and any matching results from the database, we get merely that it's mammalian *definitely*, anthropoid *definitely,* and hominoid *probably*."

"Hominoid?" Vero asked. "So that includes apes and man?"

"Exactly."

"Ah."

"Ah indeed. Unlike thistles or parrots—incidentally, Merral, that new Great Blue variant is making a real mess down on Anazubar—hominoids do not tend to share their genes across species. And in Menaya, of course, there is only one living hominoid."

"Us," Vero said, his face wearing a disturbed look. "But is it known outside Farholme?"

She shook her head. "Not in the entire Assembly. I've even checked it against the few reliable genetic records of Neanderthals and the like. No match."

"Most odd. So is it a new species?"

"It's a theoretical possibility. Hamich agrees. But . . . well, that raises all sorts of problems. There seems to be a lot of human code there, but there are also biochemical and genetic peculiarities." Anya bit her lip, evidently nonplussed. "Oh, I don't know. There may be some decomposition . . . or some contamination. But then, the biomarkers seem to be negative on that."

Vero threw a puzzled glance at Merral, then turned back to look at the screen. "Anya, would you like to speculate what has happened?"

On the screen Merral saw Anya start to open her mouth and then shut it abruptly. "No," she said firmly. "Speculation in the absence of adequate data is not appropriate. And could be dangerous." She stared at Vero.

"I understand you, Anya Lewitz," responded Vero firmly. "I am as reluctant as you are to jump to conclusions."

"Good," she answered, and to Merral's ears she sounded relieved at not having to deliver a final verdict. "Anyway, tomorrow I will make a Gate call to the best person in the field, Maya Knella on Anchala, and will transmit the data to her for a third opinion. I was wondering, Vero. . . ." She paused, as if uncertain about whether to proceed. "Yes, in view of historic sentinel concerns, if there might be someone else you think I should consult."

"Ah," Vero's head rocked gently as if something had become plain. "A generous and thoughtful gesture."

He paused. "No, I think I can wait. I hope to get more data in another forty-eight hours. I fully appreciate your desire that we do not jump to conclusions."

Merral felt that there was an emphasis to his last words.

Anya nodded slightly in response. "Which brings me to the cut branch." She sighed. "What a pair of specimens! Our invertebrate expert is sure that whatever made it was something with very large jaws or mandibles. He suggested some sort of crab and was worried what we had evolving in our seas. He was nonplussed when I said it was six hundred kilometers inland and in a wood. 'Well, it would have been twice the size of any crab known here,' he said. As if that helps."

She paused for her words to be understood, and then, with a strange look, went on. "So he is scratching his head too. But well, it may be worth mentioning that he estimates that whatever did it could put a lot of force into a shearing action. It could take an arm off, he thought, if it had the gape for it. It could certainly cut through most unarmored synthetics thinner than a centimeter. I thought you should know that."

"I see," Vero said. "I was rather hoping for one puzzle to be solved. I now find that I have two unsolved puzzles."

There was silence and eventually Merral asked. "Is that all?"

"You guys want *more*?" There was a smile and Merral felt the old Anya was back.

Merral shook his head. "*No*. Many thanks. You work on your data, Anya. We'll try and get you some more up country."

"You are going after it?"

"Or them. A hunt. The first hunt for any totally unknown land organisms for—how many thousand years?"

"Twelve or so. I don't know. But take care. Incidentally, Perena is based at the Near Station from tomorrow for some low orbit Central Rift surveys—they want to check the volcanic activity. I'll get her to watch out to the east. So smile when you look up."

"Will do. Thanks for your help."

"Thanks for a challenging problem. And keep safe, Tree Man. And you, Mr. Sentinel."

Vero bowed slightly and the screen went blank.

Merral leaned back in his chair and stared at his friend. "Now, Vero Laertes Enand, do you know what is going on here?" He was aware of a strange sharpness in his voice.

Vero looked thoughtful, shifted his lean body in the seat, and rapped his fingertips together twice as if summoning something. "Merral, I have a bad feeling. But I am worried about deceiving myself. I wish I had someone else here with my background to talk it through. If you will excuse me, I want to keep my thoughts to myself. I think things are moving to a head, and we will know better in a day or two what is happening."

"Well, if that's the way you think is best, then I won't argue." Merral thought for a moment. "But I think you know what is going on better than me. There was something that passed between you and Anya."

Vero shook his head. "No, I do not *know*. I *suspect,* but I cannot believe it. And as for Anya? Yes, I fear I know what she saw. But what it means and how it got here at Worlds' End is quite beyond my understanding."

He got up and paced the room. After some moments he turned

round and stared at Merral. "But oh, I find it too hard to believe. We will see. Oh dear."

He sat down, steepled his fingers, and stared at them, his smooth brown forehead now furrowed. There was a long silence which Merral did not feel like breaking.

Suddenly Vero got to his feet and stood upright with a stern face.

"Merral, my friend. I owe you an apology for not telling you more. I think—no, I fear—we are on the edge of something so awful that I cannot even begin to understand what it means. But I cannot be certain. The trip north will tell us whether I have found something that is beyond even the sentinels' nightmares." Then he paused and spoke in harsher tones as if to himself. "Yet it makes no sense! None at all. Oh, I must be wrong. *I must be.*"

Then he shrugged and looked back at Merral. "Anyway I must spend the next few hours making a report. I do not wish to be dramatic but I will file it in a closed format with Brenito, with instructions that if I do not report back from our expedition it is to be transmitted to Ancient Earth immediately."

Merral went to the door, finding it difficult to know what to say. "As I have said before, I hope you are wrong, Vero."

"I hope so too."

Merral opened the door to go, and as he was about to slip through Vero spoke again. "Try to get some sleep. You will not get as much as you like tomorrow."

"How so?"

"I fear we must adopt an ancient policy that has not been needed for long years."

"Which is?" Merral asked, with a sense of foreboding.

"We will have to take turns at keeping watch."

◆

Herrandown seemed deserted in the bright, early-morning sunlight as the rotorcraft pilot landed, and for a few moments, Merral found himself uncomfortably worrying whether some disaster had overtaken the Frontier Colony. Then he saw his uncle's bulky form emerge from his house and stand watching them. His posture was strangely rigid, as if uninvolved in what was going on.

The pilot swung her tight-clipped blonde head round into the passenger bay and smiled.

"Have a nice walk, fellas. I hope the weather holds. You're keeping your diaries on?"

"Yes," Merral answered, "but emergency contact status only."

"Good enough. Just so the Met Team can warn you if the weather throws a wobbly. It's been a bad year that way. Anyway, I'm off back. Hope you enjoy our countryside, Mr. Vero. It's not Ancient Earth, but it does for us."

Vero paused long enough in pulling on his backpack to bow slightly. "Thank you, Anitra. I'm sure it will do for me, too."

Then the doors opened and they were on the ground. With a gently rising whistle the rotorcraft soared away southward.

Merral looked up to see Barrand standing before them, his expression one of puzzlement mingled with unease.

"Ho, nephew. Again!"

Merral found little warmth in his uncle's tone and was struck by the stiff and cool nature of his embrace.

"And a guest. Another guest." Wasn't there a sharp edge to the voice here? Merral tried to suppress the idea.

"Uncle, can I introduce . . ."

"Verofaza Laertes Enand, *sentinel*." Vero extended a hand in formal greeting.

Barrand took it with a sort of sideways glance at Merral. "Ho. A sentinel now! Am I in trouble, then?"

Merral found the tone strange, as if his uncle had started to make a joke but had changed his mind halfway. He took his uncle by the arm. "Uncle, we are just passing through. At very short notice. Vero wants to see the north so we are going for a long walk. It suits my purposes to examine the area north of here on foot."

"I see."

Merral sensed an almost-open hint of suspicion in the voice. "So, Uncle," he said, trying to adopt a tone of levity that he did not feel, "we are going to be rude and just say 'hello' and then 'farewell.'"

"As you wish. Well, come in for a few minutes. The children are heading off to school soon so it's all a bit chaotic. It is probably best you don't stay. Things are settling back to normal here."

His uncle glanced at Vero, and Merral felt that his expression seemed to ask, "How much do you know?"

"I'm glad to hear it, Uncle."

They strolled over to the house in silence. Merral found his aunt and the children at the door and made the introductions to Vero. As he did so he found himself analyzing them, almost fearing the worst. He felt that his aunt looked tired but otherwise well. Elana seemed brighter than she had been, and Thomas appeared to have regained his former good spirits. *Perhaps the shadow has lifted off this community.* But as they moved inside, Merral caught sight of a welded metal loop against the door frame. Vero's eyes met his and there was a barely perceptible shake of the dark face.

They spent barely half an hour inside the house, and during that time Merral felt that there was little said in the conversation of any significance. It was almost, he felt, as if no one wanted them to stay for long. Merral watched for any evidence of problems, but saw little that was obvious. However it appeared to him that his uncle and aunt were now no longer the vibrant, large-scale characters they had always been to him. They now seemed to be in some way drained, and even shrunken figures, with faint shadows around them. He found himself wondering whether Vero would see anything awry.

Eventually, with good wishes and unbending embraces and handshakes, Merral and Vero were waved off up the track out of the hamlet.

When they were out of sight of the house, Merral turned to Vero. "Well, what do you think?"

Vero said nothing for a few moments and then looked at Merral with a raised eyebrow. "Most odd. They were watchful."

"Interesting. Of what? Of us?"

"No. Of themselves. Let me explain. Of course, I have never met them before. This is my first Frontier Colony, indeed my first Made World. But it is a characteristic of the Assembly that we speak what is on our minds. That we say what we think, without regard for anything other than charity. You agree?"

"But of course," answered Merral, once again wondering at the extraordinary perspective that Vero brought to bear on so many things. "Is there any other way?"

"Ah, that is the interesting thing. If you read the pre-Intervention literature or watch—if you can stomach it—their imaged data, so much of what they said was to actually disguise rather than reveal."

"To disguise—"

"Oh, come on! It comes over in the Book. For instance, when King Herod says he wants to worship the baby Jesus as well. It is a pretense."

"But he was an evil man."

"However, the principle still stands. Anyway, with your uncle and aunt I detected a watchfulness. They thought before they spoke."

"True. I suppose I had noted a lack of freedom, perhaps. But I hadn't seen the significance."

Vero adjusted his backpack and looked across with thoughtful eyes. "It was there all the same. But as I said yesterday, I didn't come here to investigate the Antalfers."

"Yes, I suppose that's fair."

Vero gave Merral a thoughtful look. "Come on; it's a long walk to the Rim Ranges."

He shook his head ruefully. "And besides, who knows what we will meet on the way?"

As the track out of Herrandown began to steepen and the weight of their packs made itself felt, Merral and Vero fell silent. As he strode up the slope, Merral reminded himself that he had been here with Isabella only a few days ago. And as she came to mind, he realized how perplexed he was there. What was going on? And yet it wasn't just her; his own feelings seemed to have polarized. A few weeks ago, there had been just a low, deep friendship. Now at least two things had happened. His feelings for her seemed to have evolved into an intensity of desire that almost scared him. And yet another part of him was counseling caution and almost screaming that there was something wrong. It was a conflict that he could not easily resolve. And to make it all worse, he had already made some sort of promise to her.

Abruptly he saw that they had come to the point where Elana had seen the creature. Merral gestured to Vero to stop and his friend looked at him expectantly. "It was here?"

"Yes."

"I thought so." He stared around at the view. "Yes, a fine vantage point. And on a day like this, a particularly pleasant view of a charming spot."

Merral agreed. There was a hint of white blossom on the apple trees now and the other trees were covered in fresh greenery. Over the whole scene the sun shone out of a perfect blue sky flawed only by the faintest high-altitude haze.

Turning their back on the view, they moved into the woods, and Merral paused at the site where he had found the cut twig. Vero took off his pack and spent a few minutes looking around the site and seemed vaguely satisfied.

"I am no bushman, and the trail is very cold and has been over-printed by others—I presume you and Isabella. But let us go on."

Cautiously, letting his eyes adjust to the lighting under the trees, with the gloom broken in places by brilliant shafts of light, Merral led them on, trying to avoid trapping his pack on the branches.

They paused briefly at the site where they had found the hair and then moved onward. Now, beyond that part of the trail that he and Isabella had examined, Merral found himself being more watchful. It was not just that the traces they were following were now faint, it was that, somehow, he found himself anxious not to come across anything unexpectedly.

The trail was still visible as a line of broken, buckled grass, vague imprints in dry soils, and torn and snapped stalks and twigs. Once, Vero stopped to examine the dents in the ground. He looked up at Merral. "Hard to be sure, isn't it? But I feel there was something heavy through here."

Merral gestured to a clumsily broken branch just above his head.

"Big, too."

"So it would seem." Vero looked up and grimaced. "I'm not sure I want to meet it in a bad mood."

"I'm not sure I want to meet it in a good one."

"True." Vero stroked his chin. "You know, I have seen wild gorilla tracks on Earth and, although smaller, they looked similar." Then he stared ahead, at the way the trail went straight along the valley side. "But were they ever so purposeful?" he added in a baffled tone.

•◆•

Over the next hour, Merral led them on at a steady pace as they went northwest under the trees, dropping slowly down toward the Lannar River. He felt a need for urgency. The trail was already very cold and he knew every extra day would make following it harder. Another rain-storm—perfectly possible within the next few days—could make following the trail harder or even impossible. Besides, they could ill afford any delay; in order to allow them to travel faster they had taken only enough food for four days.

Finally, they started to come to the edges of the wood, so that the trees became absent from the valley ridges and were confined to the base and flanks of the stream valley. There, under the shade of a gnarled, flute-barked oak, they stopped to drink water and have a mouthful of food. Vero wiped the sweat from his face and flicked a fly away. "Forester, what do you think of the track so far?"

"Interesting. Whoever—*whatever*—made it is no fool. Down in the gully itself it is very muddy and the going would be slow."

"Yes. But why not take the ridge route? You'd make faster progress there."

Merral looked up at the bare, grass-covered ridge. "Yes, a puzzle. Perhaps it isn't that smart."

Vero looked at him carefully. "Now if you had sentinel training like me—that curious way of bending your brain so that you see nothing as it really is—you might think that the ridge would be avoided because you would be open to being seen from above."

For a moment, Merral stared at Vero, then he looked back at the ridge as it lay open to the sun. "What a very curious idea. So our watcher doesn't like to be watched?"

"A suggestion. That's all."

• ◆ •

Then they moved on down the stream flanks toward the Lannar River. As the morning passed, it began to be warm and humid under the trees, and Merral began to be conscious of a sweaty feeling along his back as the weight of the backpack pressed on him. Every so often he stopped, gestured for silence, and as Vero dutifully froze, listened carefully. There was the noise of flies, distant birds in the trees, and increasingly louder as the morning passed, the liquid rustling of the river. But he heard nothing unusual.

"And what do you think, Sentinel?" he asked at one point.

"Seems like a normal temperate wood to me. Of course, it's subtly different. That beech, for example; the trunk seems wider and more ridged while the branches are stubbier. I presume that's an adaptation. A bit short of animal life, though."

"Oh, give us time, Earther!" Merral said with a laugh. "Just remind yourself that if we went back a mere twelve thousand years here you would have been choked by carbon dioxide, slowly dissolved in an acid rain, and fried on rocks as hot as any home oven. Your world has had far, far longer. In another few thousand—the Ruler of All permitting—Farholme will match old lady Earth."

Vero smiled and made a little bow as if to admit defeat. "No, you are right. Forget the Gates, forget the Library, forget our Cities-in-Space. Of all the wonders we have done with the Most High's permission, the Made Worlds are the greatest. To have turned near-molten rubble and poison gas to soil, woods, flowers, and air is—by God's grace—our race's finest achievement."

And yet, Vero's point is true enough; I still long to see, someday, the woods of which these are the copies.

• ◆ •

After half an hour they stopped to get their breath back and took their backpacks off.

Vero turned to Merral. "Jorgio's vision. What do you think about it?"

"I found it made me very uneasy. It's like nothing I have ever heard of. And, well, visions are not my line." Merral patted a birch trunk. "Trees, yes; visions, no."

"If we assume that it was genuine, then how do you interpret it?"

Merral thought for a moment. "The candles are the Assembly and the farmhouse is Farholme. That much seems beyond doubt. And in both cases, as a testing, a threat is being unleashed."

"Exactly. But a threat of what? Where?"

Merral shrugged and Vero continued. "There the vision stops and our insight fails. If we knew what we faced it would be easier to obey the charge to watch, stand firm. And perhaps to hope. But visions never tell all." He sighed. "I desperately want to talk to Brenito about all this and will do when I get back. But, in the meantime . . ." He fell silent.

"I think we need to focus on the task ahead. So let us move on. And watch," Merral said and, putting his backpack back on, set off. Vero followed him.

Ten minutes later the trees began to open out. Vero touched Merral's arm lightly and whispered. "I think we should be careful down here. We will soon be out into the open."

"I agree," Merral answered with reluctance. "Although the track still shows no sign of being younger than four or five days."

Merral listened again, but heard nothing to alarm him. Nevertheless, he felt uneasy. An intangible *something* seemed to be present. *Why is it that I don't like these woods?*

Vero seemed to sense his unease. "You're not happy, are you?"

"Ah, you talked earlier about our Assembly transparency. No, I'm not happy."

"May I make a suggestion?"

"Of course."

"From now on have your tranquilizer gun ready. I'm going to wear my bush knife."

Merral suddenly realized what lay behind Vero's interest in the knives the previous day. "A *weapon!* You're planning to use it as a weapon?"

"Not planning, *please,*" Vero looked vaguely hurt. "Preparing, perhaps. As a last resort."

For a moment, Merral could not say anything as he tried to grapple with the concept of a weapon. No, he decided, this was too much. It was important to impose some limits on what were plainly excesses in sentinel thinking, and now was as good a time as any.

"Look, Vero," he said firmly, "we need to think about this. We have no evidence at all that these things are hurtful, harmful, or even hostile. If they are sentient and can communicate we either talk to them or bring in those men or machines that can."

As he heard his words, he knew that he had pitched the tone all wrong; it came out abrasive and critical. Under his dark skin, he felt that Vero was blushing. Eventually his friend spoke quietly. "You are—of course—right, Merral. I was . . . I suppose, letting my imagination get ahead of myself."

It was now Merral's turn to feel guilty. "Sorry, Vero, I guess I don't know what's up here either."

He patted his friend on the shoulder. *He's overreacting.* But then it occurred to him that, nevertheless, to follow such a trail as this into the open might not be the wisest thing. "Okay, what do you suggest?" he asked.

"Hmm. I recollect that in the past, when there was the risk of a . . . *confrontation*, it was considered unwise to do the expected thing."

"Yes," Merral replied, wondering about the use of the word *confrontation*. "The same rule applies in a Team-Ball game."

"Quite so. So, could we go south a little way and reach the stream bank at a new point? That way we come out into the open at a different place."

Merral noted with unease the apparently bizarre way you had to think when you believed there might be enemies around.

As quietly as they could, parting the foliage softly with their hands, they made their way to a point a hundred meters downstream of where the trail would have struck the river. There, Merral motioned Vero to stay, took his pack off, and gently edged his way through a clump of young willows and bright yellow flowering irises down to the pebble strand. There he peered out of the greenery carefully. The Lannar River here was around thirty meters wide, although, he guessed, nowhere now more than waist deep. Although it had been a wet spring, the river was now at a much lower level than at the height of the winter floods, so that a sizeable strand of rough pebbles and gravel lay on either side of the water. The other side of the riverbank was tree lined, and to both north and south, the river disappeared round meanders within a kilometer or so. Feeling on alert, Merral looked once up and down the river quickly and then again in a slower, more careful scrutiny. There was nothing to see apart from some ducks out on the deeper part of the stream. Equally, apart from the soothing, bubbling flow of the water, there was little to hear except an irregular plop as a fish leapt.

Merral moved out of cover. There was an abrupt splash nearby and he felt his heart beat faster. With relief he saw a stream vole swimming away into the depths. Moments later, the ducks took off, their wings rattling against the water.

Slowly, Merral regained his composure and beckoned Vero to join him.

"A false alarm. There is nothing here."

Vero was looking up the stream. "We have to decide how to follow this trail now. These pebbles will show no tracks, and we will be very obvious walking along the stream. Anyone watching would see us half an hour before we arrived."

"I take your point. I presume whatever we are following walked along under the bank; they would be covered by trees that way. I suppose if we walked above the level of the bank we'd cover more ground quickly."

"I agree."

• ◆ •

For the next two hours they traced the Lannar River northward. So wide were the meander loops here that, although they walked a long way and cut off some meanders entirely, their progress north was not very great. The going along the riverbank was, however, generally easy. Other than a few birds and a glimpse of some tri-horned red deer, they saw nothing. They stopped once for a quiet, frugal, and brief lunch and then kept walking.

As the afternoon wore on and the sun began to sink, Vero raised a concern that was troubling Merral: Could they be sure that they were still following the trail? Shortly afterward, though, they came across a part of the river valley where the edge was marked by a large sandbar.

"Look," whispered Vero. "Tracks."

There, faintly cutting across the edge of the coarse sandbar just by the side of the trees, were impressions of footprints, clearly traceable for a length of about a hundred meters before they were lost in coarse gravel. Looking carefully around them, Merral and Vero slithered down onto the bank and took their packs off.

"*Creatures* plural, Merral," Vero announced dully as he peered at the footprints, the wonder and apprehension in his voice barely concealed.

"Yes," Merral answered in a strange, distant voice, as his mind grappled with the awesome, unbelievable awareness that he was dealing with reality, not illusion.

Merral squatted down and, staring at the tracks, reached out and stroked the edge of one gently with his finger, watching the black sand grains roll over into the depression.

"It's *real*," he said, looking across at Vero, whose wide brown eyes stared back at him with an inexpressible emotion. "Vero, let me make a confession."

"Feel free. But I think I have my own."

"I now realize that, until this moment, I didn't—in my heart of hearts—really believe in this. I don't know what I expected. I suppose I still believed that there was another more rational explanation. That it was a hallucination, a trick. Anything but this. . . ."

"Yes, I agree," answered Vero slowly. "I suppose I am more conditioned to be prepared for this, but I too find this an extraordinary moment. I, too, have had my doubts. As you have known. Maybe I have doubted too much. But come, let us examine these prints quickly and be on our way. We have some way to go, and I want to find a safe camping spot for the night."

It was odd, Merral thought, how *safe* had now acquired a meaning that it had never had before.

Vero gestured at the line of tracks. "Let's spend a few minutes separately and then get back together and share our conclusions."

Agreeing, Merral began looking at the prints and imaging them on his diary. The most striking tracks were a series of deep, widely spaced footprints with a rough similarity to a bare human foot. Wordlessly, Merral tried to match the pace. Even striding, his footprints were only two-thirds the distance apart of the older prints, and furthermore, penetrated to only just over half their depth.

To their side marched another set of prints with a much lighter impression and a very much shorter pace. In fact, they were so closely spaced that they reminded Merral of those made by a child. Curiously, the prints were bounded by sharp, angular sides and seemed not to have any clear imprint of toes.

Eventually Vero looked up from imaging them.

"Okay, Sentinel," Merral said, "you tell me what is going on."

"Going on? I wish I knew." Vero shook his head. "What I can tell you is what you yourself know. There were two creatures. The larger one has feet not dissimilar to ours, walks upright, weighs as much as you and I together, and must be—I'm guessing—as high as if I sat on your shoulders."

"And, I presume, the hair Isabella and I found comes from it."

Vero nodded. "A fair guess. If the sand were Earth quality— sorry, but it's true; it's very coarse—we might have seen signs of the fur. The other type is half the size; no, more like a third. And much, much lighter. The foot structure is, however, odd. It's bipedal too, but where are the toes? Or was it wearing shoes?"

"I don't feel so. And presumably this is our beetle-like man."

"Yes," said Vero, with a frown. "Elana is vindicated. But it is odd."

Then he looked around at the open river. "Merral, I know these are strange tracks and we could study them more, but I think we should get back off the stream. We are just too visible out here."

Merral found that he needed little encouragement to get back under the shelter of the trees. Together they clambered back up onto the grassy bank, picked up their packs, and set off again, walking thoughtfully northward.

⋅◆⋅

By late afternoon there was no doubt that both were tiring. Merral checked how far they had traveled and was far from disappointed. Indeed, he realized that he was secretly pleased with the way that Vero had borne up. His light build plainly concealed a considerable toughness.

After some discussion, Merral and Vero singled out a tree-capped hill that rose sharply above a river bend ahead of them as a suitable place to overnight. Vero examined it with the fieldscope from a distance.

"It seems fine. The banks are too steep to climb up from the river. That will make keeping watch easier."

Whether as a result of his words, his tone of voice, or both, Merral felt a shiver of disquiet. It was, he found himself thinking, both a novel and an unwelcome feeling.

Slowly and carefully, they made their way round up to the summit of the hill where, under the silver-barked birch trees, they found an almost-flat surface covered by heather and bilberry. There they took their backpacks off and, following Vero's suggestion, made a survey of the immediate area. Their examination showed that, apart from an apparently active ground squirrel set nearby, there seemed to be no life larger than a bird or rabbit in the area. The hill allowed a good view in all directions, and taking the fieldscope, they went and looked northward from the edge of the hill.

The air was clear and they could see as far as the southern Rim Ranges. With the low-angle sunlight picking out features with dark shadows, the nature of the landscape ahead was clear. For some time Merral and Vero gazed at the scene, looking at parts in detail with the scope and comparing what they saw with the map they had with them.

Not far north of the hill the landscape changed. The rolling terrain they had passed through became a broad, open plain of coarse grassland broken by dispersed patches of fresh green woodland and drabber marshlands. Through it the Lannar River flowed, no longer in a single meandering unit, but rather as an array of separate channels weaving their way in and out of each other in a complex silver braid, producing a mosaic of small, pine-covered islands. Behind this, the ground rose sharply up to the Daggart Plateau, a feature marked by a broad, steep escarpment in which lines of black cliffs could be seen. *Carson's Sill,* thought Merral as, with the fieldscope on maximum power, he could make out the white thread of the waterfall down it. And behind the escarpment and beyond the Daggart Plateau, the Rim Ranges, with high, incised, and still-snowcapped peaks, marched across the horizon, firmly marking the edge of the Lannar Crater proper.

As Merral looked at the scene, he found himself feeling very mixed emotions. One part of him was simply satisfied at the distance they had traveled today. Another part of him—he wondered whether he could call it the "old Merral"—rejoiced in the sheer beauty and grandeur of the view. And yet he realized there was another emotion: one that tainted the view and marred his enjoyment. He tried to isolate the unfamiliar feeling, seeking to name it and wondering if he had the vocabulary for the task. It was, he finally decided, *foreboding*: a feeling of unease, bordering on fear, about what lay ahead.

"See anything?" Vero asked softly.

"Anything unfamiliar? No. It all looks normal to me."

"But does it feel normal?"

"No, Vero, no," answered Merral with a shake of his head, but he did not elaborate on his answer.

Back in the heart of the cluster of birch trees, they sat down and stretched out on the heather. Vero rubbed and stretched his back, as if trying to soothe pained muscles.

"I'm out of practice, Merral. I hope I didn't hold you back?"

"Not at all. You did well for a—"

There was an enquiring smile. "For a what?"

"For a man from Ancient Earth." But as he said it, Merral realized it was an odd thing to say and an odd thing to think in the first place.

Vero seemed to sense his consternation and the smile slid off his face. "Ah," he said, "you seem surprised at the thought."

"Yes, I am. The idea just came to me that the inhabitants of Ancient Earth were, in their way, old and decrepit. Tired. That sort of thing. Sorry."

Vero stiffened and looked at him searchingly, concern written across his face. "Merral, can I ask you to think carefully? Have you ever had that thought before? Or anything like it?"

Merral paused. "No. Never. I have awe and honor for Earth's history. I suppose we look on it as the infant church looked on Jerusalem. A mother to whom we owe a debt we cannot repay, even if we now have a life of our own."

"Good. But a supplementary, if I'm allowed one. Was there another thought with it? However distant, however unpleasant?"

"An associated idea? You mean if I had continued the train of thought?" He hesitated. "Well, I suppose, it might have gone that Ancient Earth is made up of tired old men and women, and that the new worlds are now the future. It is offensive, I'm afraid."

There was a raised eyebrow. "Have you ever heard such statements before? Ever read of them?"

"No, not that I can remember. They are—embarrassingly enough—mine alone."

"I wish they were. Something very like them was said a long time ago."

"By who?"

"General William Jannafy. In a talk to his council. Around 2102. It was a famous quote: 'The tired, timid, old men of a decrepit Earth stand in pathetic contrast to the brave vigor of our new worlds.'"

"*The* Jannafy? Of the Rebellion?"

"The same. Just before declaring his independence from the new Assembly."

"Then it must be coincidence. Or I've picked it up from a forgotten history lesson."

Vero was staring at him. "Perhaps. But Barrand also effectively quoted Jannafy. That the Technology Protocols were made by man, not God, and that they were not Scripture. Jannafy said something very much the same as part of the debate on the first versions."

"I remember." *And,* Merral thought, *I remember too your alarm when I mentioned it.* "But, all that was long, long ago."

"I know," replied Vero with a weak smile. "Everyone says that. It's the standard answer."

Then he fell silent and would say no more on the subject.

◆—◆

Eventually, as the sun touched the horizon, Vero spoke out. "I think we must make our preparations for the night. I think it would be better if we do not use any lights."

I suppose, Merral thought, *it's part of being a sentinel to find danger anywhere.* He was deciding that it could get wearisome, then he remembered his own moments of unease earlier and thought of the footprints. *No, it might be better not to be taken by surprise by an ape-creature, even if it was benign.*

"As you wish."

They rapidly erected the ultra-light two-person tent and quickly made a stew from the reconstituted supplies.

As they ate, Vero poked at the food with a fork. "I suppose I had hoped that your camping food might taste better than ours. I think I shall soon get bored of this."

"There is little option. We could catch and eat ground squirrel if you wanted."

Even in the gloom, Merral could make out the grimace.

"As a forester do you have to do that? Killing animals?"

"It's part of our training," Merral said. "I've had to do it once or twice out of necessity, and we sometimes have to cull weak or sick animals. Or when we get a species that has acquired bad habits. We had some wild boar a few decades ago, they tell me: gentle creatures, ideal for the Made Worlds. Then suddenly they evolved a taste for young trees. It couldn't be allowed, so there was a Menaya-wide boar hunt. They still talk about it. But yes, I've eaten deer and so on. I don't care for killing, of course, and my experience of real meat leads me to believe that our plant protein versions taste just as good."

"Well, they are supposed to be indistinguishable at the molecular level. So you could kill?"

"It depends what." Merral hesitated, realizing that they were no longer talking about food. "Why, what are you thinking?"

"You are on guard tonight while I sleep. I suggest you take both a bush-clearing knife and your tranquilizer gun."

"Well . . . okay, if it helps you sleep better."

Merral could see the glint of white teeth as Vero smiled. "You are uncertain, aren't you, my friend? One part of you is afraid but another part refuses to let you be so." His voice was sympathetic.

"Yes, I suppose that is so. I partly think you are being ridiculously overdramatic and then—"

"You think of the footprints and what has happened to the Antalfers. And you think of what Jorgio said which makes no sense."

"Pretty much so."

"And I am the same."

Above their heads, a bat fluttered through the darkness, and Merral looked up to see the first stars.

"Vero, tell me something. I gather that what is happening does not conform with your models. So how did you expect things to happen?"

"*Expect* is too strong a word. The broadly preferred model runs something like this: You may perceive the Assembly as being in some sort of stasis with a fixed but slowly expanding state as the worlds are made. In reality, it is far more complex. There are rhythms, pulses, cycles, waves. We have a whole branch of sentinels that just looks at them. For instance, the seeding projects occur in pulses—as every child knows—and that has a major impact. But there are slow, subtle changes in such things as demand for migration and allocation of resources. There are also ill-identified things that we can only describe as being the 'mood' of the Assembly. Sometimes, it breaks the surface."

"Like the innovative three hundred years from 8120?"

"Yes, and the much less adventurous thousand years before it. I mean, how many Eighth Millennium painters or musicians can you name? Worthy men and women, but no geniuses."

"So, there are these cycles."

"Yes, cycles and pulses, and we have tried to chart them. And these great cycles work continuously within the Assembly all the time. With their peaks and troughs. Now suppose that, just once"—Merral was conscious of Vero gesturing in the darkness with his arms—"the crests were to coincide. Like the waves of the sea—the waveforms might peak together and you might get a catastrophic wave."

"So that the Assembly might be vulnerable to an internal disruption. Through a coincidence of natural events?"

Vero sighed slightly. "We could argue about 'natural events' and 'coincidence' forever. But the point is that we have been thinking about an internal phenomenon, something felt widely and traceable back to a combination of large-scale ordinary processes. This here, this Farholme phenomenon, is the exact opposite. It is localized—really just one family—and appears to be externally caused by something that—whatever it is—is not ordinary."

He paused, evidently choosing his words with care. "This is part of the problem for me. If this is a genuine event, it suggests we have been badly wrong. And if we have been wrong here, where else are we wrong?"

•—•—•

Suddenly, Merral remembered that they had to contact Anya, and a few minutes later her blue eyes were peering at them out of the diary screen. "Hi, guys. Well, there's hardly much point being on video mode as I can barely see your faces."

"Sorry, Anya," Merral answered. "But we can see you fine. Anyway it's a quick call. Do you have anything for us?"

She seemed to swallow. "Well, yes, I have. You fellows may not like this. But you may be on a wild-goose chase. I was going to call you, but I thought you might still be swinging through the trees. You see, I called Maya Knella on a truly lousy Gate line. The signal to Anchala must have gone round the Assembly several times, and it's only a hundred or so light-years away. Look, she is dismissive. She thinks we have cellular decay as well as faulty hardware."

Vero spoke before Merral could say anything. "Sorry, Anya. *Faulty* hardware?"

Anya's face acquired an uneasy expression. "Yes, Vero. She says there is the possibility that the analyzer was miscalibrated before being sent out to Farholme. She has heard of something similar."

"Anya, I can't believe she said that!" Merral snapped, unable to control himself. "That the Assembly could allow such a thing to happen!" He turned to Vero, his face just visible in the reflected glow from the diary screen. "Can you credit that?"

Vero answered in a flat tone, as if he was restraining himself. "It is indeed an odd suggestion and I agree it is very worrying. Anya, this Maya Knella is good? You know her?"

"Well, we've never met in the flesh, Vero. I've been at screen symposia she has spoken at. She is good—the best. I was . . . well, shocked myself."

Vero was speaking again, and Merral felt that he was pushing gently. "So she doesn't think there is anything wrong here? No strange, exotic, alien forms?"

Anya, after opening and closing her mouth as if struggling for words, spoke slowly. "She was—I have to say—incredibly negative about it. She implied that any other option was preferable."

"I see," answered Vero. "Was she negative about your work, in any way?"

Anya looked at the screen thoughtfully. "She did not go out of her way to affirm my competence. It was all rather odd. . . ."

Feeling irritated at this turn of events, Merral nudged his friend. "Show her the images, Vero," he said quietly.

"Not yet," Vero whispered under his breath.

"Hey, what images? What have you guys seen?"

Vero gestured out of the range of the camera for Merral to be silent. "Oh, just some tracks, Anya. We'll show them to you sometime. I need to think about them properly. Run some enhancement, computer comparison, and so on. But, I suppose, we must follow our expert geneticist's advice. Still, it's a nice stroll. Look, we better shut down for the night."

Anya peered at them. "Okay. Well, I'll check out the equipment here. But it's odd."

"Yes, it is odd. And Anya . . ."

"Yes, Vero?"

"Er . . . don't spread what Maya's saying around, will you? If it's true, it's very bad news. If it's not then, well—she's made a fool of herself."

There was a hesitant pause. "No, I'll keep it private."

The light of the screen vanished, and Merral and Vero were left alone in the dark.

Vero spoke first. "To spare you questions, no, I don't know what is going on. But I do not believe this Maya Knella. She is covering something up. She must be. Perhaps there the solution lies. Perhaps there is a problem on Anchala, too. Perhaps the Assembly has let something loose. I must find out—" He stopped suddenly. "Merral—my most tolerant friend—I am babbling. Would you mind sleeping first? I couldn't sleep and I need to think over all that I have seen and heard today. It's now nearly eight, and first light will be—if I remember—at six. I'll take watch until one and wake you."

Merral agreed, laid out his things where he could find them in the dark, slipped inside the thermal sleeping bag in the tent, and adjusted its insulation settings.

The last thing he was aware of before sleep took him was a glimpse of Vero, hunched under the tent fly sheet and, apparently deep in thought, silhouetted against the evening sky and staring resolutely northward.

$\mathbf{M}$erral felt that no sooner had he fallen asleep than his shoulder was being shaken gently and Vero was telling him that it was one o'clock and time for his watch.

"Glory! I must have been tired," he muttered, realizing that the darkness was complete. "Anything to report?"

"Puzzled badgers, or what passes for them here. I watched them through the fieldscope on infrared. A fox went down along the riverbank; some bats and an owl circled overhead a bit."

"Fine. I'll wake you at six."

The air was cool now and Merral pulled on his jacket, scrambled out of the tent, and sat on a soft tussock of heather peering into the darkness and listening to the noises of the night. After a while, he felt unable to sit still and, moving slowly to avoid tripping over tree roots, got up and went to the edge of the hill. There, under the light of the star-filled heavens, he could only make out the faintest outline of the landscape ahead. He could see the moving gleam of reflected starlight from the river's waters, and in the farthest distance, he thought he could make out the glint of light on the distant snowy peaks. Otherwise, impenetrable night surrounded him. He listened carefully but heard nothing untoward. The badgers snuffled down below him; away to the east a fox barked, and somewhere a nightjar chirred.

Using the fieldscope on the infrared and image enhancement modes, he scanned the area but saw little new. He put the scope down and sat there listening, trying to make sense of things.

Suddenly, he was conscious of a noise in the air above him, a quiet fluttering sound that was little more than palpitations on the edge of audibility. He glanced up to see something scudding through the air just above the trees, briefly blocking out the starlight as it passed. Using the fieldscope again, he tried to follow it but failed to see it. He decided that either it was too fast for him to follow, or for some reason the scope could not image it.

He put the instrument down and used his eyes as it came round again as if circling above them. It was plainly a bird of some sort, and Merral decided that it was probably the owl reported by Vero. But he found himself quite unable to identify which of the five possible owl species it might be. Then, abruptly, it was gone.

•◆•

The rest of the night was uneventful, but Merral felt ill at ease, looking here and there at the slightest noise. He often looked up at the Gate, watching for the dull shimmer of the Near Station or for the faster-moving twinkle of the other satellites. For some reason the evidence, however far away, of his fellow humans seemed to give him comfort. It was with a strange and unaccustomed sense of relief that he watched the sun rise and the darkness vanish.

After a perfunctory breakfast, Vero and Merral set off again north-ward, dropping down carefully from their hill toward the river. They made good progress, and within an hour or so of their start, they had reached the point where the broad, open plain began. Now, as the river flowed in a number of wider, sandy channels separated by clumps of trees, they had to decide which to take. Despite a careful watch, they had seen no further signs of tracks. In the end, Merral agreed with Vero's suggestion that the middle channel was the best option.

Merral found that the going seemed harder than it had on the pre-vious day and that, as they strode along the sand and gravel bars, his legs were tiring more easily. As the hours passed, he found himself sweating strongly and wiping his brow. In spite of his tiredness and the effort of walking, he maintained a careful watch on the deep shad-ows under the pines that crowded together on the gravel and pebble mounds that lay between the stream channels. But he saw nothing.

Increasingly, though, it was precisely the fact that he saw nothing that began to concern Merral. There was too little life. There were trout jumping in the water, in the distance he sometimes heard a woodpecker, and every so often a squirrel would bound away through the treetops. In general, though, there seemed to be a scarcity of mammals or birds, either because they had moved away, or because if they were there, they were hiding. Both hypotheses gave him cause for concern. He did not mention his feelings to Vero, who had been largely silent since breakfast, but noticed that his friend now kept the collapsed bush knife attached to his waist within easy reach.

•◆•

Toward the end of the morning, Vero stopped suddenly and wrinkled his nose in disgust. "I smell something. Something nasty."

Merral sniffed cautiously and agreed. Ahead of them, three black crows flew up leisurely from a tall larch tree standing on its own on a bank of brown sand.

Without a word, Merral began to walk cautiously to the tree, his eyes sweeping this way and that. He felt suddenly tense.

"Merral!" Vero whispered, his voice thick with emotion. "There is something in the tree."

Midway up the larch, a dark, formless shape lay sprawled stiffly amid green branches. As Merral tried to make out what it was, he saw Vero, his hand on the knife, slip off his pack. Not knowing what to do but aware that the time for deliberation was now over, Merral took off his pack, pulled out the tranquilizer gun, slotted in a cartridge, and thumbed the dose level up to the maximum setting of five. Vero, his eyes scanning round warily, merely nodded agreement.

Together now, they slowly walked to the tree. As they came closer, Merral could see a confusion of tracks on the sand at its foot. The stench was stronger now: a disgusting, repellent odor of decay.

Cautiously, they walked up under the tree. As they did, Merral became aware of the faint, high-pitched sound of buzzing flies above them. He stared up at the object in the branches, seeing a scrappy bundle of disheveled black fur out of which white objects protruded. Bone white objects.

"They'd lost a dog." Vero's voice, rich in disgust, broke the silence.

In a flash of sickening revelation, Merral knew what he was looking at. "Spotback. The Antalfer's dog. Poor thing." He felt a surge of anger.

"On Ancient Earth dogs do not climb trees." Vero's voice had an odd, strained tone. "On Farholme, is that rule now broken too?"

Merral looked at the tree, noting that the dog's body was nearly three times his own height above the ground.

"No, Vero, our dogs do not climb." He heard a coldness in his own voice that surprised him. "Stand watch while I go up and get him down."

He handed the tranquilizer gun to Vero and with some effort climbed the tree and levered the body out with his boot.

By the time he had descended, Vero—his face furrowed in disgust—was already imaging the body. He looked up at Merral, his eyes wide in horror. "Before you look at it, see what you make of those tracks."

He gestured to the left.

The prints on the coarse sand were of low quality and confused, but it was possible to make up some sort of dreadful story out of them. There were paw marks and the two types of prints they had seen earlier, all mixed in as though there had been a considerable melee. Then there was a rough depression, dark with dried blood, and a confused, dragging trail into another deeper and bloodied hollow in the sand, which was surrounded by the large footprints running all around in strange, intense, deep impressions. At the base of some of the prints was a dark stain.

"A fight," Merral observed, trying to sound calm. "Spotback attacked them, I'd guess. Or they attacked him. Here a wound, possibly fatal to Spotback. Then the dog crawls here. But all these prints . . .? Was the creature dancing in triumph?"

Vero gestured back at the body. "Take a look."

Merral bent over and looked at the corpse as Vero joined him and poked delicately at the pile of fur and bone with a stick. He realized that the bones were crushed into white slivers, the skull shattered into a dozen or more fragments.

Suddenly, here by this open river with the sun shining and the wind softly ruffling the green needles of the larch tree, Merral felt sick. For a moment he thought that he was going to have to go behind a bush and vomit. Then he controlled his feelings and looked up at Vero, his nausea now mixed with anger.

"It *stamped* on the dog," he said, his tone dull.

"I am no expert in such things. But I would say so. A repeated, angry stamping." Vero's tone was icy.

"Although it might be useful to try to work out the weight of the creature that did this, I think there is no point in getting this taken back to the lab. It's probably too late for a useful analysis. It's at least three days old, badly decomposed, and has been eaten by birds."

Vero looked at him. "As for the weight, I'd guess in excess of a hundred kilos. As much as two big men. I mean, could you have thrown that dog up there?" He gestured up at the tree.

Merral stared at his friend, seeing the sweat and dust on his face and noticing the strain in his eyes. "No. He was a decent-sized dog. Twenty kilos, maybe. It was a big creature that did this. Consistent with the footprints. Think of a big man and double his size."

"For a creature that doesn't exist, according to what this Maya Knella says, curiously substantial. Odd. Very odd."

"And very nasty," Merral added. He found himself looking around, trying to peer into the shadows under the distant trees as if expecting to see something. He felt an urge to shiver.

"Vero," he said, "I've seen enough."

•—◆—•

They buried the dog under a rough pile of basalt pebbles. Merral paused as he put on the last stone. *It is strange,* he thought, *how this has annoyed me: to kill this dog in such a way and then just fling the body away as if it were rubbish.* Whatever these creatures were, he decided that he already felt very ill inclined toward them.

Then, more positively, he told himself that he would get Spotback's name put on something here, some ridge or hill, when the naming commission came up this far north for the minor features.

They picked up their packs and set off again. Merral, however, did not put the tranquilizer gun away but attached it to his waist, where it banged against him annoyingly. As they walked on he found himself more than once wondering how fast he could operate it and whether it would work against such creatures. *And supposing it didn't,* he asked himself, *how quickly could I get out my bush knife?*

And, as he tackled these thoughts, he wasn't sure which disturbed him most: the idea of the unknown creatures or the anger they had aroused within him.

Merral and Vero pushed on throughout the day along the sandy margins of the river channels, taking only the briefest break at midday. They said little to each other but set a steady pace, their eyes and ears alert for any signs of the creatures. Merral noticed how they kept to the edges of the river and that when they approached large boulders they carefully circumvented them lest something be behind them. Irritated by the tranquilizer gun but with no inclination to put it back in his pack, he found himself carrying it awkwardly on his shoulder.

In the afternoon their steady pace was rewarded by good views of the steep black rock walls of Carson's Sill and the dense dark greenery of conifer woods that clung to the slopes in patches along it. And, as the afternoon wore on, the tiered rock face of the plateau edge with the white vertical slash where the Lannar River plunged down in a series of waterfalls rose before them, and it began to dominate their thinking.

"It has been climbed?" asked Vero in doubtful tones, as he stared through the fieldscope at it.

"Of course, or I wouldn't have taken this route. By Thenaya Carson first, oh, two centuries ago, and about every decade since. But not by me. It's around eight hundred meters from the base to the lip of the scarp."

"With packs, and on that surface, it won't be easy."

"The trick, I'm told from the files, is to go up well away from the river. There is a lot of loose debris and the spray from the waterfalls has smoothed the rocks, so it makes for treacherous climbing. The western side is supposed to be fine, if it hasn't slipped. There's a lot of erosion going on."

"Ah, the Made Worlds again," commented Vero with a tight smile.

"Sorry. But it will be a hard climb and we will be exhausted at the top."

"I'm tired at the thought. How much longer until we stop today?"

"Can you manage another hour?"

"Yes, Forester," Vero answered, amid a wipe of his brow, "but it can't come too soon."

They walked on, and half an hour later, as they were walking through a narrow section with high dark stands of the woodland pine on either side, Vero caught Merral's gaze. "I have noticed you listening a lot. You ought to be more at home here than me. What do you feel?"

Merral stopped, listening again to the silence around them. "*Feel?* I don't know. I'm worried that I'm talking myself into seeing and hearing things that don't exist. What with the dog, and Jorgio's warning . . ." He prodded a pebble tentatively with his foot. "But there just doesn't seem anywhere near as much wildlife as I would expect. Not here. Maybe, not since last night. The odd rabbit and the squirrel, that's all, and they seem to keep their distance. Normally, I'd expect to get within feet of them. There are fewer birds, too."

Merral looked up to see, high above them and too far away to identify, a stiff-winged brown shape circling above them. "And there's the odd buzzard. But little else."

He found it hard to put his feelings into words. "But I have to say that sometimes . . . sometimes I feel that we are being watched. Do you?"

"Yes, I do," answered Vero without hesitation, looking ahead at the ridge before them. "I was trying to avoid saying it, but I have an uneasy feeling about this Carson's Sill and what lies beyond it. I am wondering if I should just have asked a full Sentinel Threat Evaluation Team to come in and go through the whole area. With both ships of the Assembly Defense Force sitting in low orbit."

"I have to say," Merral said, "that for the first time in my entire life I consider that the Assembly may have been wise in retaining two military vessels. Not that I ever gave it very much thought."

Vero wiped the sweat off his hands on his trousers. "Yes, persuading the Assembly to maintain two armed cruisers and a hundred crew as a Defense Force on constant readiness has been a priority of the sentinels since Moshe Adlen's day. It has not been an easy task."

Then he looked at Merral. "I have not said this before, but the existence of the Assembly Defense Force makes my position tricky."

"How so?"

"This would be their first intervention ever. News of it would go throughout the Assembly, and if it was for a false alarm, then it could be unfortunate for the sentinels. But we may well have to call them anyway."

And with that he gestured Merral onward.

•◆•

By five o'clock they had reached a point where the ground had begun to rise toward the sill. Here, with the cliffs looming over them, Merral decided to stop. They had made good time and there was no way that they could climb the sill today. He had already assessed the ascent as requiring at least three hours, and with the evening fast approaching and their growing tiredness, it made sense to camp at the base and tackle the climb when fresh.

They found a suitable spot for camping. A landslide from the cliff had left an enormous mound of debris, within the angular boulders of which there had been enough fine material to make a poor soil in which stunted and tilted fir and spruce trees had grown. At the top of the mound was something of a hollow surrounded by small young firs, and Merral felt that it afforded a perfect site for camping.

In the depression, they put up the tent and then took turns bathing in the river below. As one bathed in the clear but icy river waters, the other sat by on a rock with the tranquilizer gun and a bush knife keeping watch. The troubling thought came to Merral that the very idea of keeping watch would have been inconceivable only a few weeks ago. Now, he realized ruefully, they had slipped into practicing the habit almost as a routine.

Then, refreshed by their baths, they climbed back up to the tent and, for some minutes, lay back on the soft heather enjoying the warm, gentle late-afternoon air and watching the swifts dart above them, hearing their screeching over the echoing rumble of the waterfalls and rapids. Then, taking the fieldscope and with the map in front of them they turned to look up at the rock face, trying to decide which route to take.

As Merral stared at the bulwark of rock that was Carson's Sill, he felt his spirit sink. It was an uncompromising vista; the lines of vertical cliffs of black lava seemed stacked one above another, crag hanging upon crag. Where the towering ranks of the cliff faces were broken, massive piles of sharp-edged rock fragments radiated downward and outward in vast cones of scree. Merral noted that, amid the frequent patches of firs, whole trees were toppled over or had been splintered by rolling rocks, and in the debris piles, fragments of trunks stuck out at crazy angles. The only consolation he could find was that he could see no sign of any creatures on the cliffs.

"Tough," commented Vero with a frown. "It's like looking up at your castle tree. Only the absolute necessity of my following this trail encourages me to persist."

"I agree, and I'm afraid there is another factor," Merral added, gesturing up at the sky where high in the atmosphere fine, wispy spirals of cloud were drifting westward. "I think we will find the weather changing tonight. It looks like rain coming in from the east."

"How bad?"

"Well, if it is going to be a cyclone we'll be warned by the Met Team. But we need to think about a wet-weather path."

Vero gave a theatrical groan. "Beware the weather in the Made Worlds!" he muttered.

In fact, as they looked up at the cliffs, they soon realized that their choices were limited. The Lannar River had cut something of a gorge through the top part of the plateau edge so that on either side the ground rose through forested flanks up to steep, flat-topped summits several hundred meters higher.

Merral pointed to the V-shaped notch of the stream that was sharply defined against the skyline. "So, Vero, the easiest route is to go straight up to that gorge on the plateau and then on to the Daggart Lake."

"The easiest, no doubt . . . ," answered Vero slowly and Merral sensed his disquiet.

In the end, they agreed that there was only one suitable route, an easily followed line which took them in a slow, zigzag fashion over the shiny black lava blocks, up through clumps of spruce and fir, and then upward to the western side of the gorge at the crest.

They returned to the tent and, as the shadows lengthened, ate in silence.

As the sun began to set, the gathering clouds acquired hues of purple, red, and gold so that the sky began to look like some astonishing experiment in flowing and shimmering colors.

"Ah," mouthed Vero in appreciative wonder, "you do have awesome sunsets here."

Merral smiled. "There are two explanations. One is that it is God's compensation for our being a Made World. The other is that it is the combination of abundant high-altitude dust—inevitable in this stage of our world's making—and a complex and still partially unstable multilayer atmosphere."

"May it always be that your world never divorces the two explanations."

Then, as the light faded and the stars came out, Merral said he was going to call Anya. Vero stopped him. "I think . . . ," he began hesitantly. "I think we might want to avoid saying anything very much about today's discovery."

"Fine, but why?"

"Just a feeling. We will see her in a day or two. You see," he sighed, "she is inclined to believe this Maya Knella. I think there is something very funny there. However I want to talk over with Anya exactly what was said and see the conversation replayed."

"I see."

"So I think we should play it down. We say we had a good day's walk and that's all."

The issue of withholding information made Merral uneasy and he nearly said something, but, in the end, he remained silent. These were strange events and the old rules seemed no longer to hold. *"Things have changed,"* Jorgio had said, and he felt the truth of that. If only, he found himself wishing, things would stabilize long enough, he might see his way to understanding what was going on and working out how to respond to it.

When Anya's image came on the diary, it showed her still in the office. She smiled at them.

"Good to hear from you. I noticed you made good progress earlier. What's new?"

"Bits and pieces, scraps of data," Merral answered. "We are still puzzling. Tell you about it when we get back, another day or two. Anything new on your end?"

She shrugged, her freckled face showing open puzzlement. "Well, I just can't square Maya's statement with what I've seen." Vero nudged Merral's arm and then spoke. "Anya, it's Vero. Nice to talk with you."

"Hi, Sentinel. You shouldn't call people so late. With your complexion I can barely see you in this light."

"True. I guess I'm designed for nocturnal camouflage," he joked, then changed his tone. "But look, Anya, this thing with Maya . . . I think we'll talk it over together when we get back. In the meantime, just don't let it bother you."

"Okay, but it's still odd." She paused. "Oh, yes, I checked with the Met Team people. Rain tomorrow over your area. Ninety percent probability by dawn. But passing over rapidly."

"Thanks, Anya, saves me checking. We suspected it. But it will be a wet climb tomorrow."

"You'll do it. Take care. We'll be in touch the same time tomorrow."

The screen darkened.

◆━◆

For a few moments, they sat in darkness. Merral looked up to the escarpment to the north of them, now only visible as a high, brooding mass of black against the hazy stars.

"The rain is confirmed, Vero."

"I'm used to it, as long as it isn't too cold," Vero answered, stretching himself. "Do you want first or second watch tonight?"

"I'll take second. I'm more used to the rain. But now, after seeing the remains of Spotback, I am under no illusions about a watch being a good idea."

"Yes, sadly, it is needed." Vero got to his feet. "Which reminds me, what did Anya mean about noticing us 'making good progress'? How did she know?"

Merral found himself wondering at his friend's surprise. "By monitoring my diary's location signal, I presume."

"What? Your diary broadcasts out?" Vero's voice was incredulous. "Without you telling it to do so?"

"Yes, foresters, farmers—anyone who works out in the wilds— always set their diary to emit a location signal." Merral was puzzled at Vero's tone. Suddenly a realization came to him. "Of course, you probably don't need to do it on Ancient Earth. I think it's every sixty seconds or so. Any satellite or plane can pick it up. If an accident happens, they know where to find me. Standard practice in all the low-population worlds."

A snort came from Vero. "You mean we have been radiating our position ever since we came? And I have been worried about keeping under cover!" Merral could see him shaking his head. "But why, oh *why* didn't you tell me?" His tone was now one of extreme irritation.

"Why should I?" Merral answered sharply, feeling on the edge of anger and trying to control himself. "We are dealing with animals. Aren't we? You mean to tell me that you think we face *things* with the intelligence and technology to pick up a tight-band EM signal?"

"Maybe. . . ."

"So why didn't *you* tell *me?*" Merral asked, his anger now supplemented by a definite unhappiness at the idea that what they faced might be far more than some sort of clever animal.

"Because I wasn't sure. And I am still not sure. . . ."

A sullen silence descended between them, and suddenly they both apologized at the same time.

"Sorry! I'm—"

"—No, me too."

Vero patted Merral on the shoulder. "My fault. Naive Earther that I am. I should have thought. Can you switch the thing off?"

"Yes. And I will do it now." Merral unclipped the diary and spoke to it. "Diary. Menu Command: Location signal—disable until countermanded."

The manufactured voice responded in its flat lifeless tones, "Location signal is now disabled."

Merral put it back on his belt. "So, my sentinel friend, you don't think it's animals we face? You feel there is an intelligence here?"

"It is a possibility. No more. One of many possibilities that I have thought of and some that I haven't." He sounded rueful. "Probably among the ones that I haven't thought of is the correct answer."

Merral waited for some elucidation of the possibilities, but Vero seemed disinclined to give them and said nothing more.

After some time Vero spoke in a low voice. "You get some sleep." He paused, as if listening to something. "It is quiet here, isn't it?"

"Yes," Merral said listening again. "It is. Or is it my imagination? There should be more noise. Keep a good watch, my friend."

• ◆ •

When Vero woke Merral it was raining. The air seemed thick with the incessant soft, gentle dripping of water as it trickled off the needles and branches of the firs to tap on the roof of the tent.

"What have you seen?" Merral grunted sleepily as he pulled his jacket on. In the pitch blackness of the night, he sensed his friend shedding a damp outer jacket under the fly sheet and clambering through into his side of the tent.

"I don't know," Vero answered with a strangely unsettled tone. "There isn't even any starlight now. It's pitch black and I find it very disorienting. I was careful not to go too far from the tent. In case I got lost. I wish you'd been there. . . ."

"Why?"

"I heard . . . or I thought I heard . . . sounds."

"Wind perhaps?"

"No, no. Not the wind, not the river. It was different—as if it was voices."

"Voices?"

"So it sounded to me. . . . Distant voices, as if the wind had brought them. . . ." Vero seemed to shudder. "But, as I think I told you when we first met, we are trained to be sensitive, to be able to listen to what others cannot hear, to see what others cannot see. Tonight, I wished I had not been so trained. . . ."

Merral reached out, found his friend's arm, and squeezed it gently. "You can get to see and hear things in wind and rain. Did you think they were human?"

There was a shudder. "I hope not. . . ."

"Anything nearer?"

"No, I checked around on the scope in infrared. It's too dark for anything else. Some deer by the river. I think I saw another owl."

"Again? Get a good look?"

"No. I couldn't seem to image it in infrared."

"Maybe the feathers are effective insulators. So they may not radiate enough heat to be picked up. Well, it's a theory. Anyway, let me go out."

"Watch well, Merral. The knife, the gun, and a couple of flares are under the tent awning."

"I hope not to need them. And you sleep soundly, Vero."

In the long, weary, and uncomfortable hours that followed, Merral found himself frequently thinking of the pleasant evenings and nights he had spent in the countryside in the past. Tonight, in the rain and the dark, he felt as if they might have been on another planet. Merral, trying to analyze his feelings, decided that the darkness was one factor. The night was pitch dark, unbroken by stars or even any flash of lightning, and at one point he found that he literally could not see his hand in front of his face. With the infrared mode set on the fieldscope, he could at least make out the general landscape and see the vague glow of his sleeping friend in the tent. While that was an improvement, the strange effect of seeing things in a ghostly mono-chrome only seemed to make him feel more disoriented. The rain, he felt, was another factor. It was a soft, wetting mist of a rain that not only fell, but also drifted up, under, and somehow even inside things. Despite the excellence of his garments, Merral very soon found that he was getting wet. So he stood up, feeling the cold water drip and ooze down inside his clothes, and felt miserable.

He knew, though, that it was neither the dark nor the rain: There was another factor, and that was hard to define. There was an atmo-sphere of unease, of some sort of inexpressible hostility that got on his nerves. Merral realized that he was close to reaching a level of fear that he had never known existed. Everybody was familiar with some levels of fear; you might have a fear of being crushed by a falling tree, a fear of falling off a cliff, or a fear of being caught in a forest fire. Yet that was, he realized, something normal, natural, and even good. Now, though, he sensed he was close to something deeper: a darker, wilder fear that threatened to overwhelm all logic. Was this, he thought, what they had called *terror*?

So Merral prayed for himself, for Vero and their mission, and for the strange things that were happening on Farholme. But—and he found this the most depressing thing of the night—there seemed to be no answer to his prayers. The act of praying seemed to him to be almost futile, and his words seemed cold and lifeless. It almost seemed—and he hardly dared frame the thought—as if the throne of heaven was vacant.

Through what was left of the lonely night, Merral saw and heard nothing, although once he felt sure that, over the soft, steady drip of the rain off the branches, he could hear soft, slow wing beats above him. And when, at last, dawn broke, it seemed to bring little comfort, with the blackness around merely being replaced by a formless and clinging wet grayness.

Damp and cold, Merral woke Vero and together they ate a cheerless breakfast in the tent, folded it up, and loaded the packs.

Under the gentle gray rain they set off toward the cliffs, picking their way slowly up among the wet boulders, rough grass, and tall dripping pines and spruces that obscured the cliff ahead. As they did, Merral looked around, acknowledging to himself how different things looked in the rain. In front of them, above the green-steepled firs, wisps of white cloud drifted across, obscuring the grim ramparts of rock that rose up behind. To their right the cloud, mist, and rain mingled with the spray of the waterfalls, as the Lannar recklessly and noisily plunged downward off the plateau. The very top of the plateau was obscured by a wreath of pale clouds.

After a quarter of an hour of stumbling and sliding in the mud, they came to something of a clearing and were able to take stock of the task ahead.

Merral tilted his head over to Vero. "Well, any trail is now lost, but it hardly matters. There is only one way ahead and that is the way we chose last night."

Vero nodded, shaking a large drop of rainwater off his snub nose. "Yes. But Merral, I have to say that I am worried about what we will meet on this hill. I think—I *feel*—that there is something up there. And that that something is not friendly to us or the Assembly."

He stretched out a dripping hand and pointed to the cliff. "May I make a small suggestion?" His voice was unsure. "I have studied, as all sentinels must, something of the distasteful science of warfare. Your reading of the first part of the Word will have been the nearest that you will have come in this respect. After thought last night, I have decided that I do not like the route you suggest." He traced the line up the slope with a wet finger. "It is too obvious. The gorge at the top is a mere fifty meters or so across. We will climb over the sill edge there onto the plateau, tired and weary. It would be an ideal place for us to either be seen or . . ." He paused. "Meet opposition."

"You mean it's a fine site for a . . ." Merral ransacked his memory. "An ambush. Is that the word?"

"Exactly so." Vero wiped water off his face. "Now, it seems to me that if we kept over to the left we could come onto the plateau at a higher level. Perhaps a hundred meters higher. It's hard to assess it from here. It would make for a tougher climb, but we are also more under trees. And we would not be as obvious."

"Vero, I'm beginning to feel that we are in some pre-Intervention tale."

The wet brown face seemed to wrinkle with some deeply unpleasant emotion. "I hope, my friend, you do not speak truer than you can imagine."

There was silence, and then Vero raised his head and spoke loudly in a firm voice that rang out around the trees and the rocks. "Our Father, who is the defender and ruler of your people, we fear this place and what is on it. Protect your children and go before us now. In the name of the one who is both Lamb and Shepherd. Amen."

"Amen."

There was silence, and then a dripping hand touched Merral's shoulder. "Now, to the climb. . . ."

--•--

The slope was harder than Merral had imagined. He was tired, and even though the route they took was one of a series of oblique traverses, it required continuous exertion. Where there was soil, the rain had reduced it to a soft, greasy mud so that they found themselves slithering without warning. Fortunately, the firs and scrubby bushes meant that they rarely slid down for more than a few meters. Their hands and legs soon became muddy and, inevitably, as they tried to clear the rain out of their eyes, the brown mud was transferred to their faces. Where there was only wet, loose rock, they found they had to test every step carefully lest a block roll away under their weight. Despite the drifting rain, they found that under the effort of climbing they soon warmed up, and the high humidity meant that it was not long before sweat was running off them. A few hundred meters up, Merral called a halt and sat down heavily on a slab of rock, panting for breath.

"Vero," he muttered eventually, when he had the spare energy to speak, "the idea of sliding down and asking for a ride back home in the belly of some warm, dry rotorcraft seems very attractive."

His companion grunted. "I sympathize entirely."

Then Vero looked up to the crest of the sill above them with determined eyes. "But I believe we must climb this. And, increasingly, I think we must be in a position where we can find such weapons as we have easily."

For an instant, Merral felt himself on the edge of rebellion. The words "I'm not climbing this cluttered with a bush knife and a tranquilizer gun" framed themselves in his mind. Then he pushed the thought aside and, without a word, pulled out the bush knife from his pack and attached it to his belt. With some difficulty, he was able to put the tranquilizer gun in his jacket pocket.

Then they set off again, and as they climbed on upward, weaving their way between crags and trees, slipping in the mud and bruising themselves against the rocks, Merral found the climb beginning to blur in his mind. The wet pine needles, rough tree trunks, chocolate-colored mud, and protruding razor-edged black lava blocks seemed to merge into a single slope that ran on upward forever. When, gripped by the risk of slipping down hundreds of meters to the scree below, Merral tried to watch his feet, he found instead that he walked into sharp branches that poked at and whipped his face and hands. When he concentrated on avoiding the branches, he lost his footing and slid.

Once, when they had stopped and were trying to get their breath, there was a great crash and a slab of rock fell down on the other side of the river, plunging noisily downward in a damp cloud of dust and debris. Merral and Vero stared carefully at where it had fallen from, but there was no sign of anything other than natural erosion having caused its fall.

"Beware the weathering in the Made Worlds," grunted Vero as he looked up at the crags above them, but there was no humor in his voice.

Increasingly as they climbed on, Merral became conscious of how his legs and back ached, how his lungs hurt, how he wanted to stop, and how water—he had ceased to care whether it was rain or sweat— was running down his back and chilling him. And when he looked down and back he saw, through the veil of rain and mist and cloud, a dizzying drop through green lines of trees and sheer rock ramparts to the braided, tarnished-silver line of the river.

Slowly though, they made progress, and finally, after nearly three hours of climbing up the sill, Vero nudged Merral. "Not far now," he gasped. "We are at the level of the gorge."

Merral looked to his right to see that they had indeed reached the sharp notch through which the river tumbled urgently. He breathed a silent phrase of thanks, and a few minutes later, they pulled themselves over a final rock level. There, below the wet and drooping branches of the fir trees, they could see that the ground fell away gently northward and that several hundred meters ahead of them lay the still black waters of Daggart Lake with dense pine forests clustered around it. To the left the ground rose up steeply through more trees to a steep-sided, flat-topped summit.

Weary, heedless of the rain, Merral slumped down flat on the wet mossy ground. He had to lie down, he had to rest, and he had to adjust his backpack.

Vero tapped him gently on the shoulder. "No! Don't lie down. You are too vulnerable. Sit!"

In a sudden surge of emotion, Merral felt certain that Vero was going mad and a wave of anger rose in him. *I have had* enough *of this crazy sentinel lunacy.*

He was about to say something when he looked up at Vero's mud-stained face and saw his mouth drop open and his eyes widen.

Suddenly, Vero was on all fours, cringing low on the ground.

"Stay down!" he hissed in a fierce, urgent tone.

Merral, still lying flat, pressed himself against the ground.

"S–slowly," Vero whispered, a hint of a stutter in his words, "look behind you."

Merral rolled over and stared toward the lake.

Along the water's edge, dark tall figures were moving.

For a second *figures* and *moving* were the only words that came to him because his eyes could not make sense of what he saw. The figures were large, walked on two feet, and had an upright stance, but they were not—and he knew it instantly—human. It was not just that they were a dark brownish black in color and were covered in hair, but that they had the wrong proportions, the wrong posture, and the wrong motion. Their arms seemed to reach well below the waist, there was an odd stooping character to their stance, and they had a peculiar loping gait that no human legs could ever have imitated. There was an oddity too about their heads that, at this distance, he could recognize but not define.

Merral realized with a sharp thrill of horror that these were definitely not men. But then neither were they apes; not only was the shape wrong, but there was a purposefulness, a sense of mission in their motion that he had never seen in an ape.

"Vero," he heard himself whisper, "what *are* they?"

He saw that the figures were moving toward the sides of the gorge overlooking where the river began its plunge over Carson's Sill. "I–I wish I knew," Vero answered in numbed tones. "I know less now than I did. But if I do not know what they are, I can guess what they are after. . . ."

He stared at Merral. "They are after us."

CHAPTER 13

Merral gaped at the creatures again, oddly aware that his throat was dry. The creatures were big, nearly half as high again as a big man, and they appeared to have powerful muscles. It was all too easy to imagine one stamping on a dog and hurling it effortlessly high into a tree.

Suddenly Merral became conscious of his heart pounding in his chest, his skin tingling, and his stomach twisting on itself. The deep fear that he had sensed existed last night now seemed very close. *I am really afraid,* he realized.

"T–time to get out, Merral," Vero whispered in shaken tones. Merral found a strange comfort in the fact that his friend was also very scared.

"Yes, a good idea. I have a reluctance to try and dialogue. How many do you think there are?"

"Six at least. The source of the hair you found. . . ."

Merral rolled away and looked to their left. He forced himself to ignore the thudding in his chest and to reason out what to do next.

"We must plan, Vero," he said, surprised by how level his voice sounded. "We cannot be picked up here easily by any plane or rotor-craft—there is too much vegetation. And we are too near those things for my liking."

Vero, still staring down to the lake, just nodded.

Merral looked up through the trees. "We must climb again, I am afraid. See how this hill is flat topped?"

"Yes. . . . They are dropping into the gorge."

Merral looked round to see the last of the creatures lowering itself over the rocks with a disturbingly human motion of the forearms.

"Yes, but we must move. They will find out shortly that we are gone and will trace our route."

Vero looked up at the summit, his face bizarrely transfigured by the mud. "It's another few hundred meters up. It's steep at the top. Can we climb it?"

"I hope so. I can see a crack of some sort. I think we call for a rescue pickup as soon as we can get up there. We'd better go."

They set off and Merral led the way, trying to avoid making any noise and vigilantly looking ahead between the trees. He was aware of Vero following closely behind him. They wound their way up through the firs, and soon the view of the lake disappeared behind the wet foliage. With the initial shock now waning, Merral asked himself, *Do they have a sense of smell? How far can they see? Could they track us up this way?* Mindful of his fear, conscious of tired limbs and of the soft rain wetting his face, Merral forced himself onward.

Ahead through the trees, he could see two house-size blocks of pitted, charcoal black lava that had come to rest after rolling down the hill. In between the great rocks, Merral could now see properly up to the top of the hill. The cloud was slowly lifting, and he could make out a steep, bare slope of broken rubble capped by a slablike expanse of rock. In the thick lava unit that formed the top of the hill, there was a dark, slitlike fracture in which small trees grew. Merral motioned Vero to stop, noticing that on his tired face the rain was running down and mingling with the mud. *I must look like that.*

"Look, that's the way, Vero," he said as he carefully looked up the hill. "Through this gap in the rocks, up to the crevasse, and then on to the summit plateau."

"I can see. But what if the top is occupied?" Vero's voice was urgent.

For a brief moment, a spasm of despair ran through Merral's mind. "No," he answered after a moment's evaluation of the possibility, "I think it's unlikely. It's bare rock. They like cover."

"So we believe," Vero answered stiffly. "But anyway, we have little choice."

"I'm tempted to call in a rescue now. What do you think?"

Vero thought. "Not yet," he said, pulling off his backpack and taking out his water bottle. "I must have a drink. I don't want to use a signal here. On the chance they can locate us on it. Besides, if the top is occupied, we may want to retreat back to somewhere else." He hurriedly swallowed some water.

Merral flung his own pack off his back, pulled out his own bottle, and took two hasty mouthfuls. "Fine, but let's keep moving. They may have realized by now that we aren't coming up through the gorge."

"Yes." Vero slung the pack on one shoulder and started to walk ahead.

Merral replaced his own bottle in his backpack and put it back on his shoulders. He was about to follow Vero when he stopped. Somewhere there was a noise: a faint scrabbling that made his spine shiver. Merral looked around, conscious of the darkness under the firs about him. A dozen paces ahead Vero was starting to wind his way between the high, overhanging dark rocks.

There was another noise.

Something dropped down from the top of the rocks. Something that, in the fraction of the second before it struck the ground, appeared to Merral to be like a child wrapped in shiny brown rags.

"Look out!"

Vero turned as the shape fell toward him and stepped back awkwardly. The creature landed lightly on all fours ahead of him and sprang upright.

Now the shape became clear to Merral, as if the image had just focused. It was a small creature, smaller than Vero, with squat brown legs, long arms, and hands that seemed to swing and thrust as it hopped strangely forward. Despite the small size, there was an air of menace and aggression about it.

Merral began to run toward Vero. As he did, he saw the creature suddenly bound forward with a surprising speed, holding its hands out in front as if they were weapons. Vero sidestepped clumsily, swinging his backpack off his shoulder at the brown thing. The pack struck the creature on the chest with a thud and it staggered back, flailing its arms and displaying oddly flattened hands. As Merral bounded forward, he realized that he had no strategy.

With a wild chirring noise, the creature flung the pack aside and sprung to its feet with a bounce. It began to advance on Vero, who had moved back against the side of the left-hand rock. There, realizing that he was unable to retreat farther, he reached for his bush knife. As he pulled it out, the creature leapt at him. A polished brown arm flicked out and, even as the blade extended, the knife was swept clean out of Vero's hand. It whistled overhead and rattled down against the rocks. Vero yelped and snatched his hand back. From the creature came a strange, high-pitched hissing noise.

Suddenly the creature seemed to recognize Merral's approach. It swiveled its head and looked at him with small eyes as black as shadows. Merral, coming to a halt just in front of it, could see that the head was small, vaguely reptilian in its profile, and covered with brown, waxy plates. It was like nothing he had seen or imagined.

With a fast but somehow ungainly shuffle, the creature turned round to face him, its legs clattering woodenly against the stones, its arms opening wide. Merral was oddly aware of details: the rain dribbling down the carapace, a yellow scratch on a chest plate, the black, lidless, deep-set eyes with a ring of plates around them.

The strange and terrible thought that he had to fight it came into Merral's mind. Reality seemed to have fled. Merral fumbled for the bush knife, his hand closing tight on the handle, his wet fingers reaching for the release button. With a sharp click the gray blade extended. He held it out and moved toward the thing. As if recognizing danger, the creature raised its strange arms high.

Now, as they faced each other, Merral saw the creature properly for the first time. Yet he felt that even now he saw it only as series of impressions of separate parts, as if its unfamiliarity made it impossible to see as a whole. He was struck by the polished-wood appearance of the creature and the massive segmented platelike sheets over the front of the chest that fused into a single hard vertical ridge along the abdomen. What made the most impression on him, though, was not the grotesque physical appearance, but the sense of malignant intelligence in the recessed, tar black, resinous eyes. What he faced was not simply an animal.

The hands moved slowly, and Merral saw that there were three fingers vaguely like those of a man and then a thumb and forefinger whose matching flat inner sections made a pair of blades with serrated edges like a pair of wire cutters. As he watched, the creature seemed to flick them open and shut almost as if to demonstrate them. It came to Merral as a cold fact that the gape was quite wide enough to take off an ankle or a wrist. Various deep, hissing noises came from the wide horizontal slit of the mouth, and Merral wondered if there was a language in them.

As the thing inched closer, making an odd clicking noise as its plates rubbed together, Merral waved the dull metal blade uncertainly in front of him. He saw new details: the swollen and armored joints of limbs that approximated elbows and knees and the clawlike feet that pivoted oddly at the ankles.

"*Lord,*" he prayed aloud, "I don't know what to do."

The creature took another rolling step forward, its body swaying slightly from side to side. Then it lowered itself down on bended leg joints.

It sprang.

Merral leaped aside, swinging the blade out as he jumped. The blade struck a plate on the creature's arm and, with a dull clatter, bounced off. Merral landed awkwardly on the wet grass and slid into a half crouch. In a strange hopping motion, the thing was bearing upon him. *I must not get knocked down.* With his left hand he found the edge of a rock and pushed himself upright. As he did, the creature lunged again.

Merral swung his right boot up to ward off the attack. But the creature's hand swiveled, opened, and seized his ankle. There was a sudden, sharp stab of agony and Merral kicked hard. The bladed hand opened wide and his ankle flew free. A new hiss came from the creature, and Merral wondered if it was a note of triumph. Now, less than a meter away, he was aware of a strange, unpleasant odor that brought back memories of college biology laboratories.

"*Hit it, Merral!*" Vero cried. And Merral, conscious of a surging pain in his foot, began to raise the blade again. But, as he lifted the handle, it came to him with a sharp clarity that his opponent was too armored. He had to find a weakness.

The creature moved again, this time in a crablike crouch with the head tilting and swaying this way and that, as if calculating the next attack. The broad mouth opened into a wide oval to show matching rows of sharp-pointed, brown teeth.

It is in no hurry. In a new pitch of alarm, he noticed vivid red on its left hand. A quick glance down showed blood on his right ankle and he realized that he was hurting there.

I must strike, but where? He stared at his opponent, suddenly noticing the beads of water running down the smooth surface of the creature's skin. *Skin or shell?* he asked himself and pushed the question aside. The creature seemed to stretch its head, and for the briefest of moments, Merral saw a patch of wrinkled soft yellow tissue between the hard brown plates of the neck and chest. Then the thing moved slowly toward him again, and Merral realized that he could not retreat. He knew it was going to attack again and he felt certain that this time it would go for his face or neck with those scissorlike blades.

As if from nowhere Vero appeared, bearing down on the creature with a branch in his hand. He swung it down hard on the thing's head but it was a clumsy weapon, and as it descended, the creature suddenly turned sideways. The blow landed on the armored shoulder and bounced harmlessly off. But as it did, the thing turned its flattened head upward, exposing again the yellow patch. Suddenly, with a force and speed he did not know he had, Merral stabbed the blade forward into the exposed gap. For a fraction of a second, the blade struck shell and met an unyielding resistance. Then—just as Merral thought he had failed—it juddered, turned, slipped a fraction sideways, and with an appalling sucking sound, plunged deep down into the soft tissue.

Everything happened at once.

The creature reeled back, striking the rocks with a cracking sound; the blade was snatched out of Merral's hand; a high-pitched loud rasping scream echoed out of the red-foaming mouth. The blade-like fingers began flapping and clattering in desperation at the knife embedded in its throat.

Merral stood back, clutching the rock behind him, aware of fresh crimson drops on his wet legs. He shook uncontrollably and gasped for breath.

I have killed, was the thought that pounded again and again through his brain.

Over everything the terrible screaming—surely more human than animal—was continuing.

Suddenly Merral was aware of a wild-eyed Vero shaking him. "Quickly! Now! Let's run while we can!"

Above his agony, Merral somehow recognized the truth of what was being said and began to move. He took three steps forward and looked at the creature that was now writhing like some monstrous broken insect on the wet grass.

Merral hesitated. Then, from far below, came strange bellowing howls.

"Quick!" Vero was snatching at his hand.

Merral began to run, vaguely conscious that his right ankle was on fire. He saw that Vero had recovered his bush knife and now had it ready with the blade out.

"What was it?" gasped Merral.

"Save your breath. But well done!"

Well done? Merral thought, in an astonishment that cut through his appalled and confused state of mind. *Well done! An intelligent creature is dying—is already dead perhaps—because of my action. Do we applaud such things?* Then he realized that he had had no option.

He pushed the idea out of his mind and, trying to ignore the sharp pain in his ankle, began to run as fast as he could.

They were beyond the great rocks now and were coming out of the edge of the trees. Ahead lay the open, desolate scree of the hill and above that stood the final black wall of the cliff. The cloud was lifting and the rain seemed to be dying away.

They stumbled out onto the wet piles of broken angular rock, heading for the narrow dark cleft that cut through the upper cliff. From below them, amid the trees, they heard a series of booming bellows followed by high-pitched chattering.

Merral moved forward with a new urgency. But increasingly, as they ascended over the rough blocks of the scree, pain took over: the pain of his lungs, the pained tiredness of his limbs, and, above all, the pain of his bleeding ankle.

Suddenly, Vero turned, saw him lagging behind, and threw down his torn backpack.

"Quick, Merral, let me have your pack," he said amid gasps, the sweat, mud, and rain on his face barely masking a look of intense fear. "We'll throw away mine and anything we don't need. . . . Let me carry it. Quickly!"

Merral, trying to take any weight off his injured ankle, passed the pack over and watched as Vero feverishly threw out the tent and camping equipment, spare clothes, and much of the remaining food. Vero, his eyes nervously searching the dark margin of the trees below, stuffed in some things from his own pack, which he then threw away. Putting the remaining backpack on his back, Vero turned to Merral.

"Does your foot hurt?"

"Not badly," Merral replied, his voice uneven. "I'd like to wash the cut, though."

Vero looked round. "Not here. That . . . *thing* came out of nowhere. If we can make the top we will have some respite. How fast would a pickup be?"

"Ten, twenty minutes. Make an emergency call and they will be in fast. It depends whether a ship is in the air."

"That will have to do. Anyway, it's only another ten minutes climb. You'll be in a nice sterile rotorcraft inside half an hour. Meanwhile, let's go."

They climbed on up over the unstable blocks, hardly daring to look behind. Slowly, the top cliff became closer.

The wound in his foot nagged at Merral as he moved on over the uneven ground, giving him a jarring agony at every slight twist of his ankle. Not having the pack helped, but he wished he could take some painkiller. Over his pain, he became aware that it was no longer raining and that the cloud was lifting.

Soon, though, they were in the cleft of the rock and its dark walls engulfed them. *There had better not be anything here,* thought Merral. *I cannot fight again.* But here all was silent and up at the top of the crevasse was open sky.

The crevasse was steep and strewn with boulders, and soon they were reduced to scrabbling on their hands and knees. Finally, they came to the top of the cleft, where the way to the summit was blocked by a final sheer wall of smooth gray-black rock, twice as high as a man. At one side, a pile of loose blocks of rock suggested a precarious way to the top.

Merral waited at the foot of the cliff while Vero cautiously ascended and vanished from view over the edge. After a few anxious moments, he peered back over the edge and extended a hand down.

"Fine. Smooth, level, and deserted. An ideal landing spot. Come on up."

Using his hands to help him, Merral scrambled over the blocks and, with Vero's help, hauled himself onto the flat tabletop. His breathing was coming hard and fast and sweat was dripping off him.

"Vero, that was horrible!" he gasped. "Horrible! What was that thing I killed? Should I have done it?"

"Merral, priorities!" Vero shook his head. "Yes! But let me call for help and then we'll patch up your foot. Then we can discuss what we have come across."

He slid his diary off his belt. "Watch down below while I call us a ride home. Keep your head down."

Merral crawled forward and looked down below at the dull rocks passing into the conifer woods with the gray lake waters beyond.

Tattered wreaths of cloud drifted like smoke over the treetops as a weak sunlight tried to break through. There was nothing else to see, and the noises seemed to have died away.

Behind him, he could hear Vero talking in a low, urgent way. "Diary! Priority message to be repeated until countermanded. All emergency frequencies. Priority override all other traffic. Message thus: 'Rescue immediately. Emergency.'" Vero paused. "Diary, transmit!" There was a slightly longer pause. "Transmit!"

With a terrible feeling of foreboding, Merral looked around to see Vero staring at the gray block, his expression a mixture of puzzlement, frustration, and alarm.

"Diary, transmit!" Vero looked at Merral. "Incredible! Of all the times to have the first diary malfunction of your life." He stared at the object in his hand in bemusement.

"Merral, you try yours while I run diagnostics. A general emergency call will do. See who we can call down."

Merral pulled out his diary, noting the dull green status light glowing normally on the diamond-coated screen.

"Diary, emergency rescue call! All available frequencies!"

He waited for the red signal light to flicker. Nothing happened. Merral, vaguely conscious of Vero tapping his screen, could barely believe what had happened. "Vero! Mine, too. But they always work! Always!"

Vero nodded furiously and kept flicking his finger at his screen. "It cannot or will not transmit. It is unheard of." His voice was strained.

He put it away suddenly and, after scanning the plateau around them, turned to Merral, his face a strange, sickly color under the mud.

"My friend, I apologize. Again." He gulped and shook his head. "I believe I have made a major error. A very major one."

Then, without explaining further, he bent down, slipped toward the edge, and peered over. He slid swiftly back and stared at Merral, his brown eyes wide with anxiety.

"I have indeed made a serious error. I'd been prepared for one or two creatures, even a few. But I had assumed they were dumb animals, perhaps let loose. But this technology! We cannot do this. Although blocking diary transmissions on a dozen frequencies is not a skill we have sought."

He shook his head and then said, "Perhaps we can get a message through. Low angle to Herrandown. . . ."

He peered forward again, looking over the edge of the cliff, and suddenly stiffened. "We'd better." There was a chill edge to his words that made Merral crawl forward and join him.

Far down below them, just emerging from the trees and approaching the backpack they had left behind, were three tall, dark, and ominous figures. *The creatures we saw down by the lake,* Merral noted dully, *the things with the fur and long limbs, the things with the height and the muscles: the things that kill dogs by stamping on them.* As if suddenly conscious of being watched, the creatures stood still in their tracks and looked up at the cliff. There was a curiously regimented similarity in their movements that seemed almost uncanny to Merral. For a moment, he stared back at their faces, feeling he could make out large, dark brown, impassive eyes. Then, suddenly aware of his peril, he ducked his head out of sight. Perhaps a minute later, he peered over the edge again cautiously. The three figures had turned and were now moving back under the trees. There they stopped and stood in a fixed manner looking up again at the plateau.

"Ah! They have stopped their pursuit." Vero's voice was full of relief.

"But for how long?"

"I don't know. We have probably only a temporary respite. Try this for a hypothesis: They do not like being out in the open in daylight." He paused. "So, we may have till night before they pursue us."

Merral looked around, seeing that the clouds were thinning fast and that he could make out the disk of the sun clearly now. He was now casting a faint shadow. He glanced at his watch and saw that it was now just after eleven o'clock. There were nine hours before darkness.

"Perhaps," he said. "Alternatively, Vero, they are just waiting for reinforcements. They need to be sure we are trapped. But I know nothing about how these creatures think."

Vero shrugged. "I know no more than you. I really don't. These events have taken me by as much surprise as you. We face the unknown together." He shook his head again and ran his fingers through his wet black hair. "I feel I have failed us badly. In letting us come out here to be so vulnerable. The evidence, of a sort, has been available for some days. Perhaps before. Oh, what a fool I've been!"

He stared out at the dripping green forests below them and the cloud-wrapped sharp peaks of the Rim Ranges to the north. Then his voice was more resolute. "But we have not totally failed yet. We must fight. We have got to warn Isterrane, the sentinels, the Assembly. And to do that we must think. 'Tell them to watch, stand firm, and to hope.' That was the message we had." He shook his head. "I fear we have failed on the first, and the last seems a challenge. But stand firm? We can but try."

He fell silent, squeezing his forehead as if trying to encourage his thoughts.

"I must look at your ankle. How does it feel? Your trousers look horrid. I take it that most of the blood isn't yours?"

"No," Merral answered slowly with revulsion. "It belongs to the thing. . . ." He touched his ankle and winced. "Painful. But it has stopped bleeding."

"Okay." Vero looked around. "I'd better check how we stand first. The way this hill is, I think that we can be attacked from only a few places. You keep an eye on our pursuers while I go round."

Vero set off walking round the circumference of the summit. Merral glanced up every so often from watching the creatures below to see that his friend kept a sufficient distance from the edge so that he couldn't be seen. Vero periodically dropped to his knees, crawled forward, and cautiously looked over the edge. The smallness of the summit area they were on was such that he was able to stay within calling distance all the time. *In fact,* Merral thought, *you would have difficulty playing a decent Team-Ball game on this flat plateau without the ball falling off.*

Below, the strange creatures continued to do nothing. Merral tried to call them *animals* in his mind, but the word did not seem right. He was certain that whatever they were, they were more than animals. The word *creatures* seemed more appropriate, but he wondered exactly whose creatures they were. Had they been fashioned by God, man, or the devil? If they were produced by either of the latter, he felt less guilty about killing one. But could the enemy make such things? And in this age of history?

His thoughts were interrupted by Vero's return. "Still there?"

"They haven't moved. So what's our situation?"

"Hmm. Well, we could be in a worse situation. There is really only access on two points: one we came up, and the other—almost opposite—on the western side. At our south, we go straight off the entire Daggart Plateau. It's a nasty drop: hundreds of meters. The north end appears vertical too, of course not as high. So, I think we only have two points to guard. But it's pretty bleak here. No water, no vegetation—just rock. Still, we must be grateful that it is not scorchingly hot. Although it is warming up."

"No caves? lava tubes?"

"Other than the fact that there is a low ledge on the southern side, what you see is all we have."

Merral surveyed again the flat, almost horizontal, plain of the summit surface. There were cracks in it in which a mouse or even a fox might hide, but nothing larger.

"Now," said Vero, "let's look at your foot. Do you think we can get the boot off without a painkiller?"

"Let's try."

Merral flinched as the straps were undone and Vero prized the boot off. He looked down to see that his sock was a mass of blood.

Vero reached into his jacket pocket and pulled out a small medical kit. He bent down and peered at the ankle.

"In the Divine mercy, the thing seems to have struck your boot more than your ankle, so it was unable to close tight around it. That extraordinary blade finger-thumb arrangement was sharp, but the wound is by no means as deep as it might have been. Here goes."

Vero carefully exposed the flesh of the ankle and stared at it. "Not too bad. It has almost stopped bleeding. But you can see that it has actually cut partly through the dura-polymer shell of the upper boot sleeve. You would think it had been done with a knife."

Vero washed the wound with a small amount of water, powdered it with a multi-potent wound powder, and then closed it with a self-suturing tape.

"That should be fine, unless they use some slow-acting toxin unknown to science. Let's hope it washed its hands regularly."

"Ugh!" said Merral, relieved that the wound was no worse. "Actually, that feels better already. I think I'll try and put my sock and boot back on. This isn't terrain for going barefoot in."

Vero went and peered over the edge again and came back while Merral was painfully putting his boot on.

"They are still waiting under the trees. Like machines. How do you feel?"

"The wound's okay," Merral answered. "But inside I feel lousy."

"I'm not surprised. I'm pretty shaken."

"I was terrified, Vero! I mean it; it was extraordinary! But there was more than that; I killed something there. Something sentient, alive, thinking. More than an animal. It's awful!"

Vero scratched an ear thoughtfully. "No, we—*you*—had no choice. I am totally convinced it was evil. But I understand your feelings. It was, though, an impressive action of yours. I would have slashed and slashed until I was exhausted. Why did you strike it there?"

"After my first blow bounced off, I realized that it was armored, shelled. Then—I suppose—I realized that there looked like there was thinner or missing armor just below the throat. I guess it made sense too; you can't have thick armor everywhere. So when the opportunity came . . ." He ran out of words.

"You have a gift."

"A gift! That is the stupidest thing you've ever said. A gift for killing!" Merral was surprised at the force and bitterness of his own voice.

Vero flinched and then began to speak again slowly. "But, my friend, if evil has returned in force, then there may be a place for such things. Many of the Old Covenant writers praise such skills."

Merral, calming down, remembered some of the troubling verses in the Psalms that he had passed over as "of mainly historical significance only."

"Maybe," he muttered.

"Besides, even though you were terrified, you analyzed the situation brilliantly and acted on it. To evaluate rightly and to act in a crisis is a gift."

"Well, if you say so."

"I do. I was a failure."

"Come on, Vero. You were badly shaken. And you distracted it so that I had a chance."

"Teamwork, Forester. Just like your Team-Ball games. But let's see what we have to defend ourselves with."

Vero took his jacket off and began opening the one remaining backpack. "Three flares," he announced and laid out the three stubby tubes next to his bush knife.

"And I have the tranquilizer gun," Merral said, taking off his jacket and finding the gun in his pocket.

"I'm relieved. I thought we had left that behind." Vero shook his head ruefully. "You know, it was a folly of mine leaving that pack behind. We had extra water in it, spare food, other things. . . ."

Merral felt sorry for him. "Vero, you can't blame yourself. This is a unique situation. We needed to get out of there quickly."

"I suppose you are right." Vero frowned. "Funny, I've never really felt guilty about anything before. Perhaps this spiritual atmosphere—whatever we call it—is getting to me too."

He was silent for a few moments. "But enough about the past. We have few weapons to defend us. Let us make twin stockpiles of rocks at either possible site of attack. Gravity can aid us. We must be prepared to use them to dissuade any attacker."

He looked up at the sky. "I do think, though, it will be the night when we are attacked. Whether they fear the sun or whether they are just wary of being caught on any satellite or plane images, I do not know."

Over the next half hour, as the remaining clouds disappeared and the top of the hill began to become warm in the sunshine, they scoured the surface of the plateau for hand-sized fragments of rock. They piled these up above the two points on the cliff edge where it seemed possible that an attack could come. Twice, Merral and Vero tried to make emergency calls, but each time, although incoming signals could be received, their diary messages out seemed to be blocked. They did find out that over distances of a few centimeters they could transmit between diaries, but beyond that any signal was disrupted.

"Formidable!" Vero commented. "I think whatever frequency we broadcast on they pick it up and absorb the signal within a few microseconds. I wonder what other technology they have? No wonder they are happy enough sitting under the trees waiting."

Then they took out the fieldscope, which somehow had not been left behind, and spent some minutes watching the creatures below. With the sun now shining with undiminished force, their pursuers had retreated a few meters farther back so that they were under the shade of a large pine. Merral watched them with the scope, trying to assimilate some understanding of what they were. The strange heads of the ape-creatures, with their angled, almost noseless front and the marked overhang of the skull at the rear, struck Merral as odd. *It is almost as if a human skull had been sculpted in wet clay and then— somehow—a board pressed against the front so that the whole upper part was deformed backward.* Once he caught a glimpse of a wide-open mouth with two arcs of large, dirty whitish teeth. *Are they vegetarians or carnivores?* he wondered unhappily.

Vero spoke quietly. "So, Forester, what do you think?"

"These ape things—I am struggling for a name—seem much less

strange than the other kind. These seem to be bad imitations of humans or gorillas. The other thing seemed just, well . . . weird. These I would classify as mammals, which fits with the DNA results. But what do you think?"

"I agree these things look like mammals, but do they—I ask you—have the organs diagnostic of mammals?"

Merral scanned the three as they sat on the ground. "I see no breasts. Perhaps all three are male?"

"Ah. But do you see any indication of the diagnostic organs of maleness?"

"Interesting. No, there seems to be an absence of external genitalia of any sort. I should have observed that. Are they sexless?"

Vero shrugged. "I do not know. If they are, that raises other questions. But this morning's other creature?"

"Not as easy," Merral answered, overcoming a reluctance to think about his assailant. "Definitely animal, but I can go no further. It fits into no known category of biological classification. There were elements of mammal and insect in it. That beetle-like exoskeleton is what puzzles me."

"And me. What do we call these two sorts of creature?"

Merral thought for a moment. " 'The naming of animals'? These things are 'ape-creatures.' "

"I agree. And 'cockroach-creatures'?"

"No. I am unhappy about *creature*."

Vero nodded. "Very well. I suggest that we borrow the Ancient English word *beast*."

To Merral, the word had echoes of the Dark Times with its wars and horrors, but then he realized that any such allusions were now strangely appropriate. "So be it," he agreed.

"The cockroach-beast: the puzzle creature, the fusion of man and cockroach."

"A disgusting thought."

"I agree. Anyway, I shall take some images of these ape-creatures and dictate some notes. God willing, I will be able to transmit it to

Anya in some way. And then onward. . . ." Vero paused and gestured with a thumb in the vague direction of Isterrane. "It just occurred to me: when will Anya start to get concerned about us?"

"No earlier than eight, when she finds she cannot get through to us."

"What do you think she will do?"

"I don't know," Merral answered slowly. "We can only hope she gets worried and asks for a search team to come in. Fast. Then we fire the flares and they pick us up."

Vero nodded thoughtfully. "Let us indeed pray it is so."

•—◆—•

While Vero linked his diary to the fieldscope and imaged the ape-creatures, Merral walked slowly around the perimeter of the hilltop, conscious of his aching ankle. He was becoming uneasily aware that the summit that he had thought might be their refuge was now in danger of becoming their prison. He paused at the southern edge of the cliff, noting the ledge that Vero had seen, and gazed southward over the dizzying drop off the plateau. Far below he could see where they had camped the previous night and traced the river southward until it disappeared into the haze. His eye caught the dark crescent-winged swifts as, with their effortless mastery of the air, they soared, dived, and raced noisily off the cliff edge. Merral decided that at this moment he would have given a lot to be able to fly as they could.

As he watched, the swifts suddenly scattered in every direction with wild screaming noises. Merral glanced up to see, high above him, a large, stiff-winged bird gliding round in slow circles. *A raptor of some sort*, he thought, shading his eyes as he stared at it. He decided it was a buzzard and was puzzled by the reaction of the swifts; unlike some of the faster falcons, the slow buzzards posed no threat to swifts. He made a mental note to discuss it with Lesley Manalfi, the Planning Institute's head ornithologist, then reality flowed back and he realized that he had more pressing biological problems than aberrant bird behavior.

"Now what?" he asked Vero on his return.

"Now, we sit and wait and think and pray," came the solemn answer. "We have almost no water left, a little food. And no shade."

Merral sat down beside him and pulled his jacket over his head to gain some protection from the sun. So as the hours passed and the rocks around grew warmer, Merral sat there hunched under the jacket with the sweat dripping down his face, conserving his energy and praying, in a way he had never remotely imagined he would ever have to, for deliverance.

$\mathbf{B}$y late afternoon Merral, feeling hot and increasingly thirsty, decided to try and distract himself. He turned to Vero, who still had his jacket over his head. "Let me ask you what you now think these creatures are."

"Ah. As you know, I have had a number of theories. I make the total five. One theory has been destroyed over these last two days. Namely, that the whole thing was a collective psychosis."

Merral tapped his bandaged ankle gently. "I have evidence that renders that untenable."

"Rather a shame. It was the easiest view to hold." There was a thoughtful pause. "Theory two was that it was a direct incursion of the demonic. Obviously, we have little data on how that might occur. . . ." He paused. "But did you feel it was a demon you grappled with this morning?"

Merral thought about what he had seen and felt in those terrible few minutes. "No, I don't believe you can kill demons with a bush knife. But, having said that . . ." He stopped, finding himself unable to continue for some moments. "Having said that, I felt in some way that that cockroach-beast was more than an organism. I felt there was anger in its actions, even hatred. Evil." Merral caught a sympathetic nod of agreement from his companion and went on. "I cannot express it," he added. "Not yet. Ask me again after the memory fades."

And, for a few moments, Merral sat still, staring at his shadow on the baking black rock and trying to put out of his mind the weird jumping motion, the sound of the plates clicking together, the hateful organic smell, and those staring, bottomless, tarlike eyes.

Vero spoke suddenly, seeming to choose his words carefully. "I agree. It's all too tangible. But I share your hesitation; there are some strange effects. Something has come into the worlds. I hope we can get it out. Or that, at least, it will not spread . . ." He tailed off midspeech, his face full of unspoken worries.

He slid over to the cliff edge, peered over carefully for a few moments, and then slid back. "Still under the tree." Then he leaned back gently, putting his hands behind his head, and stared up at the sky. "So we scrub theories one and two. Now theory three is that these are aliens. We are, after all, on the edge of the Assembly. 'Worlds' End' and all that. A thought which must have struck you?"

"Indeed, and been rejected," Merral replied. "These creatures do not seem to me to be alien. Certainly not the ape-creatures. And all our experience is that the probability of intelligent alien life is very small. That Earth stayed stable long enough for such life to develop has always been assumed to be a direct work of God. And, of course, despite claims, we have never found anything more than simple algae or bacteria. And no alien artifacts or signals." He paused. "At least such was the confident view I was taught. But my confidence is being eroded right now."

Vero, still staring upward, nodded. "I agree. We may have become too confident. But I can't see these things as alien. The DNA evidence seems against that too."

"No. Not aliens. They are simply not alien enough. Which leaves you where?"

"With two related possibilities. Either theory four . . ." Vero shaded his eyes a moment. "Funny buzzards you have in your world. I've been watching this one for a bit."

"Probably the same one I saw earlier. But go on."

"Ah yes, theory four. Here we have a genetic mutation of humanity. More precisely, two mutations. Natural events occurring due to some accelerated biological process; a supercharged evolution."

Merral's answer came slowly. "No, again. All we have here is microevolution, the same as you have. Some of it pretty dramatic, but it is limited. Yes, we have new species, but they are recognizably related to what was imported here. Variation on places like Farholme is about what you would expect for a world with new niches. That buzzard you are watching is probably a living example. That strange flight pattern is probably because it's moving slowly into a new niche. Another hundred generations and it will probably be more like a condor. And, as you know, human genetic change here, while it occurs, is slight. But these things . . ." He hesitated, wondering how to express his feelings. "These monstrosities would be a major jump—or a series of major jumps—beyond anything we can imagine. Anyway, the whole Assembly would hear and mourn if any parent here produced an ape-creature or a cockroach-beast as offspring. A truly horrible thought. Try me with your last one."

Vero was shading his eyes again and squinting as he looked upward at the buzzard. "Hmm. Strange how he keeps the sun close enough behind him. Yes, theory five is similar, but says that these things are deliberately gene-engineered."

"What?!" Merral could hardly contain himself. "That we have produced these things?"

"Well, that someone has." Vero had shifted his gaze sideways so he could look directly at Merral. "This is my preferred option. Reluctantly."

Indignation and unbelief seemed to flood into Merral's mind at once. "But that," he protested loudly, "is totally against everything the Technology Protocols allow. Gene-engineering up to plants—if needed—is allowed. But no further. That's enough. That's about the most fundamental breach possible. I mean, we were upset enough about modifying a long-dead human voice, but that is nothing. Nothing at all in comparison."

"Ah. . . ." Vero's voice had a sharp edge to it. "You too made the link. How interesting. This is one reason why I was trying not to feed you with my ideas."

"The link?"

"Between altering a re-created voice and genetic manipulation of human cells."

"Oh, there is no link!" Merral felt himself getting irritated. "Your overactive sentinel imagination!"

"Sorry. I'm not saying your uncle did this, too. But—what shall we say?—a spiritual climate in which one can happen is a climate in which the other can happen. Both are rebellion."

Merral could merely shake his head. "The idea that anyone could create that fiendish creature that attacked us is beyond me. Why?"

"It may have advantages that we do not have." Vero rolled over so he could face upward again. "For instan—*wait a minute*!" His voice sharpened and he froze. "Oh, the idiots we are!"

Something's up, Merral realized. *But what?*

"I wish I hadn't left my pack," Vero announced suddenly in a voice that was oddly louder than normal. He turned sideways to face Merral and began whispering with exaggerated lip movements. "I think the bird is not right. A mechanical observer of some sort. Pretend to have a conversation with me and take a look."

It took Merral a second or two for the bizarre concept to be understood.

"It's not your fault, Vero," he said loudly as he looked upward, narrowing his eyes against the brightness of the sky. "We needed to make a quick getaway, so it was quite reasonable."

He looked at the bird out of the corner of his eye. Yes, Vero was right. There was something wrong about it. It wasn't that it was a buzzard practicing to be something else. It was something else pretending to be a buzzard.

Vero was speaking. "Yes, but I shouldn't have left the water."

Merral made his mind up; all the evidence fit. He rolled over and looked at Vero. "You are quite right," he whispered. "I should have spotted it."

"It's called surveillance, and we don't want it," Vero muttered between clenched teeth. "Any ideas how we remove it?"

Over the next few minutes, in quiet asides interjected into a loud conversation about why, and why not, they should have left the pack, they plotted how they should get rid of the circling watcher above them.

"Right," announced Vero. "I'm going to see if I can get any more decent images of the ape-creatures below."

"Fine, a good idea. I shall sit here and save my energy."

As Vero walked over, peered over the margin of the cliff, and toyed with his diary, Merral leaned back next to the tiny pile of weapons and looked upward at the sky.

The bird drifted over Vero.

Still staring upward, Merral reached out slowly until his fingers wrapped around a flare tube. The bird seemed preoccupied with Vero and slowly descended to within four or five meters of him. Without looking at what he held in his hand, Merral rotated the two setting rings to give the shortest range and the maximum intensity. The flare wouldn't last for a long time, but it might be enough. If he was accurate.

One-handed, he pulled off the tab that protected the firing button.

"Hey, Merral!" Vero shouted, walking toward him, "wait until you see this."

Vero came over with his diary and put it down next to Merral, who rolled over as if to look at what his friend had in his hand.

"Ready?" whispered Vero.

"Yes."

Still staring in apparent fascination at the screen, Merral held onto the flare, carefully avoiding the recessed button. He listened until he was sure that he could hear the gentle sound of slow wing beats and see, faintly reflected on the polished screen, an image of the circling bird.

Suddenly, Merral rolled over, swung up the flare tube, aimed it, and pressed the firing button.

There was a brief, ear-piercing screech as the flare shot up, a brilliant flash of silver light, and a simultaneous bang.

As Merral leapt to his feet, he heard a falling, fluttering sound that ended in a gentle thud as the bird struck the rock nearby.

Vero bounded over and put a foot on its neck. The bird writhed and flapped; he twisted his foot sharply and the creature became still.

Vero bent down, picked up the buzzard by its wingtip, and dropped it on the rock at Merral's feet. It lay there as a curiously stiff, broken mass of brown feathers with no hint of motion.

"Pooh! It smells!" Vero said, wrinkling his nose. He bent over the bird and began poking it tentatively with a tiny pocketknife. As he did, Merral caught sight of a fine silver tracery that glinted in the sun.

"You see," Vero stated in flat, almost numbed tones, "it is a machine imitating something. A simulacrum." He looked sharply at Merral. "I presume this the first thing of its kind you have seen?"

"Of course! I have never dreamed of such a thing. The Technology Protocols forbid it. All our machines proclaim that they are machines."

"As throughout the Assembly. Since that far-off year of 2110 when the Rebellion ended." There was a strange, grim satisfaction in his voice.

Merral swallowed, squatted down, and looked in wonder and puzzlement at the creature. True, there were feathers and claws. But the beak was fixed half open, the eyes were empty holes, and beneath the vacant sockets was a pair of tiny, glinting lenses that ran back into wires.

Vero, who had been prodding gently with his knife, abruptly paused and muttered. Then he poked again. "An odd technology. Very odd. Look!"

Merral peered closer, seeing where Vero had stripped off a part of the skin and feathers and exposed a filigree of delicate silver wires wrapped over a gray substance in which thin white tubes were embedded. An unpleasant, rotting smell came from somewhere.

Vero glanced up at Merral with a worried expression. "It's not at all what I expected. There are bits of dead bird here."

"Dead?" Merral asked, suddenly aware where the foul odor was coming from.

He stared at the bird, catching sight of a tiny wisp of smoke. "Look out!"

There was a tiny crackling sound and a burst of yellow flame began to play around the body. Vero and Merral hurriedly stepped back as a black-edged golden flame flickered rapidly over the body, giving a cloud of acrid stinking smoke that twisted upward.

Flapping away the smoke with disgust, Merral stared at Vero. "What happened? Did you short-circuit it?"

"No. I don't think so." He looked thoughtfully at the fire, which was already sputtering out. "I think it was a mechanism to prevent us from taking it away and analyzing it."

"So they have clever machines, too. Do we have the power to do this?"

Vero was staring at where the abating flames were revealing a blackened skeleton over which melted wires drooped. "Extraordinary, quite extraordinary," he muttered, a great disgust evident in his tones. "The power? Maybe. The desire? Thank God, no. Disguise has never been our way. And to do it by using a dead bird? That is something very strange. No, far worse than strange. . . ." He tailed off.

"Well spotted," commented Merral, "I thought it was odd. It has been watching us for some time?"

"Yes. Probably listening, too. But good shooting on your part. You got the wing."

"I stunned it. I suppose it was that odd owl we saw."

"Yes." Vero nodded, still staring at the pile of wire and bone. "We should have realized it wasn't flesh and blood when we couldn't pick it up on the infrared."

"Of course."

Vero scratched his chin. "And what was the power source? I saw no fuel or energy cells. Odd."

Then he stood up and turned to Merral. "This bird thing is, it seems to me, every bit as significant as the other creatures. But a discussion about what it portends must wait. We *must* get a message out. Our own safety—even our survival—is quite immaterial."

Merral looked at him and realized that he was perfectly serious. Then, as he thought about what they had encountered that day, he realized that Vero's judgment was right. "I agree, reluctantly. The message must get out. That is all that matters."

Vero reached out and patted his arm. "Thank you for your support. Now we have only limited time. In under three hours or so the light will begin to go. Let us think through our options. We might be able to make a run for it now, down the other side and through the woods. How well can you walk?"

"I suspect short distances. But I am unenthusiastic. We might have to walk a long way for a diary to work. Possibly Herrandown, in fact. Not an easy task with enemies at our heels."

Vero frowned. "Well, it was one idea. Perhaps we must just hope that Anya realizes there is a problem when she calls us."

Then he sat down and fell silent.

•—◆—•

At five o'clock they divided the last of the water, had some food, and for the fiftieth time tried—and failed—to send a signal out. Then they returned to watching, Vero taking the west side of the plateau and Merral the east.

Merral, wishing, among many things, that they had more water, sat dry-mouthed near the edge of the cliff, moving forward every few minutes and peering down to the trees. There the three dark figures continued their seated vigil, and only the occasional slight movement revealed that they were not statues. The lower angle of the late-afternoon sun had enlarged their shadows and somehow seemed to increase their menace. As he stared at them, an alarming thought struck.

He rolled back away and walked slowly over the hot rock to the other side of the summit where Vero was squatting down, peering over the edge. Vero glanced back at him and gestured him down with an unmistakable urgency.

Merral's heart sank. He dropped to his knees and crawled alongside his friend.

Vero grimaced. "Well, we don't have to worry about making a run for it down here. Look."

Merral carefully looked down. Here, too, the sheer cliff face ended in a long, bare rock scree which, amid more large tumbled boulders, ran down under dense trees. Now, in the shadows of the trees and the boulders, five large figures were standing still, like distorted and blackened imitations of humanity. At their feet, equally immovable, half a dozen smaller, brown figures were clustered. Although they were too far away for him to be certain, and he was squinting against the light, the indelible impression Merral had was that all of them were staring up at the cliff.

For a moment, Merral could say little, so great was the internal turmoil this scene caused him. A part of him, detached from the cold waves and billows of emotion that buffeted him, was able to recognize that he was again deeply afraid. *What I am feeling today is true fear. What I have only read about before, I now experience.* This time, though, he knew it was different; with the cockroach-beast he had been scared, but he had had no time to think about his emotions; he had to act. *Now, I have fear and cannot act, and I can feel the fear seeping into my mind and corroding my thinking.* But, even as he thought this, another part of his mind intruded and said that he must think, and that now was not the time for analysis of his feelings.

He swallowed. "Yes. Interesting. Eight ape-creatures and six cockroach-beasts. I don't suppose sentinel training gives you any idea what to do next?"

"No," Vero muttered. "Not at all. The vision Jorgio had seems the best guide here: watch, stand firm, and hope. And, at the last, to die well and take as many with you as you can."

"I hate to add trouble to trouble, but before long, perhaps ten minutes or so, my side of the hill will be in total shadow."

"Shadow!" Vero winced. "I had forgotten. They might prefer that to darkness. I was hoping for another hour or two at least. What a mess we are in!"

"Perhaps we can hold them off until tomorrow with stones."

"Perhaps. Would they see one of these flares from space?"

"If they knew where to look they would see one. But if they knew where to look they wouldn't need a flare."

"We need a bigger flare, then." Vero screwed his eyes up. "Wait! There may be a way. If I can remember—"

"Listen!" Merral interrupted, as from over the eastern side of the hill came the faintest rattle of stone on stone.

They ran to the edge. Below, in the darkness of the ravine they had come up, two of the dark ape-creatures were climbing up with smooth, confident moves, their arms and feet working together in a powerful and coordinated motion.

Without hesitation, Merral picked a brick-sized basalt fragment and hurled it down. It hit the wall just above the head of the leading ape-creature and shattered. There was an angry rumbling growl, and the creature paused in its ascent and looked up.

They were separated by no more than twenty meters, and Merral could see the face clearly despite the shadows. It seemed to him that, despite its flattened appearance, the face was more human than ape. The large brown eyes seemed to stare at him, and Merral decided that if the face conveyed any emotion at all, it was of a cold intelligence and a determined and calculating hatred. He knew with absolute certainty that it was useless to try to communicate with this creature.

"Throw another!" cried Vero, letting fly with a rock himself. This, however, was way off target and clattered away harmlessly down the ravine.

Merral looked around and found, a few strides away, a large rock slab, the size of a kitchen tabletop but thicker.

"Quick, Vero, help me push this."

Together they tugged and heaved until the slab was at the cliff edge. Then, putting their shoulders to it, they pushed until it started to hang over the edge.

From below came a high-pitched series of wordless squeals and grunts that conveyed alarm. Merral pushed and suddenly the block began to wobble. He pushed again and the rock fell over the edge.

There was a series of booming and echoing crashes as the slab fell and bounced down the cliff. They peered over the edge in time to see it displace other rocks and cannonade down the gloom of the ravine in a gathering tumult of fragments. At the bottom of the cliff, the debris cloud exploded outward down the scree in a turbulent dark cloud of fragments. Stray rocks could be seen careening clear of the debris flow and bouncing up into the trees.

Then the rising dust cloud covered their view.

"Very satisfactory," Vero announced in admiring tones, as the sound of crashing and clattering blocks died away.

Merral, nonplussed at the effect of combining one large rock, gravity, and a fifty-meter drop, said nothing. *What have I maimed and injured now?*

As if in answer to his question, a howl of agony came from below. Although there were no words, it seemed to Merral that it conveyed an intelligence greater than any animal had. He shivered.

Slowly, the dust died away and they could see one creature standing at the edge of the trees apparently unharmed, while another sat nearby nursing a bloodied and useless arm. Of the third, nothing could be seen until Vero pointed out a red smear under a gray block of rock.

"One ape-creature and a cockroach-beast dead so far. Another wounded." Vero's voice was dry.

"Ugh! You make it sound like a sport that way."

"Unintentionally. But men once did, you know."

"I know. 'Saul has killed his thousands, David his ten thousands.' But that was another age of the world, Vero. I do not rejoice. I am answerable to their maker for those that I have killed."

Vero bowed his head slightly. "I am rebuked by your sensitivity. But I do not think that you will stand in judgment before their maker."

"You mean . . . ?"

"Simply, I do not believe that God alone made them. I believe their maker may have far more to answer for at the Final Judgment than you."

"You may be right," Merral said, wondering whether that diminished the magnitude of his killing them. "May the Most High grant us the leisure and security to debate the point further. But how do things stand now?"

"Well, this side now seems to me much less climbable than it was."

Merral looked down. Sure enough, the top part of the ravine was now cleared of boulders and was vertical for the last ten meters.

Vero rubbed his face with his hands. "Now, it has come to me that there is a slight hope. But only a slight one and it is fraught with problems."

"Go on."

Vero tapped a finger on his diary. "Do you realize how much energy these things use in the ten years between energy cell replacement?"

"No. A lot, though."

"Yes. Well, there is a way of realizing it all, of venting it all in a few milliseconds."

"You'd have an awesome explosion. I've never heard that."

"I was told it was the fourth best-kept secret in the Assembly."

"The other three are?"

"I don't know. The third is probably what the first two are." Vero's face twisted into a grin and Merral had to laugh.

"The results are spectacular?"

"So it's claimed. Mostly visible light, but a lot of electromagnetic wavelengths get a hefty kick. I was told you could see it on the moon. If you did it on Ancient Earth, that is." He paused, stroking his diary thoughtfully. "Non-nuclear. Just. I think that's what they said."

"You think?"

"Well," he sounded embarrassed, "the whole technique was given as a sort of passing comment at the end of a lecture. A piece of curious information. Any brighter ideas?"

"No."

"Well, I'll try it. It will take some time to do. It's not an easy trick. For obvious reasons."

"So I would hope."

"Quite. Now, Merral, if I may, can I download all my data onto your machine? I wonder if you could check the other side. Just in case they try the same trick."

Merral handed over his diary, and as Vero made the orders for a full data download to be made, he went over to the western side and peered into the gathering shadows, trying to see if there was any change in the positions of the ape-creatures and cockroach-beasts. Unnervingly, they were standing in silence exactly as he had last seen them. In frustration—and was it also fear?—he threw a block of rock at them, but it fell short and clattered away into the trees with no effect.

He returned to Vero.

"Still there and still out of range. But what's your plan?"

Vero looked up, his eyes showing tiredness. "We need to wait for darkness so we can guarantee being seen. If I can trigger the reaction, we will have a short delay. We find a spot where the energy can be channeled upward. Then, we get down onto that ledge at the south end. Put our fingers in our ears and, well—let it go. Hopefully, one of your satellites will notice a firework that size. You think so?"

"If it is as big as you say, I should think so. We are always on the alert for forest fires or volcanic eruptions. The Northern Menaya Monitor will pick it up unless it's helping Perena watch the rift volcanics. But will they act on it?"

"Ah. A key point. Will they?"

"They may send someone over."

There was a silence and Vero looked doubtful.

He knows, thought Merral, *as I know, that it probably will not be enough.* But as he considered Vero's suggestion, an idea came to him.

"There might be a way of making it of more benefit to us," he suggested.

Vero raised an eyebrow. "How so?"

"If the model you proposed for their interception of our signals is correct, then a blast of such a size might overload their blocking system. At least briefly. If we could get a message out immediately afterward . . ."

"*Yes!*" Vero nodded urgently. "That might work. Let's do that.

Anyway, data download is now complete. I feel happier about losing my diary now."

He handed back Merral's diary and slid open the access panel on his own. He started muttering to himself. "Now you set the toggles. Blue to green, yellow striped to orange . . . and that down, that up. Or is it the other way about? It was such a joke when I was told it. The most useless piece of information ever. Now I close the back and reset. Thus. Now, input the following codes." His forehead puckered in thought.

"Diary! Go into deep internal level four. Password is Gedaliah. Reveal battery temperature. Now, cycle energy cells one through eight."

The metallic voice that responded seemed startling in the quietness. "Under current parameters this will eventually give potentially dangerous thermal conditions in energy cells. Require authorization for procedure."

"This is the first tricky bit. Diary! Password is Eleazar! Aha, looks good."

"Authorization accepted."

"Proceed."

Vero sighed and slid the diary back on his belt.

"So far so good. Let us hope that after that failed assault, our enemies stay down at the foot of the hill for some time."

"How long before it works?"

"I can't remember. A couple of hours, at least. Anyway, we can't do anything until dark. I suggest we get some more images of those cockroach-beasts through the fieldscope. If we do get out, such evidence will be invaluable. Then we just sit and wait. And pray."

• ◆ •

An hour later Vero came over to where Merral was lying down, peering over the edge at the immobile tableau of creatures below.

"How are things on your side?" Merral asked, drawing back from the margin.

"Only the one ape-creature left; the injured one has gone somewhere else."

"Your diary?"

"At least thirty minutes, I'd guess, but it is definitely heating up."

Merral gestured westward where the remains of the morning's storm clouds hung on the horizon as the last of the rain emptied itself into the wastes on Interior Menaya. The red sphere of the sun was dropping rapidly toward them. "A fine sunset," he commented.

"I would prefer dawn," sighed Vero.

"And so would I. I feel that this side is where the attack will come from. It's a wider front. I can see various places for them to try and get up. But hopefully they will wait for darkness."

Vero got down on his knees and moved cautiously to the edge of the plateau. The setting sun had put a warm orange glow on the rocks and at the same time exaggerated both the darkness and the length of the shadows so that it was not easy to see what was happening down below among the trees and rocks.

"There are more," hissed Vero.

"Yes, I didn't feel it worth telling you," Merral added as he joined him. There were now at least six of the tall dark figures standing rigid and staring up at them, and perhaps slightly more of the cockroach-beasts, their shorter stature making them hard to distinguish from the shadows of the rocks. *It is unnatural,* Merral decided. *Both types behave like men in many ways and yet they seem to have little individuality. To act as regimented machines is not at all like us. What creatures are they?* He wondered whether Vero was right in thinking that they were modified humans and, if so, what had been taken out of them— or put in—to make them so different.

"Well, I hope they stay there longer," Vero said as he backed away. "Let me know if anything happens. I'm going to sit back from the edge and check the diary."

Merral lay down and waited, trying not to stare at the setting sun lest it damage any night vision. Finally, the lower edge of the sun dropped behind the clouds and a warm twilight started to descend. He leaned forward, stared down into the gloom, and saw that nothing had changed.

Something caught his attention. Hanging back behind the ape-creatures and all but hidden in the gloom under the trees was something new. He peered at it, recognizing another anthropoid figure, but one with a different, smaller, and somehow more familiar shape. As he strained his eyes Merral felt that, despite a size midway between the ape-creatures and the cockroach-beasts, there was somehow a presence about the figure as if it was superior to those beasts: almost, it seemed, as if it was their master.

"Vero," he called out, "there's something odd—"

There was a violent hissing and bubbling next to him. Something spat angrily and stung his right hand.

"*Get back!*" Vero shouted.

Merral threw himself backward, landing awkwardly and painfully on his hip. He was aware of a strange heat around and a smell of burning in the air.

Vero was ducked down behind him, pointing with an urgent hand at the lip of the cliff. An arm's length from where Merral had been lying the rock edge was glowing a livid scarlet and spitting vapor and drops of lava. Bubbles of rock were forming and bursting with an intense popping noise.

"What was *that?*" Merral asked as the color of the rock returned slowly to black.

Vero nodded, as if to himself. "One of a number of things capable of transmitting enough energy to melt rock. An infrared laser, a portable pulsed particle beam, something like that. Probably would just explode flesh and blood."

"So they are no longer unarmed." Sucking his hand where a small drop of molten rock had struck, Merral cautiously got to his feet, and together they moved back into the middle of the plateau. Could he be certain of what he thought he had seen? He was about to speak when there was a pulsing on his wrist.

Merral pulled his diary off his belt so fast that he nearly dropped it. On the screen, Anya was staring at him from her laboratory bench.

Thank you Lord, thought Merral in exultation, *she's called early.* "Anya! Anya!" he shouted at the diary.

To his horror, he saw her face acquire a blank, puzzled look.

Her voice was clear. "Say, what's up with you guys? Merral's location signal goes off. Now, I'm having problems even making contact."

Vero was beside him now, peeping over his shoulder at the image.

At least, Merral comforted himself, *she will realize that there is enough of a problem to call for a search tomorrow.*

She stared at the screen. "You know guys, I'm getting worried."

"That's it Anya! Go on. You get worried! *Really worried!*" Merral heard himself speaking aloud.

Without warning, another voice sounded from the diary. Although it was weirdly familiar, for a moment Merral could not recognize it.

"Sorry, Anya. We have had diary problems. Some trick of Vero's, trying to transmit data. Seems to have fused circuits on both."

Merral heard a gasp from beside him. "*Now* what are we up against?"

"Yes," the familiar voice went on, "we lost both vision and location."

"Okay, Merral. Apart from that, how is it going?"

Merral? In a dreadful, appalling moment of revelation, Merral understood why the voice was familiar. It was his own voice!

"It's not me!" Merral yelled in fury, "Anya, *it's not me!*"

"Hi, Anya," came from the diary. It was Vero's voice, but so convincing that Merral had to stare at the wide-open mouth of the startled figure next to him to be sure he wasn't hearing his friend. "Sorry. I just used too much power. Stupid sentinel trick. Anyway, we are fine."

Merral was on the point of saying something when Vero silenced him with a sharp wave of the arm.

"Oh yes," went on the voice from the diary, "we are fine. We are beyond Daggart Lake. We'll call you tomorrow night. We aim for pickup the day after. Look, we'd better shut down now, while we still have a signal. Good-bye."

It was Vero to the syllable.

The machine spoke again. "I agree. This is Merral saying good night, too."

There was a faint look of consternation on Anya's face.

"Well, okay. Sleep well. Talk to you tomorrow. Bye for now."

The screen went dark. There was a long silence, and finally Vero spoke, his numbed voice suggesting he was still absorbing the impact of what he had overheard. "Well, there have been a couple of times today when I thought we might get out of this alive. I am now repenting my optimism. It was very clever."

"Clever? It was diabolical!"

"Exactly so."

"How did they do it?"

"They have been monitoring us. Easy to do. They have had hours to prepare a voice duplicate. That will be how they did Maya Knella, of course. Anya said it was a bad transmission."

"You mean they *faked* a Gate call?"

Vero laughed quietly and bitterly. "Merral, don't you see? Whoever—or whatever—is behind this can do almost anything. They can bend and break genes to suit themselves, they can create imitation birds, and they can mimic people. Intercepting interstellar communications is a little thing. And not only do they have the means, they have the will." He seemed to shudder. "They appear to have no barriers. I would have to think carefully, but I am certain that they have broken all of the Technology Protocols and some that were never even thought of."

"I had no idea. . . ."

"No, neither had I," Vero replied, looking troubled and seeming to struggle with something. Then, without warning, he slammed a fist into the palm of his hand.

"No! We will not yield without a fight." His face acquired a determined look. "They are not immune. We will stand firm. By grace, we may win through. But everything hinges on us calling in help. We can't rely on Anya anymore. We are on our own."

He struck his fist in his palm again in resolve and turned back to Merral. "What do you think?"

"Vero, I am reeling from this morning. And this afternoon." Then Merral paused, thinking of the right words to express what he wanted to say. "But I will gladly die here if we need to. We must fight. For the Assembly and for the King."

Vero clapped him on the back. "Good! I feel better listening to you. We may have had nearly twelve millennia of peace, but if we have to fight a last stand here then I feel you—at least—will do no worse than any heroes of the distant past. And I will do what I can."

"We will try." Merral added thoughtfully, "I—well, I suppose my own feelings are mixed. I do not mind, or fear, dying, but I do not relish it. And I wish I had not killed."

"I understand, but we must do what we are called to do. Anyway, let us prepare for an early attack. I think you had best take charge of the weapons. These things seem to be your expertise, not mine."

"As you wish," Merral answered as Vero crouched back down over his diary.

Merral went over to their few belongings, put on his jacket, and stuck the two remaining flares in one pocket and the tranquilizer gun with its two cartridges in another. He grasped the knife and clicked the blade in and out, reflecting that this—plus all the rocks he could throw—was all they had. Against adversaries who outmatched them in numbers, technology, and weapons, he knew it wasn't enough.

As he grappled with the thought, he turned to watch the sunset. There was a narrow gap in the clouds at the bottom, and in it a tiny ruby-colored sliver of the sun shone out. As Merral watched, it slipped down below the horizon and, almost instantly, the shadows about him seemed to thicken.

For a strange moment, an extraordinary desire seemed to seize hold of Merral. It was a desire to lament his lot and his pending death, to grieve for himself and Vero and for the loss his saddened family and Isabella would feel. At the heart of this compelling desire was a dark yearning to give in and to admit that the whole thing was hopeless. As

CHRIS WALLEY

he grappled with the emotion, Merral tried, and failed, to label it, until suddenly the word came to him. *Despair*, he thought with a sudden recognition. *That's what I am close to. Today I have met four strange things: ape-creatures, cockroach-beasts, terror, and despair. And will death be the fifth stranger I meet?*

Then he looked up into the sky and saw that the stars were coming out and that southward the six beacons of the Gate were becoming plain. Heartened, he praised the All Highest; hope returned and the despair fled.

As he turned to go back to Vero, he remembered that the last warrior to set out to fight for the Assembly had been Lucas Ringell in 2110. He had gone to the Centauri Station to take on Jannafy and the rebels, well trained, surrounded by his troops, and armed and suited with the best defensive and offensive equipment the Assembly could devise.

And as Merral remembered that, he was suddenly aware that all he had was two flares in one jacket pocket, a tranquilizer gun in the other, and a knife. Not one of them had even been designed as a weapon.

Suddenly, the irony of the situation struck him and, in spite of all his fears, Merral smiled.

CHAPTER 15

As Merral approached him, Vero looked up, his face inscrutable in the gloom. "Nearly there," he said, his voice an urgent whisper. "It's at 37.5 degrees and lots of warnings."

Vivid red letters were scrolling across Vero's diary screen.

"Ten minutes before it is at the right temperature. Perhaps . . ."

Merral noted the uncertainty.

Then Vero spoke again. "Can you prepare a message for transmission the moment this goes off? Continuously repeating. Every emergency frequency."

Merral slid the diary off his belt and chose his words. "Diary! Prepare for a transmission on the maximum emergency frequencies and with maximum output and repetition of the following message: 'Emergency. Under attack from non-Assembly forces. Request immediate pickup from transmission location. Landing zone 100 by 160 meters and flat.'"

When, he wondered, was the last time—other than in some play or reenactment of the Rebellion—that anyone had uttered anything like those words *under attack from non-Assembly forces?*

He paused the diary and looked at Vero. "And how do I warn about the possibility that they will use weapons? My military terminology is minimal."

"Ah. How about adding, 'Attackers have beam weapons capable of damage to ships'?"

"Thanks," replied Merral as he laid the message out and checked it. Then he looked around. Night was falling quickly and it was already too dark to distinguish colors. A strange, unwelcome thought came to him. For the first time in his life, night was no longer a welcome, restful darkness in which the stars and the Gate shone, but a time when things moved, when evil stirred. What did one of the Psalms say? "You will not fear the terror of the night." With a barely restrained shiver, he realized that he now understood it.

Vero interrupted his reflections. "Up to 38.5 degrees and more warnings."

"What happens then?" Merral asked as he scanned the gloomy edge of the plateau, his mind already halfway to investing shadows with motion.

"We walk over to the ledge there." Vero gestured south. "You drop over, get under the ledge, and sit ready to hit the transmit button. I pull out the safety fuse—tricky in the dark—give a final code word, and the thing goes into a chain reaction. I put it down and run and join you. We put our fingers in our ears and close our eyes tight. And pray."

"*How* long after the last code before we get the bang?"

"Not long."

"How long?"

"Er, ten seconds. Perhaps twenty."

"You've *forgotten?*"

"Yes."

After a moment, Merral laughed. "Oh the Glory! What a useless pair we are! I'm glad I believe that the Most High graciously governs our affairs. That the fate of the Assembly might hinge on us alone would fill me with extreme terror!"

Vero echoed the laughter. "An amusing thought. I must—" He stiffened. "Wait! I hear something. It's too soon. We aren't ready."

From the western edge of the summit, where the top of the plateau was a black silhouette against the glowing and simmering purple sky, there came a faint scrabbling noise. The thought came to Merral that only brief hours ago he would have interpreted such a sound as that of a fox or badger. Now, and here, it could only be one thing.

On instinct, Merral thrust his diary to Vero. "You send the signal. I may be busy."

Then, cautiously in the dark, he ran toward the edge. Well to the left of where he had been before, he dropped down onto his knees and slid warily to the edge. He peered over carefully, half expecting to feel the hot and fatal blast of the beam weapon.

The sheer flank of the cliff was now in deep gloom, illuminated only by the waning sunset, and for a moment Merral could see nothing. He was about to run back and get the fieldscope when, with a quiver of alarm, he suddenly saw that, down to his right at the base of the slope, there was movement.

Within moments, he knew that there were at least three ape-creatures moving up the cliff. Their movements were measured and unhurried, and there was a confidence that suggested the darkness did not bother them.

Merral slid back away from the edge and turned toward Vero. "They're on their way up," he called. His mouth was now appallingly dry and he was aware of his hands shaking.

"Try to give me another five minutes."

"I'll try."

Merral slid back to the cliff margin, lay down on the rough rock surface, and prayed for help and protection. Within moments there was a further noise from the cliff below.

Suddenly, Merral felt a strange calm descend upon him. He knew what he had to do. Making sure there were some stones within reach, he coolly pulled out one of the flares and, acting from memory, rotated the settings onto short range and long duration. He primed the tranquilizer gun, flicked the safety catch off, and put it down on the ground with a surprisingly steady hand. Then he picked up the flare and waited until the first of the ape-creatures was within a few moments of reaching the top. He aimed and fired, raising a hand immediately to protect his sight.

There was a loud whoosh, and as a dazzling silver light flooded the rock surface, he glimpsed the creature turn toward him, the white teeth of its open mouth gleaming in the brilliant metallic light. As the flare struck the rock above its head, the creature instinctively lifted an arm to protect itself. Then, as the incandescent flame slithered down onto it, it gave a wailing scream and fell backward with arms flailing. It plummeted downward; the screaming ended with the sound of something smacking in a ghastly, sodden way against rock.

"Forgive me, Lord," Merral muttered, appalled at both the act and his own coolness.

Down at the base of the cliff, the flickering, sinking flare illuminated two more climbing ape-creatures. In a curiously detached way, Merral seemed to watch himself as he coldly picked up the tranquilizer gun and sighted on the next creature. As its big hands reached for a rock ledge, he pulled the trigger. There was a hiss as the dart fired. Merral ducked his head down low and flicked the last cartridge into the chamber.

He looked up, only to see that his target continuing its upward climb.

I must have missed, he realized dully, and sighted again, anxious to make the most of the fading light of the flare. As he squinted through the eyepiece he saw the thing suddenly twist its body. Then it leaned backward, flung out a desperate arm to steady itself, missed, and toppled down the cliff. This time there was a heavy thud, a slithering sound, and a succession of softer thuds. Simultaneously heartened and sickened, Merral risked a longer glance below. In the ebbing light of the flare, he could make out two other huge forms moving to the base of the cliff below and starting the climb upward.

He was reaching for the rocks, intending to throw them, when he suddenly became aware of a sizzling sound, as if he had his ear next to a frying pan. Immediately to his right the line of the cliff edge began to hiss and glow in an intense cherry red color. Merral jerked himself backward. A whiff of scalding, dusty air enveloped him and he saw that where he had been lying was now a mass of bubbling molten rock. He crawled away from the edge carefully. He had one flare left, and after that, only rocks and the blade. But if he couldn't get near the edge, even rocks would be little use.

How was Vero doing? Merral looked backward. In the darkness, he could just make him out bending over the diary's illuminated screen, his face lit by a furious red glow. *Hurry up,* he mouthed, *oh hurry.*

Beyond Vero something moved.

His heart thudding, Merral strained his eyes, scanning the starlit blackness of the surface. Along the northern edge of the summit the brilliance of the five bright stars of Reitel's Crown caught his eye. *I imagined it.* There could be no threat there: it was too steep.

The stars were blotted out.

"Vero, behind you!" Merral shouted, realizing that, once again, they had underestimated their opponents.

He began to run forward, aware that he had to put himself between Vero and the attackers. Still moving, he reached for the last flare and fired it. As he pressed the button he regretted it; the flare hit the ground and screeched along the rock surface before bursting into a blinding silvery flame. Beyond its blaze, two dark gigantic figures—each like some animated caricature of a man—were fiercely illuminated. Vero turned, realized his peril, and began to run to the south end of the cliff.

As Vero ran past him, Merral dropped to one knee, braced himself, and fired the remaining cartridge in the tranquilizer gun at the front creature. Seeing them for the first time at eye level, he now realized how big the ape-creatures were. It was a good shot and Merral saw it hit home in the chest. But his satisfaction was short-lived as the creature ripped out the cylinder, gave a horrid yell, and threw it away.

Suddenly he was conscious that behind him, Vero was shouting. "Now, Merral! Now!"

Merral began to run unsteadily over the rough surface after him. As he ran, he was aware that the creatures were following him, skirting round the flare. Ahead of him, he saw that Vero, illuminated only by the fading glow of the western sky and the light of the sputtering flare, was now standing at the very end of the cliff. Merral came to a stop next to him, aware of the drop down to the ledge just beyond and sensing more than seeing, far below that, the darkness of the plains and the feeble glint of the Lannar River.

"N–nearly!" Vero gasped. "It's almost on overload. When I shout, jump. Not too far. Hold them off until then."

"Okay. Tell me when."

Marveling again at his steady tone, Merral turned to face his enemies. The two pursuing him had come to a halt next to each other. They stood, just a few meters away, silhouetted against the dying glow of the flare like an enormous matching pair of bizarre statues. To his left the sky bore the last faint purple glow of the sunset. The creatures began slowly edging toward him, their steps almost matching, as if in some crazy dance. Over to the left and behind them, Merral could suddenly make out more movement. At least five of the ape creatures had now made that ascent. A cold dread seemed to grab hold of him.

The left-hand creature facing him made another move. Merral, still waiting for Vero's word, hurled the empty tranquilizer gun as hard as he could at it. The creature ducked and the gun went over its head and rattled to the ground beyond. Merral pulled out the bush knife, clicked it open, and held it out in front of him. Suddenly, on a wild impulse, he decided he should not fight these beings in silence. Their very monstrosity aroused his wrath and indignation.

"Creatures!" he yelled as loud as he could, his dry voice somehow echoing on the open summit. The shadowy forms seemed to freeze. "This is not your world! It belongs to the Lord Messiah, the Slain Lamb, the One who holds the stars of the Assembly in his right hand! In his Name I defy you! Go, or I will slay you!"

There was a cracked but enthusiastic "Amen!" from behind him. Then, as the words died away in the darkness, the light of the flare sank until it was little more than a glow.

Was there a hesitation among the creatures? Merral wasn't sure, but they made no move forward. Did the value of such challenges come in improving the morale of the defender or in intimidating that of the attacker? Or was it just something that had to be done? After all, had not David so challenged Goliath? Merral marveled at the irrelevancy of his questions and pushed them away. *How do I fight these things?* Positively, unlike the cockroach-beasts, they were unarmored. Negatively, their long limbs meant that they could grab his throat while all he could contact would be their hands and arms. And, if he did get close in, he knew he ran the risk of being crushed. *My only assets are speed and a sharp blade.*

Abruptly, the two creatures ahead separated and began to swing round at Merral from both sides. *A simultaneous attack,* he thought bleakly. He was aware of an urgent muttering from Vero behind him, as if his words could encourage the diary into self-destruction. The two were now barely an arm's length away. He could smell them now—an unnatural decaying smell, as if something within them wasn't working properly.

I must protect Vero. "Vero, stay where you are!" he shouted. "I have to know where you are!"

Merral took two steps to the right, aware that his ankle hurt him, and was gratified to see that the two ape-creatures followed him with a perfect symmetry. *Good, they want me.* He was relieved that he could treat it like a Team-Ball game. *That's right, don't think of what is involved.*

"Right!" shouted Vero. "Nearly there! Very nearly! Oh, come on!"

The flare was out now and the only light was the dull waning glow from the western skies. Merral stretched out his right hand and swung the blade in as broad an arc as he could. He felt a strange certainty that Vero had failed, but it almost seemed irrelevant. His one task now was to grapple with these things. With a low throbbing grunt, the creature on the left lunged forward.

Merral leapt backward and sideways to the right, sweeping hard with his blade at the same time. As the creature lurched past him, his blade connected with a forelimb, biting deep into soft, sinewy tissue, clinking on—and through—bone and out through flesh. There was a high-pitched scream and something struck the ground at Merral's feet with a sickening thud. He jerked the blade back, but before he had recovered his balance he saw, outlined against the stars, the second creature charging at him with its arms flailing wide.

Merral threw himself to the left, ducking low as he did, and the outstretched arm swung over him, foul rough fingers glancing over his back. He slashed at the creature, but the knife arced only through air and struck nothing. He staggered to his feet, aware of his first attacker writhing amid screams on the ground. The second ape-creature lurched to a halt, wheeled round clumsily, and came back toward him, its head low and its arms wide as if to claw him. Merral dodged again as a long arm swung out widely at him in the blackness. Despite his efforts to dodge it, the flat of the great hand connected with his shoulder. The force of the blow sent him reeling onto the hard, uneven rock.

Before he could regain his footing, he was aware that that creature was standing astride him, its feet almost touching his face, the stink of its fur enveloping him. Amid an awful bellowing, the creature raised a shadowy foot high, and Merral had a sudden terrible remembrance of the crushed remains of Spotback. As the foot hung there above him, Merral unhesitatingly put both hands on the knife handle. With every bit of energy he possessed, he lunged upward with the blade to where the great torso blocked out the stars.

"The Lamb!" he cried, amid a chill anger. The blade plunged deep and the creature's bellowing flowed into a hideous scream. It toppled over and the momentum tore the blade out of Merral's hands. As he tried to roll clear, a hot fluid pumped out all over him and a rough, stinking fur thrashed against his face. Everything went black. Then Merral was aware that he was free of the writhing hulk and Vero was tugging at him and yelling to make himself heard over the screaming.

"It's fused! It's fused!"

Wiping blood out of his eyes, Merral staggered onto all fours. He was aware of Vero throwing the diary and he saw it spin over his head as a pulsing, angry red block. As he moved toward the edge, Merral glimpsed in the red beating glow other figures now on the plateau. Large and small.

An army.

There was the ledge. He half jumped and half fell down onto it. Vero was pushing him down under the lip and he rolled in. Gasping for breath, aware of blood in his mouth, Merral dully remembered what was supposed to happen and turned face down against the rough rock. Then he closed his eyes and put his fingers in his wet ears. This was the end.

"Lord, I commit myself to you," Merral said quietly. He realized he had never properly said farewell to Isabella or his—

The world stopped.

Sense, feeling, thought, time, *life*. All ended.

At first there was only light. Brilliant light, the light of creation, a light that seemed to penetrate through rock and bone and eyelids. There was nothing else, and it seemed to Merral inconceivable that there ever had been anything else or could be anything else. Then there was the noise. A deafening noise on every frequency from the lowest vibration to the highest screech. A noise that bypassed the eardrums to pummel every bone, muscle, and organ in his body. Then there was the wind: a wind as solid as flesh that tore at his clothes and whipped at his hair. A wind that seemed to want to blow him off the ledge to Herrandown.

Gradually, the light, noise, and wind ebbed away.

•◆•

Merral opened his eyes slowly and rubbed them to see around him a bizarre winter landscape of snowlike ash lit by a diffuse and flickering red light. A pale figure coated in a fine gray debris coat was squatting beside him stabbing at the diary.

Over the ringing in his ears Merral could—somehow—make out Vero yelling, "Transmit! Transmit!"

He looked up to see a billowing column of dust high above them, glowing in lurid oranges and yellows and casting strange, pulsating shadows over the landscape. In the background, he could hear the diary echoing the message. "*Emergency! Under attack from non-Assembly forces. . . ."* It was getting through! *". . . have beam weapons capable of damage to ships. Emergency message ends!"*

Vero turned an ash-plastered face toward him. "It's gone successfully!" he shouted with a sort of manic triumph. In the background Merral could hear the message being repeated. Vero was speaking again now, his voice seeming distant and distorted. "You look awful, Merral. Truly awful." He reached out and carefully touched Merral's shoulder. "Are you all right?"

"Yes," Merral answered slowly, shaking his head to try and clear the noise out of his ears. "I think so. But you look like a corpse." Suddenly he heard a voice, crackling and varying in volume, coming out of the diary.

"Merral D'Avanos, Assembly ship *Nesta Lamaine* has received your message. Fireball seen. Captain is evaluating your situation now. Are you okay?"

Vero handed him the diary. Merral wiped the dust off the screen and spat to clear his mouth.

"Yes. Yes. Just about. We are on the south end of the cliff—Uh-oh!"

The screen was flashing the "Unable to transmit message" sign. He showed it to Vero who merely shook his head. "As I expected. A temporary overload. Well, we got our message out."

The diary crackled to life. "We have lost your signal. Captain advises we are coming down to you. Standard Operating Procedure is to do a Farholme orbit first. This will give two hours—"

"Two hours!" Vero shouted.

"—before we can get to you. Just hang on. Out." The signal light faded.

Merral tabbed the transmit button and shouted at the slab, "Two hours is too long! Forget Standard Operating Procedure! Make it faster!"

But the diary refused to transmit.

The gloom was descending again as above them the eerie light was fading. Merral was aware of Vero waving his hands in protest. "Can't they get in faster?"

"I know! The only ship around, this *Nesta Lamaine*, must be in high orbit or something. But I'm surprised. . . . Can we survive?"

Vero blew his nose. "Maybe, but only if there are no more attacks. You're sure you are all right, Merral? There's blood on you."

In response, Merral tried sitting up. He ran his hands over his chest and felt them come away in a disgusting mixture of dust and blood. "Praises, I think it's not mine."

"Let's get back on the main ledge then," Vero said. "We need to see if our attackers have gone."

They scrambled slowly back onto the main rock ledge of the plateau. The light from the dust cloud had almost dissipated now, but they could see that the once flat surface now bore a gentle circular depression a half a dozen meters across that was glowing a dull crimson color. They were alone on the summit.

In the growing darkness, Vero's voice was quieter now. "Those ape-creatures are very agile. To get up the northern face that we thought was impossible was an extraordinary feat."

"Yes," answered Merral slowly, suddenly feeling incredibly weary. His throat was dry, his ankle hurt, and he felt unspeakably sickened by what had happened.

As the night seemed to slip back around them, Vero coughed and spat. "Ugh! Dust! Incidentally, Merral, do you realize that you may have done what Thomas wanted you to do?"

"Sorry? Oh, you mean kill whatever had taken Spotback? Well, if it was one of those—and I hope there aren't many more—then maybe I did just that." In fact, he found the idea of little comfort.

For a few minutes they were silent. Some of the dust slowly settled around them, but much remained in the air, dulling and diffusing the light from the stars. Eventually, Vero spoke slowly. "Assuming—just assuming—they can rescue us, we must do some urgent thinking."

"You mean what happens next?"

"Yes. What we do. Earth must be told: told fast and told securely." But he said no more and fell silent.

•◆•

A few minutes later, Merral's eye was caught by a moving beam of light cutting up through the dusty air from the ground just to the west of them. Carefully, a new dread rising in his exhausted mind, he and Vero picked their way slowly over the ash-draped rocks to the western edge of the hill. Not far away under the trees, a light was drifting leisurely toward them, swinging from side to side as if searching out a pathway for feet between the rocks and tree roots. Behind it, Merral could just make out dark figures, and from their height and gait he knew they were not human.

Vero sighed. "More trouble. Not our rescuers."

"Yes," Merral answered, surprised how drained of emotion he felt. "They will be here in a few minutes. Watch, stand firm, and hope."

"The hope bit is getting harder to do. And nearly two hours before the ship arrives. . . . I wish now we had got a full message out." Vero gave a little grunt. "Huh, I really thought we were going to make it."

Then he reached out and patted Merral affectionately on the back. "But let me say—while I have the chance—that you did wonders here tonight. Remarkable. That challenge. Epic stuff. Worthy of a painting in the style of the Thirteenth Millennium romantics: 'Forester D'Avanos Faces the Ape-Creatures Alone.'"

For a brief moment, Merral felt like pointing out that a really authentic picture would have to be done in shades of blacks and dark grays. But he hurt too much.

Vero seemed to drift away into silence, and Merral, torn by his own memories of the day, tried to put his thoughts in order. They had a few minutes yet; the moving light had yet to approach the edge of the trees. Merral prepared himself to crawl to the edge and hurl rocks down until—inevitably—he was overwhelmed.

Then, abruptly, the light went off. In the distance below, near where the beam had been, Merral could hear voices, but what they said, and even whether or not they were human, he found impossible to tell. He began to crawl toward the cliff edge, wondering if he could find any rocks in the darkness to throw.

"Listen!" whispered Vero.

At first Merral could hear only the ringing in his ears.

Then he was able to make out a faint whistling noise in the air coming from the south. He stared into the darkness. Whatever it was could not be the rescue ship; that had to be ninety minutes or more away on the other side of Farholme. For a moment, he saw nothing.

Low in the southern sky the hazily twinkling stars were obscured by a shape that was growing larger every second. Merral, seized by a feeling of stark horror, stared at the blackness as the expanding silhouette rose above the cliff.

Then from his belt his diary bleeped and a dry male voice echoed around. "This is Assembly ship *Nesta Lamaine!* Prepare to board immediately! Beware hot external surfaces!"

As the shadow eclipsed more stars, four columns of white flame burst out like waterfalls of light, throwing up dust into the air. Blinking, his ears adjusting to the newly unleashed storm of sound, Merral could now make out the stained white-plated hull of a general survey craft. He wanted to cry for joy.

The ship tilted and lowered itself down vertically, thin legs extruding through the pulses of shimmering heat. A smell of steam and fumes and waves of warm air rolled over them. Above the glare of the engines Merral could make out the green light of the cockpit and the dull orange glow of heat around the stubby wings. A line of cold blue light opened in the underside of the ship and grew as the hatchway ramp lowered to within a handbreadth of the surface. Stumbling, trying to shield their eyes from the dazzling intensity of the thrusters, Merral and Vero clambered up the ramp.

"Go! Go!" shouted a voice, and a firm hand grabbed Merral's arm and hauled him into the hold. The craft swayed and bobbed like a boat on rough sea, the ramp closed, and Merral felt vibrations under his feet. Then he heard a succession of noises: the hissing of pistons closing the hatch, the tolling of a warning bell, the clamor of a siren, and then the thudding bellow of sound as the thrusters kicked in.

A big man in the deep blue Space Affairs uniform pushed Merral into a seat and strapped a belt around him. Then he was pressed first down and then sideways into the bucket seat as the ship began a series of violent motions, tilting sharply, first one way and then the other.

"Emergency maneuvers," grunted a low voice behind Merral but he was too deep into his seat to see who it was.

Without warning, a brutal rattling noise sounded underneath them. The ship wobbled briefly and, for a second, the lights dimmed. A new set of alarms sounded. With renewed force, the ship seemed to be thrown across the sky, until at one point Merral was on his side and all round him he could hear creaks and the sound of equipment sliding about in lockers. As the wild lurching motion continued, Merral twisted his head and caught a glimpse of Vero slumped in an adjacent seat, covered from head to toe in pale dust, a dirty hand over his mouth and a look of utter misery on his face.

Then it was over.

The ship stabilized, the sirens faded out, and the background creaks died away.

"I feel sick," mumbled Vero.

"Not surprised! That was rough." The cheerful voice came from behind Merral. "But can you hang on while I check out your friend? He looks bad."

Whom is he referring to? Merral looked at his jacket where the crimson blood was now brown. The crew member, a stocky bearded man with green eyes, took his wrist and applied a diagnostic unit to it.

"It's not *my* blood," Merral protested, as he felt the DU's probe gently penetrate his skin. "Except for around my right ankle," he added.

"Good. Good, you can talk, and better, it's largely not yours. Otherwise I'd have to start putting some replacement in." He glanced at the readout. "Your vital signs are good. But you're dehydrated."

A door slid open and a slender figure with short auburn hair in a night blue uniform slid in, one hand cupped around an earpiece.

"Welcome aboard the *Nesta Lamaine*," Perena said in a quiet voice. "Oh, are you all right, Merral?"

"Well, Perena Lewitz!" Vero said, a smile cracking the dust on his face. "We *are* greatly obliged."

"Perena! I should have guessed it was you," Merral added. "And yes, I'm fine. I think."

Perena glanced at the crewman. "Matthew, is he really all right?"

"Yes, Captain. Pretty much so. It's largely surface blood. But he's dehydrated."

She smiled with frank relief. "Then I should have made you wash first. And do excuse me if I don't even shake hands." Then she frowned. "But then whose blood is it, if it isn't yours?"

"Ah. I think—" Merral caught Vero's gesture and fell silent.

"Perena," Vero interjected, "we need to see your sister about that. I think she knows something. But it's an odd story. And a worrying one."

Perena wrinkled her nose. "*You* don't look much better, Vero. Matthew," she ordered, "get some water for these guys to drink and perhaps a damp cloth to wash with." She looked at them again. "I guess a hot shower with disinfectant is what's really needed."

The crewman nodded assent and left the hold.

"Many thanks, Perena," Merral gasped, realizing how glad he was to finally be off that besieged hill and in the ship. "That felt like an interesting bit of flying."

"I agree," Vero said, "even if, at the time, I may not have appreciated it. Where did you learn it?"

"It's called the Yenerag Maneuver. It's pretty specialized and normally envisaged as being for the evacuation of people from active volcanic sites—"

Perena raised a hand and seemed to listen to her earpiece. "Roger!" she snapped. "Continue on present course and speed, but watch those strain warnings. Maintain the self-sealant pressure."

As she spoke, Matthew came in with water.

"Sorry, guys. It's busy time here. Matthew, can you run up to the bridge as soon as you can? Amira may need help. I'll be up in a moment."

He gave Merral and Vero water and clothes and then left. As he did, Perena turned her cool slate blue eyes on them.

"Thank you for the appreciation. My computer is less amused and is telling me we have suffered major damage to the port lifting under-surface and minor to the starboard. From the nature of the damage and the speed of the impact, the computer has deduced that we were hit by multiple small meteoroids. It is clever enough to be puzzled as it realizes that we were flying in normal altitude near the ground and that meteoroids do not fall upward from a planetary surface. It is *not* clever enough to deduce the explanation. And, in truth, neither am I. It might be useful to know what hit us."

Merral looked at her. "A beam weapon of some sort. High temper-ature, portable. Hot enough to melt rock."

The eyes widened and she shook her head in incredulity. "Seri-ously? My ship really was fired on?"

"Yes. As we warned you."

Her face acquired a look of astonishment mingled with unease. "And what does that mean?"

"Mean?" Vero shook his head. "I wish I knew. To start with, it means we need to have a meeting. You, us, and Anya. As soon as we land. Somewhere quiet."

She nodded thoughtfully. "Fine. The self-repair systems are in operation and we are heading at high subsonic speeds—which is as fast as I dare—to Isterrane. I can't really spare you the time anyway now. In fact, I'd better get back to the bridge."

Vero, rubbing dust off his face, spoke again. "What have you said to anybody so far?"

"Nothing much. I've been too busy. Wait. . . ." She raised a hand again, her absorbed face showing she was getting another message. "Okay, Amira, I'm coming up. We'll get Matthew to check the R3 cool-ant levels manually. Initiate clearances for possible emergency glide landings at every strip between here and Isterrane."

She looked back at Vero. "Well, I've said we've got you. I've been a bit busy to do anything else. I'm afraid your alert about non-Assembly forces is being treated as evidence of delirium. Like the Youraban shuttle pilot who—oh, a century ago—was adamant that he was being attacked by thirty kilometer-long space octopods."

Vero nodded. "I remember that. May I suggest, Captain Lewitz, that you try to land as far out of sight as possible. Encourage the crew to keep silent. We don't want a panic."

"A panic?" Perena arched thin eyebrows. "No. I suppose you may have a point. I'll call Anya and have her meet us."

She turned to the door.

"Perena?" Merral asked. "Just one quick question. You said you would be two hours in arriving. You were a half an hour. I don't understand."

She reached for the guide rail and turned to him. "*I* didn't think it was delirium. And the mention of 'non-Assembly forces' and 'weapons' alarmed me. So, at first I felt it best not to say when I would arrive, and then I thought harder and decided that it might be safer—and quite legitimate—to mislead." She looked faintly amused. "I have, after all, played a lot of old-time chess."

"So you lied?" Vero asked, raising a dusty eyebrow in alarm.

"Vero, please!" Perena winked at him. "If you remember my communication, I told you that the Standard Operating Procedure would take two hours. I ignored the SOP and just corkscrewed in. Not pleasant, I may say. And risky, and we probably lost a centimeter of ablative material off all my underside plates. So, do thank my crew. At worst, I misled you and your . . . enemies." She frowned at the last word.

Then a new message came on her earpiece and she winced. "And even then it was a near thing. But"—and she gave a heartfelt sigh—"by the King's grace, we did it."

An hour later, after a landing marked by a series of bounces and an odd slewing motion, they were on the ground at Isterrane.

CHAPTER 16

As the ramp to the compartment swung down, Merral and Vero got to their feet. There was the smell of fresh, clean air with the hint of the sea, and through the doorway, Merral could see the black of the fused basalt runway below glinting under the lights of the landing strip.

Then there was the sound of feet running up the gangway, and a red-haired figure in sweater and trousers appeared. A freckled face, blue eyes blinking in the light, peered up at them.

"Hi, guys!" Anya called out, her voice soft and concerned, and Merral sensed a seriousness to her that he was unfamiliar with.

"So, you had an interesting trip," she whispered, staring at him and Vero with her eyes open wide.

With a strange throb of emotion, Merral realized that he was very pleased to see her.

"An understatement," Vero commented in pained tones, gently shaking off dust.

Anya looked them over again and shook her head. "Well, if you think I'm going to hug and kiss either of you—especially you, Merral D'Avanos, when you look like an accident in a blood bank—not a hope. As for you, Sentinel Enand, you look like you failed to get out of a quarry before blasting."

Merral looked at Vero and then down at his bloodied clothes and decided he didn't know whether to smile or shudder.

Perena's slim figure slipped in through a doorway. As she embraced her sister, she gestured to Merral and Vero. "Have you ever seen anything more disgusting?"

Anya shook her head as Perena continued urgently. "My poor ship needs a trip to Bay One for full damage assessment and repair. I've arranged for these guys to clean up at the medical center. Take them over, let them shower off, fix them clean clothes. Issue them some standard Space Affairs suits. I've asked for Doc Larchent to see them. He's under instructions not to ask questions." She gave a grimace. "Excuse me, all, I've got some weird holes to look at. See you later."

Then she had slipped away down the ramp onto the runway.

Anya hooked a thumb downward. "Out, you guys, follow me. We've an ambulance here and we'll go in by the back way. And Merral," she said, giving him a crooked grin, "if that is your blood, you ought to be dead and I want you for science. And if it isn't, well, then I want your clothes for science."

Merral clapped Anya on the back. "Only the ankle blood is mine."

She looked hard at his clothes, her eyes widening. "I'm glad of that. The rest is the blood of one of these insect-creatures?"

"There wasn't just one creature, Anya. There were many of them. And two different kinds; there was an ape-creature as well."

She stared wide-eyed at the garments for a moment before looking up at him with a colder, businesslike look. "You have both kinds of blood on you?"

"Oh, yes." Merral smiled. "I went to some trouble to get good samples for you. The left ankle and trouser leg is from the cockroach thing; the jacket and shirt blood is from an ape-creature. My contribution is the right lower leg and the sock."

"Excellent." She shook her head in mock reproof. "But next time, Tree Man, you might remember that a drop is adequate."

"Enough of the repartee, you guys," Vero said. "We need to meet together as soon as we have got cleaned up. There is a long, long chat we have to have, and some hard decisions to make."

• ◄ •

As Merral and Vero walked unsteadily and stiffly out from under the general survey craft to where the ambulance hovered gently on the strip, they could see a cluster of people looking up and shaking their heads at the underside of the stubby wings. Above them, beams from handheld lights were picking out a cluster of a dozen or so fist-sized holes with blackened edges.

Vero tapped Merral gently on the shoulder and bent his face toward him. "My friend," he said, and Merral heard the anxiety in his voice, "I ask you to pray for me. I need to make decisions now. They are hard decisions, because a wrong move now could be disastrous. If, on the summit, the weight of the struggle fell on you, it now falls on me. We will meet and discuss after you have been fixed up, but already I have to decide." He sighed. "It is not easy."

As he spoke, Merral realized that this was something he had overlooked. Vero was right; action had to be taken, but choosing the right action would be far from easy.

•◆•

The ambulance whispered through the back of the medical center. There Merral was divested of his clothes, allowed a hasty but wonderful shower, and then taken in a bathrobe to a room where he had a brief medical examination by a doctor and a nurse. His ankle was examined and the wound opened, cleansed thoroughly, and then microsutured. A bruised shoulder was treated, the small burn to the hand covered, and his eardrums examined.

As the doctor gave Merral a third different anti-infection agent, he stared at him with puzzled eyes. "I've been told not to ask questions, Forester D'Avanos, but that is an interesting wound on your foot. I've never seen anything quite like it."

Their eyes met.

"Yes, it is interesting."

Realizing that he was not going to learn anything more, the doctor just shrugged. "It should give no more trouble. Call me if it shows any inflammation."

Aware of the doctor and nurse watching him curiously, Merral headed to an adjoining room where he took a new set of clothing, including a shirt and overalls in the dark blue colors of Space Affairs. Then, feeling more human, he was shown to an empty refectory where he helped himself to fruit juice and sandwiches from a fridge. A few minutes later Vero joined him, and together, with the minimum of conversation, they ate and drank gratefully. As they were finishing, Anya came in, and this time there were embraces all round.

Then, with the gentle night air with its hint of impending summer drifting through the cab, Anya drove them across the runway in a small Space Affairs transport. Merral realized he had conflicting urges within him. His body simply wished to go to bed and sleep off recent events, while in his mind there burned the stronger longing to take action, to warn Farholme and the Assembly.

"Where are we going?" he asked Anya as they overtook the *Nesta Lamaine* being towed slowly across the runway.

"My sister asked me to take you to the Engineering and Maintenance Complex."

Vero leaned over to Merral. "While you were being patched up, I went and sorted some things out with Perena. We have set some things in motion. We need to talk in a place where we can be sure of not being overheard or having equipment intercepted. She suggested one of the engineering rooms. They are all underground."

They stopped at the end of one of the runways where a series of wide entrances and narrow doors was cut into a low hill. Perena was waiting for them and led them to a closed door.

"Captain Perena Lewitz and three colleagues," she announced to a panel at the side, and the doorway slid open.

"You have security?" Vero asked her in surprise as Perena led them through.

"Security?" The door slid closed behind them. "It's *safety*. That alone. There are vacuum chambers, laser cutters—any number of radiation-emitting processes. You can't have just anybody walking around here. Otherwise we would have space-besotted children being fried accidentally every week."

She gestured to a weighty array of warning notices on the walls and then stared at a screen. "But it's almost empty. A few engineers checking some circuits for motors in Bay Three. Six technicians preparing Bay One for *Nesta*. That's about it. Eleven o'clock in the evening is not the time for routine work."

They walked down two flights of stairs and along a lengthy corridor. At a heavy glass window at the end she stopped and peered in at a large, well-lit chamber with a vacant center space and an array of machinery around the perimeter. "Bay One," Perena observed. "Home for *Nesta* for the next few days at least. We'll have to replace a dozen undersurface plates and make sure there are no leaks. Put her in vacuum for a day or two." She stroked her chin gently. "Extraordinary," she whispered in wonderment. "Battle damage."

Then they moved on into another corridor. At the end of this was a heavy door marked Communications Isolation Room, and a notice warned that no diary communication was possible within the room. A datascreen by the side proclaimed that the room was unoccupied.

Perena opened the door and gestured them in as the lights automatically flickered on. "Make yourselves as comfortable as you can. I need to make sure we are left alone and that any com-links to this room are switched off." She gave Vero a meaningful look. "And, check on some other matters. There'll be water, coffee—everything—in the office next door." Then she left.

The laboratory was small, with a low ceiling, and empty apart from banks of equipment and testing racks. They found a table in a corner, cleared it of testing units, and pulled up chairs. Anya and Vero made coffee while Merral put his ankle upon a box.

They had barely sat down with the cups when Perena came in and closed the door behind her. She nodded at Vero. "Maybe," she said, "in an hour we will know. Just after midnight."

Then she pulled a chair up and sat with them. Merral realized that she was looking expectantly at him. He glanced around and saw that everyone else was as well.

Vero nodded at him. "I think, Merral, that you'd best start things off. It seems to be the general feeling."

"Very well. But I don't know where to begin. I am certain, though, that we should seek the blessing of the Lord first. We have been spared so far in an extraordinary way. Yet we are up against something so enormous . . ." He paused, his thoughts almost overwhelming him. "So enormous, that what we decide here tonight may have unimaginable consequences."

They bowed their heads and Merral prayed. He gave thanks for deliverance, made a fervent plea for future protection, and then petitioned for clarity and guidance in their discussion. After the resounding "Amens" he looked around and saw, as he had expected, that they were all still looking at him.

Merral turned to Vero. "You asked me to start, but if I am not mistaken, Vero, this is your hour. I know you do not understand everything, but I believe you've thought these things through more than I have. Also your background has better prepared you."

Vero looked around with a troubled face and gestured his reluctant agreement with the least of nods. "Very well. Although I must say Merral has shown a remarkable practical ability. He seems to be a born soldier."

Merral made a murmur of protest but Vero continued. "He is unhappy with that word, I know. Indeed, if he were happy with it I would worry. Anyway, let me begin, because I think there are things that I need to say. Then I will let Merral tell you what we have seen. But we must be urgent; we have decisions to make, and I think we must make them within the hour."

He paused and seemed to stare ahead solemnly into the distance for a long, heavy moment. "We have a problem. I wish I could tell you all about what that problem is—where it comes from, what it means, and how it might be countered. Description, analysis, prescription. But I cannot. I am not even sure whether there is one problem or many. To some extent it is not our task to solve it. That can be done by others. But we do need to make urgent decisions, and make them now."

There were nods of assent and Vero continued. "Let me state the problem. Something is in the north—something evil, something unknown, since at least the beginning of the Assembly. And maybe not even then."

As he spoke the words, Merral's memories of grappling in the darkness with the ape-creatures and the dreadful encounter with the cockroach-beast were stirred again. He grabbed the table's edge.

Vero stopped, creased his forehead in thought, and then went on. "There are, I think, three distinct aspects: First, there are now on Farholme two sorts of new creatures, both unknown to the Assembly. Merral will describe them. Both are intelligent and very hostile."

Merral saw the sisters share glances with each other.

"Second," Vero continued, "these creatures are connected—in some way—with a technology that is beyond ours in the area of weapons and communications." He leaned forward, his thin figure tense. "And third—and worst of all—there is an evil influence loose. A spiritual influence that corrupts. . . ."

As the words sank in, Merral stared around. In the whole history of the Assembly, he wondered whether there had ever been such a meeting as this.

Anya and Perena shared looks of silent astonishment. Then Anya turned to Vero and shook her head in such a firm gesture of denial that her long red hair flew over her shoulders. "All of this seems too much to believe. I *know* this world."

Vero tapped the table thoughtfully with his fingers for a moment. "I sympathize, Anya, and your skepticism is valuable. But, partly to help you to believe and partly to explain why we meet here, can you call up the conversation you had, what—six hours ago? When you called to make contact with us? Remember, it was just voices."

"Sure. I was impressed, Vero," she replied with a look of amusement as she pulled off her diary and put it on the table. "I've never heard of anybody managing to wipe out the main functions of two separate diaries. I was very surprised when I heard it."

A strange, ironic smile crept across Vero's face. "Your surprise, Anya, was—I'm certain—exceeded by mine. But then it has been a day of surprises. And more. But play the conversation. Please."

Evidently mystified, Anya searched for the file on her diary, and then the room was filled with the sound of her call to Merral and Vero while the sentinel stared at his fingernails. When the transmission ended, she turned to Vero. "So? Why that?"

There was a delay, then Vero lifted up his large brown eyes and stared at her. "Because, in fact, neither Merral nor I spoke." The words were hushed.

Perplexed, Anya looked at her sister, then back at Vero. "Yes, you did. We all heard you."

Catching a minute gesture from Vero, Merral turned to her. "Anya, that was not us. I testify to it. Our own diaries had been blocked for the best part of a day. Whatever it is . . . no, whoever *they* are, they duplicated our voices."

Anya's face paled. "But that *was* you. . . . I don't believe it. I *can't* believe . . ."

The troubled silence was broken by Perena's gentle and thoughtful voice. "Sister, it might help to remember that *something* burned holes right through five thick-thick thermoceramic plates on my ship. At a guess, by generating a local temperature of at least twelve hundred degrees C. And *something* cut off these guys' diary signals within seconds."

Anya, a determined skepticism on her face, merely shook her head again in exasperation and said nothing. Merral caught a tremor in Vero's fingers and knew that he was finding the meeting difficult. He prayed for him again.

Vero sighed, then looked up at Anya, his dark face strained. "I understand your reluctance to believe something so disturbing, so almost impossible. But, Anya, you must. We must all understand what we face. Now, if you could play us another diary clip. I want you to show us the interview with Maya Knella about the samples."

Anya breathed out heavily, as if in exasperation, and then pointed her diary at the wallscreen. "Very well. . . . But, as I told you, it was a bad line."

A few moments later they were looking at a grainy image of a middle-aged woman with a heavy-boned oval face, her jet-black hair tinged with gray and held in place by a silver hair clasp, and wearing a long red dress with a green leaf pattern. The background was a laboratory. The image jumped and flickered, the sound bounced up and down in volume, and there was a marked time delay between question and answer. What the woman said was more or less as Anya had reported: a denial of anything peculiar in her sample data and a suggestion that the equipment might be failing.

"F–freeze it, please," Vero ordered. "Now window the previous conversation you had with her."

"But . . . that was about a technical aspect of gene transmission in mammals. It was about nothing relevant."

"Please," Vero asked, casting a glance at his watch. "If I am right, it is an issue of greatest significance." Moments later, Maya Knella appeared again below the first image.

"Ah!" There was a note of relief in Vero's voice. "Freeze that, too!"

"I thought you wanted to hear it."

"It is not necessary. When was this?"

"About ten days earlier."

"Yes," Vero said quietly, as if to himself. "And what do you see, Merral?"

"Same woman," he answered, failing to see any cause for Vero's excitement. "But in an office this time. She's got a different dress."

Vero got up from his seat, walked over, and peered at the images, one inset inside the other.

"No, she hasn't," he said, gesturing with an outstretched finger. "This is a gray dress with brown leaves. The pattern is identical. Only the color is changed."

His finger jumped from one image to another and back. Merral heard a gasp from Anya.

Vero continued staring at the image. "See, too, that the hairstyle and combing is exactly the same. But the hair clip here is gold."

"But—," Anya protested, looking at everyone in turn as if trying to elicit support. "But the background is different."

"Standard shots of a laboratory," Vero added, his voice terse, as if he was anxious to move on. "Easy enough to provide. Careful analysis would probably show discrepancies in the angle of the shadows between her and the background."

Anya, now half standing, was leaning forward over the table, staring intently at the sentinel with an expression that seemed to fluctuate between confusion and dread.

"So, Vero," she said, her voice full of perplexity and fear, "you are saying that I never talked with her a second time. That it was made-up. That they just . . . Surely not?" She stared at the screen and Merral saw her swallow. "That they just took an old conversation we had . . . and modified it?"

Vero pursed his mouth and nodded. "S–sorry," he said.

"No!" Anya snapped and, blank-faced, sat down suddenly in her chair. She put her face in her hands for a moment and then looked around, her expression one of shocked stupefaction. "I'm appalled . . . ," she said slowly. "I mean, it smashes everything we stand for: ethics, Technology Protocols, decency—everything!"

Anya's misery was so evident that Merral was struck by a strangely potent—and perturbing—desire to comfort her by hugging her.

Anya stared at Vero with resentment in her eyes. "But . . . how did they know to do it to me?"

Vero wrinkled his nose. "I'd guess they knew because you had told us you were going to call her when we were in Ynysmant."

Anya gulped. "They listened in?"

"At a guess."

Her face flushed. "No . . . ," she continued, her face showing that she was fighting desperately not to believe what she was being told. "It can't be! I mean, how did they get the old conversation with Maya?"

Merral, who had just worked out the answer, decided that she was not going to like what Vero was going to say. But, in fact, it was Perena who told her the answer, her blue-gray eyes filled with a cold anger.

"I'm afraid that they went through your files, little sister. I'd imagine when you were asleep they just contacted your diary and pulled off what they wanted and prepared the duplicate."

Anya's face and posture showed that the disbelief had vanished, to be replaced by an anger just short of fury. "That's just . . . well, I've never heard anything so . . . wrong!" She stood up and struck her fist on the table. "I'm absolutely furious. Why, I've never been so angry! To invade my privacy. To fake that call. And I was beginning to think that Maya Knella's reputation was undeserved!" She sat down again, a look of simmering anger on her face. Suddenly a look of guilt appeared. "Why, I ought to apologize to Maya."

A hint of a wry smile played across Vero's mouth, "Amid this tale of enormous evil, I'm touched by your concern about your thoughts. Anyway, the hour is late and we have much to go through. But now you believe it, eh?"

Anya was silent for a moment and then moved her head slowly up and down in unenthusiastic affirmation.

"Now we can move on. Only, when it came to faking our forester and me," Vero said in a measured tone, "they did not have the time or data to do the job properly. So, they just faked the sound."

Perena, who had been leaning forward over the table, suddenly looked up, her eyes carefully moving round the table. "I am as horrified at all this as my sister," she said in her quiet but forceful voice, "but this means that they must have some entry into the Gate circuits. Either at the Gate itself, or—surely more probable—at one of the Gate signal relay stations." Merral saw that she was doodling with a finger on the tabletop. Then she stared at Vero. "But you see," she continued gently, "as our student of ancient history here will confirm, the Gates are the central nervous system of the Assembly. Those who control Farholme Gate control Farholme."

"Well said," responded Vero, "and that was one lesson learned in the last military action the Assembly took. In the Rebellion, because Jannafy had seized the Centauri Gate, the Assembly Force had to travel at sublight speed to get there. It took Ringell and his men six years.

Once they had the Gate, they were home in an afternoon. Sorry, but it is an episode that has been on my mind much lately."

Anya grimaced. "I really don't like that phrase, 'the last military action.'"

Vero shrugged. "Nor do I, Anya, but you saw the blood on Merral. He and—to a very much lesser extent—I fought today. *Fought . . .*" He hesitated, apparently suddenly hit by the significance of the word. "I, we, fought. Not as in sport, or as in a metaphor, but in reality, a bloody reality." He stroked his chin, as if realizing that he needed a shave, and then continued. "But, if I may say so, I have a greater—if more subtle—concern, which I feel I must express."

Merral stared at him, thinking that he needed a week to absorb all this and what it signified. But Vero was right, decisions had to be made and made tonight.

"My concern is this: They must know that they can't sustain such a scheme forever. Sooner or later Maya and Anya will correspond by paper—or even meet—and the trick will be apparent."

There was silence as the implications sank in, then Vero continued, his face now bearing an expression of foreboding. "I think it is one of two things. Either it is a desperate measure or it is a short-term strategy . . . until—"

"Until what, Vero?" queried Perena in a keen and worried tone, her head slightly on one side.

"Frankly, I don't know."

Everyone was looking at each other. *We are all out of our depth,* Merral realized. *None of us is stupid and yet here we haven't got a clue.*

Vero sipped at his coffee and stretched back in his chair. "That's me finished, Merral. But I want us all to realize at the start of our discussion that there is no question that we face a powerful foe. And also, that we cannot now trust any diary conversation. It has occasionally been a theoretical sentinel concern that our communications in the Assembly are totally open. But we have never been able to justify the use of any encrypting practices."

"Encrypting?" Anya queried.

"As in code. And not genetic. You scramble a message and disguise it so that only a recipient with the correct digital key can read it. You might do it with a personal diary."

A look of anger erupted across her face. "Yes. That makes me so—" She shook herself in a barely restrained emotion. "No, continue."

"Merral, over to you. Tell them exactly what happened."

"Very well," Merral said. "Although I'm at a loss to know where to start."

Vero shrugged. "Just begin where you first noticed anything odd."

Merral thought hard. "I would say just before Nativity."

Vero started. "*Before* Nativity?" he queried sharply.

"Yes. At Herrandown. I had a nightmare of something evil coming out of the sea. And I think—in hindsight—my uncle did, too. But he denied it."

Perena lifted her head and stared piercingly at Merral. "When 'just before Nativity'?"

"Three nights before. The twenty-second."

"The night of the meteor?"

"Yes."

"What meteor?" Vero threw a sharp glance at Merral. "Why didn't you tell me?"

For a fraction of a second, Merral was tempted to be angry. "Sorry, Vero . . . I hadn't assumed it was significant. This is Worlds' End. *Nothing* happens here. Or did."

Perena looked at Merral. "If I may interrupt. I believe that it is significant. I have been doing some checking up. For about a week before the night Merral is speaking of, one of the Guardian Satellites had been tracking a sunward meteoroid of around two thousand tons apparent mass. As soon as it was noticed, its trajectory was calculated—of course—and it was determined that it would miss Farholme by at least fifty thousand kilometers and eventually hit the sun. There was nothing alarming about either its size, speed, or path, and obviously, no action was necessary, so they just kept a regular watch on it. Just in case it broke up or did anything odd." She looked at Vero. "I should say that, at any one time, there are a dozen of this size of thing within a few million kilometers of Farholme, but they just let them through when they are certain that they are going to miss. It's a minimum intervention policy. So, the existence of this particular moving block of rock wasn't even flagged to the human supervision office in Isterrane."

Vero nodded and gestured for her to continue. "So, it was routinely tracked every fifty minutes. The last reported sighting was at 4:20 P.M. Central Menaya Time. It was still coming sunward and nearly at the point of closest approach to Farholme—estimated to be at one hundred thousand kilometers out—but was still behaving itself. When the Guardian checked again at 5:10 P.M., it expected to find it sunward of us, but it was absent from the predicted path."

"Ah!" muttered Vero. "How interesting. But I interrupt."

Perena looked at the wall clock. "Yes, we must watch the time. Machine logic being what it is, they looked around for it and, having failed to find either it or fragments, they did the electronic equivalent of shrugging their shoulders and got on with life as usual. Remember, only the presence of a meteoroid is a problem, not an absence. They did, however, tag the case to the supervisors just in case it was the first hint of a malfunction. They assumed it was and rescheduled the next overhaul sooner."

"So," Merral said, "the meteoroid changed course and came to Farholme where I saw it coming in."

"Oh, I wish you'd told me, Merral," Vero interjected. "I might have been more suspicious."

Merral, feeling tired, sighed. "It was just a meteor, Vero. An incoming pile of rock and metal. It's not rare here. It's different from the solar system: for a start we have two debris belts, one on either side of Fenniran. It was just larger than usual."

Vero looked at Perena. "And let me guess: it wasn't a meteoroid, it was a ship."

She gave him a strange, subdued smile. "Not so fast, my friend. In theory, yes, it could have been a ship, mimicking a meteoroid. But there is a timing point. It had gone by at 5:10 P.M. Central Menaya Time and Merral saw his object come in ten minutes earlier at around 6:00 P.M. Eastern Menaya Time. Incidentally, confirmed by a record of a small and poorly defined shallow-focus earthquake around two hundred and fifty kilometers north of Herrandown at 6:02 P.M. But there is a major problem."

"What?" asked Vero, looking crestfallen.

Merral spoke slowly. "I see it. It had to change course, travel over a hundred thousand kilometers, and decelerate into a landing mode in under fifty minutes."

Perena looked appreciatively at him. "Good. Let me translate. If we are right in linking the meteoroid in space with Merral's meteor, then it did what our fastest unmanned ships would take at least a half a day to do in around twenty minutes. It pushes engineering beyond anything we can envisage."

Vero closed his eyes. Merral decided that he was imagining what it must be like to be in a ship doing that sort of a maneuver.

"So there may be a ship there," he said slowly. "I was beginning to wonder about that. But can we find it?"

Perena looked at him, her face expressionless. "That is the next task. I have already ordered satellite imagery over the Carson's Sill area from the next overflight."

"Which is when?" Vero asked.

"In an hour or so. Not the best resolution, but it may show something. There's a better one midmorning."

A silence fell and Merral realized that, once more, everybody was staring at him. "Then," he began again, "other strange but apparently unrelated things happened. . . ."

For the next few minutes he described, as best he could, these other things. At Vero's prompting—and then only reluctantly—he outlined how his uncle had altered a re-created voice and how, in a subtle way, things had begun to go wrong at Herrandown. He then went on to explain, largely for Perena's benefit, how Elana had been scared by seeing a creature, and how he and Isabella had gone to investigate and found evidence that there had indeed been some sort of strange being there.

At this point Vero interrupted. "Merral, excuse me, I think this is the time for us to find out what Anya saw when she looked at that strand of hair."

Anya wrinkled her nose as if smelling something distasteful. "Well, the most obvious interpretation was that it was a mixture of two natural genetic codes: human and ape—probably gorilla. Along with some unknown, but probably artificial, segments. It was not a result I was happy with. I would have preferred almost any other interpretation."

Merral looked at Vero, who nodded gently and pursed his lips. "That would fit our ape-creatures."

A frown darkened Anya's face. "I can't believe that these things exist. But you really saw them?"

"I'm afraid so," Vero answered. "And more. . . ."

She shuddered and then looked at Merral. "Go on then. I need to hear what happened when you went north."

Reluctantly, Merral told of what had transpired over the last few days. He began with the meeting with Jorgio and his vision of the testing of the Assembly, with the command to watch, stand firm, and hope. Then Merral went on to tell of the trip north. At times he paused and had to be encouraged by Vero. In places, notably where it came to bloodier dealings, Vero had to draw out the events from him sentence by sentence. And as he recounted the tale, Merral was aware of a growing intensity to the atmosphere in the room. *It is as if the shadow has spread over us.* Where appropriate they ran the images from Merral's diary, and both Perena and Anya took copies of the images of the ape-creatures and cockroach-beasts and stared at them. When it came to the description of the imitation bird, there was horror and disgust and, despite Merral's invitation, Vero declined to talk about it. "Later," he demurred, "later. . . . In daylight perhaps."

Then, with the aid of more substantial encouragement from Vero, Merral reluctantly told of the last half an hour on the summit. With the account of the rescue by Perena's ship, he fell silent.

It was Anya, looking round the table with broad and worried eyes, who broke the ensuing silence. "A tale that is darker than I can understand. I wish it was a vision or even the result of hallucinations. . . ." She paused, her fingers locking and unlocking. "But, as with the Maya Knella incident, I *must* believe it. We have the images, the testimony, the genetic data from the hair, and will shortly have the blood results. And there is Merral's wound. . . ." She shook her head.

Perena spoke, her voice full of a restrained bewilderment as if she were thinking through a dream. "Like my sister, I would like to try and dismiss it all. But then I think of the holes in my ship." She gestured over her shoulder in the direction of Bay One.

Vero, who had been staring at his hands again, looked up. "Good, but unfortunately it is more than what we believe that is the problem. It is how we are to act. Thank you, Merral, for your account. It is, I think, obvious to you, Perena and Anya, how extraordinarily able my friend here was when it became necessary to fight these things. It is, I believe, a most significant and encouraging matter that our first contact with these things should have involved Merral."

Merral, wondering whether to protest, was aware of Anya looking at him with admiration, and the unsettling thought came to him that he found her attention pleasing.

Vero raised a finger. "Merral, time is moving on and delay may not be good for us. But I feel there may be more questions. And I want us to have all the data we can have before we decide what to do. Anya, comments on the biology?"

Anya bit her lip and shook her head. "Yes. I suppose. We have two sorts of—let's call them 'intruders.' You say, Merral, you saw no evidence of male or female with either?"

"That's right," Merral agreed. "It was less clear with the cockroach-beasts, I suppose. And we saw fewer of them."

Anya nodded. "Size variation of any type?"

"No. Each species—if that's what they were—seemed the same size."

"Like identical twins?"

"Yes."

"So they were probably cloned. Bred somehow in vitro."

Vero threw her a puzzled glance. "That's a very old phrase. I suppose it predates even basic genetics. In glass. Outside the womb?"

"Yes, laboratory generated. Very intriguing." She looked around. "Well, that does me. I'm still absorbing it all."

Vero nodded and looked around. "Thanks. Any other points about what we face?"

Perena stirred. "Just one, Vero. A question. The creatures you describe are so low technology they do not seem to use tools. But whatever weapon was fired indicates advanced technology, as does the interception of the Gate call. And maybe the ship—if it was indeed a ship—that landed. I don't see how it fits together."

Before Vero could answer, Merral spoke. "There is one more piece of the puzzle that may help. I should have said it earlier. Just before the weapon was fired the first time, I saw something in the shadows, standing back. It was a different creature."

Vero opened his mouth wide. "You mean a third type?"

"No. Sorry, Vero, I meant to tell you but, well, I was too busy afterward. I think it was a man."

"A man!" Anya's voice echoed round the room, but it was plain that the others were equally surprised.

"Well, I can't be sure," Merral answered, feeling challenged. "It just, well, looked like one."

"A man?" Vero's tone expressed surprise. "That would confirm an outlandish speculation of mine. . . . But to answer Perena, a just-conceivable scenario might be something like this: These creatures are created, I'm afraid, merely as servants. The technology and the weapons belong to the creators, not the creatures. The classic pre-Intervention slave economy."

Perena looked thoughtful. Then she glanced up at the wall clock and Merral followed her gaze to see that it was nearly midnight.

"Vero," she said, "I indicated that I would call again at twelve."

"Ah yes. But we have nearly finished. Let me tell you what I think. And then I will make a proposal."

He frowned and then looked around, his smooth face tired. Merral suddenly felt that he had a glimpse of what an older Vero would look like. "A common theme emerges. Does anybody else see it? Or is it just me?"

There were puzzled looks. "Only that horrid things seem to have been done all around," Anya offered.

Vero nodded and rose to his feet, walked to the end of the room and stood there against a battery of equipment. He stretched his limbs and frowned. "It is that boundaries have been broken. The boundaries between humanity and animals, between living things and machines." He stopped and his face showed an expression of disgust. "But there may yet be a darker twist. The bird thing. You all expressed revulsion. And rightly so. It masqueraded as a living creature. It was a machine imitating life, in contravention of all that we have ever maintained about such facsimiles. In doing so, it crossed a boundary. But there was worse. It was built on a dead bird."

Perena shuddered. "That . . . I do not—or cannot—understand."

Merral caught a look of extraordinary repulsion on Anya's face.

"Yes," Vero said, "and we can but hope they can shed light on it on Ancient Earth. But this is yet another boundary broken. And this, this monstrosity is perhaps the greatest of the breaches. The boundary between life and death. To raise the dead is the prerogative of the Messiah alone. And this—most assuredly—was none of his handiwork. On the contrary."

In the silence that followed, Vero tightened his lips and looked around the room. "But you see, this is part of a pattern too. From Merral's dream onward, through the problems at Herrandown, there is a second theme. A theme of spiritual corruption unparalleled in the long years since the Rebellion, and maybe since the start of the Great Intervention. If I had to choose between the visible genetic abominations we have seen and the less visible spiritual problems, I would choose the latter as the most worrying. But the linkage of the two is most terrible."

Merral looked at him. "So, what do we do?"

Vero smiled. "Ah, ever the man of action. In fact, I have made a decision for myself." He looked at Perena. "Can you check for me now?"

She rose gracefully. "There's a diary link point outside. Excuse me." She left the room.

Vero walked forward and leaned on his chair back. "I need to talk with Brenito as soon as I can. Then we need to meet with the representatives here, but that would take a few days to organize. And, in the meantime, Earth must know. This matter is quite beyond us here and it raises issues that affect the entire Assembly. This matter must go straight to an emergency session of the Council of High Stewards. They will doubtless summon the whole Congregation of all the Stewards, the Farholme Delegate, and the Science Panel. I have no doubt, too, that the Custodians of the Faith would be consulted about the spiritual aspects."

"And the sentinels?" Merral asked, awed at the realization that this matter would have to go so high and so quickly.

"If asked." Vero looked thoughtful. "But, oddly enough, we have served our purpose in this matter. Or very nearly. We only ever existed to watch and alert. This we have done. It could be, perhaps, that in this case we might have done better, but that is for discussion at another time."

Merral could faintly hear Perena outside talking on her diary.

"Do you think you can safely call Earth?" Anya asked.

Vero shook his head. "How? We cannot trust Gate communications. Your attempt to contact Maya Knella has taught us that. The files must be hand carried to Ancient Earth as secretly and fast as we can manage."

Anya nodded. "Yes, I can see that. But the council and everybody—what do you think they will do?"

"I think I can safely say they will rapidly muster the entire Defense Force and bring them in. There are only two ships, and even by Assembly standards they are elderly, but they—and their men—will be enough to search the north. Beyond that, I do not know."

The door opened and Perena came in and smiled at Vero. "Done. Two."

Vero seemed to breathe a sigh of relief. "So, I propose to leave for Earth on the next ship. The *Heinrich Schütz*. It departs the Gate Station at 10 A.M. Central Menaya Time the day after tomorrow—no, tomorrow now. In just thirty-four hours time. We will take tonight's in-system shuttle."

"*We?*" Merral asked, a bizarre speculation suddenly forming in his mind.

Vero walked round from his chair and grasped Merral gently on the shoulder.

"Yes, soldier," he said, "*we*. I want to take you too."

"Are you serious?" Merral gasped, his mind reeling. To Ancient Earth! He had hoped to go someday, but today? In barely hours?

Vero's smile seemed weary. "Yes, for one thing, they—whoever *they* are—probably expect us to stay here and meet up with the representatives. But the four other representatives need to fly in, so we can hardly summon a meeting today and, as tomorrow is the Lord's Day, they ought to know that we will not have any real meetings for two days. They may also be in disarray after their losses."

"But why me? To Earth?" Merral asked. "All that way?"

He was suddenly aware that he must sound stupid, and he realized that Anya was staring at him, her face a mixture of amusement and envy.

"Merral," Vero commented, "I need you. I cannot answer all the questions that will be asked. And the testimony of two is stronger than one. You have also seen and grappled with these things. If I went alone there might be a concern that it was my allegedly fertile imagination. Besides, this way, we take duplicate data. But don't you want to go?"

"Yes. . . . *No*." He gulped. "I mean, I haven't really thought it through yet. And my family and Isabella. And Henri at work. I need to talk to them."

Vero looked at him, his brown eyes showing concern. "I understand exactly. But just think what has happened to us today. And think what is at stake. It is beyond computation."

Merral thought for a moment and swallowed. The words *Ancient Earth* seemed to thud in his mind. "No, you are right. We need to go."

Vero raised a finger in warning. "Oh, and Anya and Perena can give farewells and apologies once you are gone. But, in the meantime, no diary calls."

"Okay," Merral answered. "But I need things. I mean, I'm not prepared. Anyway, there's a waiting list for places."

Vero looked at him. "You need little. Perena has sorted the places out. I wasn't sure she could do it for both of us so I delayed telling you. It would hardly have been fair to disappoint you."

Merral turned to Perena. "So that is what you were up to! But how have you done it? It must have taken one of the representatives to get you on with an urgent priority status. There's always a waiting list for spare seats."

Perena grinned. "There's one power equivalent to the representatives in such matters and that's Space Affairs. For whom I work. And you are traveling on an urgent mission."

"But you didn't tell them? Surely not?"

Vero was smiling now. "No," he said, "but while you were getting your wound dressed, Perena and I talked about this. She suggested that, in view of the curious and alarming problem occurring to General Survey Craft *Nesta Lamaine* today, it was appropriate—even a necessity—to send the plate samples to Earth. On urgent-priority status. You and I will hand carry them for her."

Perena interrupted with a gesture. "But you *will* be taking plate samples and I would like an assessment—fast. *Please.*"

"I see," Merral replied, his brain still spiraling furiously around the concept, "but won't they know if they control the information networks?"

Vero looked at Perena.

"There were," she said, "two Space Affairs engineers going—Sabourin and Diekens. They have been asked to stand down and go on the next flight." She looked at the floor, as if embarrassed. "Unusually, their names have not been removed from the manifest. Even more unusually, they are keeping quiet about the fact that they are not going. You, er—just replace them. You are even dressed for the part."

Vero gave her a look of amused respect. "Captain Lewitz turns out to have an aptitude for duplicity—I think that is the word—that worries me. It must be that chess." He wagged his head. "Be careful, Perena, that it does not get you into trouble."

"We are all in trouble now." Perena's face had acquired a wry expression. "If it is a gift, then I trust I may be careful how I use it. But the hour seems to require it. Oh, and Vero, I ought to warn you, it won't be comfortable. Space Affairs are ruthless in making their own people take the roughest seats. And in an inter-system liner, the crew seats are down just above the engines."

Vero winced. "Vibration as well. But at least only for forty-eight hours." Then he sighed, and Merral was suddenly aware of how tired his friend was and how much he was forcing himself into the giving of these orders. Vero turned to the sisters. "Oh, Perena and Anya, you ought to try and get in touch with the representatives and ask for a meeting in two days' time."

Anya nodded. "Anwar Corradon is the current chair of the Farholme representatives; I vaguely know him. My perception is that he is an unusually intelligent and thoughtful man."

Vero looked around. "That, then, is the proposed plan of action. Are all in agreement with it?"

Everyone looked at each other and nodded.

Vero looked around. "Fine. Then let me suggest the following. I think we all need at least some sleep." He looked at Perena. "If you, Captain Lewitz, can get some of those damaged tiles cut off and packaged up. And check any satellite imagery when it comes in. Oh, and any chance of a new diary for me?"

"I can get you one," Perena said.

"Thanks. Anya, if you could look at those DNA samples. Perhaps a preliminary analysis? And prepare some duplicates for Merral to take to Earth. And can I get copies of that Maya Knella data too?"

Anya nodded.

"And finally, I need to talk to Brenito. I have many questions and some he may be able to answer."

"What about me?" Merral asked.

"And you?" Vero smiled. "You rest that ankle. But I wouldn't be surprised if Brenito might want to see you."

"When do we meet again?" Perena asked.

"Here? Ten-thirty tonight? To give us all the maximum time to do what we have to do."

•◆•

As they left the room and began to walk up the corridor to the exit, Merral overheard Perena outline the journey to Vero, and suddenly he felt that he was in a dream. "You will be at Bannermene tomorrow noon. From there, you are booked on from Bannermene Inward Gate to Namidahl a couple of hours later. Namidahl is, of course, on the outer ring and you go one Gate clockwise to the Finent Node. From Finent there's a lot of traffic and depending exactly when you arrive, you should be at one of the Terran Gates with no more than two Gate jumps. Stress the urgent-priority status. So, all being well, in just over forty-eight hours traveling, you will be on Ancient Earth."

Merral felt his mind reel at the prospect. This was not a game of Cross the Assembly; this was the real thing. They were talking about his journey.

"Where are we sleeping?" he asked. Suddenly feeling overwhelmed with tiredness, he had a desperate need to lie down.

Perena patted his shoulder. "There is a spare room in the pilots' quarters for you and Vero. I'll get you another set of spare clothes each too."

•◆•

Perena drove Merral and Vero to the quarters at the edge of the complex of landing strips and showed them to the spare room at the far end of the building. It was small and its basic furnishings gave it the air of a room that was only used as a place for people to sleep; yet it was, they agreed, quite adequate.

After Perena left, Vero sat on his bed and put his head in his hands.

"Are you all right?" Merral asked, conscious that his ankle was still hurting.

"That meeting . . . I wasn't sure I could manage to lead it. I knew I had to, but it was not easy. Thanks for your support." He rubbed his face. "I am out of my depth, Merral. Making decisions; giving orders. All that sort of thing. I am an ideas person."

"You did well."

"If I did, it was by the grace of God. But we will see what happens. You nearly threw me twice, you know."

"How? I didn't mean to."

"You sprung two new surprises. That you had seen a man and that there was evidence of a ship."

"I apologize."

"No, no, it wasn't your fault. In fact, I am sure that they will help to resolve things. But I need to think about them." And with that he fell silent.

CHAPTER 17

When Merral awoke after a troubled sleep, it was midmorning. Vero had gone and there was a handwritten message on the table. *Gone to see Brenito. Back around midday. Suggest you stay out of sight and don't make diary calls. Vero.*

Merral rose, showered, and dressed his ankle again. There was food on the table and he made himself some coffee. He looked out of the window, but the quarters were at the end of a side runway and there was little to see other than bare rock baking in the warm spring sunshine. In the end, Merral went and lay down on his bed and stared at the ceiling, trying to make sense of what had happened.

Just after midday, Vero returned with food, drink, some more clothes, and a replacement diary. After checking that Merral's ankle was healing, he announced that if Merral felt he could manage it, Brenito would like to see him.

"I would be fascinated to meet him," Merral said. "His summons for help set so much in motion. And if I don't have to walk far, my ankle will be fine. How was your meeting with him?"

An odd expression slid across Vero's face. He frowned. "He listened. He was very disturbed about almost every aspect of our trip north. A number of things particularly alarmed him: Jorgio's vision, the creatures—of course, the imitation buzzard, the manipulation of the Gate and diary transmissions. Especially the bird. When I told him it wasn't a robot but was actually based on a dead bird, his eyebrows nearly flew off his head. And it was the first he had heard of Barrand's alteration of a re-created voice too. So, there was plenty for him to think about."

"Any answers?"

Vero seemed to stare at the wall.

"No, not really. He thought a lot, but he is a very cautious man. He said he was going to sleep on it when I left. He sleeps a lot. But no blinding answers. Maybe this afternoon will be better."

"You seem disappointed."

"Hmm. Oh, I suppose I had built my hopes up too much. Frankly, Brenito was far less help than I expected. I'm glad we will be at Earth in a few days; I need some answers and I think they may be able to give them to us. Incidentally, he took a special interest in my account of your exploits. 'Oh,' he said, 'I'm glad you found yourself a warrior. That's something, at least.'"

Merral shook his head. "I reject that title. I'm still very unhappy about what I did."

"I—as you know—have a different opinion," Vero answered, tilting his head. "As does Brenito."

Merral shook his head. "Nothing pleases me more about this trip to Ancient Earth than the prospect of handing over responsibility for all this. Vero, I want to turn the clock back. I want to go back to my trees."

"Indeed. I have decided I want to write and teach. May it be soon, for both of us. But in the meantime, let us eat."

•◆•

After they had eaten lunch and Vero had restored his data to his new diary, they drove over to Brenito's cottage in a small four-seater that Vero had borrowed from Space Affairs. They had the windows open, and Merral, reveling in the smell of blossom and spring, found himself wondering whether Ancient Earth would smell the same. As they drove, Vero began to tell Merral more about Brenito.

"He was very distinguished in his day as an academic historian. On Ancient Earth he wrote several studies of early sentinel history under his full name of Brenito Camsar. He was a bit of a collector of things too, as you will see. Then in retirement, he felt he wanted to spend his last years doing something else. So he came out to replace Lars Mantell, who was sentinel here."

"I see. I just call him 'Brenito'? Not 'Sentinel Camsar' or something?"

"No, he's informal enough. I call him 'sir' out of deference. You need not."

They drove toward the headland on the southwestern side of Isterrane, and every so often there were glimpses of a cornflower blue sea down valleys or over fields. Then abruptly they turned off down a pale white track between silver-skinned poplars whose new leaves rustled in the breeze. At the end of the track, nestled between two low hills, was a wooden house painted white with faded yellow shutters.

After Vero parked, they walked through a neat vegetable garden set between trimmed hedges to a blue wooden door upon which Vero rapped his knuckles loudly.

There was the sound of movement in the house, and after a few moments, the door slowly opened to reveal a large, stooped man in an old gray suit with a faded sentinel badge on the left breast and a shirt that was open at the neck. Merral had seen images of Brenito before, but seeing him now in the flesh, nearly filling the doorway, he was surprised by how big a man Brenito actually was. Once, he must have been an imposing figure, but now any muscle had turned to fat. His face was a mass of creased flesh dominated by strangely pale gray eyes capped by faint white eyebrows, and his tightly cropped white hair was little more than a pale stubble.

Behind Brenito, Merral glimpsed a corridor filled almost up to the ceiling by glass cases, cabinets, framed images, and prints.

The old man looked from Merral to Vero, and then back again with hooded eyes. Then he leaned his jowled face toward Merral and smiled knowingly.

"Ah, welcome, Merral D'Avanos," he said in a heavy, resonant voice with a hint of a non-Farholme accent and slowly extended a large, soft hand. Merral noticed that he wore open-toed sandals through which large toes protruded.

Merral bowed and took the hand. "Sentinel Brenito, it is my honor."

A wry expression played across the heavy mouth. "Ah, come, let's not worry about honor, Forester. If we ever get to that. The Assembly is in a real mess."

Merral felt that if the voice was that of a man who had lived for a century, the sharpness of the riposte indicated a mind that had no weaknesses in it.

"Now, Verofaza," he added, "you come on in too. You look tired."

"I am slightly, sir, but it will pass."

"As do all things under heaven. I'm making tea. Excuse my clothes. But do take our hero through and give him a seat."

Merral felt that the dry, humorous tone went some way to easing the burden of his being termed "hero."

Vero led Merral to a long side room. Sunlight streamed in through the large glass windows at the far end, and Merral caught a glimpse of the sea, dazzling in its blueness. But his eye was drawn away by the extraordinary collection of mementos and antiques that dominated the room. A hundred items clamored for his attention: an ancient space helmet, fragments of exotic machinery, maps of strange worlds, signed images of men and women, and piles of old paperbacks. On one wall behind glass was a worn blue flag with the gold-encircled stone tower of the sentinel insignia in the middle.

"Take a seat," Vero said, motioning to an armchair of such an age that Merral wondered if it was another heirloom.

"Why, it's almost like a museum," Merral said, carefully moving his ankle past a plant pot mounted on a thruster nozzle and lowering himself gingerly onto the chair.

"History is part of sentinel culture," Vero said. "The past must not be forgotten lest the future be lost too."

"I can see that. But, for example, what is this?" Merral tapped a dusty, black metal box on a shelf.

From somewhere in the room a voice speaking in Communal rang out. "This is the navigation unit of the Assembly Seeder Ship *Vladimir*

Hengstra. This ship seeded a total of thirty worlds from 2245–2585. Do you wish further information?"

Merral smiled. "No, thank you," he said to the unseen responding machine.

He turned to Vero. "I see. Everything is labeled. That voice is familiar."

"The younger Brenito. . . he recorded labels for all these things."

The door opened and the old man came in ponderously, carrying a tray on which were cups, a teapot, and a sliced cake. As Vero helped him put it down on the table, Brenito stared at Merral.

"Interesting, isn't it?" he said slowly. "The past, that is. But now, ironically, at the end of my earthly life, I find it is the future that preoccupies me. Now help yourselves. I still do a little cooking, and I hope the cake is to your satisfaction."

Then with sighs and gentle groans, Brenito seated himself in a massive wooden rocking chair that creaked under his weight. He turned to Merral. "First of all, thank you for coming. Increasingly, I have the belief that in summoning Vero here, I have played the part allotted to me. Now it is the task of Earth to deal with it and answer the questions. I have really, I suppose, asked you here to satisfy my own curiosity." He paused. "And yet I also want to tell you both something of what I think is going on."

"You know?" Vero asked with an urgent enthusiasm.

The big hands opened wide. "I have a hypothesis. No more than that. But as I thought about what you told me this morning, some ideas have come to me. And those tentative thoughts may give you something to think about as you travel. But first things first. Forester, shall I tell you why I summoned help?"

"Please."

"It is easy to tell: I dreamed of a field of stars and of a great red dragon that walked across them, swallowing the stars up one by one." The pale gray eyes gleamed at Merral. "The dream was repeated three nights running. It was a very powerful dream, like nothing I have ever had. And I knew that the stars were symbols of the Assembly worlds, and I knew that the first star to be swallowed up was Farholme. So I asked Earth for help. And so Verofaza came."

Merral looked at Brenito for a moment before answering. "I see. You have heard of the dream or vision that Jorgio Aneld Serter had?"

Brenito gave a slow nod and stared up at the ceiling for a moment. "The testing of the Assembly. The candles shaken by a gust of wind, a storm unleashed on Farholme. The command to watch, stand firm, and to hope. The similarities are marked, are they not? A threat to the Assembly, beginning at Farholme. But Jorgio's vision is more explicit and, I think, on Earth they will be very concerned about what it means."

Then he fixed his eyes on Merral. "Now, please, would you tell me your account of matters? If you could begin at Nativity?"

Merral began to summarize what had happened to him since Nativity. He was prompted every so often by Vero, who seemed otherwise anxious to retire into the background.

As he spoke, Brenito sipped his tea in an oddly delicate manner and listened, nodded, and frowned. Other than to dryly murmur things like "fascinating," "how curious," and "most alarming," he made little comment. Finally, when Merral had finished, he put his cup down shakily on the table.

"Quite remarkable," he pronounced. "Hearing it the first time from Verofaza was remarkable, and this second time from you is no less so."

Merral looked at the big man. "Sir, what is going on?"

Brenito made no answer but slowly rocked backward and forward. The creaking of the chair seemed to mingle with the sound of seagulls mewing outside. Then suddenly, Brenito lifted his head and stared at Merral with a strange, troubled smile.

"Ah," Brenito said slowly. "I researched the early history of the Assembly, years ago. Strictly, my period was 2120–2510, and the Rebellion was not in my scope. But you had to understand it; it cast a shadow over those years. For sentinels, as you know, it still casts a shadow. Now, I found much in your accounts that reminded me of the Rebellion, and I know that Verofaza has felt the same. When Verofaza and I discussed these matters earlier, the subject of the Rebellion kept coming up. It is almost as if Jannafy's 'Free Peoples' have crept back. But, as my young colleague here can tell you, they cannot."

Vero stared at the floor for a moment as if making a final deliberation and then looked hard at Brenito. "Sir, two points: First, the Rebellion was ended in a manner that would ensure its total termination. And all the accounts suggest a total annihilation of everything that Jannafy had set up. To use a horrid word, there was *sterilization.*" Vero hesitated. "And second, the sentinels were set up shortly afterward to guard against any resurgence of what Jannafy had proposed."

Brenito nodded. "Oh, I agree. And across the length, breadth, and depth of the Assembly there has not been the slightest hint of anything surviving these last eleven thousand-odd years. Until . . ."

"Until now?" Merral said, feeling almost surprised at the sound of his own voice.

"Indeed," Brenito said and looked at Vero. "Briefly, for my benefit and for the benefit of Merral here, rehearse again the tale of the ending of the Rebellion."

Vero glanced at Merral. "I believe he knows it well, sir."

"That is as may be, but tell it again." Brenito sat back in his rocking chair, closed his eyes, and folded his hands over the expanse of his stomach.

Vero cleared his throat and began to speak. "Very well. With the rebels in command of the Centauri Colony and the Centauri Gate, the decision was taken, very reluctantly, to end the Rebellion militarily. The assault fleet was assembled and sent in late 2104; it arrived, apparently unsuspected, after an unparalleled six-year journey in 2110. Surveillance indicated that the colony had indeed been destroyed with massive loss of life and a new orbiting laboratory station made. Preparations were plainly advanced for colonizing missions elsewhere. The decision was made by Fleet-General Denion to attack, try to release any prisoners, and then destroy the complex. A previously untested poly-element fusion explosive device was armed and fitted to the frigate *Clearstar* under Captain Lucas Ringell."

Merral noticed that at this name Brenito opened one eye and looked across at him. Vero continued, his voice dry and factual. "Ringell and his men forced an entry into the station and established from the computer that there were no surviving prisoners. There was heavy fighting, with Lucas Ringell in the forefront and many casualties made worse by the loss of air pressure as the hull was blasted open. Finally, in an end chamber they faced William Jannafy himself. In the resulting fight, Ringell shot Jannafy and killed him. In the meantime, General Denion had retaken the Gate. The assault fleet regrouped and exited through the Gate an hour before the device exploded."

"Yes. A fair—if terse—account of humanity's last battle. And the results were what?" Brenito's eyes remained closed.

"The ship *Nighthawk*—incidentally, Merral, with Moshe Adlen on board—returned through the Gate a week after the explosion when the worst of the radiation had faded. They found that the devastation was even greater than predicted and that nothing but fine dust remained of the complex." Brenito opened both eyes and nodded at Vero to continue.

"And just over four years later, when the light reached Earth, the flash of the explosion was detected by even modest ground-based telescopes. The Rebellion ended with a bang. Nothing survived. The end of the story."

Brenito leaned forward to the teapot and carefully poured himself another cup. Then sitting back in the chair he looked hard at Vero. "Perhaps." His voice rang out in the room.

"I'm sorry?"

"You said, Verofaza, that it was 'the end of the story' and I said 'perhaps.'"

Vero stared at him. "Could you elaborate, sir?"

He sipped again at his tea. "Let me go back. There were many causes of the Rebellion, although only a few are now spoken of. Jannafy, for all the evil he produced, was a clear thinker. At least, at the start. He looked at the earliest versions of such things as the Technology Protocols and foresaw—perhaps better than his contemporaries—the society that they would produce. He saw that the Assembly would be stable but that the cost of that stability would be a restriction on what could be done. To him that was an unacceptable cost; he demanded total freedom. The name of 'The Free Peoples,' chosen by him for his followers, reflected that demand. That much, Forester, you know?"

Merral nodded.

"It is the part of the story that is generally told. Yet beneath Jannafy's general request for freedom, there were, if I remember rightly, two specific issues. The first issue, about which I know little, and which may—only *may*—not concern us, was to do with Below-Space exploration. You need to talk to your pilot—what was her name?—about that. She may know more."

"Perena Lewitz," Vero said. "But—if I may, sir—we don't explore Below-Space. We never have. The Gate system is a linkage of Normal-Space tubes carved through the upper levels of Below-Space. We travel through Below-Space, not in it."

"Oh, I know that, Verofaza," Brenito said. "But it was an issue. You talk to Perena Lewitz. And when, on Earth, you have found out what the issue was, come back and tell me. And bring this young lady with you."

Merral caught the hint of a faint flush of embarrassment on Vero's face. "Er, thank you, sir. She would, no doubt, be fascinated by much that is here. You have so many old things."

"Ah, at times I feel like an exhibit myself," Brenito said, and in his slow, heavy words Merral detected a great weariness. "Now the second specific grievance of William Jannafy—'that restless mind' as he was called—was what became called 'The Alternative Proposal.' Have either of you heard of it?"

Vero and Merral shook their heads.

"Briefly, it was this: At the end of the twenty-first century, as the Assembly was forming, the whole process of making worlds fit for humanity was in doubt. They knew we could reach them—if slowly— they knew we could alter their orbits and do all sorts of things, but with the atmosphere-modifying organisms then available it looked as if it would take forever—well, many tens of thousands of years—to produce worlds where men and women could live under an open sky. So some people, including Jannafy and those associated with him, came up with what he labeled 'The Alternative Proposal.' The phrase that came to be linked with it was 'to fit humanity to the worlds, not the worlds to humanity.' In short, they proposed major modifications of our species to produce new forms. These forms included—if I remember—beings modified to handle higher radiation exposures, heavier gravities, or even low oxygen levels. The modifications were to be genetic or mechanical."

Vero furrowed his brow. "I've never heard of this. Not in as many words. It sounds appalling."

"No," Brenito said, "you wouldn't have. If you had done further studies, Verofaza, it would have come up; it is on the postgraduate syllabus. But it is in a class of knowledge that, while not hidden, is not broadcast. You could find out about it freely in the Library, but you would have to know it was there. Now, you may wish to debate the wisdom of that on Earth, but there it is. Anyway, after the Rebellion there was no desire to have the idea discussed again. And as for it being appalling, well it is, but Jannafy presented it with a great deal of skill. Anyway, the proposal was resoundingly defeated and so—at least, we have always assumed—it passed into history. But it was over these two matters in particular that Jannafy and his supporters decided to forcibly secede from the infant Assembly. And from that came the Rebellion and its suffering."

There was an intense silence that was broken by a weary sigh from Brenito. "I am tired. But perhaps you now follow my train of thought. These creatures, as you describe them, seem to be exactly what Jannafy would have created. . . ." He stopped, staring into the distance. "And yet nothing survived. Nothing. Or so we have been told."

Vero gazed at Brenito, a range of emotions—consternation, bewilderment, even anger—crossing his face. "Sir, you believe that—somehow—something of what Jannafy and the rebels created has, despite everything we have been taught—survived? For so long? But where? How?"

Brenito sighed again. "Verofaza, it is a hypothesis only. Whether it is true is for Earth to decide."

"But, sir, isn't it obvious that the rebels were destroyed? We know that Jannafy was killed. I mean, I've seen the vid-clip from Lucas's shoulder cam. Once, out of curiosity. The helmet shatters, and blood droplets float everywhere in the vacuum. He was dead."

"Just so."

Vero continued. "And no one else could have escaped in the couple of hours before the blast. And they could hardly have outrun it."

"Oh, Verofaza, I know the objections—all of them. But—and you can tell the Sentinel Council this—I do believe that, somehow, the ghosts of the Rebellion have come to back to haunt us. And if they ask whether I mean ghosts literally you can tell them that old Brenito isn't ruling that out either. Not after that awful dead bird thing."

"I will, sir," Vero said with a slight bow of his head.

"Good. And another thing. Don't let them focus totally on these beasts and creatures. It will be easy to do because you now have the DNA and the images. But it's the invisible things—the spiritual dimension—that may be the biggest threat. We can eliminate these monstrosities with swords or a vortex blaster. But spiritual evil is less obvious and far more contagious. And it is harder to remove."

"I will remember that, too."

"And finally, on Earth I want you to look at the records—the primary sources, mark you—on the Rebellion. They might give clues. What was in the laboratory? I assume no one knew, but is that true? If anyone looked at the lab it would have been the crew of the *Nighthawk*, so you might want to look at Moshe Adlen's records."

"But they were published, weren't they? Aren't they in the Library?"

"Only an edited account was ever published. And, interestingly enough, the foreword to his *Accounts of the Centauri Military Expedition* says somewhere that this 'is all the material that he felt appropriate to publish.' The central sentinel office holds all Moshe Adlen's records in their vaults, and my memory is that when I looked at them—oh, fifty years ago—I found more in them than I had expected." Brenito rubbed his stubbly hair. "In fact, I made copies of parts, and probably still have them somewhere. If we had time—and if I could find them—I would show you the difference."

"That I will certainly do."

Brenito closed his eyes and shook his head slowly. "Oh, I'm sorry. I'm rather tired."

Vero rose to his feet, "I'm afraid I—we—have exhausted you, sir. We must go."

"I am getting frail. I sent a message the other week, but, Verofaza, if you could—when you have a moment—pass on the fact that it is time to find a successor for me."

The old man rose laboriously out of his rocking chair and stood upright, his big body gently swaying. "Of course, who they choose may well depend on how this matter turns out. But yes, I think I need to lie down. You can see yourselves out."

He turned to Merral. "Forester D'Avanos, I presume you will be returning to Farholme. When you come back, I would hope to see you. I would love to hear your account of the deliberations. And as a war-rior—oh yes, I know you refuse the title—there is much here that would interest you."

"The Lord willing," Merral replied as they shook hands, "I will return. But I am not sure that what you have in mind will interest me. My concern is to get back to forestry."

There was a wry, slow nod. "May it be so. But don't go back until we let you go. Please! We may need you."

Brenito extended a hand to Vero. "And you—young Verofaza—I suppose you will not be coming back unless there is something—or someone—to bring you back."

Vero's face suddenly became void of emotion. "I have no idea, sir, what happens to me after the next few days. There are many issues for me to resolve. My father is not well. But I hope to be in contact with you at least fairly soon. I would like to return."

"I understand. Do have a good trip. I will be praying for your deliberations."

Vero turned toward the door and took a step forward. Then he turned back to face Brenito.

"Sir," he said, his face turned to the ground, "I have a confession to make."

Brenito looked surprised.

"You see, sir," Vero continued hesitantly, and Merral glimpsed his fingers wrapping and unwrapping themselves, "I confess that I have entertained, well—doubts, about the worth of our calling. The thought had often come to me, until a few days ago, that what we sentinels were doing was a waste of time. That we were watching for something that would never happen."

Then he looked up at the old man. "Suddenly, I find I have resolved my doubts. About what the sentinels do. We were right to watch. Moshe Adlen was right; those generations of sentinels—my ancestors, your ancestors—were right. Evil *was* lurking."

Brenito stared at him and nodded almost imperceptibly. Then a wide smile split his face. "I am so glad to hear it, Verofaza. Your doubts were no secret. In fact, when I asked Earth for someone to be sent, I asked for the most skeptical person they could find."

"You knew?" Vero looked startled. "But why?"

Brenito shrugged. "We didn't want someone imagining evil where there was none, did we? We couldn't afford that. Not again. You were sent here because of your vices, not because of your virtues. I hope that amuses you." He stared at Vero and smiled broadly again. "Well done, anyway."

A grin crossed Vero's face and he bowed his head. Then he turned and, followed by Merral, left the room.

• ◆ •

They had driven barely a few meters from the house when Vero began to laugh aloud.

"He knew all along! Merral, he knew! I would say that that was the funniest thing I've heard for a week, but that would be faint praise. Oh dear. I was sent here because of my vices, not because of my virtues. . . ."

Then, with a great reluctance, he seemed to push his amusement away.

"But, Merral, my friend, do you think he's right? About the Rebellion?"

Merral stared at the poplars before answering. "Perhaps. Nothing else fits. Although I find it hard to come to grips with it. To believe that we got it all wrong? That—somehow—Jannafy's people escaped and have been hiding out somewhere for thousands of years?"

"I agree it's hard to take in. One of the things that I have taken for granted ever since I first heard the story of the Rebellion was that it was distant history. It was over. Every human being everywhere was part of the Assembly. But now?" Vero shook his head. "Now, I'm not sure I take anything for granted. Perhaps, I am not skeptical enough." He looked at Merral with his brown eyes wide. "I think that's the lesson, isn't it? Remember that what you think can't happen, may happen. Assume nothing. Rule nothing out."

Then Vero turned the vehicle out of the avenue of poplars onto the main road. "But, Merral, I rejoice that it is not my battle anymore. I will willingly hand it over to whatever council of wise men and women the Assembly comes up with. With very great gratitude. And I imagine you agree?"

"I do indeed, Vero. Let's hand this over to others as soon as we can."

· ◆ ·

That night Vero and Merral arrived at the isolation room before either of the women. Vero had brought with him the travel case that held his possessions. After all, he said, there was no certainty that he would be returning to Farholme. Merral, in contrast, simply had a small holdall that contained little more than the spare clothes he had been issued.

Shortly afterward, Anya and Perena arrived bearing parcels. After greetings and inquiries about Merral's ankle, everyone sat down.

Vero gestured to Merral. "Take over. Now you know as much as I do."

Merral glanced around. "Thanks. I think it's best we go round in turns. Who wants to start?"

Anya raised a hand, reached down to the floor by her, and put two identical packages on the table. With her face creasing into disgust she pushed the packages over to Merral. "Take them away, Tree Man and Earther. Duplicates. I don't want to see them again. Let someone else deal with them. They are horrid!"

Merral looked at her. "Samples of DNA and the datapaks?"

"And the Knella images."

"What do you want to say about them? The samples?"

Anya leaned back in her chair, her sky blue eyes looking hard at Merral.

"I got three different types of DNA out of your dirty clothes. Of such things is science made. Only one is human." She smiled. "Relax, Merral, you are one of us." There was laughter, but Merral felt that it was forced and shallow.

Anya shook her head. "The other two, however, were not human. Now, I have only done a preliminary scan; after all, they will put a whole team on this on Ancient Earth." She frowned and gestured with a finger at the packages. "There is no doubt that what you carry with you will cause an outrage. It confirms what I had first suggested. The ape-creature has three genetic components: gorilla, human, and what must be artificial code. The cockroach-beast parallels it; it has human and arthropod genes and, again, artificial code."

"There's no doubt they are a creation? Not a mutation or, well, a natural hybrid?" Merral asked, knowing the answer even as he spoke the words.

"No. Simply, no. First, the human DNA is similar in both cases: as if it was taken from the same stock. In fact, the human component is odd. Natural human DNA is rather florid, baroque; it has lots of extra bits on it. This is lean and neat: a sort of optimized human genetic code. Very odd."

Merral caught the imprint of distaste on Vero's face as Anya paused, looked around, and then continued. "Second, on the basis of your descriptions, I did a quick check for where the genes for reproductive organs would be in man and gorilla. They are absent. They cannot make themselves; they must be made."

Vero stared at her. "Forgive me, my biology is basic. These are organisms?"

"In one sense, yes. Of course they are. But I think I see what you are getting at. Unless they clone themselves they are basically—I'm sorry, this is such a negative thought—little more than biological tools."

Out of the corner of his eye, Merral saw Perena's face twist into an expression of disgust.

"And the cockroach-beast?" Merral asked.

"*That.*" Anya made a grimace. "Let me correct something here. I had thought that it was some sort of giant invertebrate with an exoskeleton. In fact, it seems, at first glance, rather similar to the ape-creature. I would guess that it has, basically, a human skeleton, but a thickened cuticle instead of skin as an outer covering, a sort of organic armor. Of course, then you have to make all sorts of changes to allow for movement and sweating, but I could see how it might be done. But . . ." She shrugged. "This is beyond me. Professionally, I would be interested to know what they come up with in a more detailed analysis, but personally I would be happy never to see or think of this again. I feel I need a shower."

There was silence and Merral looked around the room. *Things now are very different from last night; then we were reeling with shock and frightened; now we are more in control and our fear has turned to revulsion and anger.*

Merral looked at Vero. "Do you want to say what we learned today?"

"No," he said. "Not yet. I want to hear what Perena has to say."

Merral looked at Perena. "Captain Lewitz, anything to report?"

Perena gestured to two oblong packages that she had leaned against the wall. "Your tile samples. Hand carry them, please; there are addresses on them. I checked for radiation and there is none." She gave a shrug of her slight shoulders. "We need to know what did it. Urgently. And what is the range of such weapons? Can I suggest that once you have gone through the Gate, I get a ruling issued giving a minimum altitude for flights over the Carson's Sill and Lannar Crater area? Perhaps three thousand meters?"

Merral looked at Vero, who nodded agreement. "Good idea. Anything on the imagery?"

Perena put her diary on the table and tapped the screen. "Here. I haven't had a chance to look at it in detail."

A landscape appeared on the wallscreen. *Thermal imagery,* Merral decided, as he looked at the browns and yellows of land cut by the cold dark blue of the lakes, ponds, and rivers. Any large creatures or a ship should show up. Used to interpreting such maps for forestry purposes, Merral saw the anomaly quickly.

"There!" he snapped, pointing a finger at a cluster of small red dots and an orange oval outline to the north of the lake.

"Well spotted," Perena said with a nod. "Four kilometers from where I picked you up. I got an enhanced blowup."

A second image, but with a more grainy texture, filled the screen. There was a large, clearly marked orange oblong with four bright yellow points at the rounded corners. To the left of the oblong were five dull red dots, two of which were smaller than the others.

"The intruder ship?" Vero said, excitement in his voice.

"*An* intruder ship," Perena said. "It is only thirty meters long. A bit shorter than my *Nesta Lamaine*."

"Too small, right?" interjected Merral. "There were at least twenty creatures."

"Exactly," Perena said, in her quiet, unruffled way. "It's far too small to be an in-system machine, let alone one capable of inter-system travel. To me, this looks to be much more like the size of an

Assembly ferry craft. That would be my guess. Carried inside a ship and used for local flights within the atmosphere."

Merral scrutinized the image carefully and caught Perena's eye. "Can you make anything of it technically?"

"A bit. It needs enhancement and an assessment by an aerospace engineering team. One other bit of data is on another image taken ten hours later. The ship has gone, but there are four scorch marks at the corner of the outline. But if I use imagination and assume that it uses a similar technology to what we have, I think here it's just landed." She nodded at the image. "Let me tell you why: The hot spots suggest four engines at the corners that are still warm. Confirmed by the corner scorch marks seen on later images. They suggest a vertical capability, probably with chemical engines. There is no hint of gravity-modification technology or anything even more exotic. There is little aerodynamic shaping; the front is only just slightly more pointed than the rear. So I read that as a low-speed craft, say Mach 2 or 3 maximum. I also find it interesting that there is no evidence of heating on what we presume are the front edges of the machine. So, no evidence of atmospheric entry. My guess is something small, subspace, and subsonic."

"And that it hasn't traveled far?"

Perena gave a pained smile, "Vero, you are asking me to pile supposition on guesswork. But normally a ferry craft wouldn't be used for a journey of more than about fifteen hundred kilometers."

Vero, leaning back in his chair, gestured at the image. "Perena, you make it sound just like one of our ferry craft."

Perena gestured at the packages by the wall. "I could be wrong. I have put copies of these for you to take; I want a team of engineers to look at them. But I *was* surprised at how familiar it seemed. It does not seem alien—whatever an alien ship would look like. But remember, it almost certainly cannot be the parent ship. You can see that by the comparison with the figures."

"I was going to ask about those," Merral said. "Are they human-sized? Bigger, smaller?"

"I did a rough check. The two smaller figures are within the range for human beings. The three others are something else."

"Ape-creatures?"

"So one presumes."

Vero looked up at Perena. "You think they are evacuating what is left of their forces?"

She nodded. "Feasible."

"And we have no idea where they have gone? where the mother ship is?"

"None. It's a big place up there, Sentinel. What? A million square kilometers?"

"Could you find it the same way?"

Perena shrugged. "It depends on how big the ship is and whether it is hidden. Remember playing hide-and-seek as children? If they don't want to be found, then it could be hard."

"This showed up fairly easily," Vero said, nodding at the image.

"This was probably an emergency mission." Perena's tone was terse. "And the area we were searching was vastly smaller."

Merral looked at Vero. "Well, that is a task for the Defense Force. But your turn, Sentinel. You better tell everybody what we learned from Brenito."

Vero started to summarize the conversation they had had with Brenito. When he came to Brenito's references to Below-Space exploration, he stopped and looked at Perena. "Can you help here? He thought you could."

Perena stared at her fingertips for moment before answering. "It is a part of space-flight history that I know little about, and I have never heard of Jannafy's name in connection with Below-Space exploration. But then, I wouldn't read too much into that. What do I know?" She hesitated before answering, apparently choosing her words. "The story is something like this: As soon as Gate technology was devised in 2068 there were efforts to use a single Gate as a portal to Below-Space. It was attractive. Building Gates gave us access through Below-Space, but to be able to fly within it would open the universe to us. Spatial physics theory suggested that enormous distances could be traveled very easily, giving speeds that were effectively ten or twenty times that of light. And the deeper you went into Below-Space, the faster you went."

Perena paused again, and as she did, Merral felt struck by the quiet, cool, and unflustered way she dealt with things. She continued. "At first remote probes were sent, but very few returned. They confirmed the theory that the vast distances and vast speeds were possible, but there were problems. Navigation was hard. Anyway, in the last quarter of the twenty-first century there were—I think—twenty human missions, with two- to five-person ships. They were all failures. Most never returned. Two came back with dead crews, and finally, one ship returned with a living crew. But they were in a poor state and died shortly afterward. The ship was called the *Argo*. I know that because there is a tradition—which still exists—that no ship is ever to be called by that name again." Her face had acquired a troubled look. "Which is odd, really, because we have lost other ships. Anyway, after that, there was a decision to abandon the research. Then there was the Rebellion, and ever since we have been content to travel through Gates. After all, once they are set up they work very well."

She looked at Vero. "I was quite unaware that Jannafy wanted such research continued. I had assumed the Rebellion was over generalities, not specifics." She frowned. "But it fits with the man: rebellious, bold, and—as events showed—someone who could be reckless with human life. I would be interested to research that data. Mind you, much of the material may have been lost in the Rebellion. The Experimental and Projects Unit on Mars was devastated."

"I will make inquiries too," Vero added. "And it may only be of passing relevance. But the thing that Brenito told us that I feel is of real relevance was about Jannafy and 'The Alternative Proposal.'"

As Vero repeated what Brenito had said, Merral watched Anya and saw that as the details were recounted, her eyes widened with evident shock. The way she kept looking at the packages she had placed on the table earlier suggested that she had made the same connections as he and Vero had.

When Vero had finished, he looked at her. "So, Doctor Lewitz, comments? Please."

Anya stared blankly back at him. "I'm appalled . . . stunned. I find it hard to imagine how someone actually proposed making the very things that I—no—we have been so horrified about. But. . . . No, the time gap is too great. Even if we allow that Jannafy didn't just propose but *did* make these things—perhaps in the Centauri Lab—all those thousands of years ago . . . could . . . ?" She frowned. "No, the Rebellion was brought to an end."

Vero spoke in a low but audible voice. "Yes, history says that nothing survived. Jannafy and his followers were killed. Their labs were vaporized in the biggest artificial explosion ever created."

Anya nodded agreement. "No, for these things to have survived and got out here is too much. It must be coincidence. Mustn't it?"

But her questioning glance received no confirming response, and finally Merral, after looking at the clock, broke the silence. "Our time has gone. We better get over to the terminal to check in. Thankfully we can soon pass the burden of all this to Earth. But it has been helpful to discuss these things here. Vero, would you summarize what you think is happening?"

Vero stared ahead. "For me the strands of evidence suggest that something survived from the rebels. Whether some of Jannafy's followers, his teachings, or even—just possibly—something of what he created. But where, when, and how will, I think, be much debated over the next few weeks." He sighed. "As will be the still harder question of what is to be done."

Merral rose. "And that, I suspect, ends the Farholme deliberations on these matters."

"Indeed," Vero said with a nod as he rose. "Well, Forester, it's time for us to travel."

CHAPTER 18

While the sisters went inside the terminal to try and ensure that formal embarkation procedures could be avoided, Merral and Vero found seats some distance from the building. Merral stared into the night. Away to his left was the main part of Isterrane City, where only a few lights remained in this first hour of the Lord's Day. Ahead, within the space terminal itself, there were lights and movement as families gathered for the imminent departure for the Gate. And to the right, spotlights picked out the curving fuselage and wings of the shuttle lined up on the runway.

"Two in the morning is an awkward time for a flight," Merral commented, as a wisp of vapor from the ramjets drifted upward and caught the light.

"I know, but to minimize the time people spend floating around at a Gate Station waiting for connections, someone has to start at a bad hour. And being the end of the line, it's Farholme. Anyway, today it suits us perfectly. We will be out of the system by midday."

Vero stopped, sniffing the night air. "I wonder," he said, "whether I will come back. I suppose they may just say, 'Thanks, Sentinel Enand, but we'll handle it from here.'"

"Do you want to come back?" Merral asked, looking at the lights of Isterrane and thinking with a sudden pang of emotion of his own town and his family.

"I've grown to be quite fond of Farholme; Worlds' End isn't that bad a place. And I have grown fond of the people; particularly you, Anya, and Perena." Vero paused, and Merral read much into his momentary silence. "But I need to go back. Above all, my task is not quite finished; I have to be sure that all this is sorted out. Then I will think of my future. I need to see my father."

Suddenly, Merral found his longing for his family more than he could bear. "Vero," he blurted out, "I need to leave a message with my parents. And Isabella. May I?"

Vero hesitated. "It will be just after one in Ynysmant. So they will all be asleep. Oh, I guess so. Just leave a message: say you are going on a private trip, that you are going to be out of touch. Whatever words you can find. But remember that your call may be monitored."

That alone, Merral thought wearily, *is cause for concern. Is privacy the first victim of these events? Until this is resolved, will anyone ever again have the confidence that his or her conversations are their personal and private affair?* He suspected from her earlier outrage that Anya would have agreed.

A new thought struck him. "What about giving them a contact? In case they need me."

"Ah. Oh, tell them to get in touch with Anya. She can pass it on. In two days she can give your address on Earth. Diaries are switched off on shuttles and liners anyway."

Merral found the mental image of his mother hearing that her youngest child—her only son—had gone halfway across the Assembly without telling her, almost overwhelming. That would raise a few eyebrows permanently. Few, if any, people in Ynysmant had been to Ancient Earth, and no one he had ever heard of had gone at a day's notice.

Merral found himself staring into the darkness as yet another new thought struck him. "But when am I coming back?" he asked, all too aware of the consternation in his voice.

"Back?" He saw Vero shrug his shoulders. "If they move quickly, you could be back in days with the Defense Force ships. They don't bother with waiting at Gate Stations. Just in one Gate and out the next. You could do Earth to Farholme in twenty-four hours. You'll feel lousy. But it can be done."

So I could be back in a week, Merral thought and wondered if he would see anything of Ancient Earth other than offices. He walked a few meters away from the seat, called his mother's diary, and was told—inevitably—that she was asleep.

"Hi, Mother and Father," he dictated. "Vero and I just got back safely from the north. But I have some urgent work to do. I will be out of touch for a few days. You can reach me through Anya Salema Lewitz at the Planetary Ecology Center. Love to you and the rest of the family. Merral."

When, however, a minute later he called Isabella, he was surprised to find that she answered in person. "Oh, er, hi, it's Merral," he spluttered. "I thought—"

"Merral! Where are you? I've been getting worried." Her smooth voice radiated concern, and the message he had prepared—similar to that sent to his mother—evaporated from his mind.

"Why, Isabella, I thought you'd be asleep. It's after one o'clock with you."

"Yes," came the answer. "I was just about to switch the diary off. I've been lying awake. Why don't you switch to visual? I'm decent."

Hearing her voice with its inviting, affectionate tone, Merral felt a desire to confide in her. He wanted to tell her the awful truth about the north and the awesome news that he was on his way to Ancient Earth. But he couldn't. *After all,* he told himself unhappily, *even now they might be listening in.*

"I'm under starlight. It's not worth it," he answered. *Just as well really,* he thought, remembering that he was wearing a uniform that was not his.

"Fine, Merral. We stay on audio then. But I have tons of questions, *tons.*" She paused. "I mean, the screen says you are in Isterrane. But how did you get there from Herrandown?"

"Ah. We had a lift from a general survey craft."

"My! That's a very odd way to travel. But it went well? What did you find out?"

With something of a shock Merral understood that the perception that he valued in Isabella were now turned against him.

"Well . . ." He paused, aware in the gloom that Vero was stirring, as if he had just realized that this was a live conversation. "Well, we have a lot of data. But it would be premature to say anything. I hope to be able to sort everything out soon."

"So, no beetle-men?" The tone was curious.

Merral hesitated. "That would be telling. But I can't talk too long. Look, I have to go away for a week or so. Work." He felt the word sounded unconvincing.

"Without coming back to Ynysmant?" She sounded shocked, even affronted. "But where? Faraketha or Umbaga?"

"No. But I can't say."

"You can't say! And you're calling me now. Truly strange. So, can I call you when you get there?"

"Er, you can try. You can get me through Anya Salema Lewitz at the Planetary Ecology Center in Isterrane."

"So this Anya Lewitz knows?" There was a hint of misgiving in her voice.

Merral could see Vero coming over to him.

"Yes, that's the way it is. Look, I have to go. Sorry."

There was a pause before Isabella answered, a pause only the merest fraction of a second long.

"Apologies accepted," she said, in a cool way. "Have a good trip. I mean, are you traveling a long time? More than a day?"

Merral was aware that Vero was waving his hand disapprovingly at him. He reached for the Terminate tab.

"Sorry. Can't say. Call Anya in forty-eight hours. Bye!"

Then he switched off.

"Sorry, Merral." Vero's tone was flustered and apologetic. "I mean . . . well . . . I wouldn't ordinarily intrude, but I thought you were just going to leave a message. I was worried you might give too much away."

"No, my apologies," Merral sighed. "Of all the times! She was still awake. I only told her I was going to be traveling for a bit."

"Did you mention how long?" There was alarm in Vero's voice.

"I suppose that I implied a couple of days. They could hardly . . . could they?"

"Oh, they could. You can get anywhere in Farholme in less than that. And why from here, Isterrane Strip, an hour before the Gate shuttle goes? If they were listening . . ."

"Sorry," Merral sighed. "I'm tired, Vero. I hope that wasn't too much."

"Well, maybe there's nothing they can do. We may have damaged them badly. Let us hope so."

Merral slid his diary back on his belt and sat down on the seat.

"How are you feeling?" Vero asked.

"The ankle aches but it's okay. I'm just tired. And numbed, I guess. The idea that next time I sit out under stars they will be those of Ancient Earth. It's all too much."

"I know. You'll find it a shock. But I think you will manage it better than me."

Then they fell into a long silence. Merral found that his mind was still racing. For some time, he sat there watching the activity around the shuttle as hatches were closed and the control surfaces on the flaring wings and twin tail were flexed. As Merral stared at it, the thought struck him that he now knew that this was not the only type of vessel to have transited Farholme's atmosphere over the last months.

New questions flooded his mind. What did this other ship look like? Did it have the same age-old lines as this? Was there just one? Did it, too, refuel in space from cometary ice, or did it have some novel energy to fuel its awesome speeds? If so, then why had it come in so fast, when it might have done so in near silence? As he stared at the vast white vessel, he was suddenly struck by the notion that the biggest issue centered on the fact that, whatever adorned the sides of its hull, it was not the emblem of the Lamb and the Stars.

He decided that he had thought long enough about the intruders and tried instead to comfort his mind with thoughts of Ancient Earth. He pictured its clouded pearl blue surface, its history, its knowledge, and its peace. He imagined the Council of Stewards: wise, concerned, and helpful. He allowed himself to picture the inevitable and solemn commissioning of the Defense Force and their proceeding at maximum speed to Farholme to render assistance.

Then realism took over, and he decided that his time would be more sensibly spent in prayer. He committed himself, his journey, and those he would leave behind into the hands of the almighty Father.

A few minutes later Perena and Anya came back. After sharing out the packages between them, they walked into the Embarkation Terminal. Merral found that there were fewer families waiting to see loved ones off than he had expected. But then, most farewells would have been said earlier in homes or at formal or informal parties. *How strange to have missed all that.*

Through the high windows, Merral could see what he assumed were the final checks being completed on the shuttle. Through its small round windows, they could see passengers taking their places silhouetted against the cabin lights. Merral noticed the name *Shih Li-Chen* inscribed beneath the cockpit in Communal and what he took to be the Old Mandarin script. Shih Li-Chen, he recollected: poet, church leader, and—unsurprisingly for early twenty-first century China—martyr.

Perena, standing next to Vero, gestured at the ship. "Normally, I would have shown you around and introduced you to the crew."

"Next time, Perena," Vero replied. "For now, the fewer who know who we are, the better."

Perena turned to Anya, who had been standing quietly by, staring out of the window, her usual ebullience apparently subdued by the impact of the night's news.

"Sister, you want to say good-bye before I see these guys into their seats?"

Anya smiled at Vero and Merral. "Safe traveling, guys. I really wish I was going for the ride."

"Personally," Vero muttered in an aside, "I wish I could miss out on the ride."

"It's a pity we can't all go," Merral said.

Anya wrinkled her nose. "Your plants will wait, Tree Man, but my animals won't. But I'll pray that you get some good counsel on Ancient Earth, and I look forward to seeing you come back with the Defense Force. Both of you."

Then Anya hugged them both in turn, and Merral fancied that her hold on him was longer and firmer than he might have expected. And was it too, he wondered briefly, more appreciated by him than it should have been? Merral was aware that, behind all the awesome news they had to take with them, there lay other personal issues that had to be resolved. His thoughts were interrupted by Perena gesturing them toward a service tunnel.

Carrying their baggage, Merral and Vero followed her along the tunnel. An approaching luggage hexapod moved to one side as they approached it, raising a forelimb in a mechanical gesture of acknowledgement. They passed it and walked through a complex hatch system that led to the rear crew compartment of the shuttle. The compartment was compact, low roofed, and rather basic, and Merral felt that, with the six or more people in uniform in it busily packing equipment, it seemed almost cramped.

Perena smiled at someone by the door who Merral took to be a steward. "The two seats for Sabourin and Diekens, please," she said, while Merral looked around, taking in the soft cream and yellow seating, the small portholes, and the neatly labeled hatches, ducts, and containers extending around and along the curved walls and between the seats. It occurred to Merral that if he had taken after his father and had had a greater affection for mechanical means of transport, he would have known far more about the shuttle and had some idea of the function that everything served.

The steward checked a listing and pointed to a pair of couches in a corner by the rear wall. Perena came over with them.

"I must go," she said, almost under her breath, "but my prayers go with you."

She hugged Merral and turned to Vero.

Suddenly, Perena's reserved and cool expression slipped, and Merral caught an emotion of fear and strain on her face that he had never seen.

"Vero," she whispered as she clutched him tightly, and Merral could only just make out her words. "We need help."

"I think help will be here soon," Vero replied in a near whisper.

"Please," she begged, her subdued voice suddenly thickened in urgency. "I can feel it. It's a spiritual concern. I feel—somehow—that there is something hateful here. Make sure help arrives."

Then she released Vero and her face seemed to regain a look of calm nonchalance. A crewman settled down into an adjacent couch and a female voice warbled from a loudspeaker somewhere. "Captain here. Five minutes before takeoff is initiated. All ground crew, please leave now."

"Vanessa Lebotin," Perena said, apparently forcing her mouth into a smile. "She nearly beat me at old-time chess only the other month."

"Perena," Vero said softly, "I note your concern. I agree. I will do all I can. See you soon."

Perena closed her eyes briefly, nodded, and then suddenly—as if to avoid revealing any emotion—turned, wove her way through the other dark-blue-uniformed personnel, and left by the hatchway.

Vero looked at Merral and sighed. Then he sat down and began to adjust his couch and, amid the sound of hatch doors closing and pumps whirring, Merral followed suit.

As Merral lay there, he decided that he should have said farewell to his family better. *My father, with that love for transport machinery that I do not share, would doubtless have endlessly briefed me about the types of shuttles and their engines and what to look out for. My mother would have worried and flustered and forced me to take spare clothes. Instead, here I am, knowing almost nothing about where I am going and what I am doing when I get there.*

He turned to Vero who was reading the instructions on a small packet marked "For Travel Nausea. Adult Strength."

"A stupid question, Vero. Where exactly on Ancient Earth are we going?"

"Incidentally, when we get there you just call it Earth. It's not pride; it's just that there isn't any chance of confusion. Anyway, where we land depends on which of the five Terran Gates we come out of. That depends on getting the best connection, just as in Cross the Assembly. From what Perena said, Beijing III is the most probable. If so, we take the long-haul passenger flier to Jerusalem. It is late spring there, too, so the weather should be fine." He paused and gave a little dry laugh. "Just as well; I've left that coat behind. Do you remember it?"

At the memory of Vero's ridiculous coat and their first meeting Merral felt an amusement stained only by a fierce longing to be back in his own bed in his own house.

* ◆ *

Then the takeoff launch instructions began. There was the hymn of the Assembly and the appeal to the Lord of the heavens for mercy and protection. After taxiing to the longest runway, there were the final commands, the rising vibrating roar of the engines just behind his head, the brief race down the runway, and the little skyward bound. Amid a rumbling vibration the ship flew upward and southward. Within minutes, though, they were in level flight, and with Merral watching their journey on the wallscreen, they crossed Hassanet's Sea at ten kilometers altitude.

Just as Merral felt himself sliding into a doze, Vero nudged him. "Hold on. We are over the equator now. Serious acceleration is about to begin any minute now."

The ship swung round to face eastward and tilted upward, with his seat rotating under him in response. Seconds later, there was a double warble from the speakers and a booming roar engulfed the cabin, making the storage cabinets rattle and the roof fixtures sway. Merral, forced down into his couch under the acceleration, closed his eyes and tried to think of something more pleasant.

Within a dozen minutes, the force and the vibration had waned, and out of the window, Merral was able to see sunlight glinting on the wingtips.

Dawn in space. It gave him an odd feeling.

He watched as Vero slowly took hold of his sleeve, lifted it, and let it drop.

But it didn't drop. It floated there, devoid of weight.

Extraordinary. Zero g.

And he fell asleep.

•—•

When Merral woke up later, it took him a long time to come to terms with where he was. Only when he stared out of the porthole to see the blackness of space and the sharp pinpricks of stars and felt his limbs float up against the restraining straps was he sure that it really was not just a dream. For a moment, he thought they had stopped because of the silence; then he heard the distant hum of the engine pumps.

Aware of a full bladder, he unstrapped himself and, mindful of the fact the only experience he had of zero g was ten minutes in a traveling simulator as a student, made his way carefully to the lavatory cubicles. Then, grateful for the fact that, despite the costs of the technology, created gravity existed in shuttle washrooms, he drifted back over to the window. Everybody else in the compartment seemed to be busy, either working on their couches or, like Vero, asleep. *At least,* Merral reflected, *traveling among people who do this on a weekly basis, I don't have to queue to look out of the window.*

As he stared through the gold-tinted glass, at first all he could see was the stars, perfect and clear against the flawless blackness. *The night sky,* he told himself, before remembering that this was the permanent reality of space. By tilting his head he could just make out the blue and brown curve of Farholme below, its edges blurred by the atmosphere.

A few minutes later the starscape rotated slowly, and Merral reached out for the wall for some sort of stability. Now, hanging above the eternal black backdrop, the sprawling silver tubes, spheres, and cylinders of the Gate Station came into view. Merral stared at it, blinking at the brilliant glitter of the silver foil-coated block of captured comet at the edge of the fuel processing section and tentatively identifying the central station complex. There, protruding delicately from the middle of the cylinders, like a mast on a homemade raft, was the matte, titanium gray, stub-ended long column of the inter-system liner. With its hexagonal cross-section, Merral realized that it looked like an enormous pencil.

But was it really enormous? The scale was impossible to tell, and for a moment, Merral had a fancy in which all he was looking at was merely some tiny but immaculately crafted model a few centimeters across. Then, floating over the fuel storage tanks and casting a tiny distorted pitch-black shadow below, he made out the shape of a general survey craft, some sister vessel to the *Nesta Lamaine*, and the sense of scale became apparent.

Then there was another course change, and one by one the dazzling bronze yellow Gate beacons rotated into view. He peered at the midpoint of the six beacons, straining his eyes until he saw, glinting dully, a minute metallic object. *The Gate*, he said to himself in awe. *I can see the Gate with my naked eye!*

The call came to return to seats before deceleration, and he drifted back and buckled himself in.

•—•—•

With what Vero sleepily remarked was "typical Assembly caution," it took fifteen minutes from the first gentle echoing tap of the *Shih Li-Chen* docking with the Farholme Gate Station until, to the accompaniment of various whistles and hisses, the hatchway opened to reveal a corridor into the station. Floating over to the exit, laden with their bags and the plate samples, they left the *Shih Li-Chen*, drifted into one end of the gravity transition corridor, and walked out of the other at the ferry car system.

After ten minutes of travel down tunnels and along corridors with only the briefest of glimpses of space and stars, Merral and Vero were unloaded at the lower entrance to the *Heinrich Schütz*. They walked into the gravity transition corridor and at the other end floated their way out into the crew and technical section.

As Vero asked for the locations of the couches for Sabourin and Diekens, Merral looked around in awe. He had, he supposed, been unimpressed by the interior of the *Shih Li-Chen*, which had seemed little more than an exaggerated and overlarge general survey craft. But this was different.

Merral knew, of course, that the *Heinrich Schütz*, as an intersystem liner, was one of that order of vessels known as the "Great Ships." Other than their size, the distinguishing feature of their order was the fact that their designers had had a freedom to work denied to them in the lesser craft that had to fly through atmospheres. He had seen many illustrations of the interior design of the Great Ships, but to be inside a real one, rather than a simulation, was somehow a very different experience. The results, honed over generations, were, to Merral's eyes, an outstanding and eye-catching triumph.

His first thought as he looked around was that it reminded him of being in some enormous and fantastic seashell with a spiral-curved floor sweeping upward above him and linking fluidly with the walls and the central column. The impression of being in a natural organic structure was aided by the scarcity of straight lines, the pale milk-and-honey coloring, and the smooth porcelain texture of the walls. Abundant lighting, whose source appeared to be everywhere and nowhere, lit the interior so that the whole ship seemed to glow as if it were a translucent shell illuminated by sunlight.

Then, suddenly, Merral's point of view changed, and he saw himself at the base of a high ancient tower with a vast snowy marble ramp sweeping gracefully through buttresses and archways up a score of levels in smooth, gentle, stepless curves. In the end, he concluded that both views were true; the interior was both organic *and* architectural.

"Over here." Vero's voice intruded into Merral's contemplation.

"Sorry. I was just taken aback by it. It's beautiful."

Vero gave his friend an amused grimace as he gestured to a pair of couches. "It's some compensation for the turbulence when we go through Below-Space. But I have to admit that the Assembly designers were surely right in thinking that a purely functional form was not an adequate response to the privilege of traversing Below-Space. You were told Horfalder's maxim?"

Merral tugged himself forward on a strap and floated over to where couches protruded at the edge of a fluted ridge curving out from the towering central column. "Horfalder? I remember something, but you tell me."

"She was head of the design team for the Composer Class; she said that as the average distance covered by an inter-system liner between Gates was equivalent to around fifty years of space flight, the least they could do was create a structure that you could live with for a half century. Even if you were only in it for a few hours."

Merral looked around again, considered Horfalder's wisdom, and found it good. Then, having stowed his holdall and the plate sample in a compartment under the couch, he lay down, trying not to float off, and stared around again. Now, though, as he looked harder, he realized that underneath his first complementary images of the shell and the tower he could see the ship as a machine. As he stared upward he could imagine the twenty-odd levels above him as distinct compartments, and glancing around he could see, concealed in one way or another, all the lockers, access panels, handholds, and information screens that such a ship needed.

With the final preparations being made around him, Merral strapped himself down and found a switch that lowered a screen down just in front of his eyes. On it he was able to read about the composer Heinrich Schütz, and he marveled again that anybody could have dedicated music to the Almighty during a war that lasted thirty years. Then as he chewed the simple food that was passed around, he glanced at the explanatory section on the ship itself.

He could easily imagine how much his father would have enjoyed reading about the Composer Class (prototype built in 9101, the

Heinrich Schütz being the twenty-fifth of the second series) and its lifespan of around a thousand years before a complete renovation was needed. Yet now, more than ever, he found himself with little appetite for machinery or mechanics. With more interest, he went through the elementary introduction to Gate travel with a well-done and elaborate version of the traditional analogy of the two ways of getting across a narrow but deep estuary.

Travel in Normal-Space, it reminded him, was analogous to the long, slow journey round the edges, while the Gate travel was like taking a shortcut through a tube running directly through the waters. It was a familiar illustration, but now, on the verge of taking that shortcut, it had a new relevance. The illustration was developed to explain some of the Below-Space features such as the notorious turbulence, which was here portrayed as being analogous to the buffeting of the estuary's water against the tube. Then, balking at a treatment of plasma engines, Merral allowed the screen to retract.

Eventually, just before ten o'clock, the last door closed and Captain Bennett gave her welcome from the speakers. After that the Assembly hymn was played and there was the traditional solemn appeal to the sovereign Lord on undertaking Below-Space travel, with its acknowledgement that such travel was a privilege and its request for safe arrival.

At exactly ten o'clock, just as the "Amens" were dying away, there was a dull thud as the linkages detached themselves. Slowly, Merral heard a gentle low-frequency rumble begin behind him and his couch began to sway ever so slightly. He lowered the screen to where he could read it and checked the flight plan. They would swing in a wide arc clear of the station to align themselves exactly above the hexagon at what was known as the burn-point. There, at 10:40, the plasma engines would ignite at full burn to start the rapid straight-line acceleration that would give them the ten-thousand-kilometers-an-hour speed needed to coast quickly along the Normal-Space tunnel linking the Gates. At 10:55 they would enter Farholme Gate, emerging a mere ten and a half minutes later at Bannermene Gate. Forty light-years away.

Merral lay back, feeling pushed slightly down into his couch by the acceleration's comforting semblance of gravity that a wall sign declared to be 0.6 g. He was still tired, and in his brain a thousand thoughts seemed to be chasing each other.

Some of the dozen people around him in this part of the Space Affairs section were busy monitoring the ship and the passenger levels, while others were plainly relaxing or sleeping. One or two were walking buoyantly from the lift section in the middle of the ship.

Eventually Merral closed his eyes, wondering if he was tired enough to sleep through both burn-point and the Below-Space transit. He was aware that some people claimed to have slept through Gate passage, but most stayed awake due to the buffeting and those various psychological effects such as disorientation that were common, but which still eluded comprehension. Merral tried to get his mind to relax and encouraged it to concentrate on nothing. *Imagine a white snow field,* he told himself, *during a blizzard.*

"Sentinel Enand? Forester D'Avanos?" The voice was urgent.

Startled, Merral opened his eyes to see a man in a dark blue uniform bending over him, clutching the side of the couch.

"Yes? I'm Merral D'Avanos," he answered, wondering with some alarm how this man knew his name.

"I'm Charles Frand, Second Communications Officer." The angular face with a thin black moustache had an expression that seemed to request immediate action. "Captain Bennett needs to see you both now. There's been an odd message. Can you both come forward to the bridge please? Immediately. We will be at burn-point in minutes."

A look of profound alarm crossed Vero's face as he gingerly unstrapped himself. "Odd . . . ," he murmured.

Together, they walked unsteadily across the floor to the elevator tube, aware of others watching them. As they accelerated up through the central spine of the ship, Vero, gripping a hold-bar tight, stared at Merral. "I don't like it," he muttered. "I don't like it at all! There is barely half an hour before we leave the system."

The door opened into the high-roofed command cabin. Merral

was vaguely aware that the spiral theme continued here, with the space being dominated by a single sweeping floorway that ran in a smooth curve from the base up to the vaulted ceiling. On this grand sweep was a series of pastel-colored consoles all facing one high, flat wall, on which an enormous image of the Gate appeared. Merral felt sure that the screen surface must match a plane of the hexagonal outer surface.

"Created gravity here, careful," Officer Frand said. "Captain's up to the right. Blue console."

Gripping the sculpted handrail they walked up the gentle sweep of the floor. As they did, Merral looked across at the screen, recognizing that the image was a computer-generated illustration showing the Gate from an oblique angle. Incomprehensible data readouts shimmered around the edges of the screen.

A lean woman with blonde hair in a tightly coiled braid rose stiffly from her seat and turned to them as they approached the cluster of three consoles grouped on the top of the slope that evidently formed the bridge. *The captain,* Merral thought, seeing the two yellow flashes on her shoulders.

She greeted them with an abrupt and rather cool handshake.

"Captain Leana Bennett," she announced in a precise, truncated way that mingled authority with perplexity. Looking at her tanned face with its fine etching of lines, Merral realized she was his mother's generation, but of a very different character. There was a tautness and precision about Captain Bennett's frame, face, and manner that told you immediately why the Assembly trusted her with over three hundred lives and an almost priceless ship.

"And you are not Engineers Sabourin and Diekens. Rather, you are instead a sentinel and a forester. How very irregular." She looked sternly at them for a second with piercing dark brown eyes. "But that can wait. This came in five minutes ago. Comms, show it, please." She pointed to a small screen on one of the adjacent consoles.

A flickering image of Perena Lewitz appeared. "Captain Bennett, this is Perena Lewitz, Captain of the *Nesta Lamaine.*" Merral strained to hear the voice, which was slightly distorted.

"This is very urgent. I am unable to access you through normal channels. I have just received an unusual message, which I think I trust. It says that your ship must not enter the Gate. Repeat: not enter the Gate. There is a peril there. The problem is related to Sentinel Enand and Forester D'Avanos who are occupying the couches of Space Affairs Engineers Sabourin and Diekens. They may be able to explain the situation. But, I repeat, I have been warned that your ship must not enter the Gate. I suggest you return to Gate Station and—"

The image on the screen froze, broke into lines of static, and faded away.

"Return to Gate Station?" Vero whispered in alarm. "But we *have* to go through. . . ." Then he stopped and stared at Merral, his eyes glinting. Intuitively, Merral knew they both had the same thought: *Is it her*?

Vero turned to the captain. "I suppose the message is, well— authentic?"

"Authentic? That's an odd way of putting it. Charlie?" The captain turned stiffly to Officer Frand who gestured his bewilderment with a shrug and an opening of his hands.

"Captain, gentlemen," he said, "all I can say is that it came in just now by one of the backup communications links. One of the old laser systems. Out to the Gate Station and then bounced on to us. It's hard to verify. I mean, we take these things on trust. But—" He turned a per- plexed gaze to the captain. "Why wouldn't it be authentic?"

"Don't ask me, Charlie." She looked bewildered. "Why are these men not Sabourin and Diekens? This is beyond me. But it looked and sounded like Captain Lewitz to me."

"Two minutes to burn-point, Captain," came a quiet voice from the console to the right. Merral glanced at the wallscreen to see that they were now nearly face-on to the hexagon and that in the bottom right corner, one set of digits had just counted down below 120.

"Helm Officer," the captain responded crisply, "proceed as scheduled."

Then her brown eyes turned back to Vero and Merral, shifting from one to the other in careful scrutiny. "Naturally, I immediately tried to contact her. I also instigated a check on the Gate and have asked Gate Control for a full update."

With a quick gesture of a finger she summoned a slight young man with cropped brown hair from a console at a lower level. He bounded up energetically toward them with an active datasheet in his hand. Then she lifted an inquiring eyebrow at Officer Frand, who had been checking an adjacent console screen with another officer.

"Captain," Frand said, "still no response from her diary. It's apparently switched off. But it's the Lord's Day and meeting time, so there's no surprise there."

"Yes. Except if she did try and call us." Captain Bennett turned her troubled face to the man who had just arrived. Merral noticed a neat yellow hexagon badge on his blue overalls.

"Gateman Lessis," Captain Bennett said in an urgent way. "review the Gate systems. In view of this message."

The Gateman turned to her, his back straight. "Captain, I report that the Gate seems normal." The tone was intelligent, confident, and unruffled. "I have reviewed all our data and that from Gate Control. All readings are within normal limits."

Merral had the impression of a man with a sharp mind, thorough training, and total mastery of his field. He would, he told himself, have expected nothing less.

"Thank you, Mikhael. Please stay for a moment. So you see, gentlemen, I have a real problem. I know Perena slightly but there is not enough evidence for me to abort. Indeed *no* evidence. If we return to Gate Station it will be at least six hours before we can reenter the Gate. That will throw up a lot of problems for connections." Captain Bennett turned pensive eyes first on Merral and then on Vero. "Do either of you have any new data?"

"Captain," Merral appealed, "I need to talk to my friend here. For a moment only."

The captain flicked a glance at the screen. The image now was of a fully symmetrical hexagon, and in the corner of the screen the seconds counter now stood at ninety seconds.

"You have just over a minute," she said politely, and turned to peer at the Gateman's datasheet.

Merral and Vero took a step back and faced each other.

"Vero, is it a trick?" Merral asked, searching to see any indication in his friend's eyes as to whether they should trust the message.

"It must be. . . . Surely it's a trick to stop us from leaving?"

Merral forced himself to think. He was aware that he was tired, aware that it was a complex matter, aware that the seconds were ticking away, but also aware that he had to make a right decision. It sounded like Perena, but now he did not automatically believe anything on a screen. And to be summoned back now? *Lord, grant wisdom and overrule if we get it wrong.*

A sudden revelation struck him. *Supposing I look at the problem the other way about, as with an inverse logic? Think like a sentinel. Put myself in the shoes of the intruders. If I wanted to stop this ship, would I have done it this way?*

"No!" he blurted out, suddenly certain. "It's a genuine message. The intruders would have faked a direct message to the captain. To do it this way makes no sense."

"Right." Vero blinked nervously. "Yes, I back you."

They turned to face the captain, who was looking expectantly at them.

"It's a real threat," Merral said with as much urgency as he could muster. "Believe me. It's unparalleled, but it's real."

Behind her he could see the screen saying there were twenty seconds left. The captain's cool, unflustered eyes flicked to Vero.

"Yes," Vero added, "a genuine warning of genuine peril. Please return to Gate Station."

Captain Bennett bit her lip and glanced at the screen. "Gateman Lessis, you are completely happy with the Gate status?" Her face stared at him, as if seeking the slightest hint of doubt.

The Gateman paused, blinked, glanced at his datasheet, and

returned the stare with wide confident eyes. "Captain, all the information I have suggests no hint of anything untoward." He glanced at the image as more words tumbled out. "If I may say, the last significant Gate problem was a generation ago and half the Assembly away. That was only a Class One failure and automatically fixed within hours. The Gate's reputation for reliability is well merited, Captain. As you know. There are at least two levels of duplicate safety mechanisms on every system."

The seconds scrolled down to zero.

The captain looked at the screen, shook her head, and then gestured to the man at the console to her right.

"Helm Officer," she ordered, "initiate burn."

CHAPTER 19

Merral stared at the wallscreen as the figure of *00:00* was replaced abruptly by *15:25* and a new countdown started immediately.

Captain Bennett turned around to face Merral and Vero with a face that bore an uneasy expression. "My apologies," she sighed. "But under standing orders I had no choice. Now"—her tone acquired an inflexible edge—"I need you off the bridge, please. Acceleration will be building up in the passenger area. But I will need a full explanation at Bannermene Gate Station."

"Yes, of course," Merral answered, trying to suppress feelings of frustration and alarm. "But I still think there is a risk. Can we still abort?"

"I'd rather not," she said, shaking her head. "Composer Class ships aren't built for maneuvers at speed."

The look on her face seemed to Merral to say as strongly as possible that the interview was over. *So that is that,* he thought despondently.

"Gateman Lessis," she ordered, "you can return to your station." But as the man started to move away, Vero stretched out his hand to block him. "Don't rule anything out," he said in a voice so low that Merral barely caught his words.

"Captain," Vero inquired in a voice that was both firm and gentle, "that image on the screen is a simulation. Can we look at the Gate directly?" Merral looked up at his friend, surprised at the determination on his face.

She frowned. "Optically? Yes, we have a scope linked to it. But the navigation simulation mode is much more appropriate."

"Of course," came the polite response. "But can we see the Gate? On screen? For just a minute?"

Captain Bennett stroked a bronzed cheek. "Give them two minutes, Gateman, and then send them back down. It's too late after that anyway." She smiled distantly at them and then turned back to her console.

As she sat down, Mikhael Lessis touched the datasheet and the image changed to one of a black, star-strewn sky in which a blurry graphite gray mass hung. It juddered slightly, came into focus, and then slowly expanded to fill the screen.

"We are still over a thousand kilometers away, so there is some vibration." The Gateman's voice was matter-of-fact.

Merral stared at the smooth metal surfaces trying to grasp the size of the structure. Only the tiny yellow marks on its dully gleaming surface that indicated the access points for visiting service vessels gave any idea of the vastness of the construction. He could see the sutures between the segments where, long ago, the Gate had been put together, and the brilliant green lights, now rapidly flashing to signify their imminent entry. Then he stared wonderingly into the still, eerie blackness at the heart of the hexagon. There was something awesome about the structure, with its palpable size and its aura of vast age. *If we had idolatry,* Merral thought, in a strange mental aside, *men and women might worship such a thing.*

"Seems all right to me," commented the Gateman, looking at Vero. "You see, Gates *never* fail. Because we can't have them fail, we don't allow them to fail." The tone was of total cool confidence. "That's what Gate engineering is about. Perfect reliability."

Merral found his attitude exasperating, but reminded himself that this young man had seen neither the falsified images of Maya Knella nor the horrid monstrosities they had met at Carson's Sill. *This man believes that the impossible does not happen. We know now that it can.*

Vero nodded thoughtfully. "Of course, only God is perfectly reliable," he answered as he scrutinized the immense mass of metal.

"I was meaning in human terms," came the defensive response.

Merral couldn't see Vero's expression, as it was fixed on the screen, but he knew that he had found nothing untoward.

Vero, biting his lip, gestured at the image. "I'd like to look at each segment. Please, one by one. Just briefly." There seemed to be an unshaken determination in his voice, and despite his own dejection, Merral felt admiration for his friend's attitude in the face of defeat. He felt he could only hope that Perena—if the message had indeed come from her—was somehow wrong.

The Gateman shrugged. "One," he said in a flat tone and tapped the datasheet.

The screen filled with a smooth, almost glassy, gray surface broken by a few minor debris impact marks and faded yellow and red markings and lettering. The thought occurred to Merral that there was less aging than he would expect for a three-thousand-year-old structure.

"Two."

Another surface appeared at a different orientation, but with similar features. Merral realized they were going clockwise.

"Three."

The image switched again, but other than the angle and subtle differences of marking, it might have been the same segment as the previous two.

"Four."

Now the alignment of the segment was back to that of the first one. *Nothing again,* thought Merral with a mounting feeling of inevitability. *Nor will there be on the rest. It looks as if, for good or evil, we are going through the Gate.* The numbers on the bottom of the screen showed him that that would now be in under twelve minutes.

He began to wonder how easy it was going to be to return to his seat in the crew section with the acceleration now building up below them.

Captain Bennett was turning toward them with a frown. Their time was up.

"Five." Another segment, exactly the same. Just like—

A fine line of intense electric blue light writhed round the edge of the image.

"Stop!" Vero's shout turned all eyes to the screen.

Merral was aware of the Gateman staring open-mouthed and of Captain Bennett turning round sharply to the image.

Another line of iridescent blue arced crazily over the smooth, still, and ancient surface of the Gate. Merral felt that there was somehow something shocking about it, as if he was seeing an act of violation or even desecration.

There was a rising murmuring around the control room.

"Gateman!" snapped Captain Bennett, rising stiff-backed from her seat, apparently transfixed by the image. "Did you see that?"

"Yes . . . Captain." The Gateman's tone was one of utter stupefaction. Merral observed in a strange, detached way that he was seeing yet another person realize that the boundary between the possible and the impossible was now being penetrated.

The Gateman continued to gape at the screen as more lines of blue curved round the surface. "There's another. And *another*. It's some sort of electrical discharge. . . ."

"So it seems," returned the captain almost brusquely. "Can you assure me it's harmless, Gateman?"

"Harmless? I have no data on that. . . . I really don't know, Captain." His eyes flicked nervously down to his datasheet. "But the Gate signals indicate plainly that it has no malfunctions." The confidence was oozing away now.

"My eyes, Gateman, tell me otherwise." Captain Bennett's voice was icy and determined. "Helm Officer, take us clear of the Gate. Minimum deviation. Mr. Lessis here will want some detailed images as we fly past, I'm sure. Say about a hundred kilometers away to be safe. And then plot us a course back to the Gate Station."

She turned sharply round on her heels, her face a mask of disbelief. "Gateman, find out what the verdict is from Gate Control. And tell them I want to know why they didn't tell us there was a problem."

As Gateman Lessis, his face pale and his eyes wide, turned away to talk into his datasheet, the captain swung back to her own console.

Merral felt a gentle change in the ship's direction, and moments later the captain's words were echoing around the cabin. "Captain Bennett here to all crew and passengers. I regret to tell you we have identified—" there was the briefest of pauses— "an apparent technical anomaly at the Farholme Gate and are returning to the Gate Station. In the meantime, I urge you to stay in your couches. Hopefully, we can reschedule our journey within a few hours. Thank you."

She turned and briefly gazed at Vero and Merral with puzzled and unhappy eyes before swiveling back to look at her readouts. Merral found the idea that they were going back to the Gate Station something that gave him both relief and concern. A moment later Gateman Lessis walked over to the captain with a nervous face. "Captain, they are looking into it. But they assure me that the Gate monitor systems are still giving perfect readouts. On my insistence they are going to switch to visual themselves."

"Perfect readouts in spite of problems?" Vero had leaned over toward Merral. "I've heard that before," he murmured.

There was another flicker of blue light on the screen, and Vero stepped forward and tapped the shoulder of the Gateman. "Excuse me, do you have any model for what's going on there?"

Mikhael gave Vero a worried look. "No, not at all. I don't know. It's not normal at all. Of course. It's against everything I've ever heard of or been taught. The diagnostics aren't telling us anything." He looked up at the screen. "I mean . . . No, there goes another discharge."

He rubbed his bloodless face as if unable to believe what he was seeing, and Merral felt a twinge of sympathy for him.

"Crazy." His tone was almost one of outrage. "There must be a major overload on some circuitry. It just doesn't make sense." He clenched his fists in frustration. "The Gate's internal monitor should have switched to backup circuits before this even happened. Straight away. And told us. But at this rate we will have a Class Two failure."

Vero peered at him. "A Class Two failure? What would happen to any ship going into it?" Merral noted an urgency in Vero's questioning.

"The Below-Space link is severed and you go straight out the other side. Harmless but embarrassing." His face wore an expression of total perplexity. "And also almost unheard of. A Class Two failure has happened only twice ever in a production Gate." Gateman Lessis nodded to himself thoughtfully, as if the words had gone some way to giving him reassurance. "And both of those were, what, ten millennia or more ago. As there are nearly two thousand Gates and on average they are five thousand years old, that is one Class Two failure per five million working years." He looked at Vero, a veneer of confidence trying to reestablish itself. "Approximately."

"Of course. Impressive." Vero glanced at the screen. "Forgive me. But what about a Class Three failure? What happens there?" There was an intensity in the question that grabbed Merral's attention. *Vero has sensed something that I have not,* he realized. *He is not content to simply go back to the Gate Station.*

"Most odd. Damping doesn't appear to be taking place." The Gateman was looking at the screen. "But it should be. Sorry, Class Three failure? There the ship hits the Gate. We've never been able to create that in remotely realistic simulations."

"At ten thousand kilometers an hour?" Merral asked in alarm, wondering if that was the peril that Perena had alluded to. It certainly sounded as if it would fit in that category.

"Yes, or thereabouts," the Gateman answered in vaguely dismissive tones. "But it's just impossible."

Mikhael suddenly tapped a corner of his datasheet. The visual image of the entire Gate now appeared on the wallscreen. It was larger than it had been and crisper.

We must be nearer, Merral decided.

There was a flicker of blue tracery on the segment at the top of the hexagon; then another echoed it along the bottom segment.

"That was on Five *and* Two, Gateman Lessis," said the Captain sharply.

"Yes. It isn't being damped. But it should be." There was now a note of bewilderment in the voice.

"What should be is no longer the issue," the captain retorted gently.

"On segments One and Four now as well, Captain," called up a voice from below. Merral stared at the screen, seeing faint moving coils of blue light around most of the Gate.

Vero cleared his throat. "Sorry to interrupt, Gateman, but is there a Class Four failure?"

His body rigid, the Gateman stayed staring at the screen as if glued to it. He shook his head. "No, not in the real world." His tone denied any possibility, however slight.

Merral saw Vero shake his head in frustration. Then he seemed to breathe in deeply and took a step toward the man. "Look, Gateman Lessis, you have already admitted that *this* is impossible." Exasperation was thick in his voice. "What *is* a Class Four failure?"

The Gateman continued to gape at the screen and just shook his head again. "It's hypothetical. Every level of fail-safe mechanism would have to be overruled."

Merral saw that the countdown on the corner of the screen had scrolled down to nine minutes. Suddenly, Vero reached out a hand, grabbed the Gateman's shoulder, and turned him round so that they were face-to-face. "What is a Class Four failure?" he shouted.

The captain stepped forward to separate them, anger flooding her face. "Sir, whoever you really are, this is my ship." In her voice, consternation and anger were mixed. "This is an outrage. . . ."

To his surprise, Merral found that he had stepped forward to meet her so that there was a strange cross-shaped symmetry with the four of them. *As if this were a dance.* His eyes locked with hers.

"And so, Captain, is that!" Merral snapped, pointing at the screen.

Over the entire hexagon a wreath of faint moving blue lines now hung, as if someone was scribbling frantically over it with a blue pen. The Captain glared at him with a look of indignation, then flung a glance back at the screen. The glance, however, seemed to become locked into a stare. Merral followed her gaze. The image showed a foreshortened Gate with the hexagon distorted and the top of the upper segment now visible. The captain opened her mouth slowly, but her curt words, when they came, were not to either Merral or Vero.

"Gateman Lessis, I order you to give this man this information. What is a Class Four failure?"

The Gateman swallowed. "In theory, Captain, gravitational instability builds up. Cycles and pulses between segments. And ultimately the Gate . . . blows up."

For a moment, the concept seemed so outlandish that Merral refused to accept what was being said and found himself sympathizing with Lessis's reluctance to mention it. A Gate, *this* Gate—*their* Gate—was something permanent, fixed, fundamental to existence. For it to "blow up" was as meaningless as talking about the angles of a circle.

Beyond his unsettling thoughts, Merral was aware of a brief moment of intense silence among them. For a fraction of second, he saw the captain, barely an arm's length away, turn to him with her brown eyes wide in a strange and terrible surmise.

"Captain . . . ," he heard Vero say, "I think—"

But he had no need to say anything because the captain was already running back to her desk and issuing a flurry of orders in tones that demanded instant obedience.

"Helm Officer! Maximum deviation and speed without compromising hull integrity. I want us to be at least a thousand kilometers away. And facing away from the Gate to minimize radiation effects."

There was a crisp acknowledgement and she took a brief breath. Merral, reeling at the concept of the Gate being destroyed and all its implications, felt the hull vibrate as power was applied. "Comms!" she snapped. "Emergency alert to Gate Station, Isterrane, and all ships that the Gate is going to blow up. Possibly within minutes. Repeat it. Have all ships and stations go to minimum radiation exposure profile. Crews to shelters. Use the solar flare drill, but make sure they realize that it's the Gate, not the sun, that is the problem. Have all rescue services on alert."

Merral noticed that on the wallscreen the perspective on the Gate was already changing as the ship's path began to curve upward. A sheath of blue flickering light was embracing the whole structure now, and as he watched, he saw the light had begun to pulse.

Around him an urgent wailing siren sounded. "Passengers and crew, alert. This is Captain Bennett." The voice was strained. "A possibility of a major Gate incident has emerged and we are accelerating out of the way at high g. Remain in your couches and strap yourselves in. Internal hull barriers will be automatically extruded shortly to provide airtight segments." There was a pause. "I would value your prayers."

For a second, a brief, intense, and awed silence seemed to fall over the cabin, only to be swept away in a wave of activity.

The Gateman looked up from examining his datasheet. "Captain, the Gate readouts now seem to reflect reality and—"

"About time," she interjected.

"—the Gate is in trouble. Serious trouble." Merral felt that the breathless and awed voice was barely recognizable as that of Gateman Lessis.

The whole ship was vibrating softly now, and every so often sharp little judders shook the frame. Merral found a support bar and held on to it. They were almost directly above the Gate now, the entrance hidden by the upper segment. Blue pulsing flickers of light were embracing the entire frame.

Captain Bennett seemed to notice it. "Helm Officer! Give us everything you can. Even if you do bend the hull. We need to be farther away."

She looked around the cabin. "Crew," she called out, "everyone take a seat and strap yourselves in. Created gravity may be unsustainable shortly."

Then, pale-complexioned but still very plainly in command of herself, she turned to Merral and Vero. "There are seats there." She gestured to the rear wall. "Oh . . ." A thought seemed to strike her and there was the briefest flicker of a smile on the wan face. "If we don't make it, my genuine apologies. To you both."

Vero, stepping back to the seat, bowed. "Apologies accepted."

•◆•

Moments later, as Merral was belting himself into the seat, the vibration reached a new pitch of intensity. *This is a dream,* he told himself desperately, *a hallucination, an artifact of the ship's computer. After all, the Gate exists and the Gate must exist. Without the Gate . . .*

Merral was conscious of the wall behind him vibrating. On the wallscreen he saw that they were still looking down on the top of the Gate, surrounded in its blue haze. But he had no idea how close they were. On the bottom of the shaking image he saw the now meaningless timing numbers reach zero and then begin to run down from 10:32. *The time we would have taken between the Gates.* He prayed that, even now, the endless backup circuits and fail-safe switches within the Gate would snap into operation.

They must. The Gates were the Assembly.

There was a tinkling chime and over the mounting rumble of noise a machine voice announced, "Created gravity termination five seconds away."

There was the sound of frantic activity as seats were adjusted and equipment secured, and then Merral was aware of an invisible something pushing on his chest and legs. His arms felt heavy and his head touched the soft pad on the wall behind him. There were thuds and bangs all around the cabin as unsecured objects slid around. The image juddered and went out of focus. There was a cry of pain from somewhere.

The vibration seemed to multiply, growing louder and deeper and occurring at more frequencies. Over it were now transposed various rumbles, creaks, and groans. Orders were being shouted. The screen image came back into focus slowly, a furious blurred squall of a thousand blue lines that pulsed inward and outward like some great slow heartbeat.

The cabin lights flickered and then dimmed for a moment. Merral glimpsed flashing yellow and red lights on the panels of the consoles. He could see the captain, bracing herself against the desk and hurling orders. The entire ship was quivering angrily now, and he had a terrifying vision of the long structure vibrating like a twig in a storm. Suddenly something broke free above him and crashed down in a pile of fragments in front of him.

The vibration continued. He slowly and painfully turned his head to see Vero, his face distorted by the acceleration, with his eyes closed, his hands clenched on the seat edges, and his mouth moving.

Merral began to pray intensely, aware of the smell of smoke, the juddering of the whole ship, and the almost deafening compound noises of the different sirens and alarms. Nearby a side panel tore loose with a bang and vomited out wiring.

On the screen image, thrashing from side to side, there was an image of the pulsing blue slab. But now the beating was faster and faster, every pulse brighter, every gap between the pulses shorter.

"It's going!" came a yell. *The Gateman*, thought Merral dully, feeling, in some strange confused way, that the catastrophe focused on this one figure.

The screen flashed a dazzling brilliant white that cast shadows around the cabin. Above the vibrating, roaring groans of the ship, Merral heard a single united awed gasp and knew that his own mouth was open and that he had contributed to it. Blue lines slowly returned to the screen as the whiteness faded. Now, though, they were less frantic, more leisurely, and their pulse seemed to be weakening. For a fraction of a second, a wild hope seized Merral, only to vanish as he saw that underneath them there was no Gate.

Awestruck, unable to comprehend what had happened, Merral stared as first one, then another, then many sharp-edged gray fragments raced outward through the waning blueness. He could hear an inconsolable gasping sobbing from somewhere in the cabin.

"The Gate has exploded," intoned Vero, his voice clogged with emotion and barely recognizable.

Numbed, Merral stared ahead to the consoles, aware of action and orders as, despite the appalling vision, the ship raced onward. Barely audible over the cacophony of sirens and ship noise, Merral could hear the captain's distorted announcement: "*All crew!* The front of the debris cloud will reach us in approximately one minute. Prepare for possible damage to hull and engines. God be with us all."

Merral closed his eyes and waited, trying to close out the brutal bombardment of sound and vibration. *The Gate has gone.* The thought rang in his mind again and again but he could barely make sense of it. It was a simple, factual statement, but he felt vaguely that the news of his own death would have been less shocking. *Be with us all, Lord.*

Something struck the ship.

There was an awesome, tearing hammer blow that broke through all the noise of the vibration like a thunderclap in a rainstorm. In a wild, explosive flurry of fragments, something burst up through the floor, ripped through the cabin, and struck the roof.

And kept going.

Most of the lights went out. A deafening screaming whistle began and a gust of air sucked across Merral. Through half-closed eyes, he could see, caught in the rays of light from the few remaining sources of illumination, debris being whipped up roofward in a whirlwind. Above him, at the apex of the spiral of dust and fragments snaking up through the weird twilight, Merral could see a hole. He was aware of a new screaming in the cabin, the screaming of men or women in extreme pain.

There was a popping sound in his ears, and he realized that through the gap in the roof he could see points of light.

Stars.

In his mind, Merral heard Perena's voice, eons ago and worlds away: *"But vacuum kills quicker than either air or water."* The sounds were dying away now.

So this is it, Merral told himself in the encroaching quietness of the vacuum. How very strange to face death twice in a few days. And, even as the idea came to him, Merral noted his ability to think irrelevant thoughts.

Then, beginning to gasp for breath, he began to make a final prayer. As he did he was aware that above him something was being extruded into the cavity from every side. The vision of stars died away as the hole seemed to shrink to nothing. Sound came back, and with it the noise.

But he could breathe.

•◆•

Lights flickered back on, and the wallscreen image slowly came to life. But the image it displayed was now a schematic plan of the *Heinrich Schütz*, and two words in brilliant red, *Pressure Crisis*, hung on top of it. Of the twenty or so sections, six were a flashing red and the rest were either a pale or dark blue. As Merral watched, one by one the flashing red blocks were replaced by shades of blue until, within minutes, all were dark blue.

The words *Pressure Restored* flashed across the top. From somewhere came a cry of praise.

Still absorbed in appalled reflection on what had happened to the Gate, Merral was only peripherally aware of how, over the next few minutes, the acceleration died away, the created gravity came back on, one by one the sirens and alarms stopped, and the screaming died away into a dull, sobbing whimper.

Numbed, Merral undid his straps, uncertain of why he did so, and got to his feet, shaking fragments off him. There was debris all around: bits of wall, thermoplastic sheet, portions of tile, shards of metal. In the roof, an ugly brown resinous mass bulged downward, showing where the hole had been plugged.

Merral turned to look at Vero, who was sitting up, his head between his hands, his face a picture of blank desolation. He was shaking. Slowly, as if in a dream, he patted Vero on the shoulder. Then, picking his way between debris fragments, Merral walked toward the three consoles on the bridge. At a gaping head-sized hole in the floor he paused and looked down, only to see that it had been blocked between decks by the same automatic sealant system that had closed the breach in the roof.

Disjointed fragments of sound seemed to drift into his mind from the frantic talking going on around him. A particular phrase seemed to be repeated and rang out again and again like a chorus. Somehow, though, its meaning failed to register with him.

He walked on. Gateman Mikhael Lessis was sitting down with his back to the guardrail, with someone bending over him, administering medicine to a bared upper arm. Merral glimpsed an expression of total vacuity on his face and a meaningless twitching of the lips. *I hope he gets better quickly and gets back to work.* In that instant, the appalling revelation struck him that there was no hurry at all for a Gateman to recover.

Staggering forward, almost overwhelmed by the thought, he came to the bridge area, now crowded with people. Merral glimpsed the captain slumping over her console with her hands to her head, her hair loose and hanging over a shoulder. As if sensing his approach, Captain Bennett turned her face up toward him, revealing tear-filled eyes.

"How is it?" Merral asked, and the words seemed to sound in his ears as if they had come through a wad of cloth.

She just shook her head. A man behind her with a single flash on his dusty uniform answered in slow, numbed words. "Five dead, twelve seriously wounded. Thirty with minor injuries. A lot of damage to the engines . . . but, God willing, we'll make it back to Gate Station."

Captain Bennett looked up at Merral with moist and appalled eyes.

"Sorry," she said, her voice almost a sob. "I have a son on Marant." It came to him that there was an odd exactness to her words, as if she were speaking in a foreign language. She swallowed and spoke again, but this time she said just two words: "Fifty years."

Fifty years.

With a stunning blow of horror, Merral realized that this was the phrase he had heard repeated—the words that had been on everyone's lips. Forty light-years from Bannermene at the maximum of eighty percent light speed. Was there ever a more simple, rigid, or cruel equation? Suddenly, as if a dam had burst, Merral realized the import of the loss of the Gate, and he reached out for the edge of the console to support him.

Fifty years, at a minimum, before there was any physical contact of any sort with the rest of the Assembly. Fifty years for a Made World to survive on its own with no external advice, no brought-in equipment, no emergency resources. Nothing out, nothing in, only long decades of silence. In forty years' time they would get the first message—already nearly half a lifetime old, doubtless with condolences, a promise of prayerful support, and probably a tentative time scale of sending a new Gate. But nothing until then.

He was aware of the Helm Officer speaking into his console and turning to Captain Bennett. "Gate Station, Captain. They are okay—just. They want to know where we are going to dock: main or engineering segments?"

The captain looked at Merral, her face bearing an infinite weariness, and then she turned back to her navigator.

"Main," she answered, and her faint voice sounded as if were from a continent away. "Engineering can wait. We aren't going anywhere for a long time." She put her head in her hands. "Not for half a century."

CHAPTER 20

On the evening of the following day, Merral cautiously made his way down to the observation bay in the crew section of the Gate Station. There he floated, his hand only a few centimeters away from a grab rail, and looked down on the browns, greens, and blues of Farholme as the night spread slowly over the Mazurbine Ocean toward Menaya. In the last dozen hours, he had found that there was something soothing about being here and watching his world. The magnificence of the view both distracted and comforted him, and whenever the enormity of what had happened threatened to overwhelm him, he calmed himself by forcing his mind to identify all the places he knew on the globe below.

The passengers who needed urgent medical treatment had been ferried back to Isterrane as priority, and Merral and Vero had been allocated berths with the crew of the *Heinrich Schütz*. In the last few hours, the *Shih Li-Chen* had returned to the Gate Station to bring back the remaining passengers and crew.

To his surprise, Merral had found that the delay had not been a problem. In part, it was because he had been in too much turmoil to think about it, but also because he was vaguely aware that it was probably as easy to come to terms with the new situation in the seclusion of the Gate Station as anywhere on Farholme.

As Merral stared down over the planet, his mind kept coming back to the events that had overtaken him and his world during the last few days. The loss of the Gate was so catastrophic that he had had to struggle not to let it push the other matters out of his mind. He wondered whether his ancient ancestors, so used to wars, rampant evil, and catastrophes, had handled such things better. *Did they just shrug their shoulders, pick themselves up, and get on with life?* If so, he envied them that, at least.

He forced himself to stare out of the glass again. From this vantage point Merral could see almost all of Menaya, apart from the extreme western Tablelands and the most northerly parts of the ice cap. South of Menaya, he noticed a swirling cluster of storm clouds gathering over Hassanet's Sea, their shadows black on the silver-tinged sapphire waters. It would, he decided, be wet and windy in Isterrane by dawn. Along the eastern coastlands, evening was falling, and inland he could make out the green swathe of the Great Northern Forest, and at its very eastern end, the tiny dirty blue smudge of Ynysmere Lake. North of the forest, the Northern Wastes stretched in lifeless shades of gray and brown almost across the entire continent, passing ultimately, on the edge of his vision, into the gleaming featureless white of the polar ice fields.

As he hung suspended there, Merral realized that even gazing at this tranquil scene gave him no ultimate escape from his problems. Normally—especially when faced with things to think about—he would have looked forward to walking out into the wilds and being alone among the forests and lakes that he could see so clearly, but so distantly, below. Only now, the wilds were no longer the invigorating and innocent spaces they had been; they had become in his mind—and perhaps in reality—haunted and shadowed places. With this somber thought, his eye was drawn inevitably to where the low-angle light was etching in black the vast broken circle of the Lannar Crater and the Rim Ranges.

There was a noise to his right, and a slight, slim form dressed in dark blue slipped down through the far opening of the observation bay. With a fluid motion, the figure glided smoothly toward him, almost like a diver cutting through water, extended delicate fingers, caught a strut, and with a practiced ease, swung to a stop an arm's length away.

"Perena!" cried Merral, lunging forward to hug her. He missed and, arms flailing, started spinning.

Retaining her fingertip hold on the strut, Perena stretched out a hand, caught him, and pulled him over so that he could reach the handrail. Then she wrapped an arm around him and hugged him. They hung there staring at each other.

"It's gone," he heard himself whisper, and he realized he sounded like a child. "The Gate's gone."

Perena lifted her gaze upward through the gold-tinted glass to where the hexagon would have been. "Yes," she replied, and there was strain in her voice. Then she added, quietly but defiantly, "Nevertheless, the King still reigns."

"Amen!" Merral answered, but felt it was an effort to say it.

Perena gave him a smile, at once determined, weary, and sympathetic. "I'm glad you agree. But it's a hard thing to say."

Funny, he thought, *she looks older now. But then perhaps we all do.*

"What are you doing here?" Merral asked, realizing how pleased he was to see her. "I thought you were getting your ship fixed?"

"I came up as extra crew on the *Shih Li-Chen* just now. They have a general survey craft here, the *Eliza N'geno,* they want bringing down, and I'm assigned as co-pilot."

She sighed and glanced down at Farholme. "A new ruling, as of this morning. All ships are to have co-pilots. Ship safety is now a priority. We can't afford to lose a single vessel from now on."

"I'm afraid I've been a bit too absorbed to take in much of the news from elsewhere. What's it like down there?"

She shook her head. "Hard to summarize. It's taking time for it to sink in. No real lasting panic, of course. Resignation, acceptance, grief: especially where families have been broken up. The day after tomorrow has been declared a solemn day of petition and fasting."

"That I had heard. But what do they know?"

She stared out of the window again at the planet below. "Only that there was a Gate malfunction on an unprecedented scale. There is no hint of intruders, or of it being deliberate—I think that is the word. To those that know of it, my warning is being put down to a premonition. I have a reputation, it seems." She smiled a shy, secretive smile. "Apparently, out of the whole of Space Affairs, I seem to be the one person that everyone feels a visionary warning might have been granted to. I don't know whether to be personally flattered or collectively ashamed."

"And was it a vision? We owe you a lot."

For a second she continued gazing out of the window. "No," she said in quiet way as she turned back to Merral, revealing a curious, thoughtful expression. "Not in a conventional sense. Something very strange happened. But I will tell you of it when Vero is with us. And how is he?"

Merral detected a deep concern in her voice and he chose his words carefully in answering. "It's been bad for everybody. But for Vero it's been an especial blow. He's said little since it happened and I've left him on his own. He's been in the chapel a lot." Merral remembered how he had last seen Vero, a brooding and disconsolate figure floating in the corner of the chamber the station congregation used for worship.

"Poor Vero," Perena said, with a sigh of sympathy. "I've sent a request for him to come and meet us here. Incidentally, the provisional statistics are that ten thousand Farholmers are trapped out of the system and just over a thousand people are trapped in. Both cases are awful."

"I can imagine. The only family member I have lost contact with is a great-uncle on Mamaria, and I've never met him. I've been asking myself, how would I take being told that I would be an old man before I had any sort of communication with my family? And Vero's father is elderly and frail."

Perena bowed her head as if in resignation. "It's tough. And how are you handling it? How's the ankle?"

"The ankle is fine, especially when I'm weightless. As for the rest, I'm trying to digest it. Bit by bit. I'm spending time in here. I find staring at Farholme consoling in some way. As if having a perspective on the planet gives me a similar perspective on my problems."

"Yes." She gave him a determined smile. "But they're *our* problems. We are together in this."

"Thanks. That is one of the things that makes it bearable. How's Anya?"

"Numbed and quiet. Which is an unusual state for her. She has lost—no, that sounds like they are dead—but you know what I mean—colleagues and friends. We all have."

She paused. "Of course, in a way it's worse for us four. Everybody else thinks it was some appalling, unexpected accident. We know—or we strongly suspect—that it wasn't that."

Merral felt himself clench the handrail. "No!" he answered, and he was surprised at the bitterness in his voice. "It was an attack! It was a deliberate, malevolent destruction of the Gate! Perena, when I think of it, it reminds me of the attack on Spotback. Multiplied a millionfold!"

"Yes," she said in barely audible tones, "and we must act. Look, I've also been sent up here to bring you both back personally. Anya's arranged a private meeting between Representative Anwar Corradon and us tomorrow. But I'd like to talk to you and Vero first."

She cocked her head sideways and listened. "Sounds like him."

There was a clunking noise from along the corridor. A pair of flailing legs descended out of the roof hatch, a groan, and a moment later, the rest of Vero awkwardly followed.

Perena launched herself toward him, smoothly curling into a tight ball and then unrolling with a final neat twist. She came to a stop with her feet against a wall strut and stretched herself out so that she lay horizontally across the corridor.

A sickly grimace appeared on Vero's drawn, weary, and unshaven face. "Perena Lewitz, the Queen of the Zero G Circus," he said in a subdued voice.

Then he smiled solemnly. "But it is very good to see you. However, bearing in mind my delicate stomach, could you please go the right way up? I would feel better about hugging you."

Perena walked down the side of the wall, stood vertical, and then reached out slender arms and hugged him. Nervously, Vero clasped his arms about her and held her tight.

"Well, Vero," she sighed as they separated, "I could wish you were safe home. Yet it's good to see you too. Very good. And I'm glad you are in one piece. The King does indeed reign."

"Yes," he answered in a hesitant tone, staring at the observation window and Farholme beyond it. "To deny that would be a greater disaster than the loss of the Gate." But Merral felt there was more determination than enthusiasm in his voice.

Then, with his legs hanging out untidily behind him, Vero hauled himself slowly along the guide rail until he was alongside Merral. As Perena made a precise glide to join them, Merral gripped his friend's arm.

"Are you feeling better?" Merral asked, heartened at Vero's appearance.

"Yes, I suppose so. It's been a bad twenty-four hours though. Extremely bad. The only way I have kept going is by trying to work out what's happening."

Vero drifted slowly forward and then peered dubiously through the glass at the stars, his gaze moving along the Milky Way until it found the location of Ancient Earth. Then he stopped and sighed deeply. "I am telling myself that I mustn't do that. Home is now down there." He gestured to the world below.

Merral felt a pang of sympathy for his friend. "We may be able to do something," he muttered.

"No." There was a sad and dogmatic shake of his head. "Don't encourage any false hopes. I have heard the commentators. And I checked it out myself. There is no chance of you—I mean *us*—making a new Gate."

Perena gestured down at Farholme. "We have the plans in the Library."

"No, Merral, Perena," he answered. "They are there to satisfy curiosity alone. Shielded Gates—Gates of any sort—are just too big. I hadn't realized a full Shielded Gate is nearly two million tons in mass.

There's one factory that makes them—in the Solar asteroid belt. Even then it takes ten years to fabricate just one. A world of thirty million people can't do it. We can't even make an unshielded one."

"No," Merral admitted, "I suppose not."

"So you see, I'd better make the most of it. Become a Farholmer." He scrutinized the world below. "Hi, home," he murmured in an unconvinced tone. "Will you have me?" he asked Merral.

"Of course." Merral patted his arm. "Anyway, we are citizens of the Assembly, not of planets. But for your insistence yesterday we would have lost everybody on the ship. We owe you a lot."

"We still lost five, or whatever the toll will finally be."

"I know, but it could have been much worse. And I had given up. You didn't. Why?"

Vero rubbed his face with his mobile fingers. "I had a terrible thought, a presentiment, that what I had done with the diary it might be possible to do with the Gate. Get into the circuitry and rearrange it. Turn the power against itself. I tried to push the idea to one side, but the phrase came back to me: 'Don't rule anything out.' As the Assembly we have never really built in safeguards against . . . sabotage." He shook his head as if the word stung. "We sentinels should have insisted that it was always a possibility." He stared silently outward. "I derive no pleasure at all from being right."

Merral turned to Perena. "You realize that we weren't sure it was you?"

"But Merral believed it was," Vero interjected, "and persuaded me it was genuine. And I just didn't want to give up. I guess I was really hoping that—by playing for time—you would get through again." Then he frowned and bit his lip. "But I wish we could have saved the Gate."

Merral stared out of the glass and thought hard. "Yes. But it seemed so impossible." He peered up to where, at the edge of the window, the three remaining Gate beacons hung equidistant from a smudge of dust that obscured the stars. "I still barely believe it. You heard poor Gateman Lessis. 'They never fail.' We never believed they could. And by forcing us to look at the visual images, you saved the ship."

"I suppose so . . . ," Vero said dully, as if distracted by the vision of the world below. He stared down, his eyes squinting as he peered toward the planet's surface.

Merral knew what he was looking at. "I know," he added, following his gaze to the edges of the Lannar Crater, now half flooded with black night. "My eyes keeping looking there too."

Vero nodded and turned to Perena. "Farholme will manage?"

For a moment, she didn't answer but merely tapped delicate fingers thoughtfully against the glass. "The short-term prognosis—that is, over months—is fairly good. But the big issue is the long term. There are a number of teams being set up to study the implications. There are so many unknowns, but the provisional word is that—if the Most High wills—Farholme may well survive fifty-plus years of isolation."

"Merely 'may well'?"

"Assembly caution," she answered with forced humor, and Merral realized that there were aspects to the Gate loss that she was still trying to come to terms with.

"Will you keep flying?" Vero asked her.

"To a lesser extent. We need to work out how much we can actually afford to do. Space flight is a major area—maybe *the* major area—where the worlds rely on the Gate system to supply spare parts. We have some supplies, but we can't make fuselages or ion engines here, let alone gravity-modifying engines or Gates. Fortunately, Assembly engineering has always gone for having long times between servicing. Of course, we don't need in-system shuttle flights or a Gate Station now. And we can recycle bits of the *Schütz*. It all may help."

"I see." Vero looked at Merral and then back at Perena. "We need to talk. I have some ideas; I think they are outrageous, but this situation is so extraordinary that it needs some explanation."

Perena gave a slight nod of affirmation. "If we have to see Anwar Corradon tomorrow, we need to decide what we are to say. And I would like to think that we have not just questions but also answers."

"Exactly," Vero said. "So first, the warning, Perena. Can you explain about it?"

Perena gazed back at him. "Explain? No, but I can tell you what happened. That was a strange matter. Very strange." Her eyes seemed to focus on something invisible that was a long way away, and Merral sensed again the depths that there were to her. Vero leaned forward unsteadily, his weary face showing an intense curiosity.

"Very well," she said softly. "After I left you I decided to stay over rather than go back into town, so I just grabbed some things off the ship and took a berth at the pilot's center. Yesterday—was it really only yesterday?—I decided to look at the *Nesta* before going over to the morning service. So I went over to the Engineering and Maintenance Complex and checked in. When I looked at the status screen at the entrance, I saw that there were a couple of people around the main offices but no one in Bay One. I'm certain of that because I'd asked that no work be started without me being there, and I remember feeling reassured that this was the case. Anyway, it was the Lord's Day. So I walked down to the entrance to Bay One, glanced at its status screen, and saw again that no one was there and that the bay was at normal temperature, pressure, and radiation. In E and M Complexes you always do that. Just in case. You don't want to walk into vacuum."

She paused, as if mentally thinking through her account. "So I went through the airlocks, put the lights on, and wandered up to the port lifting surface." She gave a tiny smile as if thinking of a private joke. "I suppose I wanted to reassure myself that the holes were really there."

She paused and closed her eyes as if uncertain about what to say next. "They were. I was staring at them when I saw, under the fuselage, that there was someone on the other side of the ship."

Merral heard a sharp intake of breath from Vero. Perena continued. "From where I was standing I could really only see a pair of legs, and the way the light was, it was impossible to make out anything about them. It was as if someone else had come in and was looking at the other lifting surface. I was, as you can imagine, pretty puzzled.

After all, I had asked that no work be begun before I had okayed it and it was the Lord's Day. And I had not heard the door open. So I walked over and peered round the nose."

She hesitated. "There was someone there. He was standing up and looking at the underside almost as I had been doing. Now, whether it was a trick of the lighting or something else . . . I have to say I can't give any sort of real description." Now her words came slowly, in a labored way. "I had the impression of a tall, dark figure. Almost a silhouette. A man, I would say. Yes, definitely."

She paused, and Merral was oddly aware that beyond the tense silence he could hear the faint hiss of the ventilation system. "He was—or he seemed—oddly dressed. As if he wore something like a loose, long black coat and seemed to have a hat of some sort. But it was hard to make out. He always seemed on the edge of my vision. And I am fairly certain that he cast no shadow; there is a lot of lighting in Bay One. He was just peering at the underside of the wing as if he was curious. No, more than that; as if he disapproved of what he saw."

Vero opened his mouth to speak, closed it, and gestured for Perena to ignore him.

"I suppose," she said, as if speaking to herself, "I knew that there was something wrong. Well, not wrong, *weird*. I think I shivered." She gave a little swallow. "Then he turned toward me and spoke. And it's hard to describe his voice, but his way of speaking was incredibly striking. As if the words were just pressed out of the air. . . ."

She fell silent, staring at the planet far below and Merral could see her reflection in the curved, coated glass.

"What did he say?" Vero asked, as gently as if he were talking to a child.

"He said this: 'Captain Lewitz, night is falling. The war begins.' But I can't give any sense of the sheer weight of the words."

She paused again and moved her head so that she was looking carefully at Merral and Vero, as if weighing them. " 'Night is falling. The war begins.' "

Vero asked, "Do you understand what he meant at all?"

She looked at him blankly. "Not then." Then she looked to where the Gate had been. "But I do now. Or think I do."

Perena turned back to Vero and Merral saw there were shadows under her eyes. "I wish I could describe the voice. It was human in its words, but not in its sound. It was emotionless; I felt there was no flesh and blood, no lungs and larynx involved, but that it was not—most definitely not—a machine voice." She shook her head. "If it was a vision, it was a remarkably concrete one. Anyway, so I said, 'Who are you?'" Then she paused and sharply corrected herself. "*No*. I said, 'Who are you, *sir?*' because there was such an authority in the voice. Then he answered me. 'I too am a captain, and I too serve.' He paused, as if to let the words sink in, then he said, 'I have been sent by our Lord the King as an envoy to you. I am to warn you that the enemy is seeking to regain his authority over your worlds. His power extends to Farholme Gate. Even now he seeks to seize your friends.'"

Merral felt himself reach for the grab rails. He glimpsed Vero gulping and, for a moment, wondered if he was going to vomit.

Perena swallowed and when she spoke again there was a great emotion in her voice. "I was nearly sick with fear, but I said, somehow, 'Can I stop it?' There was another silence and then he just said, 'You may be able to stop the ship entering Farholme Gate.' Then he seemed to start to walk away toward the rear of the *Nesta*. There he turned briefly to me. 'And remember, Perena, whatever happens, the King reigns. And stand firm.' Then he was gone."

"Gone?" Vero's voice shook and Merral was aware of his hands twitching.

She raised her eyebrows. "He just wasn't there. In the chamber. Did he move or did he vanish? I don't know."

She turned and leaned her head back against the glass and looked at them, her face pale and intense. "For a moment I froze. Then I started shaking and I had to lean back against an undercarriage leg to brace myself. I prayed. Then I realized that you were going through the Gate in just over an hour. So I raced up to the complex offices and asked if anybody else had been in Bay One. They looked at me as if I was deranged. 'Of course not,' they said. I ran to the Gate Control office. I must have been a sight for them to see. I told them to stop the *Schütz*. Turn it back, whatever. Then the fun began." She sighed, rubbing her chin gently. "They were very kind, they all knew me, but they said, 'Why?' Of course, I was in a mess, because all I could say was that I had met someone or had a vision of some sort. So they looked at each other and checked and rechecked all the Gate signals while they got me a chair." She wrinkled her face up in a rueful smile.

"Visions, I now realize, do not appear in the manuals. Nor do angels. Anyway, the Chief of Operations—a nice man—said, well, they had Standard Operating Procedures and, of course, there was nothing they could do. There was no basis to order any diversion. So I thanked him and walked out. Of course, I couldn't get you on the diary. Then I remembered something, so I walked through to Communications and sat down at the desk where they had the backup systems. There was no one about there so I sent the message that you got. I saw how it was cut off after a minute, so I just went outside and sat on a step and prayed. Half an hour later, I heard this extraordinary commotion from the Gate Control Office. I ran in. . . ." She took a deep breath. "You cannot imagine the atmosphere there. But eventually we realized the ship was safe, if damaged. As you know, a number of Gate fragments perforated it, but you were going so fast by then that their relative speed was pretty low."

She looked at them with an oddly respectful look. "I trust both of you have given thanks for great mercies. Despite our ships' excellent self-sealing abilities, most space travelers who see the stars with naked eyes find that it is the last thing they do see in this life."

Vero bowed. "I think that neither of us will overlook that."

For some moments, nobody said anything, and in the silence Merral heard the clatter of equipment echoing from one of the station's corridors. Finally Vero, his weary face marked by a bemused expression, spoke. "Extraordinary, quite extraordinary." He looked at Merral. "Are you reminded of something in Perena's account?"

"Jorgio's dream, of course. Of the testing of the Assembly; to watch, stand firm, and to hope."

"Yes," said Vero. "But Perena, I keep thinking about this appearance—this apparition. I do not have the words. What was it?"

She closed her eyes for a moment before opening them. "I wondered if it was a hallucination. I was tired and stressed. But there was a curiously solid quality to the appearance. As if it had come from somewhere else. And there were other things; I felt a moral aspect to the envoy. I felt under judgment in some way. It was—" she stared at her fingers and Merral wondered if she was blushing— "a not entirely welcome feeling."

"Was it an angel?" Vero asked. "In the Scriptures, an envoy and an angel would be the same word."

Perena shook her head. "I would not wish to claim—or deny—that he was an angel."

"That angels guard the Assembly," Vero said slowly, "is an ancient statement of faith. That, in this age of the world, they do not appear to human beings, is a statement based on equally ancient experience."

"In this age of the world?" Perena said in a sharp voice. "But if I understand Jorgio's vision—and mine—then this age of the world may be ending."

Vero stared out into space for a moment. "Perena," he said, and his tone was troubled, "I stand corrected." Then he turned to her. "Thank you twice over. Your encounter not only saved our lives; it has added another significant piece to the puzzle."

She shook her head. "There are two more things I must tell you. First, yesterday evening I did a check on the *Argo*. The ship that in 2098 went into Below-Space with a living crew and returned with a dying one."

Vero bent closer as if to hear better, swayed, overcompensated, and began to spin. Perena grabbed his arm and steadied him.

"Take it easy. No sudden movements. Anyway, very little of the *Argo's* voyage was made public. The crew names, dates of injection into Below-Space, and recovery; that sort of thing. There are some comments on the properties of Below-Space, and they provide our only real eyewitness knowledge of what happens there. The comments were that, as the remote probes had suggested, some wavelengths of electromagnetic radiation travel through Below-Space. At the upper levels you could make out stars and planets in shades of gray, but as you went deeper, it became opaque quickly. But with depth they reported a progressive and remarkable degree of mental disorientation with hallucinations and eventually delirium. Which, sadly, proved irreversible."

"Is that it? That tells us little." Vero looked disappointed.

"No, the oddity is this: That is all that was reported of the mission of the *Argo*."

"But there must have been a full report published."

"No. I checked. The full report on the voyage of the *Argo* is one of the few documents never put into the public domain in the entire history of the Assembly."

"Really? Why?"

"Ah. I then ran a search on rumors and fables of early Assembly space flight. There was one record to do with the *Argo*; simply an early post-Rebellion rumor that it had encountered 'Powers.'"

"*Powers?* Not 'power problems'?"

"The wording is precise, if ambiguous. *Powers*. With a capital letter."

"Surely it was just a tall tale?"

"The obvious conclusion but for one very odd fact. The *Argo* Review Commission, made up of a dozen men and women, met in closed session in 2099. It met for a week, adjourned, and then resumed with an enlarged board of six extra people. It met for another month. They made two recommendations: first, that the *Argo* report must remain forever unpublished, and second, that no further attempts were ever to be made to explore Below-Space. Gate links were fine, but going outside them was not."

"Odd." Vero stared at Perena with tired eyes. "Why did they enlarge the board? To put on more psychologists?"

An odd, distant expression crossed Perena's face "No, Vero, it wasn't psychologists. It was theologians."

"Theologians?"

"The six extra people were the Custodians of the Faith."

Merral suddenly felt cold. "Perena," he said, "they felt that there was something *wrong* in Below-Space?"

Perena paused, looked at Vero, and began again. "I think—and it is partly a guess—that they concluded that in deep Below-Space there were spiritual forces, elemental powers. Influences. Something like that."

Vero frowned and shook his head. "It has always been a belief that, if allowed to, human beings always go too far and become, either directly or indirectly, involved with evil powers. That is why we have checks and controls. But I had never heard that it might be so literally true. Nevertheless, Perena, I am not sure I see how this affects us now. We have more pressing problems."

Perena looked at him, her eyes troubled. "I have not finished. I have another piece of information for you. But let me first ask you a question: Assuming the intruders did destroy the Gate, why did they do it?"

Vero opened his hands wide. "It's obvious. They wanted to kill us. To stop us getting through with the news."

"I am not so sure." The voice was quiet.

Vero gave her a look of astonishment. "There are few things that I now take for granted, but that was one of them. I mean, isn't it obvious?"

"Surprisingly, no. Did either of you notice when the explosion happened with respect to your scheduled entry into the Gate?"

"I did," Merral said. "Now you mention it, it was after entry time. A few minutes later."

"Yes." Perena's firm tone brooked no argument. "It exploded at 11:07. You would have entered at 11:02, so that by then you would have been exactly midway between Gates."

Vero stared at Perena in astonishment. "I had never thought . . . What would have happened?"

"A good question and one the spatial physicists—there are two of them here—will have to work on. It has never happened. But the Normal-Space tube would have collapsed instantly and you would have dropped out into Below-Space. At the deepest point of your traverse, you—"

"—would have done what the *Argo* did." Vero's voice trembled.

Merral suddenly felt an urgent longing to be on the ground and to never, ever leave it again.

Vero, swallowing hard, was staring at Perena, his eyes open in a wild surmise. "What did this envoy say about what the enemy wanted to do again?"

"He said 'The enemy wishes to seize you.' Not destroy . . ."

For a moment Merral could only close his eyes as a wave of fear and horror broke over him. He felt his body shake.

When he opened his eyes, he saw that Vero had drifted over to the window and was gazing down at the planet. There was a long silence.

Finally, after perhaps a minute, Vero spoke. "I see why you told us this, Perena. It is horrific but is also suggestive . . ."

Vero stared toward Ancient Earth and wagged a finger slowly in that direction. Then, still looking outward, he began to speak in a slow-paced and almost dreamy voice. "Perena, Merral, let me tell you a story. About something that happened—or may have happened—a long, long time ago. As we know, frustrated by the restrictions of the infant Assembly, William Jannafy and his followers rebelled and, after much bloodshed, took control of the Centauri Gate and the colony. There, free from the restrictions of the Assembly, Jannafy encouraged exploration and experimentation into areas that had been forbidden. He had human beings altered genetically and joined with animal tissues to suit his ends—had new races made. And he sent ships deep into Below-Space. There . . ."

Vero paused, his brown eyes focused on infinity. "There they found more than they had bargained for." He hesitated. "What shall we call them? *Powers, elemental spirits?* Perhaps the older word *demons* might be better. Was Jannafy influenced by them? Did he do a deal with them then? Maybe even he held back from that. I do not know. But then, in the sudden assault at Centauri, he was slain and his men saw that their end was hours away. They chose to save themselves by fleeing to safety through deep Below-Space." He shook his head. "And what price, I wonder, did these Powers and influences exact for safe passage?"

Merral shuddered as Vero paused to let his words sink in. "So in my story, the remains of the Free Peoples fled through Below-Space to the edge of our galaxy. There they survived. But now they were bound to the Powers and they were no longer free. From them they learned— or were taught—new things, such as how to make dead creatures live again and how to use them for their ends. And as the millennia passed, their hatred of the Assembly showed no lessening."

Then Vero turned round suddenly to face them and raised his voice. "And now, they have returned to the Assembly. After long years, Jannafy's descendants are back and they bring evil with them."

Vero paused and gave Perena a questioning look. "Is this—or something like this—what you think happened?"

"Yes," she whispered, and there was fear in her eyes.

Vero turned to Merral. "My friend, you have just heard this story. But tell me, do you think it may be true?"

An urge rose in Merral's mind to deny it all, to protest that Vero's words were nonsense, a wild fiction. But he could not.

"Vero," he heard himself eventually say, "I wish I could say it was false. But what you say has a ring of truth to me."

Vero nodded but said nothing more, and in the end it was Merral who broke the silence. "So, if this tale is true, what are we to do?"

A shadow of a grin crept over Vero's face. "Ah, our soldier here asks about action. I rejoice we have you with us, Merral. I truly do. But, please, answer your own question."

Merral knew what he had to say. "If this is the case then, once more, the Assembly must fight them."

"Amen," whispered Perena.

"We fight," Merral said, aware that he was repeating himself. "We have no option. However awesome the odds and however terrible the enemies we face."

"Indeed." Vero turned to look out of the window. "The first step is that we need to find the source of these creatures. Somewhere down there is a ship."

Merral was aware that all three of them were looking where the line of night was now creeping to the westernmost edge of the Lannar Crater.

Perena gestured to the western Rim Ranges, their valleys deep in shadow. "The satellite data is coming in, but I have to say that if there are intruders there, then they are hidden. Anya and I had a quick examination yesterday; we found no settlements or landing strips."

"They will be hidden," Vero said with confidence. "Our opponents know the techniques of war. On a vast, unknown, and sparsely populated planet like this, they could find many hiding places."

Merral stared silently down, struck now by the scale of things. He felt he was seeing the immense bleak brown wastes, the vast rolling green forests, the dark pinnacled mountains, and the ever-expanding marshy deltas for the first time. *How odd, for a world entirely made by mankind, that there is so little evidence of our race's presence. Here pinpricks of light in the new darkness, there a gleaming vapor trail left by some long-haul passenger flier, elsewhere a few small, extended star shapes of the cities. So much of this world,* he thought, *has been left to evolve its own way, and all we have done is sow, watch, and—where needed—prune.* Now what he would once have seen as a glorious challenge had become an ominous threat. Farholme, and especially humanity on Farholme, suddenly seemed terribly vulnerable. *We would be threatened enough by our enforced isolation,* he thought, *even without this intruder threat. With it, we seem to be in such a great peril as to make our future a dubious matter.*

Merral spoke aloud. "Even if we were the entire Assembly, to encounter such an opposition as we fear that we face would be daunting. But as one world?"

"Yes, but we have had the encouragement of Perena's visitor. If he was not an angel himself, then his counsel was angelic. The King *does* still reign. We are to watch and stand firm. And to hope."

Merral said, "I will hold onto those words. I am grateful for them. Nevertheless we face an almost overwhelming task."

"True," Perena said, looking at her watch. "But we need to return to Farholme. There we will gather together and decide what we do. And I must go see Captain Bennett. Can I meet you both at Shuttle Dock Two in an hour? The *Eliza N'geno* will be refueled by then."

Vero nodded. "Good. We need to be back down. Anyway I'm not sure I care for this view; it's too overwhelming. Besides I want to lie down, or whatever is the equivalent when there is no down. Merral, see you at the ship." He turned to Perena and cautiously bowed his head. "Captain Lewitz, my thanks for your news and for your encouragement. And," he sighed, "for your sympathy."

Then slowly and clumsily, aided by a gentle push from Perena, Vero exited up through the hatchway. Perena shook her head as his feet scrabbled for a hold on a rung and then disappeared out of view.

She looked back at Merral. "Staying here?"

He nodded. "Yes, for a few more minutes. I just want to admire the view a bit longer. I may not get the chance again for a long, long time."

Perena nodded slowly. "True enough. But you can't stay much longer; the sun will come in at the window, then the glare will wipe out everything."

Merral stared down at the blue, brown, and green hemisphere below and sighed. "Perena," he said slowly, "you know what I have just thought?"

"No, tell me."

"Vero has lost his world and is going back now to a new one. But less obviously, I think, we are too."

"Yes," she said and her voice was barely audible. "You are right. What did Jorgio say? 'Things have changed'?"

"Indeed they have. But it is not just the Gate that has gone. It is the old Farholme. The world we knew has ended."

"Yes," she said, leaning her head against the window, and he realized that she had shed many tears recently. "I know. I fear that we will find that soon nothing is the same. But we will fight, Merral. We mustn't give in."

He found that her voice had a strange quality of resolution in it that challenged and encouraged him.

She nodded to herself, then bobbed over and patted him gently on the back. "Look, I must go. We need to start the prelaunch checks. See you at the shuttle dock."

"You will."

She touched him on the shoulder and then slid away and pirouetted up out of the hatchway with the grace of someone to whom the absence of gravity was a joy.

•—◆—•

In the silence that followed, Merral stood suspended in the chamber, staring down at the world. He watched for several minutes as twilight followed by night continued its silent and inexorable creep across the planet. He absorbed trivial details now: the smoke from the rift system volcanoes, the brown smudge of a dust storm careening across the Northern Wastes, and the light shimmering on some infant upland glaciers. Ynysmant—with his parents and Isabella—now lay in darkness, its feeble light output too small to be visible from up here. To the west, the sun had just set over Ranapert and Halmacent Cities, where pinpricks of light were forming in the purple twilight. Farther west still, the daylight was coming to a close on Isterrane, and on either side of the city the wooded headlands stood proud in the golden evening light. In the extreme west, the late afternoon shadows were lengthening over the high and rugged Varrend Tablelands with their vast lakes and coiling rivers.

Merral thought about the people that were within his field of view. With a sweep of his head he could see where half of Farholme's entire population lived. *And tonight,* he said to himself, *they will all be looking skyward for only the second day in their history to see the Gate gone and the beacons broken. And all except the very youngest will know that no Made World has ever been as alone as Farholme is now.* But of all that population, he knew that there were only four of them who realized that the threat was far more terrible than the peril of mere isolation.

"My world," he whispered, and he heard the words ring with a compassionate intensity. "I'm sorry we didn't bring back help. I'm sorry that Perena and Vero and Anya and I are all that there is. Apart from the King."

He paused. "Lord," he said in a tone so soft that he could barely hear himself, "I don't really know what is happening. And I don't know what we face, and what I've heard and seen scares me. Especially because everyone seems to look to me for a lead. But Lord," he went on, suddenly aware of his reflection in the glass, "I love this place and I hate what has happened to it. And if you can use me to save it or restore it, then I offer myself to you." He bowed his head.

Do you mean it? something—or someone—seemed to ask. Was it, Merral wondered, an inquiry that he was asking himself, or was another asking him? He hesitated, thinking of the terror of the fighting he had been involved in already, and of the possible cost.

He had no choice. He exhaled heavily. "Yes," he said, "I mean it."

•◆•

It was time to go to the ship, descend to the planet, meet Anwar Corradon, and prepare for whatever the future might bring. He drifted to the hatchway and reached up to put his fingers on the lowest ladder rung.

He took a last look at his fragile and beautiful world below.

"I promise," he said aloud. "I promise."

Suddenly, a brilliant ray of sun, unheralded by any forewarning in the dustless vacuum of space, slid into the compartment, filling the far corner with a brilliant yellow-white glow.

"Amen," muttered Merral.

Then, with a sharp tug on the rung, he propelled himself toward the shuttle dock.

ABOUT THE AUTHOR

 Born in Wales in 1954, Chris Walley grew up in northern England. He studied earth sciences at university and has a doctorate in geology. He taught at the American University of Beirut in Lebanon from 1980 to 1984 and then returned to Wales to do ten years of consultancy work with the oil industry. He began writing in the late eighties and had two novels, *Heart of Stone* and *Rock of Refuge*, published under the pseudonym of John Haworth. In 1994, along with his family, Chris returned to Lebanon to teach again at AUB. In 1998, he came back to Wales and began to make a new career in writing and editing for the Christian market. He retains his geological interests and is an adjunct professor of geology at Wheaton College. Chris and his wife live in an old cottage on the edge of Swansea and are very much involved in a local Baptist church.

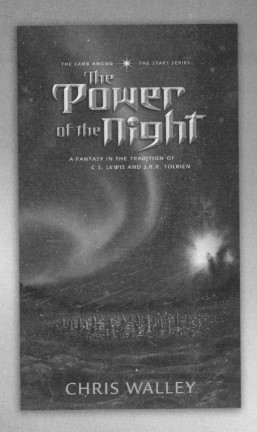

areUthirsty.com

well . . . are you?

degrees betrayal

Betrayal comes naturally—where you stand will determine who's to blame—but there's always more than one side to the story.

Revenge is sweet . . . or is it?

There's always more than one point of view—read all three.

sierra's story
{DANDI DALEY MACKALL}
ISBN 0-8423-8726-9

ryun's story
{JEFF NESBIT}
ISBN 1-4143-0003-4

kenzie's story
{MELODY CARLSON}
ISBN 1-4143-0002-6

degreesofbetrayal.com

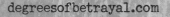